For Mom,
my fiercest protector, loudest cheerleader,
and my gentlest home.

For Dad,
who rarely found the words,
but gave me the tools to write mine.

And for Paige,
who taught me that words aren't just stories—
they're lifelines.

CONTENTS

KIDS OF KAZUMETH

THE ROOTS OF KALUNA

STEVEN RAY WRISTON

Contents

DREAMING AWAKE

EMERSON FELT AS IF he had stepped into one of his mother's hallucinations, but even they couldn't be *this* twisted. It wasn't as though he'd never wondered what it would be like to live in a mythical land. After all, he often dreamed of ancient kingdoms and odd, fantastical creatures. Yet he never imagined they would become his grim reality.

"Why did I go in that cave?" he whispered, his voice raw as the words clawed their way out. "Stupid, moronic . . . what was I thinking?"

His hand trembled against his chest as a solitary tear slid down his pockmarked cheek. He squeezed his eyes shut, fighting the sting behind them. He couldn't afford to cry—there wasn't enough of him left to spill.

The thought alone made him aware of how hollow he felt—how dry he was, how his cracked lips stung, how his tongue lay thick and useless. *When had he last had a drink?* Not since that sickly-sweet concoction had been forced through his lips on the first day at the tower.

His throat still ached, scorched by the smoke that had hung thick in the air as the forest burned. Even the cellar's cool, damp air did nothing to ease the feverish heat radiating from his skin.

Beaten, disoriented, and desperate for water, Emerson dragged his tongue across the wet, mossy substance spreading across the damp ground. He held his breath, but he could still taste the bitter, gray growth, which tickled his tongue as he tried to swallow the tiny beads of water. Almost at once, he coughed a stream of mucus across the cool, dark stones. He let out a raucous yell, the sound echoing through the high-ceilinged room.

Emerson's mind reeled, drifting back to how he'd ended up chained to the cold cellar floor in the first place: flashes of colorful fields; a beaked, furry-limbed forest dweller; and a dark cave etched with ancient symbols . . . none of which made the slightest bit of sense.

A torch flickered to life in the distance. Its light barely reached the far wall—just enough to reveal the room's curves and a twisted figure sprawled on the ground. Behind the body, a grotesque, ochre stain was smeared across the stone.

As the shape of a man came into focus, the metallic tang of copper flooded Emerson's senses. He turned away, trying to block out the desperate, rattling breaths coming from him.

"Calm down," Emerson mumbled, scratching his damp cheek with one of his chained hands. The restraints binding his arms and legs kept him in an awkward kneel—hard to breathe in yet fitting for a captive kneeling before royalty. "Just breathe. We don't even know—"

His words died in his throat as the familiar sound of grinding stones echoed through the room. His breath hitched; he'd heard that noise twice before, and each time it had only brought more pain and confusion. He had to stay calm. He had to figure out what was happening.

At the first soft footfall, a shiver crawled up his spine, tugging at the hairs on his neck like invisible fingers plucking them one by one. Emerson held his breath, swallowing the tears that threatened to spill, as the patter of footsteps drew closer. A cold wind swept through him, freezing him from the inside out.

"Emerson, do you know why you've been brought before me?" cooed a soft, faint voice from the shadows behind him.

"No," Emerson rasped. "No, sir . . ."

"Gara believed you were the savior—the one spoken of in prophecy. A mistake on her part . . . one that demands a price."

The haunting words did little to quiet the gnawing anxiety twisting in Emerson's gut.

"I've discovered you are not the heir of Ulysses Hackley, therefore not the one the Futurians wrote about. However, Gara wasn't entirely incompetent. There is something . . . unusual about you. I believe you could still be of use. Tell me, from whom do you descend? Or are you just a child of my world that the Pilfert is so eager to sacrifice?"

The man hid in the shadows, keeping his identity concealed as Emerson's heart hammered in his chest.

Emerson thought hard as strange words—*Pilfert, Futurian*—clashed against his skull. They meant nothing to him. However, *Hackley* . . . Hackley was familiar. Then, memories long buried began flooding back—diluted, but tangible.

The name spilled from his lips, fast and urgent like a wave crashing: "Hernando Garcia."

A low snicker echoed, as if the very walls were listening—relishing in his torment. Silence followed as the man stood before him, deep in thought. Emerson still refused to look at him, keeping his gaze fixed on the floor.

"Well, Emerson, with the Pilfert already poisoning your mind with lies, it seems we've reached an—"

"*No.* Please don't kill me!" Emerson screamed, his voice faltering. The tears he'd tried so desperately to hold back now streamed down his face. He needed them—they were the only thing that proved any of this was real, that he was still alive. If he let them fall—let them escape—he would be nothing but a dried-up, hollow shell, left to rot on the floor like the crumpled remains of the man across the room.

"Kill you?" the man said softly, as the sound of sniggering filled the room once more. "No, Emerson. I do not wish to waste your life. No, I believe you can help our cause. I don't even wish for you to be chained to this floor, but my guards believed it would be safer for me. Get up," the man commanded, suddenly standing inches from Emerson's ear. Emerson's body stiffened, unable to comprehend how the man had moved so fast—and without a sound.

Then, unexpectedly, he laughed as an old phrase of his mother's echoed through his mind: *If your assailant is sly, you're probably gonna die.*

As if on cue, the chains binding Emerson's arms slowly unraveled with a quiet clink, sinking back into the ground. Emerson stopped laughing at once. He pushed himself up as the circular room seemed to spin around him.

Steadying himself, Emerson avoided looking at his captor, focusing instead on a spot above the dark stain on the wall. Its deep red hues shimmered in the torchlight, and the slippery handprints smeared across the stone sent a shudder through him. Unable to bear it, he turned back to where the man had been standing—only to find he was gone.

Instead, a dilapidated, splintered mirror hung in his place, reflecting a faint blue light from the end of a long hallway. The mirror cast shadows that stretched across the walls, and as Emerson stared into the glass, a towering, dark figure slowly emerged behind him, extinguishing the warmth of the flickering blue flames.

Emerson inhaled sharply, his breath catching in his chest as he observed the figure. He was tall—taller than any man had a right to be—and unnaturally thin. He was almost skeletal, his gaunt frame a disturbing contrast to his terrifying presence.

"Turn around," the man whispered. His voice echoed around the cellar, reverberating off the stones and dripping from the ceiling.

Emerson steeled himself and forced his body to obey. A soft gasp escaped his lips.

The figure loomed before him, casting a suffocating presence over the room. His skin, once deep brown, was now charred and blackened, subtly scaled from burns that had long since healed. A maroon tailcoat clung to his wiry frame over a dark, star-speckled shirt—the fabric shifting as though it held the night sky itself. His long, narrow nose and crooked grin made him appear almost inhuman. But it was his eyes—brilliant, piercing blue like polished sapphires—that held Emerson captive.

They were unnervingly beautiful against the darkness of his ruined skin, but behind their gleam lurked something ancient, calculating, and dangerous.

"Are you frightened?"

"Yes," Emerson replied without hesitation.

"Good," the man whispered, his voice lower and more ominous than before. "Strength is born from fear."

He moved closer to Emerson, who recoiled instinctively.

"The Pilfert has undoubtedly been training you to control your magic. Am I correct?"

Emerson coughed, his throat tight with the weight of his silence. The man grimaced, and suddenly, Emerson felt a thousand needles piercing his skull, yanking at memories buried deep within him. The sharp pain subsided as his mind flooded with flashes—dancing flowers; wooden dragons; a fuzzy, wingless bird; and then the face of the most beautiful woman he had ever seen.

Each memory felt like a wave crashing against the rocks, mixing truth with fiction until he wasn't sure which was which.

"I . . . I don't know what a Pilf—" Emerson began, but as the words slipped from his lips, he realized that his captor was the reason for the sudden resurgence of memories.

"You dare lie to Akuramundo, Emerson? How very brave . . ." The man hissed through his teeth. "Now speak the truth—what did the Pilfert teach you about the Sovereign Five? You must know who Ulysses's heir is."

Emerson hesitated, his mind scrambling for an answer. He had to speak. The truth or a lie? The wrong answer could cost him everything.

"There's an old legend . . . my family used to talk about it. Something to do with Hernando. He was part of the Sovereign Five—at least, that's what my abuela said. She told me they were a radical group formed years ago to fight injustices in the workplace.

"But my mom . . .she said it was something else. She said it involved magic and another world, but I didn't listen to her . . . I thought she was just—"

"*Enough,*" Akuramundo said, cutting him off. A thread of frustration laced his tone. "Who is Ulysses's heir?"

With a snap of his fingers, four faces appeared in the mirror, projected from Emerson's mind. The faces were clear, bright, and full of life. Emerson's heart tightened.

"Jack Hackley," he answered coldly, pointing to the brown, chiseled face of the boy with earrings in the bottom right corner. Jack's face filled the mirror, and for a moment, Emerson thought he might step out of it. But then he vanished, leaving only Emerson's pale reflection behind.

The man's eyes gleamed. Before Emerson could even register the change, Akuramundo was standing inches from him.

"Thank you for that," he said softly, snapping his fingers. The chains sprang to life, latching around Emerson's arms, pulling him back into his bowing position. His face smacked against the stone, and blood began to pool beneath him.

"I hate to do this, Emerson, but you've seen too much. I'll give you two options: you can stay here like the traitor Renago," he gestured toward the man in the corner, "or you can align with me. Help me heal these worlds. Fight the Pilfert's lies. If you help me, I'll release you tonight, and we'll talk over dinner. Choose wisely, Emerson. You're extremely gifted—we could be unstoppable."

Emerson turned his head; the newly formed puddle smeared across his cheek. He knew there was only one option, but that didn't make it easier. His friends ran through his mind—Adina's stubborn grin, Jack's stupid expression, and Addison's hopeful eyes. *Were they even trying to find him?*

Emerson wasn't sure what this man would have him do, but there was one thing Emerson knew for certain: as long as he was alive, he had the power to choose what was right in the end . . . even if it meant betrayal down the road.

"I . . . I'll help you," Emerson said finally, his voice small but steady. "But . . . all I ask is that I can go home to my family in Brookville when you're done with me . . . that I can leave this world and never come back."

"Of course, Emerson. We want the same thing. You'll see."

The man waved his hand, and the chains vanished. He approached, wiped the blood from Emerson's face with a small rag, and then disappeared through the wall, leaving Emerson alone with his thoughts.

His mind raced. What had he done? Was he really going to betray everyone he had ever known? His family? His friends? How many people would he have to hurt to save himself?

The weight of the decision settled heavily on him, the pressure threatening to crush him.

In that moment, he wondered if death might have been the better option. But as his friends' faces began to fade, his thoughts shifted to the family who had been forced to forget he ever existed.

A fire ignited within him, and Emerson knew—he would do whatever it took to see them again.

Chapter One

The Crack in the Crust

A HAND WITH THE authority of a gavel came smashing down onto a bedside table, issuing a wordless decree for ten more minutes of sleep. Jack clumsily fumbled for his phone, which had fallen, and snatched it up by the charger. He clicked snooze on the autotuned pop song screeching, "Wake up!" and rolled over, pulling the thin, silky bamboo fabric over his face. Beneath the cool sheet, he constructed a surefire case: lying there, letting his muscles recover for the next eight hours, would be far more beneficial to him than anything he'd learn in school that day.

That's it, I'm staying home. And Jack rolled onto his other side, ready to fall back into the strange dream he'd been having. As he set the phone back on the bedside table, his hand brushed against a picture of his girlfriend, Emma. Through squinted eyes, he could just make out her petite frame and energetic smile. Suddenly, the idea of suffering through eight tedious lessons didn't seem so bad. At least it'd give him the chance to make out with her between classes. It would also give him a chance to change the alarm on her iPhone to a song she found equally as annoying as payback.

Jack slouched across the room to his already open dresser, slipped running shorts over his boxers, and grabbed the black hoodie he had carelessly discarded on the floor the night before.

Sitting on the bed, he sniffed a pair of socks to make sure they were clean, then pulled them over his large feet before checking himself in the mirror.

His russet-brown skin glistened in the early morning light. Jack checked his hair first, rubbing pomade through his hands before cautiously working it into his thick curls. As his fingers shaped his hair, he felt a surge of pride when he noticed how tight his hoodie fit around his arms. He shoved diamond studs into his ears, smiled at his reflection, and checked his teeth for any imperfections. Content with his image, he wiped a stray lock of hair off his slightly crooked nose—a souvenir from an aggressive hockey match, grabbed his backpack, and moved mechanically out of his room and down the stairs, still lost in thought.

Jack was trying to remember the odd dream he'd just had. A glowing blue light burned urgently in a distant land. He couldn't recall the specifics about the circular tomb he'd been in, but he could still see Emerson's frail body lying on a cold stone floor. Jack rubbed his temples and made a mental note not to mention this part of the dream to Emerson—he'd surely spend all morning analyzing it, and Jack wasn't sure his brain could handle a deep conversation until he had drunk at least three cups of coffee.

Still, Jack could hear Emerson's voice echoing in his mind: *Well obviously, Jack, the dungeon represents Brookville, and the chains are my mother, holding me back from the bright future shining in front of me.*

Bro, I need to start hanging out with my other friends. Shaking Emerson's voice from his head, he rounded the corner of the stairs, the familiar scent of his mom's famous Strawberry Pecan Waffles filled the air—a smell that somehow made getting out of bed worth it. Dropping his bag with a thud, he slid onto a barstool at the marble counter. His mom, short and round with a whirlwind energy, slid a steaming mug of black coffee and an elegantly decorated waffle in front of him. The local news murmured from the small TV beneath the cabinet, but Jack hardly noticed it.

"Morning, honey! How'd you sleep?" she asked, already hustling about.

"Alright, I had a weird fuc—" Jack stopped mid-sentence as his mom shot him a pointed look, her warm, honey eyes hardening. He quickly corrected himself. "I had a really strange dream. Some weird shit that felt so real—like something Emerson's goofy mom would rave about."

"Language," she scolded, though her curiosity quickly overtook her irritation. "What was so strange about it?"

"I don't really remember much, but I know I was in some foreign world, and Emerson kind of sold me out," Jack mumbled, not really wanting to talk so he could enjoy his breakfast instead.

"Emerson would never. You're like brothers. But also, maybe your brain's just trying to deal with everything changing. College, graduation, Emma... You've got a lot going on. It can sometimes feel like friends are selling you out for something better when they've made plans for their future—and you're, well, still figuring things out."

Jack didn't find the speech helpful. In fact, it crawled under his skin. He needed coffee—and fewer lectures about the future from people who already had theirs figured out.

"I work until six today, so if you go anywhere—especially if it involves Emma—call me first," she said, turning away to put a glass back into the cabinet. She softened as she added, "I'm serious, Jack." Her tone was gentle, but her words lingered like a rule he now felt determined to break. "You won't be allowed to visit Emma again if you keep up with this foolishness. Her father is over it. Understand?"

"I don't know what you mean," Jack said slyly, his mouth full of strawberries as red syrup dribbled down his chin.

His mother grimaced at the food-stained mess. "Oh, you know exactly what I mean, Jack. Last week's trip to New York City?"

Jack paused mid-chew, but she raised a hand to stop the excuse building behind his teeth.

"I don't want to hear that it was your five-year anniversary. You're in high school—you don't just whisk your girlfriend away on dates like that! Your father wouldn't have approved, and he certainly never would've done anything like that for me."

"There's always time . . . want me to whip out the Ouija board?" Jack smirked.

"Watch your mouth," she warned. "And you know it's not about that, Jack! You went to that dangerous city without supervision or permission. I've always been easy with you—I want you to enjoy life, but come on."

"Still, no reason to ban Emma from seeing me," Jack muttered, shoveling another bite into his mouth.

"Isn't it?" she shot back, as her hands found her hips disapprovingly. "You kidnapped their daughter, and don't forget, you terrified their youngest. That little girl had nightmares for a month after what you did."

"Oh, come on. You know that shit was funny," Jack added wryly.

"Language," his mom scolded, but her tone softened as she shook her head. "And no, Jack. You painted glow-in-the-dark eyes on a six-year-old's wall! She screamed every time they turned off the lights—and kept doing it for days. She was crying about an evil clown in her closet and slept in their bed for an entire week."

"Still funny," Jack added with a shrug.

"And maybe it was. But it didn't do you any favors." She laughed despite herself. "Got you kicked out of their house for three months."

"It just kept me from using the front door," Jack replied, winking as he took another bite.

"What was that—"

"Nothing," he said, as his gaze drifted to the TV. His mom continued to murmur as she busied herself in the kitchen—probably some lecture about his antics he'd heard a hundred times. But he didn't catch any of it. Something else had stolen his attention: *Breaking News – Brookville High School* flashed across the screen.

"Hey, Mom, can you turn that up? Something's going on at my school," Jack said, curiosity piquing.

His mom jumped at the mention of his school, the dish in her hand clinking against the sink. Her fearful eyes lingered on the screen for a second before flicking to the kitchen clock. She let out a short breath, grabbed a towel, and wiped her hands as she reached for the remote.

An old, gangly woman with gray, matted hair—tied back with a flowered bandana—filled the screen. Her sunken eyes darted back and forth, swiveling like she was watching a tennis match. Her mouth, tight-jawed and deeply wrinkled, opened as she stepped toward the microphone. When she spoke, her voice was loud and strained, as if she were trying to be heard across a busy street.

"I heard it this morning! There was a loud cracking—coming from in there!" She jabbed a finger at the forest lining the yard. "It sounded like the world was splitting in two! My dog started barking, so I got up to tell him to can it, and then—bam! I'm at the window, and the whole house starts shaking!"

The screen cut back to a news reporter. Her red hair framed a pale, almost amused face, a smile still clinging to her lips as though she'd just stifled a laugh.

"Last night's events of what has been described as 'the world splitting' have led to the discovery of a cave deep within the ground right here in Brookville. Protruding from the earth is a hole that seems to stretch deep into the crust. It's currently under investigation, and we've been told that no one is allowed near the site. This is truly history in the making, and it's happening right here in Brookville."

The footage cut to jagged stone jutting from the ground as fog unfurled from the earth's broken seam. Above it all, trees loomed, silent as sentinels, their roots gripping the soil like claws. At the base of the hole, delicate white and purple flowers were crushed beneath the rocks. The camera zoomed in, but the light barely penetrated the swirling haze. Jack stared, mesmerized, wondering if it was deep enough to reach the center of the earth.

"We've just learned the cave is around two hundred feet deep," a scientist explained in the live shot. Jack's excitement deflated instantly. "But the length of the cavern below is extensive . . . we're still working on . . ." He paused mid-sentence, eyes drawn off-camera. He bolted toward the jagged rocks, with the camera crew scrambling behind him, their gear bouncing as Jack sat back on his stool, watching.

They leaned over the hole as a high voice rang out from below.

"Sam, you're not going to believe this! I . . . I can't believe it!" a woman's voice hollered animatedly. "There are markings down here—actual paintings, carvings, odd symbols—whatever you want to call them. The walls are covered. You need to get down here, Sam. Right now."

The scientist peeled off his jacket before glancing back into the camera. "I'm sorry, but I'll have to cut this interview short. If you could pack up, we've got work to do. Thank you." His attempt to mask his excitement failed as the smile on his lips betrayed him.

"Thank you. We'll keep you updated on this 'groundbreaking' discovery. Now, let's check in with Ralph for the weather," the anchor chimed in from behind her desk.

Jack's mother switched off the TV, her hand over her heart as fear and concern overtook her face.

"Mom, are you alright? What's wrong?"

"Oh . . . nothing, dear! Just strange, isn't it?" she added coyly, a small laugh escaping her. "A cave bursting through the ground like that . . . It just made me think about your father, that's all: dark secrets concealed by a rock for ages—just sounds like him." Her voice took on a darker edge, and she laughed again, though it sounded almost manic. She rushed out of the kitchen, still clutching her chest.

Jack watched her go, a new feeling creeping over him. For the first time, he felt his mother had, like the earth, cracked. *It was only a matter of time. Being a single mother, raising me . . . no one could handle that weight forever. She lasted longer than I expected, though.*

"Well, Mom, I'm off to school. Just grabbing ten from your wallet—should cover lunch. Thanks, love you, bye!" Jack yelled, yanking a bill from her wallet and bolting out the door. His mother started to chase him, but stopped at the sliding glass, watching as Jack disappeared halfway up the street. She swore under her breath, then slid the door shut, sealing herself off from the chaotic world unfolding beyond.

Jack sprinted down the road, his footsteps pounding against the pavement as he tried to stay ahead of his mother. He didn't stop until an engine roared behind him, making him dive into the woods lining the street. Slumping behind a tree, he watched a silver blur zoom past that was definitely not his mother's red Nissan.

Ah, she gave up early today!

Already in the woods, Jack veered off the path, cutting through the underbrush on his usual shortcut to school. He pushed aside thick branches, stepped over fallen limbs, and crunched through dry leaves until the trees began to thin.

Ahead, bright yellow caution tape fluttered in the breeze, wrapped around the trunks of tall, thin trees. His view was partly obscured by a line of parked vehicles he didn't recognize. The forest—usually his quiet sanctuary—was now teeming with activity. Photographers, scientists, news anchors, police, and officials bustled about, none of them paying Jack any mind as he gaped stupidly at the strange stones jutting from the ground—the very same stones he had just seen on TV

A jolt of awareness snapped through him: he was supposed to be heading to school. But as he started to turn, a voice whispered, faint but unmistakable, threading through the air and freezing him in place.

"Jack," the ethereal voice called, deep in his mind. He spun around, his eyes locking on the rocks. As if on cue, several other voices began beckoning for him: a ghostly chorus of voices whispering words in foreign tongues he couldn't understand. His heart hammered as he felt a chill rip down his spine. Without thinking, Jack began inching closer to the opening in the ground.

It felt like walking down a city street on a cool winter night, the wind pushing against him—yet somehow, he glided forward, impervious, as though on a moving walkway. The crowd he'd seen earlier had vanished. He was alone.

The voices grew louder, more insistent, drawing him closer. Jack's fear evaporated, replaced by a strange sense of longing. He wanted to know who they were, to thank them for their song—and he was certain he could do that once he jumped into the hole.

Jack brushed his hand against the cold, jagged surface of the rocks as he scanned the area. *Where had everyone gone?* Jack hesitated just a moment before climbing onto the edge of the stones.

"What the hell do you think you're doing? Get the hell away from there!" a gravelly voice shouted, cutting through the hypnotic pull of the song.

A moment later, the sharp noise of engines and shouting erupted as the man called over his shoulder, "Barney, are you sleeping on the job? There's a kid on the rocks! Security, can you—"

But by the time the man turned back around, Jack was already gone—a flash of muscle, his black hoodie clinging to his back as he vanished into the trees.

Jack tore through the woods, branches slapping at his arms as he ducked, jumped, and finally dove behind the widest tree he could find.

Gasping, he peeked out from behind the tree. No one had followed. With a sigh of relief, Jack brushed himself off and continued toward school—now wide awake. His mind raced, replaying everything that had just happened. Sweat beaded on his forehead.

How had he slipped past all those reporters and scientists? Where had they gone? And what were those voices?

Emerging from the forest, Jack spotted the prison he'd be trapped in for the next eight hours. His foot hit the asphalt of the parking lot, and the familiar sights and sounds of school began dragging him back to reality—

EEEEEP!

A high-pitched horn blared as tires squealed across the pavement. Jack spun around, ready to yell at the driver. But instead, he sprinted toward the yellow Beetle, vaulted over the passenger door of the convertible, and passionately kissed the golden-haired girl behind the wheel.

"You know," Jack said, grinning. "You don't have to run over pedestrians to get a little mouth-to-mouth. I'm always here for you."

Emma cringed at his cheesy line but kissed him again anyway.

"Did you end up getting your graduation outfit last night?" Jack asked as he settled into the seat, grateful for the distraction.

"Mom got called into work, so we're picking it up tonight," Emma replied, clearly frustrated. "I won't be free until late. Late, late." Her annoyance was palpable—graduation was next week, and she still didn't have a dress.

Jack's face fell into a puppy-eyed pout as they pulled into her usual parking spot. That meant he wouldn't see her for the third night this week. They exchanged a silent glance before Emma leaned in and kissed him again, pulling away only when the warning bell echoed across the parking lot.

Jack opened the door for her with a flourish, and she grabbed her bag from the backseat. Hand in hand, they walked toward the old brick building. The moment they stepped inside, Jack sensed something had changed. The usual whispers and stares had faded—like the school had moved on to bigger drama.

For four years, they'd been the 'it' couple at Brookville High—the pair everyone whispered about in hallways and watched at lunch. Some students bitterly hoped Emma would get pregnant, convinced it would shatter their flawless image. Others wished Jack would get bored and chase after them instead. But now, with graduation looming, the tension had shifted. The school's focus had turned to the impending shake-up in the social hierarchy.

Together, Jack and Emma made their way down the hallway toward first period—one they'd intentionally scheduled to share.

"Alright class, pull out your books, we'll be discussing the final act today."

A collective groan rippled through the room as everyone dug into their bags for their copies of *Hamlet*. Jack glanced over at Emma, who'd just pulled a notebook from her bag. She quickly scribbled on the top of the page, "I thought we were doing our presentations today?"

She tore out the page and slid it over to Jack, who replied, "That's tomorrow." Without skipping a beat, they began their daily routine of practicing their grammar skills in the form of note passing.

As class dragged on, the teacher began pacing the room, making it difficult to discuss more pressing matters, like what was for lunch or the dress Emma's friend Stefani had bought over the weekend. With no other distractions, they were forced to pay attention.

Jack sighed as he scribbled down something about a queen possibly murdering her husband, a mad king, and an evil uncle—none of which made any sense. He was ninety percent sure none of it was connected, and one hundred percent sure he was going to fail the test.

The teacher droned on about Shakespeare's influence on Gothic literature, but Jack's attention wandered. He unconsciously turned around and glanced at the dark-haired girl with the average build in the back of the room. To his surprise, she was already staring at him.

Emma, noticing Jack's movement, quickly turned to see what had caught his attention. When she saw the girl—whom Emma was certain was a Satanist—she shot her a warning glare before placing her hand on his arm. The girl lowered her gaze and mumbled something under her breath.

By the time the bell rang, Jack was half asleep, and Emma was folding the notes they'd passed earlier, planning to stash them in an old Valentine's chocolate box when she got home.

"That was the longest forty-five minutes of my life. How about we ditch the next few classes and go make out behind the bleachers?" Jack added slyly, waggling his eyebrows.

Emma rolled her eyes. "Jack, I can't. I have choir practice for graduation, and then I'm rehearsing my speech during study hall. It's our last week, and we still have so much to do. You really shouldn't be skipping either—not when you're barely passing."

Jack shrugged nonchalantly. He tried not to be bothered since he knew Emma was highly active in her day-to-day school life. However, her social agenda had become so packed she barely had time for their relationship.

Jack kissed Emma as he sought a change of subject, and the change of subject just happened to be walking toward them.

The dark-haired girl from the back of the class glared at Emma as she strolled past.

"Did you see that freak staring at you? I think she was trying to cast some kind of love spell on you or something," Emma said childishly, with a toss of her hair.

Jack scoffed. "A love spell, eh? Well, now that you mention it, I do have the urge to go make out with her." He bit his lip coolly. "Maybe I'll ask her to meet behind the bleachers since my girlfriend won't."

Emma smacked him hard on the chest. "Don't joke about stuff like that. It's unnatural!"

"Says the girl who's obsessed with that musical about two witches . . . or as I remember it . . . the three longest hours of my life!" Jack grinned. "But whatever, I'll see if Emerson wants to go with me."

"Now *that* I'd like to see," Emma smiled playfully.

"Yeah, that's never gonna happen, perv. I was just talking about skipping. See you at lunch."

Jack kissed her goodbye as he walked down the hall, where he saw Emerson picking up papers that were scattered across the floor.

"Move over and let me help you with that," Jack said, bending down and scooping up several thick packets with his large hands.

"Thanks, I was up late last night. I think I was sleepwalking," Emerson replied, pointing to a deep gash under his eye. "Not sure where I wandered off to. It's weird though, right? I've never been injured while sleepwalking before."

"Yeah, that's weird. It looks awesome, though," Jack said, tracing his finger lightly under the cut, admiring the strange shape. Emerson shrugged.

"Kiss," Emma shrieked as she strolled past, causing the group of girls she was with to burst into giggles. Jack quickly pulled his finger away from Emerson's cheek and blew Emma a sarcastic kiss. She snatched it from the air and tucked it into her pocket.

"Well, that was nauseating. Why did she yell that?" Emerson asked, his face flushing.

"Oh, I asked her to skip with me so we could smooch behind the bleachers, and when she said no, I told her I'd ask someone else. She interpreted that as you," Jack said with a grin.

"Well, that's never gonna happen," Emerson shot back.

"That's what I said!" Jack exclaimed, lightly smacking Emerson in the chest. Emerson's frail frame wobbled slightly. "But wait—what's that supposed to mean? You don't find me attractive?" Jack added, puckering his lips and adopting a hurt voice.

Emerson's face turned a deep shade of red, and he bit his lip, hastily shoving the remaining papers into his bag without responding.

"Well, anyway, I had a weird night too—strange dreams. You were . . . I mean, it felt like a dream you'd have, with all the weird stuff you're into," Jack started, trying to backpedal. "I was in a dungeon, being tortured by this really tall guy, and I'm pretty sure I was in another world."

Jack went on, tweaking the details so that he was the one being tortured—but in the mirror, it was Emerson's face staring back at him.

"You gave my name up just like that?" Emerson blurted.

Jack shrugged, nonchalant. Without wasting any time, Emerson dove into his own dream saga, clearly excited to share.

If you were to look at Jack and Emerson, you'd never guess they were best friends. Emerson had a long, thin face with piercing greenish-brown eyes, and long blond hair that he draped over one side of his face like a curtain. He wore thick, square-shaped glasses, and his skin was dotted with tiny red marks—battle scars from his war with puberty. Emerson was also taller than Jack, and his awkwardly long limbs made him an easy target for teasing.

"Oh crap, I forgot my English book," Emerson exclaimed, yanking open his locker and digging through the mess. "By the way, did you feel the earthquake last night? Everyone at school's talking about it. I didn't feel a thing, but hey . . ." Emerson froze mid-thought. "Maybe that's how I got this!" He lifted his hand to show Jack the cut on his cheek. "Maybe I was walking from the bathroom and fell into the banister while it was happening."

He shook his head and moved on. "Anyway, I saw the cave on the news. I'm so curious about those paintings on the walls—how old do you think they are?"

Jack just shrugged as Emerson withdrew the book he'd been searching for.

"I didn't feel the earthquake either," Jack said. "But you don't want to go to that cave. It's kind of weird. I passed by it this morning."

Emerson's eyes lit up. "Wait—you saw it? Tell me everything!"

"Alright, calm down," Jack replied, sensing Emerson's interest in seeing the cave for himself. "But, yeah, I could've sworn . . ." He stopped mid-sentence, unsure how to tell Emerson what happened without sounding crazy. What if Emerson didn't believe him and asked to go see the cave for himself? Jack felt it would be stupid to return after almost being caught. But if they did go—what if Emerson didn't hear anything? What if Jack really had imagined it all? Reasons upon reasons as to why they shouldn't go were stacking up like a wall of bricks.

"Mm, it's really not worth going there. You can't even really get near enough to see anything," Jack lied dully.

"When do you ever turn down the chance to get in trouble?" Emerson shot Jack a knowing look. "You're hiding something."

Jack struggled for a response—he needed to know if he'd imagined it, but was it worth the risk?

"Alright, let's check it out. We'll skip the next few classes and get back just in time for lunch. I've got a date with Emma then."

Emerson's face relaxed, but his body stiffened. Skipping class wasn't something he took lightly, especially with finals around the corner. Emerson's eyes flicked over him; Jack felt a crack split through his confidence, hoping it didn't show on his face.

"Alright, let's do it," Emerson said as he shoved the book back into his locker, with an excited grin. "This is the last time I'm skipping, though. School ends next week, and I'd like to leave with at least one good memory of this place."

"Right, you've been saying that for the last three years," Jack teased. As they walked down the hallway, Jack stole a glance at the "witch" from his English class. She was applying dark lipstick in the mirror attached to her locker door.

"What's her name?" Jack asked, brows slightly raised as he watched her trace the lipstick with steady precision.

"Adina Maynard. She transferred here at the beginning of the year. Doesn't seem to care about making friends. Honestly, I don't blame her—people here aren't the kindest."

"Even when you're insulting others, you're still polite. People are assholes to you, my dude. You can say it."

Emerson grinned.

Jack's heart began to pound harder as they neared the doors leading to the faculty parking lot. He wanted Emerson to confirm that he hadn't imagined it—that Emerson could hear the voices too—but he also didn't want to go anywhere near that cave. Just as they reached for the door handles, a voice called from behind them.

"Hey!" Jack's friend Addison called, jogging up to them. "Where are you two headed?" He glanced at Jack's devilish grin and raised an eyebrow. "Again? Are you even going to graduate? I don't think you've been to a single class this quarter."

"I think I've made it to a few," Jack replied brightly, shrugging. "How else am I supposed to secure the title of 'Worst Case of Senioritis' if I'm constantly being lectured? By the way, did you catch the news today?"

"The cave thing?" Addison asked.

"Yeah. Apparently, there was an earthquake too, but neither of us felt a thing. We're actually going to check it out now."

Emerson chuckled and rolled his eyes. Jack knew that look—it was the one he gave when Jack was laying it on too thick, and he was trying not to laugh. Jack opened his mouth to defend himself, but Addison cut him off.

"Yeah, I overheard my mom talking to my grandma about it this morning. But I probably wouldn't have felt it anyway—I was too busy shaking the mattress with Jamie last night." He winked, clearly proud of his double entendre.

"And Jamie is the name of what? Your left or your right hand?" Emerson blurted out, the words hanging awkwardly in the air between them. His face flushed with heat, embarrassment blooming in his chest.

Addison blinked, clearly taken aback by Emerson's sudden bluntness. The tension lingered for a beat, then he met Emerson's gaze. His lips pressed into a tight line, like he had something to say—but chose not to. Instead, he just offered a casual shrug.

"Well, go have fun playing cave explorer with your little architect friend. See you at lunch."

Addison tossed up his usual two-finger adieu. As he passed, Jack was pretty sure he heard Emerson mutter under his breath, "Anthropologist, dumb ass."

It only took Jack and Emerson a few minutes to sneak past the school security guard who was escorting two giggling girls who reeked like skunks back into the building. Jack and Emerson snaked across the parking lot, dodging behind parked cars, until they were finally safe in the quiet shade of the forest.

"I honestly don't think I've ever heard you call someone out—well, someone other than me—for being a douchebag before. I'm finally rubbing off on you," Jack said proudly.

Emerson snorted. "God, I hope not. I just can't stand how Addison talks about women. Aside from Stefani, I doubt he's ever even been with a girl—he just talks a big game. And . . ." Emerson launched into another tangent about how disgusting it was when guys, like Addison, objectified women.

Jack, however, had already tuned him out. His mind wandered, still stuck on Addison's smug comment about "Jamie." It wasn't that Jack believed him—but the way Addison said it, so casual and confident, got under his skin, as if he were somehow behind.

His thoughts drifted to graduation night: Emma in a lacy nightdress, candles glowing softly around the room. He imagined her lying beside him, his arms around her waist, his lips tracing the curve of her neck. The thought of their first time made his pulse race, blood rushing through him, a mix of admiration and selfish desire.

Emma had promised to stay a virgin throughout high school—a vow Jack respected, but secretly resented. And now, with graduation just a week away, he couldn't stop thinking about what came next.

OOMPH!

Jack snapped back to reality just in time to watch Emerson face-plant into the forest floor, courtesy of a tree branch he had severely misjudged.

"Who put that there?" Emerson grumbled, rubbing his forehead as Jack helped him up.

Emerson dusted himself off and froze, his eyes catching on something a few yards away: a line of yellow caution tape.

Emerson's face lit up. "This must be it," he said.

The excitement surged through him, but the energy of the scene only amplified how inexplicable this cave must be to have so many people already on-site.

The boys raced to the police barrier, following it around, edging closer for a view of the jagged rocks. The ground was flattened by the footsteps of the adults who had once circled the area—all of whom now seemed to have vanished into thin air.

As they crept closer to the threshold, their hearts began to thud—beating together rhythmically, pulling them forward as if they were strung on invisible thread. Both boys' faces seemed to sink, their eyes widening as they stared at the unfurling fog ahead. The only thing that mattered now was whatever lay beneath the stones, barely beyond their reach.

Then, without warning, voices filled the air, singing in an unfamiliar, ethereal language. The words sounded ancient, and yet something about them felt familiar, almost comforting. Without thinking, they both reached forward, lifting the caution tape. They stepped closer, mesmerized, each unaware of the other, pulled forward by something they couldn't explain.

A sudden gust of wind slammed into them, sending their hair flying in all directions. But they didn't hesitate. They moved toward the cave, as if the wind itself were encouraging them. They moved effortlessly, as if the earth itself were drawing them in, their steps falling in quiet, unthinking rhythm.

Jack's heart was pounding so loud it felt as if it had replaced the brain inside his skull. This was it—he knew what to do. They had to get inside. If they just jumped in, everything would be OK.

When Jack glanced to his side, he saw Emerson already dangling over the edge of the cave's opening. A flash of panic surged through him as he looked down to gauge how deep it was. But before he could stop him, the force erupted again—stronger than the wind—and sent both of them crashing to the ground.

A blood-curdling scream tore through the air, and both boys froze, their hearts slamming in their chests. They exchanged a wide-eyed look, fear flickering between them. Then, a voice called out from behind them.

"What the hell do you think you two are doing?!" a man shouted, spinning around to face them. "That's it—who's about to lose their job?!" His voice rang through the trees as he stormed toward them. "No one is allowed back here without one of these!" He stopped and thrust a plastic ID badge in their faces.

But then, as recognition dawned, his expression shifted into a grin. "Oh, it's you again." His yellowed, gapped teeth gleamed in the dim light as his face wrinkled into a smug grin.

He reached into his pocket, but before they could see what he was about to withdraw, the boys had jolted to their feet and were already sprinting through the forest.

They dove under the yellow tape. Jack glanced back just in time to see Emerson weaving and zigzagging, dodging policemen as they gave chase. They didn't stop running until they reached Jack's house, unaware of their destination until they were standing in the front yard, gasping for breath.

Emerson, still panting, doubled over and retched onto the grass. Jack looked at him, his chest heaving.

"Did you hear that? *Did you hear that?*" Jack gasped, still struggling to catch his breath.

"You heard it too?" Emerson's voice was shaky, his face pale.

"Yeah, of course I did! How could you not?"

Emerson swallowed hard; his gaze distant. "I don't think that man did, or else he wouldn't have been so focused on us. I think . . . I think it had something to do with the weird trance we were in . . ." His voice trailed off as he shuddered, his eyes still unfocused, like the scream was still echoing behind his eyes.

Jack shook his head. "Well, even if that's the case, we can't tell anyone. If we do, we'll have to explain how we got past security, and no one will believe us about what we felt. Whoever screamed down there—it was probably one of the scientists. I'm sure someone's already gone in. We can't be the only ones who heard it."

Even as he said it, the words felt hollow.

That night, Jack stayed up late, scrolling through the web, trying to find any updates about the cave. His eyes burned from staring at the screen for so long, but there was nothing new—no reports of an accident, no mention of the scream, no sign that anything unusual had happened at all.

The silence in the news didn't ease his growing anxiety. What if Emerson was right, and they really were the only ones who heard it? What if the voices only reached those who were somehow drawn to the cave? His mind raced with questions that had no answers, that gnawed at him, making it impossible to sleep.

Someone was down there. What unsettled him most was the feeling that they might already be dead. But there were no reports—so why would anyone cover it up?

He was so lost in hunting for information that when his mother snuck into his room, he almost fell out of his chair at the sound of her voice. *Get a grip, bro.*

"Why are you still up, baby? You need to get some rest," she said as her neck stretched over his shoulder trying to see what webpage he had quickly clicked out of. "There haven't been any new updates, just the ones they've already released," she whispered softly, relieved that this was the information he'd been looking at. She massaged his shoulders as he let out a long exhale, unaware of just how tense he had become.

"I know, Mom. It's just . . ." He struggled to find the words. "I have something to tell you."

Her brow furrowed. "What is it, honey?"

"I skipped school today with Emerson . . ." Jack began, but his mother's disapproval was immediate, her posture stiffening as she crossed her arms. "I know, I know, that's not the point. We decided to check out the cave. Well, when we got there, I heard voices . . . and Emerson did too. I swear, I'm not crazy," he added quickly, more to reassure himself than her.

"Anyway, as we got closer, everything around us seemed to stop existing. The scientists, reporters, and police—everyone—just disappeared. Or something. I can't really explain it, but it was like the cave was pulling us in, inviting us to come closer. Then, when we looked inside, someone

screamed from below. One of those horror movie screams."
Jack's voice trembled. "I think someone might've been hurt.
But as soon as we heard it, a man started yelling at us. He was
reaching for something, so we just ran home. I made Emerson
swear not to tell anyone, but now I feel like we should. I'm afraid
the person might not have survived. I'm afraid it's all being
covered up."

His mother's face softened as she wrapped her arms around
him. "I love you, son," she whispered. She pulled back just
enough to study his face. "It's best not to dwell on it right
now. You need to get some sleep tonight. Tomorrow, when
your head's a little clearer, we can talk more about it. Just know
this—if someone had died, it would have been national news.
This isn't some small thing happening in our town. This is
bigger than you realize."

She kissed him on the cheek and stood up, leaving him with
more questions than answers.

Jack rose and crossed the room to stand in front of his mirror.
This morning, he'd felt comfortable and mature as he stared
at his reflection, but tonight all he saw was a confused, young
child staring back. He wasn't sure why this was affecting him
so deeply, but somehow, he knew that a piece of his destiny lay
beneath those jagged stones.

That's crazy. You need to relax.

A loud buzzing sound echoed from across the room. Jack
looked over to see his phone glowing as it wiggled across his
desk. He picked it up, seeing a notification from Emma flashing
across the screen. His heart skipped a beat. He'd completely
forgotten to respond to her—he hadn't even gone to lunch or
answered any of her twenty texts. She must be furious.

He clicked on the message thread, and his eyes locked onto
four simple words: *Come over, it's urgent.*

Chapter Two

Break-ups and Briberies

Jack re-read the text several times, trying his best to figure out the tone Emma meant. He was quite used to Emma's emergencies consisting of stress over tests he knew she'd pass, the latest cheating scandal involving the Kardashians, or Taylor Swift's ongoing drama with a guy named Scooter. However, today had been so strange, he knew deep down she wasn't crying wolf.

Moving as quietly as possible, Jack slid open his bedroom window, removed the screen, and carefully climbed onto the thick branch hanging outside. After a few Tarzan-like maneuvers, he dropped to the ground and sprinted toward the road.

He tore down the street, his shoes slapping against the worn pavement, until he reached an old, narrow graveyard tucked at the end of the block. Muttering a quick apology, he hopped over gravestones on his way to the fence at the far side. He scaled it without thinking and took off again, sprinting down a dimly lit lane and cutting through yards he had crossed countless times before.

When Jack finally arrived at Emma's large, white country home, a tightness settled in his shoulders. As he glanced toward the neighbor's house, he caught sight of a thin hand pulling back a curtain in the upstairs window. A thin-faced woman with watchful eyes stared down at him.

His heart jumped. Anxiety swelled in his chest, and he kept walking—just far enough to slip out of view—before looping back toward Emma's house. The last thing he needed was to get arrested while his mom lay awake, worried about his mental state.

He crossed the expansive lawn, watching Emma pace inside—her silhouette shifting in the soft glow of a polka-dotted lampshade. Jack climbed the lattice that connected the deck to her balcony. Once he swung himself over the railing, he glanced down, surprised he hadn't crushed any of the flowers interwoven through the lattice.

Jack was nearly to the door when Emma spun around, her body tensing, hand flying to her chest. A moment later, her face softened with recognition. She flung open the door and ran straight into his arms.

"What's wrong? Why are you crying?" he asked as she broke into a hysterical sob. Jack pulled away slightly to take in her appearance. Her usually sleek hair was now tangled, and her perfectly manicured nails were chipped and broken. He pulled her back into a tight embrace, her tears soaking through the cotton, warm against his chest.

Then, just as suddenly, she pulled away and bolted into her room, throwing herself dramatically across the bed. Reaching toward the pillows, she grabbed a picture and hugged it to her chest, her fingers curling tightly around the edge of the frame. For several uncomfortable moments, Jack stood frozen, watching her cry as she clung to it. Finally, he stepped forward, took her by the shoulders, and made her look at him.

"Jack . . . something's wrong with Stefani."

Jack's eyes widened in surprise.

"I—I've been calling her all day, but she hasn't answered any of my calls." Emma sniffled, her voice quivering as she wiped her nose. Jack reached up to brush the tears from her cheeks.

"She hasn't responded to any of my texts, and she wasn't at school today either." She paused, closing her eyes and rolling her head from side to side, trying to release the tension. "Her mom called me, asking if I'd seen her. Said she never came home after leaving this morning."

Whatever Jack had expected, it wasn't this. He pulled Emma close again, cradling her as fresh tears streamed down her cheeks.

He couldn't stop his mind from drifting back to the scream he'd heard earlier that day.

Surely . . . it couldn't be.

No—he couldn't think like that right now.

As he held her, Jack struggled to think of anything to ease her worry. Comfort didn't come naturally to him. Pain, he could manage—he'd learned how to carry it without showing much. He hadn't cried over anything since he was a toddler. He wasn't sure if that was because he'd never been deeply hurt or because he felt the need to be strong for his mother.

Still, Jack couldn't deny the slight twinge he felt anytime he thought of the father he never knew. He had learned to ignore that pain long ago, knowing it would only hurt his mom more to answer questions about the man who died the same day Jack was born.

As Emma's sobs escalated, Jack snapped back into the moment, his nerves beginning to fray. He feared waking her parents—and when he heard a soft cough from the other room, he knew he had to intervene.

"I'm sorry, Emma. Maybe she snuck off to see that guy in Clarion—it wouldn't be the first time," Jack suggested.

Emma scoffed sharply, her eyes narrowing. "She would've told me. I mean, I *am* her best friend!"

The sudden rise in her voice set off a chain of events that made Jack's heart plummet: the lights in the house next door flicked on, a door banged open down the hallway, and Emma scrambled off the bed, tossing the picture frame to the floor with a crash as she attempted to lock the bedroom door, which was already swinging open.

Emma's dad stood in the doorway, tall and scrawny, his narrow eyes flicking to the bed where Jack had just been. He stepped into the softly lit room, his gaze sweeping the space. Nothing seemed out of place—except for the wild wisps of silver hair on his head, which he caught in the mirror above her vanity.

"Ju ok, sweepee?" he mumbled, voice dry and crackling with sleep.

Tear-streaked and breathless, Emma quickly replied, "I'm fine, Daddy. Nobody's in here."

Jack groaned softly from beneath the bed, but Emma didn't miss a beat. "I'm just upset about Stefani. Her mom didn't call back with an update, and I still haven't heard from her. This is so unlike her. I'm just worried."

Her eyes followed her father's as they landed on the broken picture frame on the floor.

"I guess I panicked and knocked it over. If you hear anything else tonight . . . it's just me trying to calm down."

Another groan slipped out before Jack could stop it. Tonight was going to be a long one. Emma was spiraling, and now he'd be forced to offer support when all he wanted was to act.

The scream from earlier had started replaying in his mind the moment he crawled under the bed. It kept cutting through everything else—louder now, sharper, and sounding more and more like Stefani each time.

Had it always?

With her missing, the pieces were starting to shift in his mind, and he hated the picture they were forming.

Maybe it wasn't connected. Maybe he was just reaching.

But what if he wasn't?

"It's a completely healthy coping mechanism, Daddy," Emma added, catching the skeptical look on her father's face as his eyes flicked toward the off-white bed skirt—which had just fluttered, as if stirred by a breeze. He teetered forward, sitting down on the bed, and patted the space beside him. He placed an arm around her, and they sat together in a slightly awkward embrace, staring at their reflections in the mirror.

"Emma, I know you're scared," her father said gently, "but Brookville is safe. Maybe she just needed a break or wanted to go somewhere without anyone knowing. She could've turned off her phone so her parents couldn't track her. It might not mean something's wrong. Didn't you say she's been secretly seeing a college boy?" he asked, trying to hide his disapproval.

Emma didn't reply, only dabbed at her cheeks with her sleeve.

"She'll be back," he continued, steadying his voice. "I know it doesn't feel like it right now, but people disappear for all kinds of reasons that aren't . . . final. It's not like she's dead."

Under the bed, Jack winced at his wording—but couldn't help feel a flicker of relief that, for once, he wasn't the one fumbling through Emma's feelings.

Mr. Rhodes reached out, brushing a strand of hair behind Emma's ear. "If you don't hear anything by tomorrow, we'll get people involved. But I really think she'll show up. You may not remember, but this isn't the first time you two have caused a little panic sneaking off in the middle of the night."

That finally earned a tiny flicker of a smile from Emma.

"And when she's back," he added, standing, "you can invite her to come with us to California this summer."

Emma's eyes lit up. "Wait—are you serious?"

He nodded. "Graduation present."

Emma let out a shriek and hurled herself at him, squeezing him until he let out a wheezy laugh.

Jack, still under the bed, blinked at the whiplash of emotion.

Mr. Rhodes chuckled, clearly pleased by how quickly he'd lifted her spirits.

"Try to get some sleep, sweetie. We'll figure this out tomorrow." With a final glance around the room, he shuffled out and gently closed the door behind him.

Jack waited a beat, then finally slid out from under the bed—only to be met with a face full of pink fluff.

"That's for being completely heartless earlier," Emma muttered, retrieving her little pillow as Jack sat up.

He raised an eyebrow but didn't argue.

"Thank goodness for my daddy," she added, pulling the blanket around her shoulders. "If it weren't for him, I'd be a total mess right now." Then, brightening again: "Did you hear that? I'm going to California this summer."

Jack stared at her, nonplussed, still trying to keep up with her sudden turns.

Emma twirled the corner of her blanket. "I mean, I guess I was overreacting. But it still doesn't feel right. Stefani wouldn't just vanish. Even if she needed space, she'd say something."

She turned back to him, eyes wide with excitement. "But oh my god—I'm going to California."

Jack watched, stunned, as Emma launched into her plans like nothing had just happened. She pulled out a notebook and began jotting down everything she wanted to see, rambling about road trips, beaches, and Hollywood stars, while Jack stayed laser-focused on the hallway, listening for any sound from her parents' bedroom. If he got caught here in the middle of the night, his relationship with Mr. Rhodes would be beyond repair.

After what felt like an eternity, Jack knew he had to silence her; he could sense the restlessness from the room down the hall. Leaning in, he pressed a soft kiss to her lips, then pulled back, his mouth lingering just a breath away from hers. His gaze locked onto her cornflower-blue eyes, which were full of hunger and longing. All at once, the events of the day melted away.

Jack moved his lips to her neck; the smell of her hair made him crave every inch of her body. Emma pulled him tightly on top of her as he started kissing her feverishly. Her back arched around his arm as he slid it beneath her, pulling her even closer. Their bodies melded together into the perfect heart. Jack moved his lips down her thin neck to her collar bone and immediately felt her body stiffen, causing him to pull away slightly more aggressively than he had intended.

"What's wrong?" he asked.

She was breathing fast, her chest rising beneath him. Jack could feel the tension in her body—the way she arched into him one second and froze the next. She looked at him—eyes wide, lips parted—as if her body wanted to say yes, but something inside her had hit pause.

Her gaze searched his, silently pleading for him to understand.

Jack moved to the edge of the bed, letting his feet brush the floor. She crept up behind him, wrapping her slender arms around his thick neck, her breath soft against his ear.

"Sorry," Jack whispered, frustration and embarrassment coloring his voice.

"Shhh," she murmured, her tone firm yet soothing as she studied his face. "You have nothing to apologize for." She paused, her fingers tracing the line of his jaw. "It just can't happen tonight. Not here. Not with my parents so close. Not like this."

Jack forced a smile, but it was strained—so obviously false that Emma looked as if she'd been struck. "Jack, I'm . . ."

"It's fine," he said, his tone sharper than intended. "I love you. I've been waiting for years. I guess I can keep waiting."

The words hung in the air, edged with frustration he didn't fully understand. He did love her—so why was he acting this way? Why did hearing "no" make him feel like a spoiled child who'd never heard it before?

Was it peer pressure? *No, that definitely wasn't it.*

There was only one other explanation he could think of: it was the overwhelming mix of lust and love pulsing through every inch of his body, flowing through his veins, his bones, every part of him. He simply couldn't think of any other way to release it. It was a dangerous combination.

Feeling slightly awkward from the turn the night had taken, Jack cleared his throat and asked softly, "Should I go?"

"No. Stay just a little longer. We can talk," Emma said softly. "I haven't even asked about your day. Who did you end up skipping with? You never showed up to lunch."

She fell back against the pillows, and Jack moved in beside her. He wrapped an arm around her, pulling her close as he quietly recounted everything—the eerie calm at the cave site, the voices, the scream he was sure he'd heard. However, he didn't tell it with the same vigor he would've had just moments ago.

"Well," Emma offered gently, trying to sound rational, "if it wasn't reported, maybe you guys heard something else? That man who yelled at you—maybe it was just him. Your mind probably filled in the rest. Besides . . ." she hesitated, brushing her fingers against the blanket as she looked into Jack's eyes, answering the unspoken fear behind them. "I doubt it was Stefani. My dad's right—she's fine. She was with that guy in Clarion last weekend. Lied and told her mom she was staying with me again. It's just odd she didn't give me a heads-up this time. I've never minded covering for her."

Jack stiffened, the urge to say, *"But what if it was her?"* burning at the back of his throat. But Emma clearly didn't believe there was anything to worry about.

So, he said nothing.

"So, tell me, Emma. What would you say if I took you on a getaway this weekend? You and me, to my grandparents' old farm?" Jack asked, trying to steer the conversation to a lighter note. Emma pulled away slightly, creating more space between their bodies.

"I just want to be with you alone. It doesn't have to be anything sexual," he continued, his voice softening. "Not saying I'd be opposed or anything," he added with a mischievous grin, pulling her back into his arms, "but I really just want to spend a night with you where I don't have to rush home before your parents wake up."

"Yeah, that sounds nice," Emma said dreamily. She'd wondered what a full night alone with Jack would be like. "But . . . I don't know. Are you talking about that old, abandoned farm by my parents' church? Are you even allowed in there? I'm surprised it didn't collapse during the earthquake."

"Yeah, it's only abandoned because no one's really gone in to fix it," Jack explained. "I've worked on one of the rooms. Me and the guys hang out there sometimes, play games, you know. Addison's even brought dates there. It's not bad, I promise."

"Wait, what?" Emma's voice was sharp with disbelief. Jack knew immediately he'd stepped on a landmine. The mention of Addison was always a trigger, and he knew the explosion had finally come.

"You want me to stay the night in a place where Addison, the man-whore, brings naïve girls to hook up? Um, no thanks. That's completely insulting." Her voice grew more heated. "And with everything that's going on with Stefani, you're going to bring him up? She might have pretended to be okay after the breakup, but Jack, she wasn't." She stood up abruptly, crossing the room and opening the door to her balcony. "I'll call you in the morning. Good night."

Jack stood, forcing the same smile he always wore after losing a hockey game. He leaned in for a kiss but was met with the warmth of her cheek instead. Without a word, she locked the door behind him.

Dumbstruck, Jack began his journey home. He moseyed down the dimly lit street, eyes alert for any sign of movement or approaching headlights, his thoughts tangled in the night's events. *What had gone wrong?* He racked his brain, trying to make sense of it. One thing was certain, though: he had to fix this. He just didn't know how.

But why should I apologize? he thought bitterly. *I'm one of the few guys in my class with a girlfriend, yet everyone else seems to have gotten a lot further, and I've been stuck in the same position for five long years.*

He shook the thought away and glanced around, trying to get his bearings.

That's when he heard it: a strange voice calling to him as if from the end of a long corridor. The voice grew louder, and the same sense of captivity he had felt that morning flooded through him again, this time heavier, as though it were anchoring him to the spot.

Jack fought not to blink as he stared into the dark, foreboding trees. A cold wind brushed against him, and then—silence. The voice stopped.

A long-fingered hand grabbed his shoulder. Jack jerked around, ready to swing his thick fist, but his feet slipped on the gravel, sending him sprawling to the ground. Panicked, Jack crawled backward, watching the shadowy figure move into the dim glow of the old streetlamp.

"Did I scare you?" came a light, teasing voice. Jack blinked and saw the bright, spotty face of his best friend.

"Didn't you hear me calling your name? What are you doing out here so late, Jack?" Emerson asked, his tone oddly cheerful.

"Just leaving Emma's. What are you doing out here, punk?" Jack shot back, trying to sound cooler than he felt. He studied Emerson's appearance—he looked . . . alive, more so than Jack could remember. There was an excitement in his expression that seemed almost out of place.

"Oh, you know, just taking a midnight stroll."

Jack raised a skeptical eyebrow. "You look pretty damn cheerful for a midnight walk. Everything alright?"

Emerson grinned. "Yeah, everything's fine. You, on the other hand . . . you look upset. What's going on? And why were you staring into the forest like that?"

The two boys began walking down the road together, and for the first time in a long while, Jack took in his surroundings. He couldn't help but notice how eerie his town seemed at night: the shadows stretched long, and the quiet felt heavy, as though the night was holding its breath.

"Oh!" Jack exhaled sharply. "It sounded like someone was calling me from in there."

He paused, hopeful. "Wait—you said you were calling my name, right?"

Emerson nodded, clearly amused by his friend's paranoia.

"It's been an odd night," Jack continued, deciding to push the unsettling image from his mind. "Emma kicked me out . . ." Jack stopped suddenly, his face lighting up as a plan formed behind his furrowed brow. "Hey, I've got an idea. Could you write me a poem to give her tomorrow? I'd do it, but you're way better with words than I am. I'll give you fifty bucks . . ." *in the graduation card my mom gives you,* Jack finished in his head.

Emerson shot Jack a look of annoyance. "I do your homework for you, and now you're asking me to fix your relationship? Seriously, what do you do with your time?"

Jack made an obscene gesture, prompting Emerson to elbow him while frowning in discomfort.

"You're disgusting," said Emerson.

Jack pouted, which only made Emerson's face twist as though he'd eaten a sour candy. "Alright, alright, I'll write it—on one condition," Emerson added, holding up a finger. "You promise to never make that face again."

"Deal!"

"It'll be in your locker first thing in the morning."

They reached Emerson's house first. Jack watched Emerson, his skin luminous under the crescent moon, walk up the stairs to his porch. Once he disappeared inside and the door shut behind him, Jack finished the walk home, wondering if the voice he'd heard earlier had been real—or if he'd imagined it. Now that he thought about it, he could only hear Emerson's voice in his mind.

When Jack finally reached his own house, he crossed the yard and started up the front steps, but his way was blocked by a fat, ginger cat sitting stubbornly on the top step. As he stepped over it, the cat pawed at his leg, tugging gently. He smiled at its desperate attempt for affection. Sitting down on the step, he watched as the cat brushed up against him.

"Having a rough night too, little buddy?" Jack asked, and the cat answered with a contented purr. Jack absentmindedly stroked the cat as he thought about how to fix the communication issues with Emma.

Suddenly, a loud sound like thunder echoed from inside the house. The cat, startled, jumped down the remaining steps and darted into the night. Jack immediately sprang into action, diving behind the bushes in his front yard. He peeked through the window nearest to him.

Inside, his mom was wandering around the kitchen like a drunken college student on a late-night snack raid. She had several loaves of bread tucked under her arms, a glass of water in one hand, and a bag of Doritos in the other. Jack watched as she bumbled up the old rickety staircase.

Without hesitation, Jack sprinted to the backyard, climbed the tree with practiced ease, and slipped through his bedroom window. He quickly reinstalled the screen, tore off his shirt, and flopped onto the bed, pulling the covers over his head in case she decided to do one of her surprise check-ins.

Jack listened intently as his mom padded back into her room and shut the door with a loud bang. He exhaled, finally allowing his mind to replay the night's events: Emma crying and kicking him out, the walk home, the strange voice in the trees, and Emerson—the happiest he'd seen him in months. Jack had been so caught up in the events of the evening that he didn't even notice the ache in his pelvis until it became undeniable. He swung out of bed and bolted down the hallway, barely making it to the bathroom in time.

Relieved and on the verge of succumbing to sleep, Jack slunk back down the hallway, using the railing as his guide. He was just passing his mother's door when he heard her mumbling inside. Curiosity got the better of him, and he pressed his ear to the door.

"No, I'm not ready to let go . . . I'm not ready for a new life . . . the stories are false . . . lies," she muttered, her voice muffled by the pillow.

The old, unlatched door creaked open slightly as Jack leaned in closer. He reached for the knob, readying to pull it shut, when his mother tossed herself onto her back, her body stiffening as she whispered Stefani's name into the night.

A sudden, bright light flared at the mention of the name, flooding the room with an unnatural glow. Jack's heart raced as he sprinted to his mother's side, her frantic screams filling the air as her body flailed around. He grabbed her shoulders, trying to keep her still and desperate to pull her back to reality—his own heart pounding fast and hard. He pulled her head into his chest as he collapsed to the floor with her. Despite his efforts, she wouldn't wake. Her chest rose with each breath, but her eyes remained shut. Jack frantically scanned the room for her phone to call for help, but it was nowhere in sight.

He bolted down the hall, his breath coming in ragged gasps. He flung open his door, rifling through the mess on his bedside table. It wasn't there. His hands trembled uncontrollably as he dug through the clutter. Then, a loud BANG—like a gunshot—echoed from down the hall. Something massive crashed through the house, its footsteps thundering so loudly that Jack knew it couldn't be his mother. It was coming for him, clanging against the walls as it moved.

A soft buzz sounded at the foot of his bed. Panicked, Jack threw himself onto the mattress as his hand raced toward his phone. He almost had it when the bedroom door suddenly burst open, flooding the room with light. An unseen force slammed into him, knocking him onto his back.

"Jack?!" a soft voice called from the doorway.

He scrambled to his feet, heart pounding, fists clenched—only to find his mom standing there, looking bewildered.

"What's all this noise? Are you having a bad dream or something?"

Jack blinked at her, then at his phone lying at the foot of his bed. *What is happening to me?* Manic laugher burst from him as he struggled to catch his breath. His mom stared, brows drawn, eyes wide, lips parting like she was about to speak.

"Mom, I think I'm losing my mind," Jack gasped, still laughing, unable to stop. *How could any of this had been real?* He felt sick. He lay back on his bed, trying to calm his racing thoughts, questioning whether the entire day had been nothing but a fever dream.

"What's wrong, honey?" his mother asked in caring whisper. "No, lay back down." She brushed his damp hair away from his forehead. "What happened to you? You're soaked."

"I'm not sure," Jack muttered. "I don't even know what's real anymore."

"Well then," she said, sitting down beside him, "what do you think happened?"

Jack hesitated, then decided to play along. "Well, in my dream . . ." he began slowly, trying not to sound completely unhinged. "Emma and I got into a fight, and on the walk home, I kept hearing this—" But before he could finish, his mother's head snapped toward him so fast it looked like she was mid-exorcism.

"On your walk home? You mean to tell me you snuck out of this house and went over to your girlfriend's place in the middle of the night? Are you out of your mind?" she snapped at him.

"I said it was a dream . . . but Mom, that's not the point. Let me finish, please." Jack continued with his story, telling her about the voice in the forest and running into Emerson. His mom muttered something about how kids think they can do whatever they want, but Jack ignored her. When he got to the part about her room filling with light, she interrupted him again.

"Well, clearly you must have been dreaming." She waved her hand dismissively. "Rest assured, I'm in perfect condition, and nothing paranormal happened to me tonight." She paused, then added, "As for you, well . . . you're grounded."

"But it was just a dream," Jack protested, though his mind whispered that it wasn't a dream at all.

"You sneaking out doesn't sound much like a dream to me. You're grounded for the next two weeks. Sneaking out of the house? Let me tell you . . ." Jack didn't fight her on it; he knew she was terrible at following through with any sort of punishment. Jack let her deliver the usual lecture while he tried to stay awake out of respect.

The room fell silent, and Jack took his cue. "Alright, I understand. It won't happen again." His mother seemed to have been waiting for that response, because she bent down and kissed him on the head.

He lay back on his bed, but as he closed his eyes, his mind raced with the memory of his mother whispering Stefani's name in her sleep. He had to ask her about it in the morning. But for now, he turned off the light, hoping sleep would finally claim him.

Chapter Three

King of the Hallways

The next morning, Jack stood vigil at the window like a meerkat on high alert, head swiveling between the student parking lot and his phone as he searched for any sign of his girlfriend. Jack didn't notice the gossiping students behind him, speculating about their supposed breakup—rumors sparked by Emma's emotional Instagram post earlier that morning. Though the post seemed to confirm everything that had happened last night, Jack still needed to talk to Emma in person. There was too much he didn't understand—about her, about them, and especially about Stefani. He couldn't shake the thought that it was her scream he'd heard in the cave. Maybe Emma had heard from her. Maybe there was still a chance it wasn't what he feared. So, he kept his watch over her parking space, sending message after message—void of text, but full of punctuation.

No reply came. That was all the confirmation he needed. Last night had happened. Emma wasn't the type to leave her phone unanswered. Frustrated, Jack made his way to his locker. He yanked it open and watched as a folded piece of amber paper drifted to the floor. He bent down, grabbed it, and read:

Jack, I'm still very upset about last night. I know I overreacted a bit. It's all so fuzzy. However, I will stay with you at that old disgusting farmhouse this weekend. I'm sorry for writing you this note, but I just feel like we need to spend the day apart. I shut off my phone and gave it to Sarah when she picked me up for school today. I didn't want to further escalate things. I hope you understand.

I still love you, always,
Emma Rhodes

Jack chuckled as he reached the end of the note. A surge of intoxicating excitement washed over him. She was going to stay with him—finally! Jack was about to get the chance he'd fantasized about for years. He shoved the note in his pocket and glanced down the hallway, spotting Emma talking to a short, dark-haired girl with a strong build.

I shut off my phone and gave it to Sarah when she picked me up for school today.

That's odd. They haven't spoken since seventh grade. He remembered vividly when Sarah had accused Emma of stuffing her bra and basically bullied her off the gymnastics team. What was Emma doing hanging out with her now? Jack wanted to ask her, but he knew he should respect the space she'd asked for. He headed off to first period, alone.

Entering the room, Jack made his way straight to the back of the class, where Emerson sat, smiling.

"She's pissed! But guess what?" Jack said, slamming the note onto Emerson's desk. "It's finally happening. She's agreed to spend a night alone with me at the farmhouse!"

Emerson scanned the note with judging eyes, and then pulled out a neatly folded sheet of paper from his bag, waving it in front of Jack. "Guess you won't need this then?"

"That's where you're wrong," Jack exclaimed, peeling open the note and eagerly reading. "Dang, bro, this is good. Real good," he said, grinning. "I think I changed my mind about that kiss." He lunged toward Emerson's face, but Emerson pushed him back, his face turning bright red.

"Fine! But seriously, thanks. I owe you," Jack said, tossing the note back on Emerson's desk. "Hey, fold this again for me. I can't do it."

Jack watched as Emerson folded the paper back to a tiny and elegant origami fold, all the while averting his eyes away from the door as Emma entered.

"So, did you do the homework?" Jack asked, changing the subject. "Sorry, I forgot sonnets were due today or I wouldn't have asked you to write that."

"It's fine. I wrote a few last night. I polished one up this morning that I think I'm going to use. I was actually inspired by this," he said as he flourished the poem in Jack's face before placing it back on the desk. "What did you write yours on?"

"Hockey. I copied it from some website."

Emerson scoffed, as he always did whenever Jack brought up sports. He hated them, which Jack figured was because Emerson was terrible at anything athletic—aside from fencing, which he'd picked up at summer camp a few years ago. Jack found fencing boring, but it suited Emerson, who always seemed to be chasing some fantasy he'd read in a book. "No one gets redeemed in a football game. No one saves the world with a bat," he'd once said.

"What's yours about?" Jack asked.

"It's a secret . . . well, more like a revelation. Fortunately, I don't present mine until tomorrow, so I've got more time to rehearse." Emerson grinned.

Before Jack could ask more, the bell rang, and their teacher bounded into the room, his energetic presence overwhelming the students.

"Good morning, class," he called.

The class groaned in reply.

"Before we begin today's presentations, I've got last week's quizzes to hand back. Most of you did well, and some of you . . . well, let's just say it wouldn't have hurt you to actually read the play instead of relying on your good friend SparkNotes," he said, his gaze lingering on Jack.

The room broke out into hysteria as Mr. Pruitt walked around, placing the quizzes upside down upon their desks. Some students leaned in to peek at each other's grades, while others picked up conversations that were rudely interrupted by their teacher's presence.

"What did you get?" Emerson whispered to Jack.

"Fifty-eight. You?"

"One hundred. Jack, you really need to start cracking down. Finals are next week."

"Exactly! Why waste my time now?"

"Your life, I guess," Emerson said, shrugging.

"Alright, who wants to begin today's presentations?" Mr. Pruitt asked, scanning the room for a volunteer. Instead, he was met with a sea of downcast faces. All of his students seemed to have discovered something quite fascinating on the floor. Sarah James, the valedictorian, raised her hand and marched to the front of the room.

"Alright, Sarah, thanks for volunteering," Mr. Pruitt said. "Let me take my seat, and you can begin when you're ready."

The class dragged on slowly since Jack had no other option than to give his full attention because of Mr. Pruitt's deliberate proximity to him. There was nothing entertaining whatsoever about these sonnets, until Adina Maynard stepped to the front with hers in hand and a small, sarcastic grin on her round face.

"Alright, Ms. Maynard, you're up," Mr. Pruitt said.

"OK, just a heads-up. My sonnet contains some strong language, but know my art comes from the heart," Adina said, pulling her dark hair out of her face and flashing a forced smile at the class. She cleared her throat and began reading:

I Hate Sonnets, by Adina Maynard

I hate sonnets more than I hate you all.
They're dull as hell, my brain begins to ache.
Shakespeare's overrated—thank God he's gone,
Six feet under, no longer awake.

Each rhyme's a trap, a damn cage for my thoughts
A box that locks me in; no room to think.
I'd rather scream my mind out, fuck this rot—
Let poetry run wild, not so succinct.

I'll mock the rules and toss them to the floor,
I won't conform or bow to their demands,
For art should never be a fucking chore.
I'll paint my verse with raw, unsteady hands.

And though they preach I'll never bend the knee
My words will fly, unchained and wild, like me!

The class erupted into awkward laughter, some students staring in disbelief while others looked absolutely dumbstruck. Jack, who couldn't contain himself, stood up clapping passionately with fervent woos.

Mr. Pruitt, however, sat calmly with his hands folded on his desk.

"It seems you have a basic understanding of how a sonnet is constructed—though whether intentional or not, you broke quite a few rules, both in the poem and in my class . . ." he added grimly.

"We'll discuss this further during your detention." He paused. "For the rest of the week. You can run down the attendance sheet when you go to the office. Let them know I'll be down to discuss this with Principal Harris after class."

Adina glared at him, unfazed, then grabbed her bag and slung it over her shoulder with force.

"Just because you're a senior does not give you the liberty to curse in my class," he called after her, as she snatched the pink slip and white paper from his hands and stormed out of the room.

Mr. Pruitt moved to the front of the class. "OK, so today's readings went rather well. We will resume tomorrow. Take the last five minutes to rehearse for your presentations. Also, don't forget to fill in your study guides . . . you may have to re-read certain portions of the play, and for some of you," he said as his eyes shifted back to Jack, "read them for your first time."

"What the heck just happened?" Emerson exclaimed as the entire class broke into loud chatter and stunned whispers—none of which had anything to do with practicing their sonnets. "She's absolutely insane."

"It's cruel that I'm just noticing her for the first time," Jack said, clearly impressed. "I'm half-tempted to go down to the office and bail her out. Actually, scratch that—I think I will." He tucked the note and his poem back into his bag before slinging it over his shoulder. His eyes scanned the room, looking for his teacher, but instead, they landed on Emma, who was cackling like a witch and mimicking Adina's hand movements.

"The bell's about to ring. Why don't you wait until after lunch? You know she'll be down there all day. They'll probably move her to the in-school-suspension room anyway," Emerson suggested. "Also, when do you plan on giving Emma her poem? I'm curious to hear what she thinks."

"I'll wait until after school," Jack replied, not out of respect for her space this time, but out of annoyance. "I want her to realize what she's missing."

The bell rang, but it was drowned out by the sound of chairs scraping across the vinyl floor as students rushed for the door. Emerson and Jack parted ways, heading to their lockers in opposite directions, as Jack had swapped with another senior to be closer to Emma. He grabbed his hacky sack and a notebook, then shoved his bag into the empty space.

As Jack walked down the hall, he noticed a crowd growing around Emerson's locker. He quickened his pace.

"Hey faggot, I heard they're finally taking your loony mother in today. Is that true?" a muscled teen with fiery red hair taunted. Emerson, clutching his books tightly to his chest, inched closer to his locker as the bully pushed up against him, his oily nose leaving a smear on Emerson's cheek. "I asked you a question, pizza face. Answer me."

The boy shoved Emerson's books from his hands, scattering them across the floor. Emerson felt a sudden rush of heat as sweat started to bead down his sides. The bully savored the fear in Emerson's eyes before slamming his fist hard into a locker, a mere inch from Emerson's left ear, which now flushed brighter than the bully's hair.

Jack barreled through the crowd, shoving the junior aside, and positioned himself in front of Emerson.

"Oh, you've come to help your boyfriend, huh?" the freckled boy shouted, drawing the attention of the onlookers, all of whom raised their phones to capture the scene.

"You're mighty clever, George, now move aside before this turns into something you can't handle. Emerson, let's go."

The gang of students seemed to mishear Jack. Instead of stepping aside, they closed in, cracking their knuckles and staring menacingly into Jack's cool eyes.

"Did you not hear me?" Jack asked, his voice calm.

"Oh, we heard you. But we're not going anywhere. You're not the king of these hallways, bro. We can stand here and talk to your little sissy friend if we want to."

Jack let out a long exhale as he handed Emerson his notebook and hacky sack. When Jack turned back around, his chin collided with something hard and fleshy. Before George could land his second blow, however, Jack was ready; he caught the swinging fist and slammed his forehead into George's long nose. As George cried out in pain, Jack twisted his arm behind his back.

"You afraid I'm going to mess up your face, pretty boy?" the boy teased through gritted teeth and bated breath as he struggled to get loose. Jack rolled his eyes as he shoved him to the floor. The boy bounced back like a tennis ball and grabbed Jack around the neck, forcing his head beneath his sweaty armpit as his bicep constricted around Jack's face.

"I didn't realize a healthy skin routine was a bad thing," Jack said as he pulled himself free, slightly winded, punching his attacker who fell heavily to the floor this time. Jack pushed through the gathering crowd to get closer to Emerson, who was sprawled on the floor. A kid sat straddled on his chest and was gearing up to punch him again when Jack ripped him off by the collar and extended his hand to Emerson. "Let's go, Em."

Emerson reached for Jack's outstretched hand when the rest of George's gang surged forward. A tangle of legs crashed down on Emerson as he lay on the floor, each blow landing harder than the last. He felt a sharp kick to the head, and for a moment, it felt like his vision was wrapped in gauze. He heard the distinct sound of his glasses skittering across the floor, their lenses spinning away from him.

The hallway erupted into a cacophony of noise; students screamed as arms and legs flailed in every direction. Jack was beating his way through the kicking students, trying to get to Emerson. Teachers poured out of their classrooms, shouting at the students, but their voices were drowned out by the relentless chants of "Fight! Fight! Fight! Fight!"

It took several teachers and security guards to finally pull them apart. Emerson and Jack complied more easily than the others, who continued to thrash in the grips of their captors. Blood stained the floor as the disheveled boys were escorted away. A tall, birdlike woman with a bob of graying blonde hair and a hooked nose led Emerson and Jack toward the office, her heels clicking sharply against the tile.

"What happened, Emerson? How are you feeling?" she asked, as she waved at several students to get to their classes. Turning to Jack, she snapped, "Hold him tighter. We need to have him checked out."

Emerson leaned more heavily on Jack's shoulder, his weight sagging further as they moved down the hallway.

"They attacked me, Mrs. Stone! I . . . I don't think anything's broken . . . Please, can we go to the office before you take me to the nurse?" Emerson's voice cracked slightly.

Mrs. Stone shot him a questioning glance, which he met with a look of consternation. She studied him with pity, but it only made Emerson feel worse.

Once they reached the downstairs office, Mrs. Stone led them into a small waiting room. She gently bent down to lift Emerson's head. "You have nothing to worry about, Emerson. None of this was your fault. Principal Harris will be right with you." She stood, smoothed her skirt, and walked past the other people in the office, offering them a warm, professional smile.

Jack sat nearby, rubbing the back of his neck. The gang of boys who had attacked Emerson were being shuffled into another room. To Jack's surprise, Addison was among them.

"Barbarians," Emerson murmured. "I could've handled that myself Jack; you didn't have to help me."

"Shut it. I wasn't going to allow some grease-faced farm boy push you around. They weren't holding back at all. But, how are you feeling, buddy?" Jack asked with brotherly concern.

Emerson shrugged, his legs bouncing nervously, and the reality of the situation came sharply into focus, as if he had just woken up and was putting on his glasses for the first time.

"Do you think this will be on my criminal record? Do you think they'll think I started this?" Emerson asked, his voice filled with anxiety.

"Emerson, you don't have a criminal record. And honestly, with the way you look right now, they'll know you didn't start this. One of the few perks of being different in Brookville," Jack replied with a reassuring grin.

Just then, the door to the principal's office slammed open, and a rush of untamed dark hair shot out. Adina, looking disgruntled, knocked a stack of papers from the secretary's desk, sending them scattering across the room as she rushed by with her arms flailing. She kicked a few papers as she sprinted into the hallway and out the front door, pausing only briefly to turn around and raise both her fists in a one finger salute to the security cameras above the arch.

Jack burst out laughing as he watched the chubby security guard—who'd been flirting with the school counselor, Mrs. Starwell—slip on the papers as he chased after her.

Jack's laughter intensified as he watched the scene unfold on the camera screen, like something from an old cartoon. Adina had managed to vanish from the grounds as the security guard comically looked both ways, scratching his head, before running in the wrong direction.

"Oh my god, we're screwed. I'm going to be in trouble for something I didn't even do." Emerson exhaled as he stared at the cameras blankly.

"We're fine! Just let me do the talking. You know I have a way with words. You read that poem I wrote earlier."

"I wrote that, you idiot. I have a way with words. Jack, actually, please don't speak."

The principal stood in the doorway while the guidance counselor whispered in his ear. He glanced at the boys, then back at Mrs. Starwell, raising an eyebrow in genuine surprise.

"Boys, please come into my office," said Principal Harris, a lean, bald man with a gravelly voice, as he stepped aside to let them pass. The guidance counselor gave the boys a small encouraging smile as she made her way back to the secretary's desk and bent down to help gather the scattered papers.

Jack and Emerson sat down, both dropping their heads as the principal stared sternly at them. "Before we talk, are you sure you're okay, Emerson? We'd really like to have you looked at by the nurse."

Emerson lifted his head, but his response caught in his throat. He was in pain, but not just from the physical wounds. It felt like he was the root of every problem; his mother was the town loony, known for raging around in kitchen strainers and military hats, screaming about a war brewing in Kazumeth—a battle Emerson felt was only in her mind.

But it wasn't just her. The boys at school knew he was different. He'd always been different. It wasn't just his love for fantasy and anime that set him apart from the other guys in his grade; he also liked guys—something only his best friend, Jack, knew, and the others merely guessed.

Not only that—he was white, yes, but also the only Latino in a town that liked its boxes neat and its labels simple.

"I'm fine. But you know what? This is trash," Emerson snapped, his voice louder than intended. Both Jack and Mr. Harris looked up, startled.

"They came up and started trashing my mom, calling her loony, throwing names at me—and now *I'm* the one sitting here like *I* did something wrong? You're going to question *me* because of *their* ignorance?"

His voice was rising now, his ears flushed red. "How much longer do I have to take this? I keep my head down. I don't even answer questions in class just so people won't notice me. Do you know what that's like? Being too afraid to *speak* because you know it'll just make you a target?"

He gestured wildly, emotion surging. "While that asshole douchehead—"

"Emerson." Mr. Harris raised a hand gently, his tone steady but firm. "First, you were never going to be suspended. Let's be clear about that."

Emerson's mouth snapped shut, his breathing heavy.

Mr. Harris continued, more quietly now. "Second—bullying is real, and it's painful, and I won't pretend otherwise. But it's also, unfortunately, a part of life. There will always be people who try to make you small, because they're afraid of anything that doesn't look or sound like them. That's not a flaw in *you*. That's a weakness in *them.*"

He leaned forward. "What they don't understand is that your differences—your voice, your passions, even the way your mind works—those are strengths. The world doesn't need more people trying to blend in. It needs people who stand out. It needs people like *you.*"

Emerson blinked, his jaw set tight but eyes shimmering.

"Every teacher here speaks highly of you. You've got a brilliant mind, and a future that's yours to shape. Don't give their ignorance the power to shape it for you."

He smiled, the expression genuine and soft. "One day, the very things they mock will be the things others admire."

Emerson gave a shaky nod, his pockmarked cheeks lifting slightly in a smile that trembled under the weight of it all.

Jack shifted awkwardly in his seat.

"Right, so uh . . . we're good to go?" he asked, making his presence known.

Mr. Harris nodded. "You're free to go, both of you."

Jack waited with Emerson as the nurse checked him over and cleaned his wounds. She reluctantly let him leave shortly after. As they walked back to their lockers, they could feel the eyes of their peers on them—students watching to see if they were grabbing their things to head home or preparing for their next class. Jack turned around and gave a sarcastic smile, causing the group across from him to quickly return to fiddling with their locks.

As Jack pulled his bag out, Emma marched up to him, grabbed him by the ears, and kissed him, her lips landing softly on his.

"That was so brave of you to stand up for Emerson like that. Very sweet, Jack. I sometimes forget how much you care about others—even if you do it in . . . stupid ways." She raised an eyebrow, clearly referencing the fiasco from the night before. "I'm really looking forward to spending the weekend with you. Anyway, I was wondering—if you haven't been expelled—would you want to skip your next class? Maybe walk with me to the football field?"

"Sorry, can't skip. Apparently, I'm the king of the hallways—I've got a few decrees to pass before lunch," Jack replied flatly.

Emma's eyes dropped. Jack smiled, unable to hold his grudge. "Emma Rhodes, are you really asking me to skip? Why are we still standing here?" he teased, swooping in to kiss her.

Emerson, who had just walked over, stared at them in repulsed amusement. He rolled his eyes, waved goodbye, and shuffled off to class, his shoes squeaking as they slid across the floor.

Used to escaping the confining halls of his high school, Jack led Emma to the field and under the bleachers without anyone giving them a second glance. They peeked out from beneath the stands as a tenth-grade gym class ran laps around the track. Jack began offering a crude commentary on the event, and Emma couldn't help but join in.

They stayed there for the rest of the class, Jack holding her in his arms as they laughed at the sophomores running slowly in circles. And for a moment, Jack felt like everything had returned to normal. Surely, Emma would've heard from Stefani by now—otherwise, she wouldn't be here, joking with him like nothing had happened.

When the class began to march back toward the school, they kissed passionately, finally alone and undistracted.

"I can't miss this class," she whispered in his ear, pulling away to catch her breath. Jack's face fell at the mention of her leaving, and he gave her his signature wide-eyed puppy-dog look.

"But this has been a very, very nice break from everything," she said, her contagious smile spreading across her face.

"I love you," he whispered. "But before you go, have you heard from Stefani yet?"

Emma's finely trimmed eyebrows rose. "Who?" she asked.

"Umm . . . your best friend?"

"Oh, Sarah. I thought you said Stefani! Yeah, I was with her all morning. Didn't you see us?"

Jack blinked, stunned. Was she serious? Messing with him? Or was this some inside joke he didn't understand? But her expression wasn't playful—it was blank. Unbothered. Like Stefani had never even existed. Just last night, Emma had been convinced something terrible had happened to her. And now . . . it was as if none of it had ever happened.

His stomach twisted.

The scream he'd heard in the cave kept replaying, sharp and jarring, like a splinter in his memory. What if something had happened—and her life had been erased from everyone's mind but his?

What are you even thinking, dude? That's insane. Why you, of all people?

By the time he opened his mouth to ask more, Emma was already gone, melting back into the crowd.

Jack stood there, alone beneath the bleachers, the weight pressing in—Emma's blank stare, Sarah instead of Stefani, the cave, the scream. None of it made sense, yet the world kept spinning, like nothing had changed.

He stayed for the rest of the period, lying on the unused mats, earbuds in, music turned low. He skipped lunch without even realizing it; it didn't matter to him—his mind was only craving answers to the questions racing through his head.

When the final bell rang, he wandered the halls in a daze, eventually finding his way to Emma's locker.

She was already gone. Turning, he saw Emerson's tall, skinny frame approaching, trailing behind several other students.

"Hey, what's up?" Emerson asked as he neared.

"Thought you might want to walk home, talk about what happened today or something," Jack said, knowing that wasn't really what was on his mind. Emerson nodded, and they set off toward the shortcut through the woods.

As they walked, they talked about the fight and Emerson's return to the nurse's office after lunch when his head had begun to throb. He had called home, but no one had answered. Jack half-listened, waiting for a moment to tell Emerson about his brief date with Emma under the bleachers. As Emerson took a deep breath, Jack took control of the conversation, rushing through it as fast as his tongue would allow.

"And when I brought up Stefani, it was like she had no idea who I was talking about." Jack finished his story as Emerson absentmindedly played with a leaf he'd ripped from a tree.

"Mental illness runs in my family, but even this sounds strange. Do you know if her family has any mental health issues?" Emerson asked.

"If they don't, Emma's definitely starting that trend," Jack replied.

"Hmm . . . well, that's all I've got. I have no idea what to tell you."

"By the way, I'm sorry about what they said about your mother . . . are they really taking her away?"

"Nah, they were just talking nonsense. Well, unless Abuelita isn't telling me something. Come to think of it, she has been acting kind of odd lately," Emerson said as he pushed past the last few branches blocking the road that led to their homes.

"Also, Emerson, I wanted to let you know you're the coolest kid I know. Gay dudes are—" Jack stopped mid-sentence as a blond streak whipped past him.

"Mom," Emerson screamed into the still air as an ambulance pulled out of the driveway a few yards ahead, a white van following close behind. "Abuelita, where is my mom? Did they just take her?" he yelled as he rushed toward his grandmother, who was sitting sobbing on the top step of their porch. She held her wrinkled face in her hands, tears dripping between her gnarled fingers onto her lap. "Abuelita, answer me. Where is my mom? Did they take her? Where are they going? WELA!" He grabbed her shoulders, forcing her to look up.

"Tenía que hacerlo, Emerson, lo siento mucho," she sobbed.

In an instant, Emerson sprang from the steps and sprinted like a leopard toward the vehicles already disappearing around the distant curve. Jack raced after him, watching helplessly as his friend crumbled to the ground, screaming. Jack had never heard a sound so painful in his life. He placed one large hand on Emerson's thin, flailing arm, gently bringing it to rest.

"Just leave me alone, Jack. Go home, please," Emerson hissed, his voice cracking under the strain. "I don't want you to see me like this. I don't want anyone to see me like this . . . Jack, just GO!" His voice grew angrier with each word. Jack tried to look into his friend's tear-filled eyes, but when Emerson turned his head, he understood the unspoken dismissal.

"Be strong, kid," Jack whispered as he turned to leave.

As Jack made his way home, images of Emerson running down the street filled his mind, ripping at his chest as he thought of his friend's breaking heart. He was so lost in thought as he passed Stefani's house that it took him several moments to notice that the home was no longer beautiful, but falling apart, as if no one had lived there in years.

CHAPTER FOUR

MISSING

THE FOLLOWING FEW DAYS turned out to be uneventful in the tiny humdrum town of Brookville, Pennsylvania. The investigation was still underway at the site where the world seemed to have split open, but no new information had surfaced. Life went on—people went to work, sent their children to school, gossiped with neighbors—and no one seemed to notice that something unsettling was happening right under their noses. No one noticed—except Jack.

Jack Hackley had been thinking of little else besides the cave since it had erupted into his life. Whether he was lifting weights at the gym, walking to class, smooching his girlfriend, or engaging in any other of his usual activities, his mind always wandered back to the woods and beneath the ground where something odd was transpiring. In those moments he could hear the haunted choir calling his name—and every time, that familiar, inexplicable floating sensation took over him.

When he wasn't obsessing over the cave, he was thinking about the friend whose life seemed to have been wiped from everyone's memory. Jack had been shocked—and excited—to discover that Emerson was also unaffected by the strange lapse in memory that had befallen their town.

"Jack," Emerson said, sprawled out on Jack's bedroom floor. "I was flipping through the yearbook yesterday . . . and I noticed something strange."

He slid the open book across the floor. It stopped at the foot of the computer chair where Jack sat shirtless, staring at the screen while cooling off with a tiny fan attached to a shelf. He picked up the book and glanced down at the page, his eyes scanning it as Emerson sat on his hands, rocking with anticipation.

"What am I supposed to be looking at?" Jack asked, his eyes still skimming the page.

"Stefani Campbell," Emerson said, practically vibrating.

"She's not on this page," Jack muttered, flipping through the pages to find her photo. But it wasn't there. Emerson watched as comprehension slowly dawned on Jack's face.

"She's not in here at all, is she?" Jack asked eagerly.

"Exactly." Emerson's eyes gleamed. "Check the index. She's not listed in the back either."

Jack flipped to the back of the book and scanned the page for her name. He mouthed a few swear words as his fingers skimmed the "C" column multiple times.

"I think . . ." Emerson began, then hesitated, afraid Jack might laugh at his theory.

"What?" Jack pressed.

"I don't think she moved, Jack. I think you're right—something is happening, and it's connected to that cave. I know it sounds kind of crazy," he blurted out, noticing Jack's scrutinizing look, "but it all adds up. Look, as far as we know, we're the only ones who remember her, right?" Jack nodded. "And Emma, her best friend—the one who knows her best—doesn't even know who she is? What if her new friendship isn't new at all? What if Sarah has replaced Stefani in every shared memory? I know it sounds a little insane—"

Jack scoffed, but his eyes betrayed him, revealing to Emerson that what he was saying was exactly what he'd already been thinking.

"One more thing. What if Stefani went into that cave? What if the reason we still remember her is because we were the ones who heard her last? What if that was her screaming inside that cave?"

Jack's mind, muddled with anxiety and confusion, struggled to grasp Emerson's theory. He stood up, walked over to the old, dingy area rug and sat down beside Emerson, tossing the yearbook back toward him. Emerson, to Jack's surprise, caught it.

"I'm positive that scream was Stefani's, but what you're saying is completely nuts, you know that, right?" Jack said, shaking his head.

Emerson slumped a little, discouraged.

"Loco, but right," Jack added, his voice softening. "Stefani's life has been erased, and somehow, we weren't affected. For some reason, we're the only ones who can remember her." Jack paused and stared out the window, overwhelmed. It was too much all at once, and he didn't know what to do with it. "I want to make sure we're completely right. We need more proof."

Emerson sat up straighter. "And how are we going to obtain that?"

"I have a plan. I'm going to check Emma's house first," Jack said, his voice steady. Emerson gave him a quizzical expression as he sank back into the floor. "If Stefani's missing from the yearbook, she's probably missing from other photos too, right? Emma has a ton of pictures of them together—she was holding one the other night when I was there. I'll do a little digging and let you know what I find."

"Sounds good," Emerson agreed. "But if we're right, what then? Report it?"

Jack smirked. "We figure it out ourselves. Who the hell is gonna believe us? We'd end up locked up just like your mom, and with her condition . . ." Jack gave Emerson a sympathetic look. "You wouldn't stand a chance." Emerson's heart plummeted at the mention of his mother, his ache for her release overwhelming the jab that Jack had just thrown.

"Really Em, would you believe someone if they told you a magical cave had taken one of their classmates, but no one else could confirm it because there was no proof she'd ever existed?" Emerson shook his head. Jack nodded in reply. "Exactly. It's up to us."

"You do realize this will require some serious research, right? You can't rely on me for everything. I'll be just as lost as you are."

Jack nodded, shaking off the tension as he braced himself for the long road ahead.

"God, I just need to clear my head," Jack said, massaging his temples. "I've never felt like this before. How do you do this every day? Wanna play a game? I just need to stop thinking for a bit."

As they raced through a spaceship, trying to avoid being slaughtered, Jack pestered Emerson with questions about his secret dates. As usual, Emerson skillfully changed the subject each time. Jack figured it was either because the other person wasn't comfortable being open about it—or because Emerson had made them up to feel less lonely. However, he didn't voice his suspicions.

It was just after eight when Jack's mother called them down to take Emerson home.

"Remember," Emerson said, slinging his bag over his shoulder, "call me if you find anything."

The moment Emerson ducked into the passenger seat of Jack's mother's car, Jack dialed Emma's number.

"Hey, baby, I haven't heard from you all day."

"I've just been hanging with Emerson," Jack replied. He heard Emma inhale, preparing to respond, but he cut her off.

"Look, Emma, can I come over tonight? I really need to see you, even if it's just for an hour."

"Sure, I'll leave my balcony door unlocked like always. Jack—"

"Thanks, babe. I love you," he blurted out before hanging up.

It was eleven-thirty when Jack's mother finally fell asleep—later than usual, but he knew Emma would still be up waiting for him. He climbed down the tree and immediately broke into a sprint, unwilling to waste any more time. The anticipation of uncovering the truth behind Stefani's yearbook disappearance surged through him, propelling him forward with a speed and recklessness he wouldn't normally allow.

As he turned his head to check his surroundings, he tripped on uneven pavement and went skidding across the dark road. Jack cursed under his breath as he pushed himself up, feeling the sting of a shallow scrape, the slow drip of blood around his knees, and, worst of all, the bruise to his ego.

As Jack slowed his pace, he couldn't help but notice how eerie the forest looked, swaying ominously with the wind on his right. The branches creaked, and the fluttering wings of bats rustled from the foliage as they darted toward the moon, which was hidden behind a dark cloud lazily hanging in the sky.

He was getting close to Emerson's home, which still had several lights on. As he passed the olive-colored house, a bright white light spilled from an upstairs bedroom window.

No wonder your eyesight's shot, Emerson—with lights like that.

Jack squinted, blinking as tiny black dots swam across his vision.

He averted his gaze—only to see a towering figure standing in the middle of the street just a few yards ahead.

He stared at the frail, shadowy outline of a man who seemed to be looking directly at him with glowing white eyes. Jack inhaled deeply, eyes locked on the figure, as he cautiously reached into his pocket and withdrew his phone. He flicked on the flashlight, but the light was swallowed by the thick darkness.

"Emerson, is that you?" Jack called hesitantly.

The man said nothing. His wide, white eyes blinked, briefly darkening the street before returning to their eerie glow. He continued to stare at Jack, whose heart began to pound in his chest.

Refusing to let fear take over, Jack lifted his foot, but before it touched the pavement, the figure darted off the road and disappeared into the trees without a second glance.

Fuck this, Jack thought, bolting down the street. A sharp pain flared in his knee, but he kept running, glancing left and right for any sign of pursuit.

When he finally reached Emma's house, he let out a sigh of relief and began climbing the lattice toward her balcony. Inside, she lay casually on her bed, laptop open to an article titled "The Ten Must-Dos While in LA." Jack knocked lightly.

"What took you so long? And what happened to your face?" she asked, letting him in. Her tiny hands gently brushed a cut on his cheek he hadn't noticed earlier.

"Mom took forever to fall asleep, but I'm here now. Oh, and, uh, I kind of tripped on the way. Don't laugh," he added, just as her face broke into a grin. He exhaled, letting her smile steady him. Everything else—the man in the street, the real reason he came in the first place, that desperate search for a single image of Stefani—could wait. Right now, he just wanted to feel something real.

Jack lifted her into an embrace; her lips pressed against his. He sat her back on the bed, brushing her sleek blonde hair aside as he kissed her face, then slowly moved to her long, silky neck. He was just above her collarbone when she grabbed his head and pulled him up playfully.

"So, *this* is why you wanted to see me," she purred.

Jack moaned, biting his lip. Like a lioness with her prey, she shoved him off and pounced on top. They wrestled between the sheets, each trying to gain the upper hand. Victorious, Emma pinned him down, guiding his hands to her waist as she straddled him.

Jack groaned as she leaned in and whispered, "Shh . . . my parents. We have to be quiet."

Emma yanked the blankets over their heads, and they curled into their usual spooning position. Jack breathed her in deeply, savoring the soft scent of her fragrant body wash.

"I love you," he whispered into her ear.

A warmth bloomed in his chest as he noticed she was wearing one of his old hockey shirts. She rolled over so they were face to face, sliding one smooth leg between his. Her hand moved gently to his lips, and he kissed each of her slender fingers in turn.

Jack lay there, admiring every inch of her. As he stared into her eyes, he noticed something had changed. They were sadder—lonelier than usual. She might not remember Stefani, but her body did.

"Hey, babe, could you get us a glass of water?" Jack asked, remembering the mission that had seemed so important earlier but had been forgotten in the heat of the moment. "I could use some after that run."

Emma kissed him softly before slipping out of bed and into the hallway.

As soon as the door clicked shut, Jack sprang into motion. He moved silently around the room, rifling through drawers and checking every frame. There was no sign of Stefani. He paused at her vanity, where he was sure there used to be a picture of the two girls together. It was gone. In its place was a photo of Jack and Emma at homecoming. He couldn't tell if that was a good or bad sign.

Just as he bent toward the floor to check under the bed for the broken frame, he heard footsteps returning. He dove back under the covers just as the door swung open.

"What were you doing?" Emma asked, eyeing him suspiciously.

"Nothing."

Emma raised an eyebrow. Jack knew he wasn't going to find what he needed tonight. "Thanks for the water. I know I said I wanted to see you, but I shouldn't stay too late. I can only hang for another twenty minutes. It's been a long day, and that run kind of wiped me out," he mumbled, annoyed he couldn't think of a better excuse.

Emma crossed her arms and sat on the bed, turning her head away from him like a child. Jack was just leaning in to nibble her ear when something in the vanity mirror caught his eye. Above his head, he spotted a photo he hadn't noticed earlier. It was different. Where Stefani had once stood in the picture, there was now a shorter girl with frizzy hair and wire-rimmed glasses.

Jack, careful not to draw attention, waited until Emma wasn't looking. He reached up, peeled the photo from the mirror, folded it quickly, and slipped it into his pocket.

"Hey, do you happen to have that picture frame you broke the other night?" he asked casually.

Emma turned to him with a raised brow, then pointed to the glittery dresser a few feet away.

There it was. A frame that had once held a photo of Stefani—her dark braids swinging as Emma laughed—was now filled with a picture of Sarah, carrying a much taller Emma in her arms.

"Has that always been the picture in there?" he asked, keeping his voice casual.

"Yes! You didn't care about any of this the other night when I was crying over graduation. Why are you concerned with my pictures all of a sudden?"

"Just wanted to see if you got it fixed. I was going to pick up a new one for you, but I forgot the size," he lied smoothly.

"Right. Well, good night. You were leaving, don't you remember? I don't know why you bothered to come over just to check on a frame. You could've asked me about it over the phone." Her tone was sharp now, arms folded tightly across her chest.

Refusing to take the bait, Jack slipped on his shoes, doing his best to hide the nervous excitement rising inside him.

Emma walked him to the door and watched as he climbed down the lattice and dropped to the soft ground below. He blew her a kiss, but without waiting to see if she caught it, he ran off. He didn't stop until he reached the tree outside his window. He climbed up, stripped off his jeans, tossed his shirt into the corner, and dropped into bed.

Grabbing his phone, he scrolled through his contacts and tapped Emerson's name, trying to steady his shaking hand as he held the phone to his ear.

Voicemail.

He tried again.

Voicemail.

And again.

Each call gave him the same result. Finally, he gave up and sent a lengthy, frustrated text message instead.

Jack closed his eyes, but the images and noise wouldn't stop: Stefani lost in the cave, the scream, the altered photos. He knew he wasn't going to sleep tonight, but he didn't care. He was ready to spend all night trying to figure out any logical explanation for how a cave could make a person disappear and an entire town forget her.

Jack's alarm rang loudly from his bedside table, but he didn't need its warning—he hadn't slept a wink. Thankfully, he could smell a fresh pot of coffee brewing downstairs. Jack listened for the sound of his mother sweeping around the kitchen, but the house was silent, save for the steady patter of rain and the rattling of the screen in his bedroom window.

He slipped on an old t-shirt and walked downstairs, where he found his mother staring blankly at the TV, bathed in the solemn gray haze that filled the kitchen.

"What's up?" Jack asked, observing his mother's altered morning routine.

"Oh, nothing, honey," she replied in a flat tone, flopping from the barstool and walking across the room to pour him a bowl of cereal.

"Didn't sleep well last night, did you, Mom?" he asked, as she slid the bowl in front of him and returned to her seat. "Oy, woman, you forgot my milk."

She walked absentmindedly to the fridge, pulled out the almost empty gallon, and poured it into Jack's bowl—milk spilling over onto the counter.

"Alright, Mom," Jack said, grabbing the jug from her hand. "You didn't even yell at me for calling you 'woman,' and now you're flooding the kitchen with milk. What's going on?"

"Yeah," she muttered, "just need to finish these dishes."

Bemused, Jack glanced at the perfectly stacked pile of clean dishes.

"I'm fine, Jack, really," she insisted, as though just realizing where she was. "I've just been thinking about your father lately . . . about the family . . . and how you must wish your dad were here to see you graduate . . ."

She forced a weak smile. "It just gets hard," she finished, her voice cracking. Tears brimmed in her tired eyes.

Jack placed a hand on her back. "I do think about him," he said quietly. "But I've never wished for more than what I already have."

She turned away to wipe her face on the collar of her shirt.

Jack returned to his cereal, chewing slowly, as his mom left the room. She was right . . . it was hard. He often thought about his father, but he avoided the conversation with his mom, not wanting her to feel inadequate. She occasionally told him stories from their short time together, and during those rare moments, Jack would ask as many questions as he could.

Though he always longed to know his father, he meant it when he said—she was enough.

"We need to get you to school," Jack's mother said as she returned to the kitchen, grabbing the keys she had left on the counter. Usually, Jack would refuse her offer of a ride, but the gray skies and soggy ground made him accept. When they pulled up to the school, Jack leaned in and kissed his mom goodbye before hopping out and waving over his shoulder.

Jack pushed through the throng of people flooding into the school, all of them scrambling to close their umbrellas before stepping inside to avoid seven years of bad luck. He bypassed them all and went straight to his locker.

He wasted no time—he hung up his bag, pulled out his phone, and began pacing the hallway as he repeatedly dialed Emerson's number. After the fourth try, Jack still didn't get an answer. Annoyed, he sent several texts, calling Emerson every curse word he knew. Jack walked down the hall, propping himself up against the skinny blue door that held Emerson's notebooks. He was prepared to wait for him all day if he had to.

"Hey," a high-pitched voice called from down the hall. Jack turned to see Emma running up, wearing her graduation gown. "Why didn't you pick up your robe this morning?"

"I forgot," Jack answered truthfully. With everything going on, graduation—the only sane part of his life—seemed to be the farthest thing from his mind. "Am I still able to pick it up?" he asked. She nodded and grabbed his hand, pulling him excitedly toward the office.

"Back again?" the secretary asked with a forced smile as Emma walked through the door. "I already told you—gowns need to be flowy! I can't alter them . . ."

"Yup, I'm back with company this time," Emma chirped. "Jack Hackley forgot his robe this morning!"

The secretary smiled with relief and handed Jack his square package.

"Hey, do you happen to know if Emerson Garcia picked up his robe yet?" Jack asked casually.

The secretary traced a finger down the list, raised an eyebrow, then gave a small shake of her head.

"Oh, well, thanks," Jack said, turning toward the door.

"Hey, Emma, I'll meet up with you in class, okay?" Jack said as he scrambled down the hallway. When he glanced over his shoulder, he saw Emma staring at him with a befuddled expression. Her attention was quickly diverted as Sarah came bounding down the hallway, flaunting the same robe they all now shared.

Jack returned to his post beside Emerson's locker, praying he hadn't missed him during his short absence. Students were now hurrying down the hall, racing to avoid being marked tardy.

Jack rolled up his graduation robe and slid it under his head, making himself comfortable on the floor. As the halls emptied, he absentmindedly fiddled with a hole in his jeans, all the while continuing to dial Emerson's number. *Emerson, you never miss first period. What's going on?* Though, deep down, he already knew.

"Hey," an authoritative voice called from somewhere to his left. "Get to class, Mr. Hackley! It's the last day before finals, and most of us are reviewing important material. You of all people are going to want to take advantage of this."

It was Mr. Wright, Jack's favorite teacher, waddling down the hall toward him. "You know this attitude won't work in college! Now get off your ass and get to class."

Jack didn't argue. He simply picked up his belongings and headed toward first period. He gave the teacher an excuse and took the open seat at the back of the room. Jack avoided Emma's concerned stare as he slouched into the chair, his bag slumping to the floor beside him.

Under the cover of his desk, Jack continued dialing Emerson's number. He was so consumed by his phone that he jumped when the dismissal bell rang. He bolted to the front of the room, bumping into other students who had just stood up, and ran down the hall to return to his post.

He waited several minutes, but Emerson still didn't show. Knowing he couldn't be caught again, Jack decided it was best to hide in the bathroom until second period began. He paced around the bathroom, receiving several curious glances from underclassmen at the urinals. He counted down the minutes until it was safe to resume his watch.

As Jack walked in circles, he couldn't help but envision Emerson walking out of photos, his name vanishing from records, and every yearbook page rewriting itself without his best friend. Jack was deep in thought when a seventh grader entered, carrying a hall pass.

"What are you doing?" Jack barked.

"I . . . um." The boy trembled. "I was just . . . I just need to go to the . . ."

"Right, sorry, dude. Make sure you wash your hands when you're done."

Jack walked out of the bathroom and back down the hall. He couldn't wait any longer—he needed to know. Checking to make sure the coast was clear, he pulled the plastic lock off the handle of locker number 112. He slid it into his bag and pulled the door open. As he peered inside, his face dropped in horror. Nothing but a dead fly, lying upside down in the corner, filled the once-packed space. The images of ancient wizards, Einstein, and all the unique things Emerson had once plastered inside were gone.

It felt like the ground had dropped out beneath him. He refused to accept it. He slammed the door shut, walked briskly down the hall, and yanked open his locker. Jack grabbed his hoodie from the hanger, slung his bag over his shoulder, and sprinted out the side door. He dashed across the slippery parking lot and into the thick foliage lining the school's perimeter.

Mud splattered up his jeans as Jack plowed through the underbrush, breaking through branches as he plunged deeper into the trees. Halfway through the forest, the ground suddenly seized his foot, sending him tumbling across the sodden earth for the second time in two days. The contents of his bag spilled everywhere, and the humid scent of marshland filled his nostrils.

He didn't bother gathering his things. There was only one book that mattered now—just one book he needed to see: last year's yearbook.

His feet soon found pavement. Jack moved down the street until he rounded a small curve and his eyes landed on an old, overgrown olive-green house.

No. His jaw dropped. He knew this house all too well. It was the lively home where Emerson had lived just yesterday. Now, its welcoming façade was faded. The paint was peeling, revealing moldy wood beneath. The foundation had sunk into the earth, and every window was boarded up with planks of wood.

Without thinking, he walked up the rotting stairs of the front porch.

Jack peered through a narrow gap between the planks on the window as his foot slipped on the moss-covered floor. Inside, the room was filled with old, forgotten furniture. There were papers scattered across the floor and a thick layer of dust. The air reeked worse than a neglected litter box. Tiny bones scattered the floor, and animal droppings coated every surface. Tipped on its side was the couch Jack used to sit on while playing video games—now riddled with holes, soaked in filth, and claimed by some creature as its nest.

Jack tore a few boards off the window and squeezed inside. The once-high, white ceilings were now stained brown and cracked, with tiles scattered across the decaying floor.

His heart thudded in his chest as he climbed the broken staircase and pushed open the half-hinged door to the room where Emerson used to sleep. All that remained was an old chest beside a moth-eaten mattress. Jack pulled the chest open, only to be showered with cockroaches and flies. An old, mildewy stuffed animal lay inside, maggots squirming over its limbs and crawling out through its abdomen.

Jack slammed the chest shut and raced down the stairs. As he jumped the last few steps, his arm knocked an old, jeweled cane from the wall. It clattered to the floor, but Jack didn't stop to put it back. He had to get out.

He climbed out through the window and sank onto the porch, an overwhelming weight settling into his body. His mind raced while everything around him seemed to slow. How could this be real? How could any of this be happening? It didn't make sense. The only explanation he could come up with was magic. *But magic didn't exist.*

Did it?

It was time to let someone in on the secret; he needed to tell his mom. But how could he convince her that what was happening was real? How could he make her believe something he wasn't sure he believed himself? Then he remembered: the yearbook. Maybe that would be proof. Maybe, like Emerson could remember Stefani, his mom would still remember the boy who had spent countless weekends in her home, acting as if he were a second son.

As Jack neared his house, a cool, clasping pressure gripped his insides, twisting with increasing intensity. The bile rising in his throat threatened to spill across the blacktop.

He climbed the stairs to his room, his mom's voice floating up from the living room as she vented about work. Jack knew she'd be up soon to scold him for skipping school, but he didn't need to give her an excuse today—he must look feverish and strung out by now. With every step he took, his stomach churned harder, the fire in his muscles more intense than any workout.

The thought of what he might find in the yearbook consumed him entirely.

When he entered his room, Jack spotted the yearbook beneath the windowsill, shining like a beacon against the dark world outside.

He flipped through it until he found the page with his and Emerson's picture.

Gone.

Emerson's photo wasn't there—nor anywhere else in the book.

Jack slammed it shut in frustration and shouted.

"Everything okay, honey?"

"I'm fine," Jack called back, hearing her just outside the door. "Sorry, just a rough day. I wasn't feeling well, so they sent me home early," he lied.

His mom opened the door, and with one look, could tell something was wrong.

"Oh, honey, you need to take a nap. We can talk when you wake up." She crossed the room to pull the curtains shut. "I'll go grab you some water."

Jack tore off his damp clothes and changed into gym shorts. He then crawled into bed after his mom had brought in a glass of water and closed the door behind her. He stared at the ceiling, letting his mind unpack the boxes of endless possibilities he had been too afraid to open—the ones Emerson lived out of every moment. The ones that held the secrets of the world, so vast that even peeling back the lid felt like an exhausting endeavor. Only someone truly remarkable could be brave enough to uncover what lay inside: magic, the supernatural, the secret of existence. All of it was waiting for Jack to understand.

Jack wanted to tell his mom now, but she was already in her car. He assumed she was off to the store to buy him some medicine. As he considered what he might say to her, he wondered if she'd even believe him. After all, he had a reputation for making up outlandish stories to avoid trouble. And how could he be taken seriously without another witness—particularly one with a knack for turning the strange into the plausible? Someone like Emerson.

A vein throbbed in his temple as he struggled to think. He'd never felt anything like this before—and hoped he never would again. His pocket buzzed, vibrating against his leg, but he had no urge to read the message from Emma. Instead, he lay there, zombie-like, staring at the ceiling, the cracks snaking down the walls seeming to grow wider with every second. Jack tried to sit up, but at that exact moment, a loud splintering snap resounded through the room. His hands shot above his head instinctively, bracing for falling debris.

When Jack opened his eyes, the floor beneath him had vanished, replaced by a blanket of hardened snow. He looked around, realizing he wasn't in his room at all. The walls were gone, replaced by tall, white trees with exaggerated limbs that hung low, blocking out the sky. Snow fell in soft puffs around him, and a crackling sound filled the air, followed by the distinct noise of breaking glass.

Jack jolted upright, ready to fight—but there was no one there. The snow felt strangely warm beneath his bare feet as he walked among the trees, scanning for the source of the footprints pressed into the snow. As if in response, a voice called behind him, sending a spike of adrenaline through his legs. Jack moved faster, and soon, through the trees, he saw the pale, blotched face of his best friend.

"Emerson," Jack called out, his voice carrying through the stillness. "Emerson, there you are!" But the boy didn't react; he just continued to stare through the thick trees as if Jack weren't even there. "Emerson . . . bro, can't you see me? Em?!"

"I'm lost! I don't know where I am . . . please, I want to go home." Emerson's voice trembled, his eyes wide with panic. But he wasn't looking at Jack—he was staring past him, into a wild bush Jack hadn't noticed before.

"You are home, in Kazumeth, Heir of Hernando," a squeaky voice chimed in. "I'm sorry to inform you, there is no returning to the land you've left behind."

Jack stepped closer to his friend, placing a hand on Emerson's trembling shoulder, but Emerson gave no sign he'd been touched. The bush suddenly shifted, moving toward them. As it came into focus, Jack realized it wasn't a bush at all, but a furry creature that barely reached his waist, hunched over an old, twisted walking stick.

The creature wore a strange diadem resembling a third eye, a black stone glowing like a large, unblinking pupil between its wide, yellow eyes. Its mouth curved into a small beak, and oversized ears jutted out from the sides of its head, twitching with each sound. Wispy, gray fur covered most of its body, except for its birdlike legs and feet. Its fuzzy fingers—more human than animal—rested lightly on a twisted wooden staff. A leather satchel was slung across its narrow chest. There was something about the creature—odd, ancient, and slightly comical—that made Jack both uneasy and intrigued.

"Come with me," the creature urged, extending its hand to Emerson, who hesitantly grasped it, rising from the snow-covered ground. "Let me take you away from these miserable winds to a much quieter wood: O'Keen—my home."

Jack followed, trudging through the snow behind them, but the moment the winds picked up again, his senses were drowned out by a wall of white. When the blizzard subsided, Emerson was gone. Jack stood alone in the snow.

As it cleared, Jack saw his bed—his headboard nestled between two towering pines. He rushed toward it, leaping back onto the mattress, expecting to wake the moment he hit the covers.

Nothing changed.

He closed his eyes, picturing his room as vividly as he could, but when he reopened them, he was still surrounded by swirling flurries and trees.

The sound of breaking ice cracked through his thoughts. A deep grunting followed, then the thunderous sound of a stampede tearing through the forest. The ground trembled beneath him, shaking his limbs as cold shivers crawled down his spine. Finally, a hand touched his head, and Jack rolled over, coughing violently—to find himself back in the dim light of his bedroom.

His mother was leaning over him, gently brushing the hair from his face, her voice tinged with concern.

"Jack, are you alright? Why didn't you call me to pick you up if you were feeling this sick? What's going on?"

"No . . . I didn't think about calling . . . Mom," Jack murmured, his foggy brain clinging to the memory of the night before—a flash of clarity cutting through the haze. "The other night, you said you'd tell me something in the morning... What was it you wanted to talk about?"

Her eyes widened with fear as she stared at him.

"Does it have anything to do with Kazumeth?"

She gasped, rushing across the room to slam the door shut, as if afraid someone might overhear. "How . . . how do you know about Kazumeth?" she asked, her voice trembling.

Jack shrugged, not eager to share his dreams with her. She sat on the bed, her expression torn, and after a long pause, she finally spoke.

"Jack, I . . . I'll tell you everything I know. It's very tricky business, and until recently, I barely believed it myself." She had never shared the strange dreams she'd had, nor the final conversation with Jack's father before his death. She had never mentioned the other world she'd known about for most of her life.

"Mom, just tell me. I think I'm going insane. Please—tell me I'm not."

She stared at him, overwhelmed by the pain she saw in his eyes. She exhaled deeply, allowing those forbidden words to finally spill from her lips.

"You remember the legends I used to tell you? The stories about the Sovereign Five?" Jack nodded, urging her to go on. "Well . . . your father was part of that group. I know you've never been one to believe in magical places, but—"

"Mom, at this point, I'm willing to believe anything," he interrupted. "Are you telling me my father was part of some secret covenant?"

"Yes—and no. I don't know much about that part, Jack. You have to understand. When your father and I first met, I started having strange dreams—almost like hallucinations—about a world called Kazumeth. A tiny creature warned me about what was coming.

"When I finally told your father, he didn't laugh. He told me that's where he was from. That he carried a deep magic in his blood, enhanced by a Vocation Stone—magic that always passed to the youngest in a family line. He said one day that magic would pass to you, and when it did, his body wouldn't be able to survive here anymore.

"Without the magic, he'd die—unless he was called back to Kazumeth before your birth. Then, instead of dying . . . he'd simply disappear."

Her voice cracked. "I thought he was joking. But soon after you were born, he died."

Jack's stomach twisted. "Then why didn't you ever tell me?"

"I didn't want you to know," she said quietly. "I wanted you to live freely without this wild idea of your untimely death or fading from our world hanging above your head. I cried myself to sleep. But the dreams kept coming—always of Kazumeth, always of that creature . . . a Pilfert."

She paused, her voice growing more strained. "The other night, it returned. It told me you'd be called back to Kazumeth—that a cave would be discovered, and you'd be drawn to it. That you'd fade from this world, just like your father had said all those years ago. It told me my memories of you would be replaced and that I'd move on as if nothing from my life was missing at all. It's all part of the magic cycle in a world that refuses to believe."

Jack's mind was spinning. "I'm going to disappear?"

"Yes," she said, tears spilling over. "But you won't die. I know that much. The children of the Sovereign are being called back to Kazumeth—to restore balance, to heal both worlds. I thought I had more time. I thought I wouldn't lose you unless you became a father. Thankfully, you've never shown much interest in that."

Jack stared at her, wide-eyed. "So, I don't have a choice?"

She smiled weakly, brushing a tear away. "I wish you did. But your destiny—your bloodline—it calls you to Kazumeth. And the others might already be there."

His chest tightened. "Mom . . . I think Emerson might have passed through already."

She blinked. "Who's Emerson, dear?"

Jack's heart sank. "Never mind," he whispered. She had already forgotten. Soon, she'd forget him too.

"I'm going to lie down," she said softly, kissing his forehead. "I suggest you do the same."

Jack sat on his bed, staring into space. Everyone he loved—his friends, his mother, even Emma—would soon forget all about him. He pulled out clean clothes for tomorrow, grasping at some last shred of normalcy as he ignored the cold air hardening in his lungs. He thought about the weekend ahead and prayed he wouldn't disappear before then.

His phone buzzed. A message from Addison lit up the screen: *You and the weasel skip again?*

Jack's fingers trembled as he typed: *Do you mean Emerson? He's not with me. Why?*

He waited, heart pounding. Twenty minutes later, the reply came: *Yeah, I just assumed he was with you. He wasn't in my last period. What are you up to tonight?*

Jack's chest clenched. He fired back: *Meet me after school.*

He shoved his phone in his pocket and stepped out into the drizzle. His feet carried him past Emerson's house again, dread pooling in his gut. He had an hour until school let out—no need for shortcuts today.

As he walked the quiet streets, Jack's mind drifted back to the dream he'd had days earlier—Emerson, chained to the floor of a dark dungeon, wincing in pain as a shadowy figure loomed above him. At the time, the names Pilfert, Sovereign Five, and Kazumeth meant nothing—just strange words that dissolved the moment he woke. But now, with pieces falling into place, Jack's fear only grew. He didn't know what had led to Emerson being chained up, or whether anything he'd said—like revealing his name—might put him in danger too. But if that dream had been more than just a dream—a warning, perhaps—then time could already be running out.

In truth, he didn't even know what any of it meant. This wasn't about betrayal, nor was it about protecting himself from some unknown evil. It was about his best friend possibly being in danger. And if there was still time, Jack had to save him.

He waited by the school gate until Addison's tall frame finally appeared. Jack gave a small nod toward the woods. Without a word, they turned and headed into the trees, their boots splashing through puddles. Jack's heart skipped a beat, knowing that his fate—and possibly Addison's—was tied to the stones just meters ahead.

CHAPTER FIVE

THE GIRL IN THE FLOWERED DRESS

JACK TOSSED HIS YEARBOOK aside and grinned as Addison's mouth dropped open in disbelief. Without missing a beat, he flicked a crumpled gum wrapper straight into it.

Addison gagged as he spit the wrapper onto the floor. "So, you're telling me we're part of some magical cult? Bro, I thought you gave up smoking months ago." He raised an eyebrow at Jack, clearly unconvinced. "Because this? This is some stoner-level nonsense."

Jack flipped open the yearbook again and flipped through the pages, pointing at the empty slots for Emerson and Stefani, as if no words were necessary.

"How do I know that's not just a conveniently misprinted book?"

"Check yours when you get home," Jack replied casually, leaning back against the headboard of his bed. "This might be real, it might not, but whatever is going on, it's happening because of that cave—I know it. At this point, I don't see how you can deny magic is real. I've shown you proof right there with that book and with Emma and Sarah's picture. Just ask your mom, maybe she'll know something, just like mine did."

Addison gave him a skeptical look. Jack understood why: Addison's mother had become distant ever since his stepfather was killed. But this was important—it was about her past and present. Addison couldn't think of a reason she shouldn't share this with him, her only son.

"Also, there's another reason this might be real," Jack continued, pausing to study Addison's unreadable expression. "I think Emerson and I heard Stefani the day she disappeared. The day she passed through the cave and into Kazumeth."

"Fine. Say I believe . . . whatever all this is. What are we supposed to do about it?" Addison asked, sounding less skeptical, but still not convinced.

"I've been thinking, and I know you'll think it's nuts—but I think we need to go into the cave. It's the only way to figure out what all of this means. The other day, the news said there are writings on the walls inside. Maybe everything we need to know—the instructions on how to pass through, or whatever—maybe that's what's carved on the walls. Look," he added, noticing the hesitation in Addison's eyes. "I know you don't care about Emerson, but you and Stefani have a past. Just go with me, please? Something's not right down there, and we're the only ones who know what's really happening. We're the only ones who can fix this. I'm sure of it."

Jack wasn't really sure of it. He was also not sure where the words had come from, but he was relieved to have said them, because Addison's expression had shifted from scrutiny to excitement. Once again, Addison seemed confident, even eager.

"Alright, I'm in. Do you want to go now?" he asked as he ruffled his auburn hair.

Jack thought about it. He needed to uncover what was happening in his town—needed to find Emerson and save him from the fate he'd seen in that cellar. But another part of him, one he'd suppressed for so long, was roaring to life. It begged him to wait. Tomorrow night was his date with Emma.

What was one extra day, anyway? Emerson was with that little Pilfert creature—surely he was safe.

Plus, one question still lingered—who was the fifth? Maybe if they waited, that person would reveal themselves. The group was called the Sovereign Five, but only four had been accounted for.

Jack thought of Emma but quickly pushed the thought aside. It couldn't be—not if she could forget Stefani so easily. The idea made his stomach churn, his heart grow cold, and his mind catch fire.

"No, not tonight. Emma and I have a date tomorrow. If this is my last one, I want to remember every detail." *Even if she won't.*

"Sunday, then. Let's meet at five. If this is what you think, it'll give us time to get in our final goodbyes," Addison said. Jack could tell he was trying to be brave, but deep down, Addison was just as scared as he was.

After Addison left, Jack pulled out his phone and called Emma. As they talked, he let himself believe that nothing had changed—that he was just Jack, the senior dating the most beautiful girl in the world. When the conversation ended, he heard his mother call from downstairs.

"I'll be down in a minute," Jack called as he walked to the window. It was raining again. Staring through the fog, a branch banged against the window, drawing his attention back to his reflection. His brown skin looked gray against the glass. His stone face, once sharp, now looked tired. Turned off by his appearance, he looked away, focusing instead on the street where a red car sped by, splashing water over two kids who screamed in delight. Their mother, shower-capped and robed, stood on the porch, yelling at them to come inside, but the kids ignored her, continuing to race around the yard.

Jack's mother called again, and with a solemn expression, he descended the stairs, afraid to face her, and the quiet weight of everything still left unsaid.

To his surprise, she was in a spirited mood, as if their earlier conversation had never happened. "Do you want to eat in the living room and watch a movie?" she asked brightly as she emerged from the kitchen. Her sudden mood change made Jack feel uneasy.

"Um, no, I was hoping we could talk."

She smiled warmly at him, her skin glistening as if she had just come in from the rain. She placed his plate on the table and sat down across from him.

"Are you feeling better . . . from earlier, I mean?" she asked.

"Yes," Jack replied. "Though it does freak me out, you know . . . that you will—well," he trailed off awkwardly, "that you're going to forget about me . . ."

"No magic in the world could ever make me forget my beautiful boy," she said, her eyes glassy with emotion, her smile soft and steady. "You've been a gift to me. Jack, my miracle baby."

Jack squirmed in his seat. This conversation was about to take a cringeworthy, but necessary, turn.

"You've accomplished so much here. You've always been a hero to me. I prayed that you'd go off to college, never have kids, so I'd never have to let you go—but I always knew that was an irrational dream. You're more special than you could even imagine."

Here come the tears.

She quickly composed herself and added, "Just know, whatever happens, I'm proud to have had you as a son—even if you were a pain sometimes. You are, and will always be, the one good thing I did in this life."

"I love you, Mom," Jack said, his voice suddenly thick with emotion.

They fell into a comfortable silence that not even the rain pounding the windows could shatter. Jack stared at his full plate, his stomach heavy and tight, leaving no room for the food his mother had spent all evening preparing. "How about we put that movie on? I'm sorry, I know you made this, but I'm just not that hungry."

"First time for everything," she said with a chuckle. His mother took his plate into the kitchen, wrapped it in plastic, and grabbed an old favorite DVD from the shelf.

While Jack watched her laugh and cry at the fictional couple's ups and downs, he felt completely empty and isolated, as though he were watching from the other side of the world, high in a tower with no one else around. His heart seemed to sink into his chest, resting on top of his stomach. Still, he pushed the ache aside, holding onto the little time they had left.

It was as if his head had barely hit the pillow when the sun began to blaze against his face, urging him to get up. His night had been plagued by dreams of dragons chasing him down the streets of Brookville, swallowing him whole, and spitting him into the air where he would land on tiny, unstable planets. They would wobble beneath him until he lost his balance, sending him spinning endlessly through space.

Jack rubbed his eyes as the sound of his phone rattling on the floor reached his ears. He saw it poking out from the pocket of the jeans he had worn the night before. He crossed the room more carefully than usual, determined to remember every single detail of the space where he'd slept for the last eighteen years.

The cold, dark wooden floor beneath his feet felt as cool and soothing as walking on the wet sand of a beach; the clean clothes piled in his hamper smelled fresh from the dryer; the intricate woodwork covering the base of every part of the house gleamed as rays of light filtered through his curtains.

As he bent down to grab his phone, he looked at the vintage images of tatted women and beautiful blondes that flooded his walls, noting how much he'd miss Amber, who was kneeling on a beach, posing nude with just a sheer cloth covering her breasts.

"Good morning," Emma called excitedly into the phone. "Did I wake you?"

"No," Jack answered groggily, but truthfully. "Do you want me to pick you up already?"

"No, not yet," she replied to Jack's relief—he still had quite a bit to do this morning. "I was thinking you could pick me up around eleven, if that's alright?"

"Yeah, no, that's perfect," he responded, grateful for the three extra hours, one of which he hoped to spend back asleep. "I'll see you then. Love you," he added before tossing the phone to the bottom of his disheveled bed. He bent over to set his alarm for an hour, then flopped back onto the mattress. It felt like he had just shut his eyes again when the alarm went off.

Jack showered and dressed in his favorite pair of jeans and a short-sleeved flannel shirt that clung to his biceps. He stared into the mirror, concentrating as he tamed his thick brown curls. After unbuttoning a few buttons to expose the top of his he chest, he sprayed a few spritzes of cologne, then walked downstairs.

It wasn't until he stumbled forward and landed spread-eagle in front of the door that he realized his mother had been sitting at the foot of the stairs. Jack quickly got to his feet and extended a hand to her. She grasped it weakly, her seafoam green robe draped over her elbows, revealing a soaking wet shirt. As he turned his face toward hers, he noticed her eyes were puffy and red. The coffee she had been holding had spilled across the floor, but neither of them moved to clean it up.

Jack took a deep breath and cradled his mother in his arms. He was starting to feel overwhelmed by the emotions that had been building up over the past few days—and by the new emotions stirring inside him, emotions he didn't know how to deal with. He didn't like it. He began to think he'd feel much more relieved once he was gone, when the world would forget he ever existed. At least then, his mother's heartbreak might heal, and his own, well . . . it would be distracted, which was what he preferred.

"Mom, you've got to stop this," he said softly, as her body began to tremble. He stayed with her as long as he could spare, comforting her and trying every trick to make her smile. In the end, she managed to offer him a sorrowful "have fun" as he finally walked out the door.

"Hello, Mr. Rhodes," Jack said as the disgruntled, willowy man reluctantly stepped aside to let Jack enter his home half an hour later. He walked into the living room, fully aware of Emma's father watching him with pure loathing.

But Jack wasn't focused on Mr. Rhodes. His attention was entirely on Emma, who'd just appeared at the top of the stairs. A mischievous look must have crossed his face because, in an instant, his view was blocked by Mr. Rhodes's unruly, dust bunny-like hair. Jack sidestepped him as Emma began to descend.

She wore a simple floral dress that hit just above the knee. A belt was tied around her waist, accentuating her figure. Her sleek hair was pulled to the side, with a white and gold flower tucked behind her ear. Her cheeks were flushed with makeup, and her lips, painted bright red, looked fuller than usual. As she reached the living room, her father placed a thin red cardigan over her shoulders, his hands lingering as he held her close.

"Dad, please," Emma whispered softly as his thin fingers retreated, reluctant and slow.

"You look beautiful," Jack murmured as he kissed her gently on the cheek.

"Thanks," she giggled sweetly. "Daddy made reservations at the old country club in town. I figured we could have lunch there, then do our picnic for dinner. Is that okay with you?" she asked, though Jack knew his answer didn't really matter.

"Of course, thank you, sir," Jack said, grasping Mr. Rhodes's frail hand a bit too firmly. "And thank you, ma'am," Jack added to Mrs. Rhodes, whom he hadn't even noticed had followed Emma downstairs. Mr. Rhodes opened his mouth as though to say something but, seeing the look on his wife's face, he swallowed his words and gave Jack a curt nod instead.

"You just have her back here by nightfall," Mrs. Rhodes said, breaking the tension that hung in the air. Jack nodded, though he felt slightly confused. He took Emma's tiny, freshly manicured hand and led her to the car, opening the door for her and helping her inside. After climbing into the driver's seat, he waved at her father before reversing out of the driveway and onto the main street.

"What did she mean by 'Have her back here by nightfall'?" Jack asked, feeling defeated.

"Don't worry, I've got it all figured out. I'll just say we ran into Sarah at the mall." Jack opened his mouth to protest, but she shushed him. "We're not going to the mall. It's just a cover story. I'll tell them she invited me over, and I'll be staying at her place. If he calls, she'll tell him I'm taking a shower or something and that I'll call back later. Then I'll call him from my phone and say she's grabbing snacks or something." Jack raised his eyebrows, and Emma added, "But I'll really be with you. Thank God you're pretty," she added condescendingly, patting his face.

Jack felt as though they were in a bubble. The soft glow from the spherical lights cast tiny rainbows around the dining room of the country club as they lost themselves in conversation. It was as if they were the only ones there, and time passed in a blur—they didn't even realize the bill had been sitting on their table for over an hour. At last, the impatient waiter arrived, his sour expression relaying his annoyance.

"Glad you're enjoying yourselves. I just didn't know we were running a bed-and-breakfast now."

Just like that, the bubble popped.

"You've been done for an hour. My shift ended forty-five minutes ago."

Jack reached for his wallet, completely in shock at the bluntness of this waiter. However, Emma had already withdrawn a card.

"Daddy gave me money for this," she said. "Don't worry about it. You've taken care of everything else; this one's on me."

"Fine, but I'm leaving the tip," Jack replied, feeling slightly emasculated but determined not to let it show. He slid a twenty-dollar bill into the crack of his seat and left a note on the table: "Your rudeness doesn't deserve a tip, but I'm not a shitty person, so if you find it . . . it's yours." Emma scolded him as they left, but Jack didn't hear. He was too busy watching the waiter scurrying around the table, his face growing redder as he searched for the bill.

"That was rude, Jack," Emma scolded again once they were in the car. She slammed her seatbelt into place, staring at him with an incredulous look.

"He was rude. No, actually, he was a dick. If I hadn't challenged his bad service, who would? Consider it my civic duty," Jack said, hoping his words would soothe her.

They did not.

Realizing she wouldn't let it go, he got out of the car, went back inside, and walked to the table where a backside was sticking out from underneath. Jack grabbed the twenty from the seat and dropped it under the cloth. The body immediately emerged. The server gave Jack an exasperated glare as he waltzed back to his station, grabbed his bag, and moved to sit at the bar.

"Happy?" Jack asked as he reentered the car. Emma nodded, and he slid his seatbelt over his lap.

The drive to the farmhouse felt heavy in Jack's stomach. His nerves had finally caught up with him as he realized what was about to happen. When they pulled into the wide driveway that curved around to the back of the decaying barn, Jack jumped out and rushed to the passenger door before Emma had a chance to reach for the handle. She stared at the barn, its roof damaged, with random branches poking through.

"Regretting coming here now?" Jack asked as he watched her lift her small nose toward the sky.

"No," she said, not fooling him.

They continued walking to the porch, and up the stairs, where Jack helped her avoid the soft spots in the rotting boards. Once they reached the door, Jack tried to lighten the mood by scooping Emma into his arms.

"Close your eyes," he instructed as he opened the door. He carried her through the dirty, dilapidated house, up the stairs, and into the one room he'd completely remodeled.

"OK, open them," he said, setting her down and flicking on the lights.

Her eyes widened in shock. The room was a soft symphony of blues, with candles lining a blanket spread across the middle of the floor. Jack watched her face, wondering if she was as impressed as he'd hoped—and *not* wondering how he managed to light all the candles. Addison's name would only kill the mood.

The warm glow of the flames reflected off freshly polished mahogany baseboards. She walked around, running her hands over the dust-free walls, marveling at the circle lamps hanging from the ceiling. Each lamp was a different color, adding a whimsical touch to the room. A small white couch sat at one end, beside a TV and gaming system. Her gaze shifted from the couch to the picnic, and then to the bed. Her mouth parted as she took in the smooth walnut headboard, decorated with photos from their relationship, each clipped up with tiny clothespins: snapshots from dates and dances, photo booth strips, and MacBook selfies—a carefully arranged wall of memories.

"Wow, Jack, I'm . . . speechless. You did an incredible job. I . . . you did do this, right?" she teased, crossing the room with a seductive sway. She moved toward the bed. "Well, don't just stand there. Come here and kiss me," she said in a soft, sensual voice he had never heard from her before.

His body responded instantly, a surge of blood rushing through him. He moved toward her, almost leaping to her side. He kissed her with a fervor he hadn't felt before, pulling her closer by her sweater as he allowed himself to fall onto the bed. She fell with him, landing lightly on his chest.

"Wait a second," Jack said, sitting up. She slid to his side as he reached behind him and pulled out a blue pen with a TARDIS on top.

"What's that doing here?" Emma asked, puzzled.

"I don't know . . . it's Emerson's lucky pen. He must've left it here when he helped me clean the other day."

"Addison has a lucky pen?" Emma teased.

"No—" Jack started, then stopped. His stomach plummeted. Of course she thought he said Addison. "Yeah. Addison," he said, forcing a smile. "And you have a lucky hair clip," he shot back, moving past the Addison name drop as smoothly as possible.

"Yeah, and every time I wear it, everything goes my way," she taunted.

"Well, you're not wearing it today," Jack pointed out with a grin.

"I don't need it," she whispered, leaning in close. "You're in control," she added, her breath warm on his neck, sending tiny shivers down his spine.

Jack took her hands and placed them on his shoulders. Her cool fingers traced down his shirt, slowly unbuttoning each one. Jack let the shirt fall off as her hands slid to his thick chest. Using the edge of his jaw, he tilted her head, guiding her gaze from his body to his eyes. He kissed her softly as he positioned himself above her.

His lips trailed down her body as he gently let her dress fall to the floor. He paused, admiring how their skin melded together. This was it. Jack gazed into her eyes, an unexpected fear creeping over him. What if he wasn't good at this? Real life was nothing like what he'd seen online. He relaxed as he saw the fear mirrored in her eyes. In that shared moment of understanding, the spark between them reignited. He kissed her softly, love and desire intertwining into a single, indescribable feeling. He gently lowered himself onto her, completely enveloping her. Their kiss deepened with passion; they were both lost in each other—fear and doubt forgotten.

Sunday morning unfurled in the distance as soft beams of light crept across the wooden floor in scattered patches. The two lovers lay entwined in the disheveled sheets, still and silent, their faces so close they could have been conjoined. The forgotten basket sat on the floor, and the candles that had once dotted the room had burned out, leaving pools of wax stuck to the floor. Jack gently brushed Emma's blonde hair from her face.

"Good morning, beautiful," he whispered, the words he had longed to say for years. She pulled the sheet tighter to her bare chest and smiled.

"Thank you for last night," she said, giggling as she spoke. "Am I supposed to say that?" she added with another laugh. "I mean it, though. It was perfect." She kissed him, then rolled over, yanking the sheet from beneath him. She wrapped it around herself and crossed the room to gather her clothes, which were scattered across the floor. After dressing, she grabbed her phone and noticed three missed calls.

"Oh no! They're going to kill me," she muttered, checking her phone. "Daddy called. Get dressed. I'm going to go talk to him downstairs." She opened the door and stepped into the sunlit, mildew-scented hallway. "This place is disgusting!" Jack heard her yell as she stumbled over a loose floorboard.

Feeling relieved and peaceful, Jack began to get dressed for the day. He reached into his pocket for his keys when he felt his phone vibrate. Still wrapped in his contentment, Jack pulled out his phone—only for his moment of serenity to be suddenly ripped away.

Make sure you're here by five! The message from Addison flashed across the screen, dragging Jack back into the bedlam he had momentarily forgotten.

"Got that cleared up," Emma said as she reentered the room. "Ready to go?" she asked. Jack wanted to protest, to ask her to stay with him in this room and never leave, but the words didn't come. Instead, he nodded.

"Are you alright?" Emma asked as she slid into the car.

"Yeah," Jack replied, his eyes fixed on her. "Emma," he began, his voice tense. "I want you to know that no matter what happens in the future, last night was beyond perfect. I can't even tell you how amazing it felt and how happy I am. I know I'm getting all sentimental here, but I needed to say it. I love you more than anyone else in this world ever will. I want you to understand that, Emma Valentine Rhodes. I love everything about you, so don't ever compromise who you are, no matter what may come. Never, ever stop being you."

She stared at him, her eyes searching his face as if she had missed something.

"Are you breaking up with me, Jack Hackley?"

"No, of course not! I just wanted you to know, in case something happens and I . . . disappear forever, I just want you to know that you are wonderful, and not to change—that's all."

They fell into silence, the air heavy with everything left unsaid, until they reached Sarah's house, where she stood outside, shifting nervously by her car. Emma gave Jack a half-hearted kiss, her brows slightly furrowed, before jumping out. She paused, mouth open like she had more to say, then decided against it and shut the door.

Jack watched her walk toward Sarah's passenger door, catching her gaze briefly when she turned back, an uncertain expression on her face.

He wished, with everything in him, that this cave would turn out to be a hoax—that he'd wake up from a coma caused by a skating accident or something. But he knew the truth.

He drove home with an emptiness in his chest. It was the loneliest he had ever felt in his life.

CHAPTER SIX

THE FEAST OF OGOF

ADDISON SAT IN AN overstuffed armchair, his gaze fixed intently on the magnificent grandfather clock in the corner of the lavish living room. He watched, unwavering, as the hands came to rest on six and twelve. The chimes rang loudly through the high-ceilinged room and out to the porch, where the person he'd been waiting for finally arrived—exactly one hour late. As if on cue, the doorbell rang.

Addison sprang from the chair and bolted across the freshly polished floor, scuffing it with his shoes as he slid into the foyer. His mother's voice rang from her office, yelling at him, but he ignored her and flung the front door open.

"You're late," he hissed.

Jack shrugged, scrunching up his thick eyebrows and smiling innocently.

"Sorry, but the last supper ran a little longer than I expected." He chuckled half-heartedly at the poor attempt at humor. Addison tried to ignore the comment, but the chill crawling down his spine made it difficult. The thought that they might never leave the cave haunted him—visions of their dead bodies decaying in the depths flashed behind his eyes.

"Right," Addison said, forcing a smile. "Let me go say goodbye to my mom, and I'll be right out."

"Take your time," Jack replied, his voice sympathetic as Addison turned and walked down the empty hallway. Jack shut the door to give them privacy and made himself comfortable on the top step. He stared out at the pond across the road. A tiny fox sipped from the misty water, and two swans glided by. The road was eerily empty, so the only sound Jack could hear was the rustling of trees as the breeze moved through them. As he watched the fox, he marveled at how beautiful the small creature was. For a moment, the world seemed perfect.

Then, suddenly, Jack saw movement in the trees—a lean, dark shape slinking toward the fox. He stood on the step, frozen, but it was too late. The coyote lunged, its teeth sinking into the fox before Jack could react. He turned away, disgusted and shaken.

Was that what they were walking into? A world where they wouldn't even know they were prey until it was too late? A sharp pain spread through his body, his mind overwhelmed with the uncertainty of what lay ahead.

What would happen when they entered the cave? Would there really be an entrance to Kazumeth? How would they survive in this new world? And if they did pass through, could they find their friends?

Jack was just beginning to wonder if they'd gotten it all wrong when a soft voice behind him pulled him from his thoughts.

"Are you ready?"

Jack snapped out of his reverie and turned to find Addison standing there, his expression unreadable.

"Yeah, I think," Jack lied, his voice tight, knowing deep down he wasn't ready at all. Addison handed him a checkered green backpack and slung another over his own shoulders.

"What did you put in here?" Jack asked.

"Rope, flashlights, and a few things from the kitchen in case we get hungry . . . I wasn't sure how long this would take," Addison replied, as though he still half-expected to be home in bed by nightfall. They shared a brief, silent moment of understanding before heading down the road together.

"So, do you believe yet?" Jack asked.

"That this is some kind of portal to another world?" Addison replied skeptically. "Yeah, I'm not quite there with you on that yet." Jack shot him a disgruntled look. "I'm not ruling it out. Clearly, something strange is going on . . . I just find it hard to believe that's what it is."

Jack felt a flare of irritation, but he had to admit, it did sound ridiculous. A portal to another world in his town? And he was supposed to be part of it, of all people? Still, deep down, he knew it was true. He believed his mother—he'd had similar dreams. Why would she lie about something like this?

They chatted about Jack's night with Emma as they made their way down the winding dirt road that stretched from Addison's house to the edge of the forest. Jack thanked him for lighting the candles ahead of time, and Addison raised an eyebrow.

"How'd you even convince her to go through with it before graduation?"

Jack shrugged. "Still not sure. She never questioned it." A sly smile crept across his face. "Honestly, I think she wanted it more. And it must've been good—she initiated round two in the middle of the night."

Addison smirked, clearly entertained. "Big guy's finally trying to catch up to the rest of us, huh?"

Jack gave a cheeky wink. They veered off onto the less-worn path, ducking beneath low-hanging branches and kicking aside fallen limbs. With every step deeper into the woods, Jack's unease thickened.

Jack had long since turned off his emotions—something he had mastered over the years—but these last few days seemed to bring up everything he'd never allowed himself to feel, especially as he thought of those who would soon forget him. He cleared his mind. He had a mission—to save Emerson, and then possibly the world. But as that thought drifted through his mind, he couldn't help but realize how absurd it sounded. *How could someone save the world when they didn't even know what they were saving it from?*

"Here we are," Addison whispered as they reached the yellow caution tape. "Where is everyone?"

"They're here. It's just how it works," Jack whispered back, eyes fixed ahead. He was beginning to understand how the cave operated. Every time he came here, it called to him. Whatever magic was inside—it wanted him there. The cave made him invisible to the guards, and them to him. The key was not breaking his concentration.

"Just focus on the cave and our task," Jack reminded Addison. "Don't break it or they'll be able to see us."

Addison stiffened next to him and began to walk forward awkwardly. Jack chuckled softly as he followed.

They moved in tense silence, holding their breath as they neared the uneven rocks. They peered down into the dark, foreboding hole. No scream issued from the cave this time. Jack stepped forward, hoisted himself onto the edge, and prepared to jump.

"What the—are you crazy?" Addison exclaimed. "You can't just jump! Do you not remember how deep that is? I brought rope. We can tie it to this rock and lower ourselves without cracking our skulls."

"It's fine. Stop thinking or they'll see us! Just trust me. We won't need rope."

Jack somehow knew the drop would be like missing the final two steps of a staircase.

"I'm going in first. If it doesn't work—get help."

Addison shot him a look like Jack had lost his mind.

Jack took a deep breath and plunged into the shadows. It only felt like a short fall, but when he looked up, he could barely make out Addison's silhouette leaning over the now miniscule hole.

"I'm alright! Come on down," Jack shouted as he brushed dirt off his jeans. Seconds later, he heard a thump and knew Addison was beside him, already rummaging through his backpack for a flashlight.

"Wow," Addison exclaimed, shifting the light around and pointing it up at the spot where they'd jumped. "OK, now I'll say I believe. There's no way I fell that far," he said in awe.

A moment of silence followed as they both took in the enormity of what they had just done. Both were imagining their lives being erased from the memories of everyone they knew.

"Right," Jack said, clearing his throat, "let's get to work."

Addison aimed the flashlight directly at Jack's face, who swatted it away.

"Get that out of my face, p—" Jack stopped as the beam of light caught the opposite wall. A giant crack split the cave, branching outward in the shape of the letter "K." Images and words were scrawled and painted all around it.

"Well, that was fast," Jack muttered. "Let's check it out."

They splashed across the floor, ducking under stalactites as Jack pulled a second flashlight from his bag.

They stared at the size and intricate details of the images. After a few moments, they decided to split up to examine the cavern's vast walls. They called out to each other each time they found something interesting. However, after Addison's sixth trip to Jack, he finally told him to only call if he found something useful—not just because there was an image resembling a penis on the wall—one that Addison suspected Jack had drawn himself.

"Hey, Stempinski!" Jack shouted.

"If this is another rock dong, I swear—"

"It's not. Just come here!"

Jack pointed his light at a massive wall mural as Addison came running up. It depicted a colorful village sprawled across a large hill that ascended out of a vast body of water. At the top of the hill sat an elegant golden castle, flames sparking from every rooftop. They flickered in the dim light, casting shadows as tiny people and creatures Jack had never seen before ran down winding roads that flowed like rivers down the hillside. A towering figure rose at the peak, its upper half shaped like a man, the hillside town spread below like a vibrant cloak. As the light flashed over it, Addison could have sworn the figure's electric blue eyes flickered with flames.

"Creepy," Addison muttered. "But how will this help us find the entrance?"

"There's more."

They turned to see another image: a man on the ground, a sword at his throat, blood trickling into a growing river of corpses. The same hooded figure grinned grotesquely above it all.

"Whoever painted this could give Tarantino a run for his money," Addison said.

"Right, and look—there's this word carved right here: 'AJESA' . . . I've seen it scrawled all over these walls," Jack said, his hand trembling as he held the flashlight.

"It was written down there too. There were a bunch of words and symbols I didn't recognize. And there was this picture—a giant snake, the word 'Ogof' etched into its skin. It was positioned like a wall. On one side was Earth, and on the other, a red-shining letter 'K' . . ." He stopped, the final word lodging in his throat

"Blooood . . ." Jack said, slipping into a thick, prolonged Romanian accent.

Addison shot him a withering look, his face reddening.

"I'm serious. This isn't the time for jokes, bro. I was actually about to call you, but you yelled for me first," Addison said, his voice tight.

Jack pursed his lips, lost in thought.

"Hm," he grunted. "Take me to it."

They carefully made their way to the other side of the cave, navigating slimy rocks and jagged stalagmites. With every obstacle, Jack couldn't help but be impressed by the speed and agility Addison had shown earlier.

"Here it is," Addison said, shining his light on the wall.

Jack stared at the image as his hand skimmed over it. He pressed his palm against the ominous red "K" and whispered the word beside it.

"Ogof," he read aloud, his fingers brushing over the snake's coils.

As if reacting to his voice, the serpent's head turned, and its body began to slither. Addison stumbled backward, crashing into something hard and wet. His flashlight hit the ground with a shattering crack.

He spun around, frantic, but then saw that it was just a stalagmite.

"What the hell, dude?" Jack barked, his heart pounding, blood thundering in his ears. Fear gripped him as he realized his flashlight was now their only reliable light source—aside from the weak glow of their phone. His grip tightened as his palm grew slick with sweat.

"That snake just moved. That snake just moved! Did you see that? What the fuck?" Addison yelled, breathless. Jack flashed his light toward Addison's face, which had gone paper white.

"I did," Jack said. "Do you just want to get out of here? Forget this whole thing?"

Addison nodded.

"Well, that's too damn bad. There's no getting out. We came down here for a reason. And in case you forgot—we jumped in. We need to figure out how to get—" Jack turned to shine his light on the snake, but it was gone.

"The snake's gone." Jack's voice tightened as he swept the beam along the wall, scanning in frantic arcs. But the image had vanished. As he turned back toward Addison, something strange happened: the red ink coloring the letter "K" lifted from the stone, leaving behind a deep, widening crack as it spilled down, mingling with the image of the world, flooding its oceans with blood.

A faint hissing rose from the crack, slithering through the air like steam escaping a kettle. Jack's heart dropped.

"Jack, let's get out of here. Come back here with that light!"

"We can't!" Jack shouted, his feet pounding the stone as he surged forward, desperate to escape the cave—and forget everything about it.

And then something happened.

A massive force struck the backs of Jack's legs, knocking him off balance. He swung his arm toward the impact, but nothing was there—only an odd stone archway, shaped like the entrance to an ancient church.

"Hurry, Jack! I think something just slid past me," Addison gasped. "I think something else is in here. I think we woke it up," he called in a harsh whisper.

Addison watched Jack's bobbing orb of light flicker toward him like a frantic strobe. When Jack finally reached him, Addison snatched the flashlight and swept it across every shadow and crevice, searching for movement.

"Right. Let's get the fuck out of here."

Addison grabbed his bag, and the two of them hurried back toward the center of the cave. As they walked, Jack was strangely relieved by Addison's hysterical behavior—he seemed on the verge of a breakdown, spinning in desperate circles, shining the light in every direction. Somehow, Jack even found it somewhat amusing.

When they finally made it back to the entrance, the light from above filtered down, casting pale beams across their faces.

"I told you we should've used the ropes! We could've just climbed out if this didn't work. But no—'Just jump in,' you said. 'We're magical!'" Addison bellowed, pacing back and forth as he searched for an escape. "Ugh! This whole thing was a waste! And now we're stuck down here. Thanks, Jack. We can just sit here and rot or get eaten! Fuck you, dude—I knew I shouldn't have listened to you."

Jack felt his body heat up as his hands began to shake. He was glad it was dark—he was sure the look on his face would've scared Addison. Though he was embarrassed by the mistake, he was also overwhelmed with the urge to punch Addison in his stupid, red face. Instead, he took a deep breath, wrung out his hands, and replied through clenched teeth, "Well, you didn't have to follow me. You could've tied the rope and tossed it down if you were that concerned. So don't pin this all on me. You believed just as much as I did."

They started shouting, blaming each other—voices echoing into the abyss. Insults flew, obscenities spat. Then, finally, laughter.

"A magic cave—honestly, what the hell were we thinking, coming down here?"

"Wait—what if we break our focus? That's how Emerson and I became visible again."

"Even if we could think of something else for a while, I'm not getting arrested for trespassing. My mom wouldn't even bail me out."

"Really? You'd rather be eaten than arrested?"

Jack watched as Addison's eyes lit up, panic replaced by the spark of an idea.

"Wait," Addison said, "What about our phones? We could call your mom—have her talk our way out of this. The police would probably do anything to cover up the fact that two kids slipped past their security and ended up down here."

"Sure," Jack muttered, frustration boiling over—as if he hadn't just suggested this himself. He yanked the bag off his shoulder and, without meaning to, slammed it into Addison's chest. The impact knocked the flashlight from Addison's hand, sending it clattering to the ground with a heart-sinking crash.

"What the hell, dude?!" Addison's voice echoed sharply through the cavern.

Ignoring him, Jack dropped to his knees and dug into the bag, fumbling for his phone. Once he had it, he shoved the bag aside. Addison, visibly irritated, scooped it up and hugged it to his chest.

The glow from Jack's screen cast a faint pool of light around them. He scrolled through his contacts and tapped the name he needed. Holding the phone to his ear, he waited.

After a few seconds he pulled the phone back—and there it was, the dreaded message: *Call Failed.*

"Shocker. No service," Jack muttered. The pale blue light flickered across Addison's sunken face. "Well? Didn't you bring yours?"

"I was in a rush . . . I left it on the charger . . ." Addison's voice trailed off.

"I'm sorry," Jack said suddenly. "This was a stupid idea." The weight of their situation pressed down—they were trapped, invisible, and two hundred feet underground.

"Should we start yelling?" Addison asked, not quite ready to give up.

"Haven't we already . . ." Jack started, but then he caught a glimpse of Addison's scared expression in the faint glow of his phone screen and couldn't bring himself to finish. "Yeah, sure. That'll work."

Jack was furious. He'd been so sure they could pass through—that this was the key to bringing their friends back. This cave had already taken two brilliant, talented people. He had to end it. But he didn't know how. He still believed the cave was a portal to another world. And if they made it out, he'd come back. Alone.

"On the count of three, make as much noise as you can," Addison said, his voice firm.

"One . . . two . . . three!"

The boys screamed at the top of their lungs, shouting obscenities, stomping their feet, and clapping their hands. The sound echoed off the cave walls, building into a cacophony that reverberated around them—growing louder and louder. But it never disturbed the hole above.

They stopped and listened, hoping for any sign of a response, but the only sounds were their own voices bouncing back at them. The echoes grew so intense that they were forced to cover their ears.

"Well, looks like we're screwed. I'm sorry, Addison," Jack muttered, glancing toward the spot where his friend should have been standing. "Addison? Bro, where'd you go?"

He pressed a button on his phone and swung the dim light through the darkness, scanning for the tall, ginger silhouette. Nothing.

"Addison!" Jack's voice tore through the still air. "Where are you, dude? Say something!" he yelled into the vast cavern.

No response.

He started walking, palms outstretched in front of him, the faint light from his phone casting an uncertain glow in his right hand. Blindly, he navigated around the crowded stalagmites. His foot slipped into a deep puddle hidden between the stone arches he had noticed earlier, but he kept the phone above his head, careful not to let it get wet.

Panic was rising within him like smoke in a sealed room—thick, choking, impossible to escape. Addison was missing, the flashlights were broken, and here he was, stumbling blindly through a tomb of stone and silence, screaming into the dark like it might answer back. The whole rescue had curdled into disaster. Jack sank to the ground, burying his head in his hands, and let out a raw, frustrated yell.

"Addison, if you made it through to that place without me, I'm gonna rip you apart when I get there, you selfish dick." Something slammed into him, sending him sprawling across the damp floor. His phone cracked on impact, but he snatched it up and shined the feeble light in the direction of the hit. Nothing was there. The phone light flickered once, then died completely. Jack let out another yell of frustration—but immediately regretted it. Something crashed through a stalagmite behind him at the sound, and he heard the scrape of scales on stone.

Desperate, he tried his phone again, and with some incredible luck, the light flicked back on. There it was—illuminated in the weak glow—a long, yellowish-orange snake coiled in a massive loop. A single, acid-green spike jutted from between its eyes.

Jack screamed, scrambled to his feet, and ran—eyes locked on the creature, sprinting blindly into the dark.

SMACK!

He slammed into a pillar. His phone flew from his hand—there was no saving it now. Dropping to his knees, he scrambled across the slick floor, fingers fumbling across knotted rock.

Suddenly, a blinding white light flooded the cave, then shifted to an eerie green glow.

Jack looked up—and froze.

The snake had circled around him, its thick body encasing him like a trap. It lowered its head and opened its wide mouth. There were no fangs, but Jack knew death when he saw it. Grabbing its massive head—thicker than his torso—he twisted it into a headlock. The snake didn't resist. Jack slammed its skull against the rock, then scrambled over its body and bolted toward the center of the cave.

He screamed for help, but the cavern offered nothing in return—only his own voice echoing back mockingly. The snake lay still a few yards away, knocked out—or so he hoped. But Jack's terror grew. His gaze flickered, catching a shifting shadow in his peripheral vision. Then, just as quickly as it had appeared, the light and heat vanished, and he was swallowed by darkness.

Jack stumbled behind a boulder, making himself as small as possible, trying to control his breath.

"I'm going to die," he muttered, eyes squeezed shut. "If I'm going to die here, I'd rather not see myself get ripped in half."

Out of nowhere, the snake's tail struck him. Jack was hurled into the air and slammed down hard—but somehow, he caught hold of its jagged spike. Gritting his teeth, he swung himself onto its back, clinging tight. The serpent thrashed, crashing into the cave's ancient stone, desperate to shake him off. But Jack held on. He wasn't letting go.

He lasted only moments before his head slammed into a low-hanging stalactite. His grip loosened, and he crashed to the ground with a heavy thud. Dazed and aching, Jack stared at the creature, which seemed transfixed, its attention on him filled with an unexpected kindness.

Jack watched in horror as it opened its massive mouth, unhinging its jaw. It slithered closer to his feet. Jack screamed, trying to crawl away, but deep down, he knew it was hopeless. A long, eggplant-colored tongue unfurled from inside the creature, curling around his soaked shoes, slowly drawing him in.

He grasped the rock beneath him, kicking and screaming as loud as he could, fighting for his life. But his strength was fading. This was it. The world would know him no more. He was nothing more than snake food.

CHAPTER SEVEN

KAZUMETH

JACK OPENED HIS EYES to an extraordinary light, and to his relief, the sight that greeted him was not the acidic interior of a snake's stomach, but vast, beautiful branches with large, colorful leaves. The orangish-yellow glow lingering between the colossal trees dimmed as his eyes adjusted. His body was twisted beneath him, pain pulsing through every muscle and bone. The only other time he remembered hurting like this was when he was seven and jumped from the tallest tree into a pile of leaves. That was the first time Jack had broken a bone—though certainly not the last.

He lay there, his breathing shallow as he tried to fill his lungs. It took several minutes, but once he felt he could breathe again, he pushed himself off the ground, his trunk-like legs trembling beneath him.

Ignoring the sharp pain ripping through his body, Jack marveled at the massive trees. The bark shimmered with warm tones, and spongy, grayish-green moss sprouted along the roots. Around the trunks, brilliant flowers and mushrooms bloomed with a spectrum too rich to be natural. They swayed in the breeze, giggling as wind blew dust over them. Suddenly, the flowers sneezed, releasing tiny, scented clouds into the air—a strong floral fragrance mixed with hints of clove, wood, and sugar. A smoky haze lingered in the forest, and the filtered light from the colorful canopy cast an ethereal glow.

Is this heaven? I expected pearly gates and cotton-candy clouds, but this is definitely more my style.

With each step, a sharp pain shot down his left leg, but Jack did his best to ignore it. *But if this is heaven, shouldn't all my pain be gone?*

Jack gawked at the girth of the trees as he stood barefoot on the soft soil. Sun-colored, stained rocks littered the forest floor, but they were so smooth he didn't flinch when stepping on them. In the distance, he spotted an old, boarded-up cottage built around the trunk of a tree. Its thatched roof seemed to meld seamlessly with the bark, and an opening at the top led to a spiraled staircase ascending to a deck. From there, rope bridges stretched toward neighboring homes suspended twenty feet in the air.

Jack approached the nearest hut, all fear spent. If he was already dead, what else could possibly happen? He crept toward a planked window, the ledge sagging under mangy white leaves.

He tried to peek inside, but the boards were sealed tight. Glancing over his shoulder to make sure he was alone, he yanked a panel loose with a loud snap. Several birds scattered from nearby nests in a flutter of wings and panicked chirps. Jack didn't flinch. His eyes were already sweeping the interior of the overturned home.

Whoever had lived here couldn't have been very big—the ceiling barely reached his shoulders, and the furniture looked sized for a toddler. Sooty stains covered the walls. Burn marks streaked across the floor, which was littered with torn book pages, smashed bookcases, broken tables, and tattered furniture. The crisp, cool air outside was no match for the sulfurous stench burning his nose inside.

Dead or alive, Jack didn't like the look of this place.

Unwilling to turn his back in case something moved inside, he inched back—right into a small, hairy something.

"Watch it, you," snapped a sharp, pious voice. Jack froze as fuzzy fingers gave his hip a firm nudge, guiding him just out of the way.

He blinked down at the small creature before him, its oversized eyes shining with irritation beneath its crooked diadem.

"You," Jack exclaimed, jabbing a finger at it rudely. "You're that . . . that thing that took Emerson in the snow. You—wait—does that mean he's dead too?"

The small creature scoffed, snapping its beak. "You're not dead, you bloated bag of imp seed." It smoothed the tangled fur on its chest, looking unimpressed. "You're in Kazumeth."

Jack swayed on his feet. "I'm in . . . Kazumeth?" He repeated the word like it was foreign on his tongue. "But the snake—it ate—" His mind reeled. "I—bu—am I in another world? You mean this place is real?"

The creature clacked its beak in frustration. "Of course it's real. Does this look like the inside of a seminarion's stomach to you?" It tutted. "Blue dwellers—always so slow to catch on."

Jack barely heard him, thoughts racing. "But the snake . . . it swallowed me whole."

"Yes, swallowed. Not ate. There's a difference." The creature rolled its eyes and hunched over its wooden staff. "Ogof is an old friend—one of Kazumeth's greatest protectors. And you, my dull-witted blue dweller, should be counting your blessings."

Jack opened his mouth, then shut it. He didn't feel particularly grateful at the moment.

The creature suddenly stiffened, ears twitching. "No more questions. Not here. We'll talk when I get you home." It placed a long, thin finger to its beak—or what might've been a mouth.

With an eager clap of its long-fingered hands, it grinned. "We've got another boy to collect. Two at once! How delightfully unexpected."

"I'm not in the best shape to walk. My leg . . ." Jack gestured, just as the pain reminded him that he was definitely still alive.

"Here." The Pilfert rummaged in a small, leather sack. "Eat this."

It offered a pulsing, oozing tablet that smelled like rotten eggs and burnt licorice.

Jack gagged. "Uh, yeah—hard pass."

Jack didn't have time to react before the Pilfert leapt onto his shoulders and shoved the squirming tablet down his throat.

Jack choked, stumbling as warmth surged through him. The pain vanished. "Wha—whoa. I feel amazing." He bounced on his heels.

The Pilfert, now leaning casually on its staff, sighed. "Don't do that. You're not healed—just patched up until I can fix you properly." It spun. "Now come on—"

Jack hesitated. "Not to be rude, little guy, but what *are* you, exactly?"

It snorted. "A Pilfert. And 'little guy'? Please. I'm more of an *it.*"

Without another word, it marched down the path.

Jack followed, his eyes drawn to the diadem on its head—an eye-shaped band with a large, black onyx at its center. Four empty sockets circled the gem in a jagged, incomplete ring. *Fitting*, Jack thought. The Pilfert itself seemed to be missing a few stones.

No sooner had the thought formed than the Pilfert turned and whacked his leg with its staff.

"I can hear your thoughts, boy. I suggest you focus on your surroundings. Think less. From what the girl's been saying, that shouldn't be too hard."

"Wait—what girl? Stefani? Do the others know I'm coming?" Hope lit in his chest.

"We've known for days. The boy—Emerson—said you'd uncovered Kazumeth's secrets." The Pilfert didn't turn. "Now hurry!"

Jack's pace quickened. He didn't understand half of what any of it meant—but he didn't care. It was real. He wasn't crazy.

And Emerson was alive. He was safe. Far from the cold, circular cellar floor Jack had dreamed about just a week ago.

They stopped before the thickest, strangest tree Jack had ever seen. Overgrown roots twisted like a jungle gym, and vines curved into odd shapes—some even burrowing back into the earth. Nearly every branch was adorned with large leaves, lantern-like pods, and amber-tipped blossoms.

"Wait here. I'll only be a minute. You're safe in these trees. I'd take you along, but I can only carry one person at a time," the Pilfert said, then promptly disappeared before Jack could respond.

Jack paced, his excitement building. He and Addison had actually made it. Their terrible plan had worked. Whatever came next could be dealt with later.

He spotted a neatly cut branch lying nearby and picked it up, twirling it in the air.

Nothing happened.

Feeling slightly embarrassed, he tossed it aside and resumed pacing.

For the first time in his life, Jack wished he had a notebook to write down all the questions racing through his mind. How was this world possible? Were there others beyond Kazumeth and Earth? What was magic like? How did someone produce it?

But most importantly—*could he?*

"Quick, take off his shoes," the Pilfert barked, appearing suddenly out of thin air.

Jack, lost in thought, jolted and yelped at the sight of the small creature cradling a wet, blood-soaked sack the size of Addison in its arms. The Pilfert set it down with a grunt, unwrapping the cloth covering Addison's body.

"Had to cover him. He can't touch my fur. None of you can."

"What happened?" Jack demanded, rushing forward to carefully pry Addison's waterlogged shoes off his blistered, red feet.

"Dwarves." The Pilfert's voice dripped with exasperation. It looked furious, slamming its staff against the nearest tree. The trunk quivered and twisted, slithering into a small, round hole at its roots.

"Get in."

Jack eyed the plate-sized hole, then flicked a doubtful look at the Pilfert. "Yeah . . . I don't think I'm gonna fit."

"I told you to stop thinking." The Pilfert jabbed its cane into Jack's back. "We need to heal this one. Now! Move!"

Jack scowled but stepped toward the hole, baffled by how this would work. He wasn't sure why he trusted the creature but questioning it wouldn't get Addison the help he needed. Besides, weirder things had already happened today.

The moment he placed his foot over the hole a strange sensation rippled through his right side. His bones shrank to the size of pasta noodles; his muscles dissolved into water. Jack sucked in a sharp breath, stepped forward—and before he could exhale, gravity pulled him under.

He spiraled through a twisting chute of roots, flashes of light bursting through the tangled walls as he rushed past. Then, just as suddenly, Jack's body stretched back to its normal size as he tumbled onto a pink, fuzzy carpet with a soft thud.

Immediately two pairs of hands pulled him from the floor.

"Emerson," Jack exclaimed, staring at the pockmarked face of his best friend, who was already wrapped around him in a hug. Jack clung back so tightly Emerson's frail frame looked ready to snap.

"I'm so glad you're okay," Jack said, relieved that he could finally forget the battered images of Emerson that had haunted him this last week.

As they pulled apart, a flicker of sorrow crossed Emerson's face—but before Jack could register it, he'd already turned to the other person who had helped him up.

"Adina, isn't it?" Jack extended a hand.

She rolled her cool, lily pad-green eyes and turned away, dropping back into the chair she had just vacated.

"Well, thanks for helping me up," Jack called after her. "That thing up there has Addison. He's hurt. I don't know what happened—"

Emerson flopped onto a thin wooden stool that had sprouted from the weaving roots of the floor, cradling his head in his hands.

Jack frowned. Why wasn't anyone acting with urgency? No one seemed concerned that they were finally together —or that Addison was injured.

Just as he opened his mouth to demand answers, the snapping and groaning of wood filled the room. He spun just in time to see the radicles twist apart, forming a large, arched doorway.

Something whizzed through and flopped onto the rug—tiny, hairy arms flailing beneath a tangle of limbs and a blood-soaked sheet.

Jack bent down, lifting Addison like a sleeping child.

Then, without missing a beat, the Pilfert tossed away the sheet that had been lying between them and twirled its tangled staff overhead. Books slid back into place, chairs stacked themselves neatly, and a bed scraped across the floor from an alcove near the kitchen.

Jack turned, taking in the space. A tiny stove sat against the far wall, with two large pots steaming on top. Pans hung from the ceiling, and a small sink rested beneath a curtained window that—somehow—bathed the kitchen in warm autumn light, even though they were underground.

Adina, who had just toppled from her chair as it slid out from beneath her, puffed the pillows on the bed as Jack carefully laid Addison down.

"Jack, go lie down in there," the Pilfert said, its voice suddenly tender as it pointed to a small, circular room off the newly formed archway. "You need rest—you'll feel better once you sleep. I'll fix your leg when I've finished here."

Adina held Jack gently by the elbow and led him into the firelit, untidy chamber where a bed waited beneath a storybook mirror. Its edges were gilded in golden branches, with soft pink blossoms crowning the top. The glass itself held a greenish-blue tint, smudged and darkened by age.

"Drink this," Adina said, handing him a small wooden goblet. "I helped the Pilfert make it yesterday. It'll help you sleep."

Jack brought the cup to his lips, letting the sweet juice flood through him. Sleep washed over him like a warm bath on the coldest night. The goblet slipped from his fingers, spilling a soft stream of lavender liquid across the floor, as his body collapsed onto the cushions. His mind fell blissfully blank.

"Hey, wake up," a voice whispered from the end of a long, narrow hallway. Jack stirred, but his eyes refused to obey the command.

"Hey dude, get up. I want to talk," a second, more familiar voice called to him. Jack twitched and briefly opened his eyes, but the weight of his eyelids was too heavy.

"Let me try," said a cool, soft voice that reminded him of Emma. The moment he thought of her, he felt a tug in his gut. Jack barely had time to process this when a loud crack filled the room, and the right side of his face began to sting.

"I thought that might work," cooed the familiar voice of Stefani, giving Jack an innocent smile as she lowered her hand.

Jack stared, open-mouthed, as Stefani moved to sit on his makeshift bed.

"The Pilfert went to get food. When it returns, do us a favor and tell it we didn't wake you."

"We'll see how my face feels when it gets back," Jack smiled, rubbing his cheek. "You look good," he added truthfully. Her dark skin looked stunning in the firelight, and her full lips spread wide to reveal her expensive smile, as her stepdad always called it. However, something felt slightly different—Stefani would never wear an outfit like this.

"I know, right?" she said, noticing where his eyes lingered. "But I'm not going to travel somewhere and not respect the customs."

Stefani wore a long purple cloak draped over her shoulders, its hood lined with golden trim that shimmered like snakeskin. At the peak, a serpent biting its own tail formed a perfect circle. Beneath the cloak, she wore a tan dress with sleeves so long her thumbs poked through like holes in a glove. Golden jewelry glinted in the long strands of hair that framed her hooded face.

"I won't lie; I was really bummed when I realized you'd be the one joining us. I hoped to see Emma again . . . But I'll make do with what I got," Stefani said with a wink, though her eyes lingered too long to match the playfulness in her tone.

"I've been here a week now and still don't understand everything happening. All I know is . . ." She averted her gaze and let out a muffled cough that moistened her eyes.

Jack wiped the tears starting to spill down from her high cheekbones, and she responded with a soft smile. She gently moved his hand from her cheek, then crossed the room, crouched on a circular cushion that faced a twisted skylight, and began to scribble on a sheath of parchment.

"She's been like this ever since I arrived," Emerson whispered. "You always said she was fun, but I think it'll take some time before that side comes back. Come on—let's get out of here. The other room's a bit cozier anyway."

Jack looked around and understood what Emerson meant. They sat in a dimly lit space among nests of books, maps, stacked furniture, and strange, oblong objects he'd never seen before. Jack gestured for Stefani to follow, but she shook her head and turned away, now staring into the glowing flames of the hearth, the quill poised beside her cheek as she thought.

"Well, come out when you feel up to it," Jack said, tripping over a book that lay forgotten in a crack on the floor. The cover depicted an old woman with wispy, gray hair standing over a bubbling cauldron, her head tilted to the moon in manic laughter. The title, *Spellium Toegrown's Recipes for Elixirs, Goulash, and Antidotes,* gleamed in gold ink. Jack chuckled at the title as he ducked under the low door frame into the luminous room where Addison sat propped up, beaming.

"Evening," Addison said brightly, looking completely unperturbed. "How did you sleep?"

"About as good as your mother on New Year's," Jack shot back, recalling the time they'd found her passed out on the staircase after a night of heavy drinking.

Addison gave him a sharp look. "Dude, what the fuck."

Jack winced. "Sorry. I wasn't thinking."

They exchanged a look—half annoyance, half amusement.

"What else is new," Addison muttered, shaking his head.

Jack plopped onto a wobbly stool near Addison's bed, where the others sat positioned around him.

Adina, sitting nearest to Addison's feet, kept eyeing them with disdain.

"So . . . what were you guys talking about?" Jack asked.

"My feet," Addison said. "Adina was just telling me how to properly wash them, you know, in case I wasn't aware." He said it in a tone that questioned Adina's sanity.

"Well, I'm just saying, if you washed them correctly, the room wouldn't smell like *Eau de Toe Fungus by Stempinski,*" Adina said in her best perfume-ad voice, wrinkling her nose.

Jack smiled at the banter, though at the same time, something stirred uneasily in his gut—a sensation that started as a tickle but soon erupted into a sharp pain that shot through his abdomen. He glanced around the room, trying to distract himself from

Adina's intense gaze, unsure whether it was her presence or the situation causing the discomfort.

Trying to ignore the pain, he scanned the room. It was just as cluttered as the one he'd slept in: clay pots and pans hung from the ceiling, marked-up maps framed the tangled walls, and a stone basin the size of a kitchen sink bubbled over a fire in the small hearth. Jack's eyes landed on an old book, its gilded pages burning like a candle on a stand. The open page depicted strange illustrations of a dragon hiding between rocks and men with four arms dancing around a fire.

"Right, well if we're done discussing your feet, I want to know what happened to you. The Piflit—uh, I mean, that creature, the Pif . . ." Jack began, fumbling for words.

"Pilfert," Emerson interjected.

"Yeah, thanks," Jack replied graciously. "Well, the Pilfert said that you were captured by elves or something. What happened?"

Jack noticed the circle around him straighten up, the attention to the conversation now sharper than a knife.

"It didn't say 'elves,' you idiot, it said 'dwarves'," Addison corrected. Jack shrugged, giving a what's-the-difference sort of look, and nodded for Addison to continue.

"Well," Addison began, his voice taking on a theatrical tone as he saw the group lean in. He let the silence hang for just a beat longer than necessary, reeling them in further.

"I guess the Pilfert was the one who rescued me?" He shrugged, playing up the mystery. "I don't remember much. I remember the snake—then me screaming for you—but it was like my vocal cords were glued shut. The creature slowly pulled me into its throat. It got super dark, and the next thing I knew, I was completely submerged in water. Drowning. Sinking deeper and deeper."

He let his voice dip into a low, eerie whisper, relishing not just the tension in Emerson's shoulders, but the way all eyes were suddenly on him.

"I pushed against the water as hard as I could, and suddenly, spheres of light burst to life, swirling around me in a ghostly shimmer hummed with something I didn't understand. I swam harder than I ever had before, racing toward the surface. The lights raced with me—until they shattered through the water like shooting stars. My head broke through the surface, my lungs gasping for air . . . but then—"

His voice dropped, and everyone leaned in.

"Then what happened?" Emerson asked, his voice barely above a breath.

"I'm getting there," Addison said with a sly smile and a wink. "Something grabbed my leg—next thing I knew, I was yanked back under. I swallowed so much water I thought I'd turn into a human sponge . . ."

He trailed off, glancing around the room.

Adina let out a slow, unimpressed sigh and rolled her eyes, making it clear she found the showy storytelling more than a little much.

"Whatever had me was strong—and my energy was running out fast. Things started to go dark. I reached for the little, white orbs dangling above the water, but they were too far. And just when I thought, *Well, I guess this is how Addison goes out—tragic, beautiful, heroic*—I saw him."

He dropped his voice again, savoring the moment.

"A bearded man. Swimming toward me. Sword in hand."

Jack's eyes widened. Emerson looked enthralled. Adina looked annoyed.

"Right before I blacked out, I caught a flash of silver steel—and then nothing. Darkness. Next thing I know, someone's pounding on my chest, forcing the water out of my lungs and onto the sand. As I came to, I remember seeing someone sprinting away. Then, as I'm lying there, dragging air into my lungs . . . the white-haired man who saved me straddles my chest . . . and spits—right in my face."

He wiped at his cheek like he could still feel it as a collective sound of disgust rippled through them.

"Don't worry. It gets worse."

Stefani had just appeared in the crooked doorway, watching with an unreadable expression.

"The last of the water flew out of my lungs and onto his beard—so, you know, karma. But this guy? He looked mutinous. Started shouting, demanding answers, asking me my name and how I ended up in the Willow Wisp Sea. It took me ages to process what he was saying, and when I tried to respond, I realized—I still couldn't speak."

He lowered his voice again.

"That's when I saw them. Bearded men. A whole group of them. Some taller than others, but none higher than my chest. They became increasingly hostile, and finally, they tied me up with these thin, white ropes. My skin started burning the moment they put them on me." Addison lifted his shirt slightly, revealing deep red burn marks across his pale, freckled abs.

"The pain was so bad, I finally managed to scream. My voice came back. I told them my name and started answering all their questions, hoping they might let me go. But the moment my name left my lips, they lifted me into the air. Axes in hand, blades grazing my back, they carried me toward a cave in the mountain.

"That's when the Pilfert arrived. A blast of light flared from its staff, and the ropes untwisted from me and coiled around my captors instead. The last thing I saw before blacking out—*again*—was that ridiculous, tiny, furry thing standing there, staff in hand, looking far too pleased with itself."

He sat back, arms folded behind his head, smirking as he basked in the weight of his own legend. Adina couldn't help but smirk at his bravado—for being rescued and having done absolutely nothing.

Jack sat in stunned silence, feeling fortunate that he hadn't suffered anything like that—yet slightly jealous that he hadn't.

He started wondering if the others had faced similar fates when they arrived, or if they, like him, had been immediately rescued by the Pilfert.

"Well, I'm glad you're okay," Jack said finally. "I don't know if I could have lived with myself knowing that I was the one who made you enter that cave."

"You didn't make me do anything; I chose to tag along," Addison shot back.

"You guys entered the cave willingly?" Stefani asked quietly from behind them. They all jumped at the sound of her voice.

"Yeah," Jack and Addison said together.

"That's odd," Emerson commented. "When I came here, I remember being in the cave, but I don't have any recollection of how I got there. I remember I had just been chatting with my wela about . . ." Emerson broke off, his voice cracking. "About my mom. I was getting ready for bed when I heard something calling me. I didn't realize what was happening until I was already being swallowed by that horned serpent. I ended up in a snowy forest. I was screaming for someone to help me, but there didn't seem to be any life there whatsoever. The trees looked gnarled and dangerous, and the whole place just made me feel suffocated. It was creepy." Emerson shivered, as if he could still feel the cool breeze on his neck.

"I started running, searching for someone because I kept hearing these loud noises, but no one was around. Then the Pilfert revealed itself, brought me here, and explained everything it could. It wanted to wait until everyone else arrived for the full story," Emerson said, his tone a bit sharp as he finished.

"Interesting," Stefani said. "I remember everything. I was in my room, watching Homecoming. I was in the middle of gettin' bodied—like full-on Beyoncé mode—when my mom barged in. I remember yelling at her to knock next time when all sound vanished—except for a chorus of soft voices repeating my name. I had that weird feeling, like running down a never-ending hallway in a bad dream. I ran right past my mom, who looked horrified, her mouth gaping in shock as she stood in my doorway. Some force was pulling me away from my house, and my whole body fought against it. Then, after the snake . . ." Stefani paused, watching their hungry faces. "I blacked out and don't remember a thing until waking up in this place."

"You don't remember what happened when you arrived in Kazumeth?" Adina asked skeptically.

"No, I don't," Stefani said so sharply that the others knew her part of the conversation was over. Adina raised a brow but didn't press the matter.

"What about you, Adina? Why don't you tell us what happened to you when you arrived?" Emerson suggested.

"Nothing that exciting," Adina said coolly. "But, let me set the scene for you," Adina said, slipping into a near-perfect imitation of Addison.

"I woke up on a hill overlooking what looked like a cathedral—except it wasn't just a cathedral. It was more like a small castle. A long stone bridge stretched from one side of the ravine to its grand arched entrance. Behind it, mist rolled down the peaks like a moving curtain, and warm, golden light poured from its windows—like it was expecting someone." She added with a spooky flair.

"All along the mountain path leading toward it were steep-roofed cottages nestled between trees, their windows glowing with golden light. Giant pumpkins lined the trail like lanterns at a festival. The whole place—called Strega Academy, I later learned—felt unreal. Beautiful, but eerie."

She shrugged. "I walked the path and entered through the massive front doors. A woman was waiting inside. She brought me into a side office, and the Pilfert showed up a few minutes later. And now I'm here."

She leaned back, arms crossed and glanced at Addison with a smirk. "How'd I do? Not quite the three-act structure your monologue had, but I figured someone had to add a little ambiance since you were clearly handling the drama."

Jack let out a quiet laugh, shaking his head. *This girl really didn't hold back,* he thought, remembering her sonnet performance from a few days ago. He studied her features: dark hair casting shadows across a moonlike face, pond-green eyes that held a tragedy he longed to read, and just above her lip sat a tiny scar. She was oddly beautiful. But as that thought formed, images of Emma flickered through his mind, making his heartbeat faster and his stomach twist.

"Hey, does anyone know if it's possible for other people to enter Kazumeth?" Jack asked, mostly directing the question at Stefani since she had been here the longest.

Stefani's gaze softened. "You're thinking of Emma, aren't you?" She reached for his hand.

Across the room, Adina's expression changed, as if every muscle in her face had stopped working.

Stefani sighed. "I don't know. I've already told you, a lot of this still doesn't make sense to me." She offered him a small, understanding smile. "I miss her too. But from what I've gathered, it's the Sovereign Five . . . so I think this is it." She gestured toward the others.

Jack's heart sank. Even though this wasn't news to him, he didn't want to believe that Emma couldn't follow.

Before anyone could respond, the room was interrupted by the cracking of shifting vines as the archway formed again behind them. The Pilfert came zooming down the chute, landing on its large, birdlike feet.

"Ah, you're up," the Pilfert said cheerfully. Then, with zero regard for the mood in the room, it jerked its beak toward the bed. "Off. We need a place to eat."

Addison's feet had barely touched the floor when the bed began to fold itself into a large wooden table. The chairs that had been hanging from the ceiling dropped carefully behind each of them. They all grabbed one and pushed it to the table, waiting patiently as the Pilfert placed several boxes on the twisted surface.

The Pilfert then moved its hands in complicated gestures, like an orchestra conductor. The ceramic plates and bowls, which had been piled beneath a small window in the kitchen, moved gracefully across the room, following every motion of the Pilfert's hands. As the table set, the white boxes unfolded to reveal several silver dishes brimming with delectable food.

Jack's eyes widened with excitement as the smells of garlic and ginger, cinnamon, and freshly baked bread filled the air. His gaze traveled up and down the table, surveying the exotic dishes. In one bowl, long strands of sausage were entwined with wild berries and drizzled in honey sauce; a small cauldron still bubbled, holding a creamy golden soup with strands of white meat, exotic vegetables, and sprigs of greens; and directly in front of him, sweet, twisted breads were covered in a white glaze. The smell reminded him of his mother's famous waffles, only somehow a thousand times more pleasant.

"Well, dig in."

Adina reached across the table, grabbing the dark red dish in front of her.

"Oh, that one's my favorite," Emerson said, as he slid the small cauldron to Jack. Jack eyed the strange-colored beans bathed in creamy sauce, piled high with chunks of slow-roasted meat and golden corn. He grabbed the spoon and scooped a hefty serving into a bowl.

"I think it's made with dragon meat?" Emerson continued, turning toward the Pilfert, clearly expecting confirmation.

The small creature barely paused mid-bite of the sweet bread it clutched in its fuzzy hand. "Wyvern meat, Emerson," it corrected, licking a sticky glaze from its beak. "Though wyverns are part of the dragon family, there's only one true dragon left on the mainland of Kazumeth—one many have tried to slay, but none have prevailed. Actually," it added offhandedly, "that dragon will be part of your tale." Then, as if it hadn't just dropped something important: "Wyverns, on the other hand, are everywhere and, frankly, a far bigger nuisance. One of them can feed a village for a month."

Emerson shot a shifty look at the Pilfert at the casual mention of them meeting a dragon before taking the dish from Jack.

"What's this called?" Jack asked, still chewing on the succulent bread he'd been eyeing since they sat down.

"That is a dreamroot pasty. It's topped with a glaze made from brightveil flowers," the Pilfert explained between bites. "Brightveil flowers help clear a clouded mind. Very useful." It tapped a tiny sack tucked beneath its left arm, almost invisible against its fur.

"Most potion makers grow their own—the fresher the flower, the stronger its properties."

Jack nodded absently as he chewed, the sweet glaze lingering on his tongue.

"You should try dipping it in your wyvern stew." The creature shivered with a purr. "Sweet and salty."

Jack hesitated, then ripped off a piece of bread and dunked it into the rich, creamy sauce. He took a bite and his expression lit up.

"Well, why aren't the rest of you eating?" the Pilfert asked as they all sat there, momentarily entranced by its words, forgetting their full plates.

Jack's gaze drifted to Stefani, whose head was bowed in prayer.

A flurry of hands scurried over the table, and the sounds of clinking silverware filled the air. They enjoyed their meal amidst light conversation, mostly focused on the food they were devouring. Jack was the last one to finish eating, only because he had filled his plate five times. Once he finished, the Pilfert cleared the table with a sweep of its staff, and the rest of them watched as the table sank into the floor.

"Sit," the Pilfert suggested as the rooted floor creaked. There was a series of *whoomphs* as thick cushions sprouted into place, settling with a soft, breathy hush.

"I know you're all bursting with questions, and in time, you'll have answers. But tonight, I'll explain what the three of you already know to Jack and Addison. After that, we'll see what the night will allow and how much more I feel like sharing," the Pilfert said, causing the others to share sideways glances, unsure if the creature was trying to make a joke.

"What you two need to know is that our history extends further than the history of your world, simply because we have existed far longer—and, if I may say so, much more successfully—than those we refer to as 'blue dwellers.'

"When your world burst into existence, it caused a deep rift and an unsettling disturbance to the balance we once had here in Kazumeth. It tore a hole in our atmosphere, creating a gateway through which we could pass into these new lands. At first, we weren't sure what to do about it. The High Kings of Kazumeth debated endlessly—should we venture into this new world or seal the rift before it became our downfall? Many argued for sealing it, remembering the horrors of the first gateway discovered long ago. But in the end, greed and curiosity triumphed. The Kings sent forth our greatest explorers."

The fire crackled, casting twisting shadows against the walls.

"They found your world untamed, brimming with monstrous creatures—beasts unlike any we'd ever seen. We lost men to the wingless dragons that roamed your lands, but the survivors returned, bearing stories beyond imagination.

"Camora, a gifted witch who was part of the expedition, buried half of her scepter deep in the soil of your world, allowing us to observe it from afar. It sprouted into a great tree which became known as the Eye of the World."

Jack raised an eyebrow. "A . . . tree?"

"A very special tree," the Pilfert corrected. "One that let us see beyond our own lands—yes. By the time we ventured through the gateway again, your kind had already reshaped the world. Cities and kingdoms rose from stone and sweat, where once only the wild things roamed."

The Pilfert tapped its staff against the floor, and the roots responded—shifting slightly, as if alive.

"But something unexpected happened. When our explorers stepped through the gateway, their magic surged. Spells cast through wands, staves, and daggers grew stronger, more refined, something not even the witches of Strega Academy had seen at the time. Upon returning to Kazumeth, their power did not fade—it only flourished. This revelation changed everything.

"The Kings panicked. They saw potential—but also danger. If the youth of Kazumeth learned they could become more powerful simply by crossing over, how long before the gateway was abused? How long before ambition unraveled the order they had spent a lifetime maintaining?"

The Pilfert sighed. "So, they sealed it for our safety and to curb the growing greed within the youth of Kazumeth. Amity was restored—or so we thought. A secret resistance began to grow among those who felt the gateway should remain open. They saw it not as a threat, but as a gift. Their voices grew louder, and soon, Kazumeth fell into its second great war."

Jack gripped the arms of his chair.

"The war ended in fire and ruin. The Seven Kings abdicated; their rule shattered. Seven became five. The remaining territories were either absorbed into stronger kingdoms or collapsed under the weight of war. Five new rulers rose, forming a fragile alliance to prevent further chaos. The war had left scars—and the portal . . . the portal remained an ever-looming presence.

"After the war, the portal was reopened. We spread word of our existence to certain men we had been watching—those we believed could become ardent protectors of both worlds, from local threats and those from other realms where previously opened gateways had since been sealed.

"For a time, our knowledge was welcomed. We shared magic, and in return, blue dwellers gave us sanctuary—places where witches, elves, and scholars could refine their gifts. Grand, magical schools were built across your lands."

Adina and Emerson shared an eager look.

"But as history has shown, all golden ages are temporary. The blue dwellers found new scriptures to follow, and those who once sought our wisdom turned against us.

"The birth of the great books marked the beginning of the end. Fear spread. Hatred followed. Our schools were abandoned, our existence erased from the minds of men. And as your world waged war upon itself, the very fabric of Kazumeth began to unravel. Entire islands off our coast were lost—including my own. Dark clouds began to shroud and poison our lands."

It paused, eyes flickering with something unreadable. "This, of course, is one of Akuramundo's—among other politicians'—favorite stories to twist for personal gain. But we'll get to that.

"We left the gateway open. For study. For understanding. For reasons I'm sure made sense at the time."

"And then?" Emerson prompted.

The Pilfert let out a sharp, hollow laugh. "Then, of course, someone fell in love.

"Time went on, and around the early 1800s—your time—Camora fell in love with a blue dweller she had hired to work the fields of her private school. She trusted Francisco beyond all reason, and in her foolishness, she brought him into our world and allowed him to drink from the Fountain of Etervida. Just one sip can make a man immortal. This was an illegal act, as the fountain can corrupt even the strongest of minds. And it did. It doomed them both.

"Some blame the fountain for the changes in our world, others blame the gateways. But one thing is certain: Natural magic changed. Our healing springs could no longer work without ingredients and incantations. The Fountain of Etervida dried up. And our seasons have been erratic and unpredictable ever since.

"But long before the drought, Camora had several children with the blue dweller."

"Her poor ancient vagina," Stefani muttered in awe and discomfort.

Jack, who had just grabbed his drink, choked on his water—but the Pilfert didn't miss a beat.

"The children were raised in secret between the two worlds. But as Francisco's age progressed and his body did not, questions arose. The secret was eventually exposed. Both Camora and Francisco were sentenced to death.

"Years later, before the new century dawned, the youngest of Francisco's grandsons crossed into our world with his closest friends, desperate to uncover the truth of what had been done to his family. Entranced by our lands and impassioned by our teachings, they became more than wanderers—they became restorers. In the aftermath of war and betrayal, they helped reshape Kazumeth, breathing life back into our world. They gave us a new beginning. They restored Kazumeth to some of its former glory."

The Pilfert paused, tilting its head. "They never returned home—not even when Hernando, Francisco's grandson, finally learned the truth of his family's crimes and of Francisco's execution."

"They were educated at Strega Academy, where they studied the magical arts. Their thirst for knowledge and deep love for this world led them to surpass most inhabitants of Kazumeth in magical understanding. After leaving Strega, they traveled together through Kazumeth for several years. Not much is known about their journey, but what the Pilferts managed to gather was that they were in search of the infamous Vocation Stones, stones created by the Oracle of Burkank that could only be wielded by the true protectors of the lands—what we have come to call the Guardians."

Addison smiled dopily as Jack leaned in further, giving more attention to this little creature than he ever had to any school lecture.

"Eventually, they all found residence in communities they cherished most. Within the community they built lives and families of their own.

"But time passed quickly for them here—so quickly that their human years began to catch up. Fear crept into the hearts of the Kings of the land. What would happen when the ones who had reforged Kazumeth were lost to age and death? Fear is the great corrupter of reason, and so the Kings, filled with fear, abandoned all reason and sought to make them eternal. The High Kings christened them the Sovereign Five."

Jack's eyes widened. He whipped toward Addison, giving him a *Didn't I tell you?* smirk.

The Pilfert chuckled, its body shivering with amusement. "I see your mother has done as instructed. So, you know? You understand now that the Sovereign Five are your ancestors? The same magic that flowed through them flows through you—it sings in your veins even now."

The Pilfert's tone darkened. "But let me make something very clear. Even though you were granted this gift, if you do not learn to control it, it will destroy you. Magic untamed is a death sentence—it will consume you faster than a seminarion bite."

Emerson swallowed hard and squirmed uncomfortably in his seat.

"Anyway," it continued breezily, as if it hadn't just issued a dire warning, "after they were knighted as the Sovereign Five, the Kings made them an offer—one as dangerous as it was tempting: the very drink that had once doomed Hernando's father."

Jack stiffened. "The Fountain of Etervida? But I thought it had dried up."

The others gasped, inching closer. Emerson, however, stared at Jack in awe for his rapt attention to a history lesson.

The Pilfert gave a knowing nod. "It had . . . but the elves had stored some away. Kept in the most secure place in Kazumeth—seeking it would be a death wish. And there is only one key-bearer who can access it.

"Many years later, four siblings crossed into our world. Foolish and trusting, the men of Levestin welcomed them, hoping they would rise like the Sovereign Five before them. And at first, they seemed promising—eager, curious, harmless. But then terrible events began to occur." An ominous chill crept through the room as the Pilfert lowered its voice.

"Villages were set ablaze, riches were stolen from Kings, and murders occurred in every village they visited. It was violence Kazumeth had never known outside of war."

The Pilfert leaned in, eyes gleaming like embers as if it were seeing it all unfold.

"The children fled, vanishing into the night as the witches of Strega chased them through what is now known as Dartmoor. Three of them made it back through the threshold, slipping into your world like ghosts. But one . . . one remained."

It paused for effect, surveying their faces.

"The youngest girl was left behind—confused, frightened, and abandoned. She hid herself in Levestin, severed from her brothers.

"The Kings ordered the Pilferts to close the portal forever. But not before one of the boys came back in search of his sister. His name was Akuramundo."

The mention of the name fell upon them like smothering smoke.

"You've mentioned his name before, like he's still alive," Jack said, cutting his way through the tension. "Who is he?"

Addison snorted. "I don't care who he is. I want to know who the hell names their kid Akuramundo?"

The Pilfert went on as if no one had spoken.

"As time went on, Akuramundo grew stronger. He has had a long and mysterious rise to power, vanishing from history for long periods, gathering power in the shadows. When he finally struck, he already had a large and faithful following. He took Dartmoor in a storm of blood and ruin around forty years ago.

"He was—and still is—after the Vocation Stones."

Jack's stomach twisted, but he wasn't sure why.

"His hunt led to the Great Burnings. He killed every last Pilfert in a ruthless attempt to uncover the knowledge we swore to protect. I was the only one who survived. From there, his atrocities only worsened—he'd discovered how to kill immortals."

The Pilfert's beak clenched.

"Well, then, they're not actually immortal, are they?" Emerson said with folded arms. "Immortality means unending life. If he found a way to kill them, then that makes their immortality invalid."

"Death does not define immortality, Emerson, nor does life," the Pilfert said affectionately. "The Sovereign sought the Pilferts for guidance. They begged for our help, for we—the wisest and most ancient creatures of Kazumeth—held one of the greatest secrets. It was I who told them of their only chance to survive; it was I who showed them how to escape Kazumeth."

Jack furrowed his brow. "But I thought the portal was closed for good?"

Adina rolled her eyes. "Well, obviously not. We're sitting here now, aren't we?"

"The Pilferts left only one way for someone to leave Kazumeth. And only one way to enter." It fixed them with a knowing look. "I believe you're all familiar with our seminarion, Ogof?"

Jack's stomach lurched at the memory of the cave serpent. He shared a glance with Emerson, who seemed to be quite unnerved by the story.

"When Akuramundo's army came hunting them, the Sovereign Five turned to us once more. And, of course, we assisted. We opened the threshold, and they sent their youngest predecessor through. With spells and enchantments in place, their descendants began their quest."

A pause. The fire crackled softly.

"With their youngest alive and filled with their magic, the others went into hiding, scattering the Vocation Stones and shielding them behind enchantments and beasts.

"It wasn't long before Akuramundo found our families—yours and mine—and murdered them during the Great Burnings I mentioned earlier."

The room was so silent Jack could hear his own pulse.

"Years passed in gloom, until a light ignited on the hill of Burkank, where a prophecy was made—one stating that the Guardians of Kazumeth would rise again. They'd be the ones to end Akuramundo's reign and bring peace to Kazumeth. Or, at least, that's how it's been interpreted."

The Pilfert recited the words, its voice lilting like an ancient song:

> *The return of the Guardians will be swift and sure,*
> *As they are trained by one whom the enemy immured.*
> *A rift will form, yet bind anew,*
> *Upon the mountain where fate holds its due.*
> *With beating wings and a blaze of fire,*
> *Walls will burn as the lost draw nigher.*
> *A weapon claimed by a Guardian's son,*
> *Shall bring an end it once begun.*

Stefani raised an eyebrow. "Mm. That sounds more like bad poetry than a prophecy."

The Pilfert grinned. "Indeed. But that's beside the point. Here I am now, in my home, speaking with the last surviving members of the Sovereign Five line." Its beak curled up as it made an odd sound, somewhere between a howl and birdsong. Its body shivered with excitement.

"For twenty years, despair has ruled this land. Kazumeth, once perfect, has become the playground for Akuramundo's army.

"Now, I know you have many questions, and with the first sun beginning to set, I will answer as many as I can. I give my word that I will explain more soon, but for tonight, you will need your rest."

"Oh, I have so many questions," Stefani began. "You briefly touched on the second war, but what about the first? You skimmed over that little detail. Also, what do you mean by 'spells and enchantments were put in place' when the Sovereign sent our parents into our world?"

"And why is he after the stones? What makes them so important?" Emerson blurted out just as the Pilfert started to open its beak.

"I have a question too," Addison added, shifting uncomfortably on his red cushion. "When that snake ate us . . . did we—uh—did we die?"

"A lot of questions. Good." The Pilfert smiled, turning to Addison first. "Tell me, do you look dead? Do you feel dead?" It paused for effect. "No. Does your blood still sing in your veins?" Addison nodded hesitantly. "Then I'd say you're very much alive . . . in this world. But in yours? As you already know, you've ceased to exist—every trace of your life, your legacy, erased. All memories, friendships, relationships—gone.

"As for your mothers—" Emerson's eyes widened in horror, but the Pilfert continued, "Oh, don't worry. They're fine. Their lives, however, have been drastically altered. All their memories have been rewritten, their pasts reshaped. They now live as if a piece of their soul was never missing."

The Pilfert turned its gaze to Stefani. "Which brings me to your questions about spells and enchantments. Your parents were able to live a normal life in your world, but their true responsibility was to ensure the family line survived. Magic still bloomed in their blood. Once they had a child, they were called back to our world—because, you see, their bodies, and yours, cannot survive on Earth without it. Your magical abilities are tied to the Vocation Stones, which can only inhabit one member of the family line at a time. The others may learn magic, but in your world, where magic has been forgotten, your bodies are unable to survive the strain. Once the child is born, magic like what you've experienced with your passing is set in motion. They were cursed to either die with the birth of a child or come home to Kazumeth and have theirs lives completely erased."

Its eyes lingered on Stefani. "Now, about the first war. The first gateway to our world opened into a dark realm, teeming with monstrous creatures and vicious demons. Before we could seal it, our world was attacked. Killing these creatures would've been the greatest sin, so we captured them instead, imprisoning them on islands far from Kazumeth's shores. The gateway was sealed, its key hidden. To make way for the prisons, many races and species left their homes behind and started new lives on the mainland."

"That snake," Jack said suddenly. "Can it hurt people?"

"Of course," the Pilfert replied. "That is part of being alive, isn't it? But seminarions are clever. They can hide things well. Only those tied to Ogof and Kazumeth can enter. Should an intruder appear, Ogof will defend this world better than any gate or guard dog."

"So . . . it kills intruders?" Stefani asked, her voice tight.

"Yes," the Pilfert said simply.

"That's awful." She trembled as the warm shadows flickered across the room. Jack knew she must be thinking of Emma, maybe even imagining her being torn apart. He shook the image from his own head.

The Pilfert clicked its beak. "So many big questions you should be asking, yet you fixate on a seminarion. Perhaps we should continue this discussion tomorrow when your minds are clearer. We leave at first light for training."

A nervous energy passed between them. Jack, who had slept all day, couldn't imagine dozing off again. Emerson looked pale and uneasy.

"Clear your minds tonight," the Pilfert instructed. "Tomorrow, I'll answer any important questions. For now, rest." It extinguished the last candle, casting the table into shadow.

Jack followed the others into the side chamber, where roots and vines snaked down from the ceiling, weaving into hammocks beneath the great tree's sprawling branches. As the roots froze in place, blankets and pillows popped into existence on each hammock.

Jack stripped off his shirt and jeans, grabbed the tiny crystal vial of shimmering violet liquid resting on top of his pillow, and hopped into the highest hammock on the right.

"Whoa," he murmured, settling in. "Weirdly more comfortable than my bed."

The Pilfert entered just as Addison picked up his vial. "Drink up," it said. "A sleep elixir. It will clear your minds and help you rest. Lights out."

As if on cue, the fire flickered and died, draping the room in soft darkness.

Jack lifted his vial, toasting silently with the others before drinking. The room went still; the only sound was the soft clink of glass bottles hitting the floor. One by one, they drifted off to sleep.

CHAPTER EIGHT

THE ROOTS OF KALUNA

JACK AWOKE THE NEXT morning to the sound of a sizzling pan and the sweet scent of cinnamon curling through the air. *Of course it had all been a dream.* He was in bed, sunlight creeping through his window while his mother made his favorite breakfast. Relieved—but just a little disappointed—he opened his eyes and stared up at a sea of tangled roots.

With his pulse quickening and a grin tugging at his lips, he hopped out of the hammock and ducked through the crooked doorframe into the room where they'd eaten the night before.

At once, Jack noticed that the space was much tidier and cozier than the previous afternoon. The table, once askew, was now back in place with a bouquet of autumnal flowers in the center. The pans that had hung above their heads the night before were now all in use on a stove barely wider than a nightstand. The window above the sink was bathed in warm golden light, and pouf-like chairs in flamboyant colors were scattered throughout the main den.

The Pilfert was toddling between the kitchen and the gilded book Jack had noticed the night before. He watched as the creature scribbled quickly with a quill, then darted back to the kitchen, where it rummaged through a tall, sky-blue cabinet filled with herbs and spices, which it poured over the food in a cloud of fragrance.

Adina and Emerson sat by the fireplace, hunched over books and completely oblivious to the bustling Pilfert behind them, while Addison and Stefani stood conversing in the corner.

"Morning! How'd you sleep?" Emerson asked as Jack squatted beside them.

"Great," Jack murmured through a yawn, stretching his arms toward the tangled roots above. "How about you?"

"No nightmares, no bathroom breaks, and no checking on my mother," Emerson said, forcing a lighthearted tone. But the flicker of guilt that crossed his face betrayed him.

Adina offered a sympathetic smile before shifting her gaze to Jack, eyes wide, giving a subtle nod toward Emerson.

Jack barely had time to register the silent plea before the Pilfert called them to the table for breakfast, sparing him any awkward attempt at comfort.

As soon as they sat down, plates glided onto the table with effortless grace. Jack's stomach growled as he took in the feast before him—fluffy scrambled eggs, thick strips of fatty bacon, and a heap of colorful, pointed berries. Without hesitation, he piled his plate high, ready to devour every bite.

"This looks great, thanks," Jack called to the Pilfert before biting into a handful of berries. Their delicate skins burst between his teeth, flooding his mouth with a rush of electrifying juice—sweet and sharp, like a taste of childhood.

"My pleasure," the Pilfert replied. "The spark fruits are freshly picked, and we got fresh eggs this morning as well. My dear friend Greynook—a goblin from Ealu—snatched them from a stymphalian's nest just last night. Sold them to me for only a couple of selacs. Always gives me a bargain. He still comes by every morning with his cart, even though the forest is empty now. Habit, I suppose. But I imagine he's pleased to have extra customers again."

The Pilfert noticed Jack's mouthful. "The blue dwellers from years ago really fancied spark fruit; they said it was a real treat compared to the fruit of your world. They'll actually be quite useful today. A handful of these can help sustain energy and give you an extra burst when your body starts to wear down!"

The Pilfert looked around the table and noticed that Adina hadn't touched her eggs. "Is everything okay?"

"No." Adina paused, meeting the Pilfert's yellow eyes. "You told me when I arrived—during our conversation about how the food is prepared—that all of it was granted to us and that it never came from any inhumane source." The Pilfert smiled like it recalled the conversation clearly.

"Stealing eggs from a mother's nest doesn't sound very humane to me."

The table fell silent, but Stefani looked intrigued. Jack knew that the way animals were farmed and killed was the main reason Stefani no longer ate meat.

The Pilfert's beak curled into a satisfied smile. "Very noble of you to think that way. However, these eggs come from a dangerous creature with a large population. Scavengers hunt for stymphalian eggs to protect us from them. The stymphalian is a mutant creation bred by a retired professor from Strega. If you wish, we can all say the Prayer of Fortune today. It's usually up to the hunter to make this prayer, but if it will relieve you, Stefani here can lead it, as she has been doing every meal."

Holding out her hands to her sides, Stefani urged Jack and Adina to take them. Then, clearing her throat, she began:

I grant thee peace in thy tired flesh,
With your miraculous wonders,
You make life fresh.
For thee I thank and bless thy flight,
Go forth, live on,
And ignite the night.

"That was very nice, Stefani. Thank you," the Pilfert said, clapping its hands together.

"It actually feels insincere since they never had a chance to grow tired," Adina said, staring off into the distance. She cleared her throat and turned to face the Pilfert. "One last thing: a stymphalian is a giant bird, right? I've read about them in class."

"That is correct."

"When did we ever talk about giant birds in class?" Jack asked, staring across the table, his fork loaded with scrambled eggs. He was dumbfounded that his school had ever taught him something this exciting.

"Maybe if you'd actually done your schoolwork instead of having me do it all the time . . ." Emerson started, but Jack cut him off.

"Alright, no need for lectures, Mom," Jack said coolly. "School never prepared us for this." Emerson looked ready to respond but stopped when Addison shook his head.

"That's wild, though. It's like a sign or something. Like our lives were leading to this very moment," Jack said, cramming more eggs into his mouth.

Addison exchanged a knowing look with Emerson, and Stefani rolled her eyes. Adina, however, looked at Jack curiously.

As they continued eating, the Pilfert disappeared into the tiny alcove across the room. The moment it left, the room erupted into a mess of overlapping voices.

"So, what do you think it'll teach us today?" Emerson's voice cut through the chatter.

"It's not what it's teaching—it's how," Stefani said, looking worried. "I don't feel the least bit magical, so how am I supposed to learn it?"

"Hopefully, it's not as boring as school," Jack added, shifting in his seat. He'd already spent way too much time asleep in the last twenty-four hours, and the thought of sitting through long lessons made him restless. "And I really hope it doesn't take forever—there's too much to explore."

Their conversation spiraled into wild theories about what they'd learn: Addison suggested they'd start off simple by conjuring rabbits from hats, while others hoped for more exciting ventures like summoning storms and battling fire-breathing dragons. Then the excitement shifted to concern: What were they even supposed to do here? Why had they been chosen?

Emerson's voice broke through again, quieter this time. "Do you think we'll have to do any type of combat?" His fingers tapped absently against the table. "I used to fence with my uncle whenever my mother . . ." He trailed off, his hands suddenly trembling.

Jack caught Adina's sharp glance in his direction—another unspoken plea. What was he supposed to do? He wasn't exactly good at this kind of thing. Still, he nudged Emerson's shoulder.

"I'm sure fencing will pay off, bro," Jack said, hoping it was the right thing to say.

Emerson forced a smile, blinking rapidly. Jack could tell he was trying to shove thoughts of his mother aside. Jack understood. Emerson had spent years looking after her, caring for her as her mind unraveled. Jack knew it was hard. After all, he had only been gone for a day, and already, thinking about his own mother—or Emma—twisted something deep in his gut.

"Ah! Good, you're all done," the Pilfert chirped as it lumbered back in with several sacks in its arms. "Excellent, excellent. I've brought you cloaks, tunics, dresses, leathers, and some light under armor." It threw a sack onto the floor, and the kids scrambled around, pulling out several pieces of clothing none of them, except maybe Emerson, would've worn.

"Go get changed in the other room and then join me when you're done so we can make our short trek to Kaluna Fields."

One by one, they grabbed what fit and slipped into the tiny alcove to change. When Jack came back in, he noticed the Pilfert filling a tiny pouch with a handful of beans.

"My dad used to grow the most wonderful weetle beans in Kaluna," the Pilfert stated, noticing Jack's reentrance. "We Pilferts used to take great care of various fields across the lands before the Great Burnings. Did I tell you? I'm the only one left," it added so nonchalantly that Jack blinked. He wasn't sure whether to feel sympathy, shock, or just go with it.

"Ah! Good, you're all dressed," the Pilfert exclaimed, looking them over as Addison tugged at the collar of his tunic, the dwarven embroidery itching against his skin, his usual ease dulled by the weight of a cloak.

Jack wore a long, brown cloak that reached his ankles, a red shirt laced with gold string, and a leather band that tightened under his chest. His pants, in earthy tones, accentuated his legs. Emerson sported an earthy tunic embroidered with a delicate pattern along the sleeves and neckline, paired with dark trousers and supple leather boots. The look was finished off with a deep-blue ombré cloak that was fastened with an intricately carved wooden clasp.

Adina and Stefani were draped in dark dresses with golden plates covering their shoulders and chests.

"OK, let's go," the Pilfert called, marching toward the archway.

One by one, the tree swallowed them like a popsicle before spitting them out beneath its branches above.

They traipsed through the beautiful forest. As they passed rundown homes, Jack couldn't help but wonder if they were built this way to be more mindful of the trees—or if the forest had simply overgrown these abandoned structures. He imagined how it might've looked when a colony of Pilferts lived here—walking the pathways, swinging on bridges, cooking and laughing near firepits outside the circular cottages. An odd knot formed in his stomach as his gaze shifted to the lonely creature leading them.

"These trees used to be the home of so much life!" the Pilfert announced, as if reading Jack's mind. Then Jack remembered—it probably had. "So much magic lingers in these trees, a history worth telling—and one you shall know in time. Life was much different before the Great Burnings occurred. A tragic time for all magical creatures."

Jack swore he heard its voice crack slightly.

"There were many more of my kind years ago, but he destroyed us all—every last Pilfert. He tried torturing secrets out of us, but our loyalty runs deeper than our knowledge. There's so much he didn't know. Akuramundo killed my family and friends. But his time is coming. His reign will end."

The darkness that lingered on its tongue sent a shiver through the group.

"My, my. Have I said too much? You must excuse me—I've lived a very long life."

Stefani, who was closest to the Pilfert, moved to hug it, but it jumped back before she could make contact.

"You must never touch my coat," it snapped. "It's extremely important that you all remember that! The sentiment, however, has been noted." It squeezed her hand gently. "Ah, looks like we've arrived—right through those trees." It pointed to a large, egg-shaped opening between the voluminous trunks.

They ran toward it, with Addison leading the way. As they flew through the opening, Addison came to a sudden stop. Jack ran right into Addison's back, and Emerson collided with Jack's shoulder. They all stared around in awe at the vast field before them.

To the north loomed a rocky mountain, draped in every shade of green, with dabs of trees climbing its sides. To their left, on a small hill, sat a tiny, stone cottage, overgrown with ivy. The field was alive with colorful flowers, swirling and dancing as their sweet scents filled the air. The flowers stretched for miles, creating a vibrant landscape like nothing Jack had ever seen before. White fluff drifted from their petals, floating upward like snow falling in reverse. Jack watched, entranced, as the flowers settled back into the dirt, brushing their leaves like smoothing a ruffled dress.

His gaze was locked on a massive, wooden dragon puppet standing several yards away, surrounded by golden grass. The puppet was larger than a two-story house.

Beyond it, rising like a guardian of the land, stood a colossal tree. Its silver roots sprawled across the earth like veins of moonlight, its luminous leaves catching the light as if woven from stardust. It looked ancient, otherworldly—a beacon in a world already steeped in magic.

"What's that?" Jack asked in awe as the Pilfert toddled up beside him.

The Pilfert followed his gaze and gave a knowing nod. "The Kaluna Tree."

"Which means . . ." Jack prompted.

"It's believed to be the birthplace of Kazumeth. It grew from a seed that fell from a star. It unraveled and created the beautiful world we live in. Its roots connect every living being."

Jack said nothing, his gaze fixed on the silver-tinged bark.

"It will do anything to protect every living thing on its land. To those it deems worthy, it offers a silver vegetable called the Kaluna root—bestowing powerful magic. Sometimes," the Pilfert added, "it can be coerced . . . but only when the intention is pure.

"What's truly remarkable is what lies beneath its canopy—the Listening Ground. Those burdened by grief come here, press their skin against the trunk, and the tree listens . . . then helps them let go."

As they walked further into the field, Jack's attention moved to the ivy-covered cottage with its cracked windows and no light shining within. Then, as if answering his unasked question, wisps of smoke began unfurling from its chimney.

"Who lives up there?" Jack asked the Pilfert, watching a squat, bearded man climb the ivy on his house, then stretch out on the slanted roof, gazing toward the sky. The man wore a pinstriped suit in watermelon pink and seafoam green, and fashionable, pointed sunglasses adorned his round face.

"Up there?" The Pilfert raised an eyebrow in amusement. "That's my dear friend, Barticus Balumi. He's descended from one of Kazumeth's greatest protectors. It's unfortunate for Barticus, though—he inherited none of her magic or warrior talent. An old, dull gnome, really, but what he lacks in power, he makes up for with his heart and mind.

"Now, gather around in a circle, please. As gifted as you all may be, it'd be fruitless to train you without first understanding exactly what we are up against.

"As you learned last night, Akuramundo has risen to a high place of power in his slow conquest of Kazumeth. He wishes to extend our borders into the world you left behind. His seizure of Dartmoor proves that he has discovered where the gateway is, but thankfully he does not yet have the means to open it. The Vocation Stones hold the power—but only through you can they be claimed. Because of this, you're in grave danger. We must keep you safe as we train each of you to wield the skills sewn into your bloodline and passed down by your ancestors. I've put enchantments around this field, and Barticus will be watching the skies for the next few weeks. By then, you should all know enough for us to begin our journey.

"So, before we begin, there's something else I'd like to mention. One of the ways Kazumethians travel from city to city is through the hopper stones. At the bottom of the hill, as you head north, you'll find a purple tree standing next to a tall, pointed archway. Should anything happen, and we're forced to flee, just walk through the arch, and it will take you to the gates of Ealu, our safe hub. Don't worry," he said, sensing the wave of tension that swept through the circle, "it's just a precaution."

"But enough of that," the Pilfert continued, waving off their furtive glances. "The first thing I wish to teach you is how to shield yourselves. This will be the most important lesson you'll ever learn. As citizens of this world, we rarely engage in violence.

But times have changed, and in these dangerous days, we must do everything we can to protect ourselves and those loyal to the Elders' way of life."

Adina, who had been brimming with questions for the last week, had had enough. "I've got a lot of questions: Why does Akuramundo want to take over our world? How does magic work here? Are there spells to learn, or should we be feeling something? I've been here a week, and I haven't seen any reason to believe I have 'magical blood' in me at all. Don't you think you should explain all of this first? And what are these things?" She gestured to the strange obstacles around them.

The Pilfert gave a knowing smile. "Ah, it's really quite simple, Adina. Your bloodlines are so strong that they alone will be ready to . . . react!" it declared, raising its staff.

Before anyone could process what was happening, it slashed the staff through the air, sending flames straight at Adina's chest.

Jack tensed, ready to shove her out of the way, but before he could move, Adina sprang into the air, soaring high above the treetops with a speed that stunned them all. Then, she dove straight for the Pilfert, hands outstretched. A wall of water erupted from the ground, forming a barrier between her and the Pilfert's flames. The fire slammed into the water, vaporizing into dark mist that coiled around them as the water rained down in gritty drops. Adina landed gracefully on her feet, staring at the Pilfert as the others cheered. She was breathless, but her eyes sparkled with excitement.

"Very good, very good. A true heir of Anneva, no doubt," the Pilfert exclaimed as it stumbled toward her, clearly impressed. "Now, do you see? The magic flowing through your body is so advanced that you need only react. For you, Jack and Emerson, spells will come naturally. For Stefani and Addison, skills in weaponry, hunting, and combat will be their reflexes. But don't worry—you'll all have access to both magic and combat in time. Your advantages depend on your stone and your ancestry."

The Pilfert gestured at Adina, who was still dripping with water. "It takes students of Strega years of study to come close to what you just did, Ms. Maynard."

Adina, still processing what had just happened, asked, "But how did my body know to react that way?"

"Blood. Blood is the deepest, most powerful source of magic in our world. Blood connections can do the most extraordinary things—good and bad. It's a complex subject, and to be honest, I don't have all the answers myself, as it's an ever-changing science," the Pilfert explained. It paused, its yellow eyes searching their faces. "What you need to understand is that you are powerful because your ancestors were incredibly gifted, and the stones helped store those gifts directly into your veins. It is said that the Vocation Stones could only be used by those whom the Oracle had destined to find them. These stones possessed all the secrets, magical gifts, and histories of the five different sources of magic in our realm at that time. A diamond from the witches, born in the Hills of Strega, was destined for and found by Anneva Maynard."

"My ancestors were witches? Wicked," Adina interjected, her mouth curling into an excited grin.

The Pilfert chuckled. "Ah, your ancestor was a blue dweller—though, yes, the blood running through your veins is laced with witch magic. But don't forget, your ancestors were blue dwellers who studied the magical arts. Their power was glorified and enhanced by the Vocation Stones—as well as by the lost magic of your world."

It turned its attention to Addison, who stood just behind Adina. "The ruby of the dwarves was found by Victor Stempinski, master of the mines. That's why it was no easy task rescuing you from the dwarves. Their treasures and weaponry are sacred to them, and they believed you belonged to them. I think they were hoping to offer you to the enemy in exchange for protection."

Addison nodded, his face twisting in disgust at the thought of his kin's actions.

"A sapphire for the elves to Hernando Garcia," The Pilfert turned to Emerson, who smiled warmly at the mention of his ancestor.

"An emerald reserved for Leidy Campbell, tied to the people of Levestin." It looked at Stefani, who seemed dissatisfied by the notion that her ancestors were merely men. "Don't look down on them, Stefani," it said. "The people of Levestin, men and women alike, were masters of different kinds of magic: agricultural, potion-making, and combat. They taught us all how to fight during the first war. You have plenty of magic flowing through your veins, child. Do not despair. We will talk more about Levestin in the months to come, but it'll be your responsibility to restore the island's magic and put an end to the regime that has devastated their people. You alone will be able to achieve this. I feel it."

Stefani smiled bashfully. Jack noticed a shift in her posture that drew a smile across his face.

Lastly, the Pilfert turned to Jack, its eyes gleaming. "A piece from the onyx of Kazumeth for Ulysses Hackley. This stone is linked to the Pilferts." Jack fought to keep a neutral expression, but inside he was bursting with excitement. The Pilferts' species were renowned for their wisdom, and Jack could barely contain his joy at being attached to them.

"Well, clearly, the stone must be broken," Addison said with a smirk, nudging Jack. "No way this guy's descended from the so-called wisest creatures in the land."

"The stone is alive and well," the Pilfert replied, its voice firm. "I felt it the moment I laid eyes on Mr. Hackley. The presence of a Vocation Stone can be sensed by both its bearer and those who draw power from it. Each of these stones is protected—and rightly so. If they were ever destroyed, the consequences would be dire. You'd lose all instinct, and the magic in your blood would dry up. The centuries of strength woven into your lineage would vanish, leaving you to relearn magic from the very beginning. For a blue dweller like you, even at Strega Academy, that could take your entire lifetime.

"As long as the stones remain safe, so do you. But if someone were to seize them, they wouldn't just wield the magic within—they'd control you as well. You would become their puppet."

The group sat in stunned silence, absorbing the gravity of what they had just learned. No one spoke or moved until the Pilfert cleared its throat. "Shall we continue? Emerson, would you please come forward?"

The gangly boy moved past his friends, his shoulders stiff as he moved into the center of the circle.

"Now, I want to show you how to defend yourself the right way. A shield won't always be your best option." Its voice was calm, deliberate. "As guardians we only attack when absolutely necessary. But when that moment comes, you need to know how to."

The Pilfert turned its sharp gaze to Emerson. "If you would, please—attack me. Not with your hands. With your mind."

Emerson's jaw clenched.

"Using magic as a weapon isn't natural in Kazumeth," it continued, "but it can be done. And it starts with intent. You must want to cause me harm. Not in theory. Not in practice. Truly want it. Do whatever you need to move your mind into that darker space."

There was a beat of silence at these words as all eyes flashed to Emerson.

"When you get there, focus. What's around you? What can you use? Magic doesn't always require incantations or spells. Elven magic is organic, tied to the earth itself. Tap into it." Its voice dropped, steady and commanding. "Now—close your eyes and go there."

Emerson obeyed, but the moment he felt the shift inside him, the moment his mind coiled around something raw and furious, his eyes snapped open. His breath hitched.

The Pilfert was watching him with an unreadable expression.

"Nothing you attempt will be difficult for me to negate," it assured him, almost amused. "You're gifted, but I'm a Pilfert! And there are only three ways to kill a Pilfert, and none of them are present in this field.

"Now. Do as you're told."

Emerson closed his eyes again. He let his mind wander into the dark recesses where memories lived: bullies spitting slurs, their laughter sharp as knives; his mother, strapped to a stretcher, her eyes vacant as they wheeled her away after another psychotic break; his abuela, trembling as a group of men hurled insults at her in the supermarket for speaking broken English.

He had wanted to hurt them all.

The rage ignited like dry kindling, shifting toward the Pilfert—the very one who'd ripped him away from his family when they needed him most. The one standing there now, still pushing him, like it hadn't already ruined his life.

Heat surged through Emerson's body as his heart thundered in his chest. His long fingers curled into tight, trembling fists. His eyes snapped open, a flicker of red glinting beneath the usual greenish-brown. With a sudden motion, he thrust his right hand forward. The brittle grass around him quivered, then stretched—longer, taller—ten, twenty feet—like rubber bands pulled to their limit. Then, with a sharp snap, they recoiled. The grass whipped into motion, twisting like serpents, lashing around the Pilfert's body and yanking it into the air. The creature flailed like a rag doll before slamming into the ground with a heavy, jarring impact.

As the grass tightened its grip, it hoisted the Pilfert once more, preparing to slam it into the earth again. But with a swift flick of its tangled staff, the Pilfert severed the bindings. The blades of grass, sliced cleanly as if by an unseen machete, slithered back into the ground, taking root.

The small creature landed lightly on its feet, unshaken. It twirled its staff in an intricate motion above its head, its movements precise and practiced. Then it spoke—its voice striking a strange chord between beauty and terror, the words both haunting and mesmerizing.

Before it could finish, a thick, brown whip of grass lashed out, cracking through the air. It struck the Pilfert's staff, sending it flying. The tangled wooden rod tumbled end over end before plunging deep into the ground, far beyond the Pilfert's reach.

Roots—thick and serpentine—erupted from where it had fallen. The ground cracked and shifted like scorched toast beneath them. The Pilfert staggered, its large feet kicking into the air as the roots coiled around its body, pulling it back down. It clawed at the earth, straining to break free, and Jack caught a flicker of fear in its wide eyes.

The field erupted into chaos as everyone screamed at Emerson, whose face was darkening with rage. Overhead, the sky churned, thick clouds rolling in like ink spilling across the heavens. A stinging, warm rain began to fall. The clouds swirled, gathering in thick layers as the rain formed a translucent barrier, like a pane of glass separating Emerson's friends from the Pilfert.

Addison pushed through the wall, his skin immediately breaking out into painful boils that rapidly healed. He lunged toward Emerson's thin form, but Emerson was quicker.

A blinding white bolt of energy erupted from the ground between them, sending a crackling shockwave across the field. Addison tried to dodge it, but the force caught him, hurling him backward. He hit the ground hard, skidding across the dirt.

Pandemonium broke out as the others rushed forward, each breaking out in fiery boils and encountering the same fate as Addison. Lightning flashed everywhere.

Jack had just staggered to his feet when he caught sight of the Pilfert, standing motionless amid the chaos. Slowly, it raised something thin and silver to its beak—a tuber, glistening in the storm light. It slurped it down like a worm, and in that instant, the world seemed to freeze.

Its staff shot into its outstretched hand, and a blinding light erupted from the twisted top. Emerson gasped. The fury vanished from his face, leaving him pale and wide-eyed. His limbs trembled, his breath coming in shallow gulps. The storm above wavered, the swirling mass of darkness thinning into pale gray streaks. The barrier shattered into mist. The roots twisted one final time before retreating back into the earth, the broken ground sealing behind them as if the destruction had never happened.

A heavy silence fell.

The Pilfert leaned against its staff, its gaze unreadable as it studied Emerson. For a long moment, no one spoke. Emerson curled into himself, his body shaking, his face buried in his knees.

And then, to everyone's shock, the Pilfert clapped.

"Very well done," it said, its voice smooth, almost amused. "You've reminded me of the most important lesson I will teach you here. Control. More specifically—emotional control."

"Power is easy," the Pilfert continued. "Restraint is the true challenge. You wielded anger—the most volatile and dangerous emotion—the hardest to master. True strength lies not in unleashing power, but in taming it. That is what made the Sovereign exceptional—no other blue dweller has ever shown such discipline when faced with temptation.

"Emerson, you did exactly as I hoped. There is no shame in struggle. Do not hide your face."

Emerson hesitated, then lifted his gaze, which was somber and uncertain.

"Why don't you come back over here and stand with your friends?" the Pilfert said, motioning gently.

Slowly, Emerson stood and shuffled toward them, his shoulders hunched. He kept his eyes down, unable to meet their gazes. Stefani reached out, rubbing his back in quiet comfort. He looked down, his eyes filling with tears.

"I'm sorry to have pushed you so hard, Emerson," the Pilfert said. "But if you don't mind me asking . . . what were you thinking about?"

Emerson swallowed, looking away. "I was . . ." His voice faltered. "I was thinking about how I'll never see my mom again."

A pause. The Pilfert's voice softened. "I see."

There was a shared pain in its tone. "I'm sorry that you were chosen for this fate. It is a cruel magic—to be torn from your family, knowing their lives continue without you. A cruelty we failed to consider when we hastily set it into motion during the Great Burnings."

The Pilfert gave him a small, knowing smile. "But rest assured, Emerson. Your mother is in good hands."

Emerson didn't smile back.

"We mustn't dwell on our grief," the Pilfert continued. "Not when there is still so much to learn. Come—let's get back to it."

No one moved. All eyes remained fixed on Emerson, and for a brief moment, empathy hung thick in the air. The flowers around them stirred, releasing snowy tufts that drifted lazily, their calming scent settling over the group like a whispered lullaby.

"Time is limited," the Pilfert declared, its voice crisp and absolute. "Every second must be spent mastering the arts and the ways of this world so that you may protect those you left behind. Time stops for no one." And with that, it leaped into the air, its staff raised high. A jet of red light shot from the tangled end of the staff like a bolt of lightning.

A siren voice rang out. Then, as though from the abyss, a godlike hand wreathed in red flame reached toward them, its smoldering fingers outstretched with violent intent.

Jack instinctively threw himself in front of his friends. His body ignited—heat racing through him, spreading beneath his skin before erupting outward—ten . . . twenty . . . thirty feet. A wave of deep emerald burst from within, swelling into a dome around them.

The fiery hand struck. Fingerlike flames crashed against the shield, and the sky exploded with perilous bursts of red and green—a collision of heat and magic, like living fireworks.

As the hand sizzled into nothingness, the Pilfert limped forward, its eyes gleaming, wide and animated. It seized Jack's arm, patting it enthusiastically before snapping its beak open.

"Never let your guard down," it boomed, vibrating with excitement. "That! That's exactly what I was looking for. Brilliant, boy, brilliant!"

It threw a hand into the air, as if basking in the glow of victory. "Not only did you protect yourself, but you extended the shield to guard your friends! That's instinct! That's strategy!" The Pilfert nodded, satisfied. "Now—go sit down and rest. There's water and goblin ale in that bag over there. We'll get you some oil for your boils later. The rest of you can join him after you conjure an equally effective shield."

Jack moved away from the group, his body trembling as he reached the supplies and flopped down. His clothes were soaked in a freezing sweat, but he didn't mind; the coolness felt good against his burning skin. He opened the bag and pulled out a long, thin canteen full of water, then let himself collapse on the grass, exhaustion pinning him to the spot.

He lay there, watching his friends fight off fire, water, daggers, and the other dangerous objects the Pilfert hurled at them. Still, none had managed to create the protective force he had. Two hours passed before Emerson and Adina joined him on the hillside, both looking just as drained as he felt.

"Great job. I was beginning to think I'd have to entertain myself all afternoon. And trust me, I'm not that fun. This no-phone business ain't it," Jack said, smirking as they sat beside him.

"I hate to admit it, but I keep reaching for it too," Emerson mumbled, still avoiding their gaze.

Adina took a long drink. "You can speak up. Attempted murder makes things awkward, but we're all about growth here."

Jack chuckled. "Seriously, Emerson. Just because you almost killed our mentor doesn't mean we're mad at you. Any of us could've been pushed that far."

"Mentor . . . right," Emerson muttered. He frowned, his voice dropping. "I don't know why, but something feels off about it." He glanced around, then leaned in. "It always dodges direct questions. Didn't you notice? It only answered one of the concerns you brought up earlier. There's so much that doesn't add up. I just feel like—"

He didn't get to finish. Stefani and Addison suddenly appeared above them, Stefani practically bouncing on her heels, too jittery to sit still.

"Rest, rest," the Pilfert said, materializing beside them.

Adina popped the stopper off a bottle of goblin ale and held it out to Stefani, who waved it off, reaching for the water canteen instead.

"We'll start the obstacles soon," the Pilfert announced.

The groans from the group didn't go unnoticed. The Pilfert's beady eyes darted between them before it clapped its hands together.

"Ah, already feeling fatigued. Eat the crackers—they'll restore your energy. Oh, your burns. Right. Let me get the oil." And before anyone could react, it was gone in a blink.

They sat on the hillside, drinking and munching on the delicious crackers, which had the faintest hint of chocolate and hazelnut. They seemed to forget about Emerson's earlier outburst as they joked about their shields.

"I just wish my mom could see all this," Emerson said, suddenly quieting the group. "She knew. She knew for so many years. If only she were here. But, if I'm lucky, maybe in this new life she's no longer sick."

Jack looked around and saw the smiles slide from everyone's faces, landing heavily in their laps. It was the second time "home" had come up today—a subject they were all quietly avoiding. Life on Earth felt like a distant memory to Jack, though he had only been in Kazumeth for a day. It felt like a lifetime had passed. Now, however, images of his mother and Emma erupted in his mind, and his heart sank. Jack turned to look at Stefani, who had tears falling from her high cheeks.

"Alright, are you ready for the next lesson?" the Pilfert asked, reappearing and handing them bottles of oil without looking at them. When they didn't move, it noticed their solemn expressions, and its beak curled into a frown.

"What happened here? Aren't you interested in trying out the course?"

"Emerson killed the mood talking about family," Adina said flatly, rubbing the thick oil onto her reddened skin, which quickly returned to its fair complexion.

The Pilfert's eyes filled with remorse. "I'm so sorry. Truly. Losing everything is a wound that never fully fades—I understand that. However, there is a time for sadness and self-pity, and a time to rise above it. And right now, we must rise.

"Healing will come, but dwelling on the past will not bring back what is lost. If we allow ourselves to be consumed by the past, we risk forfeiting the future. There is still so much to fight for—so much still unwritten."

Silence. The Pilfert didn't look pleased.

"We must continue forward, because danger does not wait for us to be ready. Akuramundo has been waiting. He has known of your coming for months—that is why I sent Ogof to retrieve you before the date the Futurians suggested. He will make his move, and when he does, you must be prepared. Not just for yourselves, but for all who will one day look to you for strength.

"Training is not just for survival—it is a promise to those you have left behind that you'll keep them safe."

"Make his move? This isn't a game of chess. This is our lives," Emerson exclaimed.

"Exactly. We cannot stand still. He has armies searching for you. He's been waiting. This war may be new to you, but it is not new to us. We have been fighting for longer than you can comprehend, and every moment wasted is a step closer to our undoing."

The Pilfert paused, scanning their blank stares, then sighed.

"I know it's overwhelming. You were thrust into this without warning, without choice. But war does not wait for understanding. Whether you accept it or not, the battle has already begun. And if you are not ready when the moment comes, there will be no second chances.

"Now get up. Phase two begins now."

They stood and moved toward the circle with less enthusiasm than before.

"We'll practice the shield again," the Pilfert instructed. "Focus on pushing your limits while conserving energy—strength without endurance is futile. After that, we'll move on to defense—learning how to disarm weapons from predators and combat creatures like dragons, ghourians, and mermaids."

With heavy hearts, they began their work.

As the day wore on, Jack became increasingly aware of their differences in skill. He had managed—just for a moment—to slip inside Addison's mind, hearing his thoughts as clearly as if they were his own; he could even speak through them if he focused hard enough. The Pilfert had explained that this ability was something only Pilferts could do.

And though Jack was decent with spells, he struggled to produce things from thin air like Adina could.

Then, during another shield drill, Addison faltered. He raised his hands too late, leaving his barrier incomplete. The wooden dragon puppet reared back and exhaled a burst of fire. The flames struck him head-on.

Panic surged through the group. But, as the fire engulfed him, Addison didn't flinch. Instead, he watched, wide-eyed, as fresh skin knitted itself over his burns within seconds, erasing the damage as if it had never happened.

"Why can't I fly like Adina?" Emerson burst out, after attempting to jump high into the air, only to fall straight into long wooden pincers that jutted back and forth.

"I understand it's frustrating, but the magic you produce stems from the stones. Elves don't fly, but that's not to say they can't learn. Elven magic, which you possess, is nothing like the magic of the witches of Strega. You'll each face obstacles and have much to learn before mastering other forms of magic. It takes time. This is why talismans and bloodlines are used to store magic—so your hard work isn't lost when you venture on."

They spent the evening learning to disarm opponents both magically and physically, and how to heal minor wounds—though Addison liked to point out that his dwarven blood would allow him to self-heal deep wounds. They worked until hunger and exhaustion started to take their toll.

The journey home was even more beautiful than the journey there. Soft, red light beckoned between the tall, colorful trees. The ground was littered with leaves, and the abandoned tree homes seemed to breathe. The rustling of animals and the beating of wings filled the still air.

"Go inside. I'll be a minute. Get ready for bed, and we'll feast by the fire. Emerson, would you be so kind as to escort me to Ealu?" the Pilfert asked as they reached the swirling knot entrance of their home. Emerson nodded, and in the blink of an eye, he and the Pilfert disappeared.

After changing, they gathered around the fire, too tired to speak. The Pilfert eventually returned, carrying several dishes. It set them down in the center of the table, watching as the friends devoured their meals. The only sounds in the small, fire-lit den were the clatter of silverware and the sloshing of food.

After dinner, they crawled into their hammocks, ready for sleep. But Jack found it impossible to drift off. He lay awake thinking about Emma, wondering how her new life was unfolding—if she had a new home, new friends, a new story that no longer had space for him. When he finally closed his eyes, he painted her face across his eyelids, trying to memorize the slope of her cheekbones and the way her eyes lit up when she laughed.

Then his mind betrayed him. It conjured someone else beside her—faceless, unknown. A stranger written into the space where he used to be. Jack tried to picture what he might look like, but the thought lodged like a stone in his chest. He couldn't help but wonder if he loved her as much as he did right now in this moment.

The ache was unbearable. Jack climbed out of his hammock and sidled into the main room, where Adina was curled up by the fire, staring into the dying embers.

"You can't sleep either?" she asked, her voice low.

Jack shook his head. "Emma."

Adina smiled faintly. "Missing her?"

"Of course," Jack answered, as if it were a silly question. But the pain he was feeling went far beyond missing. Worse was the knowledge that while he remembered every detail about her, Emma was waking up not even knowing who he was.

They sat for a long moment in a comfortable silence, watching the flames pulse and flicker.

"It's wild how fast the world moves on."

Jack glanced at her, catching something unreadable in her expression. There was a weight in her words, something personal—but her body language made it clear she wasn't ready to share. He looked back at the fire instead.

"How is Emerson?" Adina asked Jack.

"I'm not sure. I feel like the Pilfert pushed him too hard, and he's still beating himself up."

"Yeah . . . but it was a bit scary." She hesitated, picking at a loose thread on her sleeve. "Has he always had this much anger?"

"I'm not sure," Jack said after a pause. "His life wasn't exactly easy in Brookville, but he never said anything to me."

Adina sighed, staring into the fire. "It didn't just feel like anger, though," she murmured. "It felt more dangerous. Untamed. Like, what if next time, he can't stop?"

Jack didn't answer. His mind flashed back to the field—the way the earth had split open, the roots writhing like living things beneath Emerson's fury. The force of it had been wild. Unchecked. And Adina was right: it was dark and dangerous.

Then his thoughts drifted to the dream he'd had before entering Kazumeth—Emerson chained to a cellar floor, Akuramundo's questioning, and the betrayal. He needed to tell the Pilfert. Because if it *was* a premonition, could he save Emerson in time? Before it was too late? Before he destroyed them all?

A slight creak of wood brought Jack back to the present. They both froze, eyes fixed on the doorway to their room.

Nothing was there.

"Maybe we shouldn't talk about this tonight," Jack said at last. "He's our friend."

"Sure," Adina said before returning her attention to the crackling embers.

Later, when they finally rose to return to their hammocks, the earlier easy silence was now a heavy curtain between them. Jack didn't know what to say, only that he hoped Emerson hadn't heard their concerns.

But part of him feared that he had.

Chapter Nine

Silfrado's Flute

The following weeks passed quicker than flying axes and fluttering fairy wings. No one was quite sure how long they had been in Kazumeth, but Jack felt certain it had been at least a month. Their days were spent training in the vast valley where Kaluna Fields stretched between the O'Keen Forest and the village of Ealu.

Mornings were dedicated to hand-to-hand combat and weapon drills, while afternoons were filled with spells, charms, and curses. During the few breaks they were granted, Adina pored over spellbooks, mumbling incantations under her breath until they were burned into her memory. The others spent their time studying maps and history books—or, more often than they probably should—talking about everything they missed from home.

Emerson fretted over his mother, but even more so about his abuela, who barely spoke English and relied on him to translate. He could only hope that in her rewritten story, his mother's illness had vanished, leaving her strong enough to care for his grandmother.

Addison didn't miss much, but he often found himself hoping his little sister was finally getting the love and attention they'd both gone without since their stepfather died.

Jack, though he felt guilty for it, mostly spoke of Emma, knowing deep down that his own mother—strong and unshakable—would find a way to be okay, no matter the circumstances

Stefani still caught herself reaching for a phone she no longer had whenever the Pilfert said something confusing. It frustrated her to no end that she no longer had all the answers in her pocket. More than anything, she missed music; she'd break into song at all hours of the day—much to Adina's annoyance.

Adina, however, rarely joined in these conversations. Whenever talk of home came up, she buried her nose in books or busied herself with the additional tasks the Pilfert had given her. She learned how to brew and store potions, how to summon powerful roots from the Kaluna Fields—roots that couldn't simply be dug up, including the elusive Kaluna root, which had strengthened the Pilfert during its fight with Emerson. She also studied the magical properties of everyday items and refined her magical combat skills under the Pilfert's watchful eye. The only one who seemed to keep up with her was Emerson, who had gained a far greater mastery over manipulating nature.

Stefani, despite envying their magical abilities, had proven herself just as formidable. She had bested the Pilfert in a long sparring match, becoming highly skilled with a blade. And though she lacked Emerson's and Adina's magical finesse, she had achieved something none of them had yet—she had made herself completely invisible.

Jack and Addison, on the other hand, had become masters of physical combat. Addison, wielding the raw power of the dwarves, had become a deadly axe-thrower, and with his ability to heal almost instantly, he rarely lost a match. Jack, with his ability to enter minds, tried to use it to his advantage in combat, but maintaining control long enough to make a difference remained a challenge.

Jack, however, was learning something the others envied above all else: the Pilfert was teaching him how to shift through space, appearing in different locations—a rare magical technique called *fading*.

It took weeks of relentless practice, but Jack had finally managed to fade from the field to the forest home and back again. The success was exhilarating, but the cost was brutal. Each attempt drained him completely, leaving him so exhausted that even fruit and crackers barely took the edge off.

The Pilfert assured him it would get easier with time, but it offered a stark reminder—all magic had its limits.

That evening, they had each been taking turns dismantling the wooden dragon in the field. Jack had been the first to behead the beast, narrowly avoiding a deadly blast of flames that shot from its wide mouth.

"How much more training do we have to do?" Jack asked, voicing an opinion he'd been holding for over a week. "We've improved so much already. I think it's time we get on the offensive before it's too late."

The Pilfert looked at him with a frown. "It's not that simple, Jack. We cannot just march into Dartmoor and expect to overtake the capital and have Akuramundo surrender. If it were that easy, do you think I would not have done so already? After all, I'm much cleverer and far more skilled than you."

Jack tried not to look offended, for he knew the creature was right.

"Besides, we won't be marching into battle. We have allies to gain—and your stones to collect."

"Our stones?" Emerson blurted out.

"Correct, Emerson. These stones are well hidden and protected by deep magic. However, Akuramundo will use each of you to retrieve them—because only those linked to a stone can claim it." The Pilfert's large eyes gleamed. "If we collect them first, we can store them where he will never be able to reach them."

It hesitated for a moment, then added, "Of course, it is ultimately your choice whether we move them there . . . though I think it's rather important that we do."

Addison frowned, arms crossed. "So why didn't our families hide them there in the first place? If our entire being is poured into these stones, they should've given them this grand protection before."

"They didn't have time." The Pilfert clicked its beak, shaking its head. "During the Great Burnings, we had no choice but to secure them elsewhere—our original plan was impossible because of how quickly they were being hunted. The Sovereign placed the stones with purpose, knowing they would remain untouched until those who were worthy came to reclaim them and finish the plan we had intended. That moment has arrived," the Pilfert said, though Jack noticed something distant in its eyes—a quiet sparkle, like it was holding back more than it said.

"You have two choices—trust me to see this through, to protect them so they'll never be touched again, or destroy them. Any other path and Akuramundo wins."

The Pilfert's words did not settle easily. Uneasy glances passed around the circle, doubt flickering between them.

Stefani's face tightened with concern. "And what will that do to us? The other day, you said without the stones, we'd be powerless."

"Correct," the Pilfert said simply. "Without the stones, you will no longer wield magic as you do now. That is why, once we collect them, you will have a choice—destroy them immediately to ensure Akuramundo never possesses their power or trust me to hide them where he can never reach."

It let the words settle, scanning their faces. "But understand this—if we hesitate, if we falter, we risk everything. There is no third option. Either we take control of the stones' fate, or he does."

Emerson scoffed. "So, we're just supposed to trust that you'll hide them, keep them safe, and not exploit them yourself? Or destroy them and be left powerless in a world still full of magic?"

The Pilfert's beak clicked. "Magic has never been about power alone, Emerson. It is about trust. It is about choice. And you will have to make one."

A tense silence followed. Uneasy glances flickered between them, the weight of the Pilfert's words pressing heavily on their shoulders.

Then, as if sensing the shift, the Pilfert suddenly brightened. "Now, I'd like to congratulate you all on how far you've come in such a short time." It clapped its fuzzy hands together. "I suspect we'll be on our way to the first stone in just a few short days!"

And with that, it winked and faded from view.

"Something isn't right," Emerson muttered at once. "The Pilfert is hiding too much. Why should we give up the very gifts our ancestors left for us? Why should we willingly become powerless, stripping away our only defense in a world that's so volatile and dangerous now? This isn't a choice—it's an ultimatum."

Adina crossed her arms. "An ultimatum? No one's forcing you to choose either option, Emerson. But pretending like we can hold onto this power without consequence is just as reckless. The greatest heroes in history made sacrifices for the greater good—why should we be any different?"

"We've sacrificed enough already." Emerson's voice rose through his clenched teeth, his fists curling in his lap. "We gave up our entire lives to protect the people we love, and they don't even remember us."

The weight of his words settled over the group like a thick fog. No one spoke. No one moved.

Jack felt the silence press against his ribs. He wanted to say something, to reassure Emerson that their sacrifices weren't meaningless—but what could he possibly say to make it better?

He glanced at Adina, who met his gaze briefly before looking away. She didn't have an answer either.

Jack exhaled sharply, running a hand through his hair. "Well," he said, forcing a smirk, "since we're all in such fantastic spirits, how about a round of Gladiator?"

The others shot him a look that said, *read the room,* but Adina only raised a brow like she was considering it.

"You're not afraid to get your hands dirty, are you, witch girl?" he teased.

Adina hopped up, grabbed one of the wooden swords lying in the grass, and swung without hesitation.

Jack had already snatched up another, meeting her strike with a dull thwack. Within seconds, they were weaving across the field, their swords smacking together in quick, hollow knocks. The others watched, their earlier unease melting into laughter and cheers.

Adina swung wildly, missing every time. Jack doubled over, laughing at her sloppy attacks—until something solid slammed against his shoulder. He barely had time to react before the blunt tip of her sword slid to his neck.

"Checkmate," Adina said smoothly, resting her sword across her shoulders as she walked away triumphantly.

"That doesn't count! I was too busy laughing at how bad you are!" Jack protested.

Adina smirked. "Like Pilfy always says—never let your guard down." Then, with a playful glint in her eyes, she added, "But if you want a rematch, why don't we do it up here . . ."

Before he could react, she leaped effortlessly into the air, twirling high above their heads.

"Oh, wait." She laughed, soaring higher. "You don't know how to fly."

Jack watched in stunned silence as she danced through the sky, her dark hair swirling around her pale, moonlit face. She moved effortlessly, gliding and twisting, her blue dress trailing behind her like ghostly ribbons. The fabric rippled with the wind, undulating like a school of exotic fish drifting through an endless sea. When she landed beside him seconds later, he felt a surprising pang of disappointment.

Adina grinned, her cheeks flushed with exhilaration, just as the Pilfert waddled over, beak stretched in a wide smile, and clapped her on the back with a proud thump.

"Big deal, you can fly. That's not nearly as useful as my visions," Jack gloated, feeling a foggy sensation lift from his mind.

"Visions you can't control?" Adina teased.

"Visions that came to me before we even got here. You couldn't do any of this back in our world!" Jack shot back. "Come at me again."

"Oh, suck it," Adina huffed.

Jack grinned at her—until he caught Stefani's raised eyebrows over Adina's pale shoulder, her expression unreadable but pointed. His smile faltered, shifting into a frown as he quickly looked away.

"You've been here six weeks and have already become exceptional in the art of magic," the Pilfert said, beak stretching into a wide grin. "Some of you are born fighters! I'm impressed with how quickly you've learned to control your magical abilities. Just a few more days and we'll head out to collect the first stone."

"According to my insiders, many of Akuramundo's supporters have been spotted in the city of Alors for months now. That said, we need to go over what's expected of you." The Pilfert's tone turned firm.

"In four days, we'll travel to the Sabana Mountains, which stretch through Alors, to retrieve the blue sapphire of Hernando Garcia. But before that, we have a brief meeting with the elves in Veilage Platts."

It paused, tapping its staff against the ground. "The stone is protected by a dragon. And while you've been trained to defend yourselves against dragons—and, if necessary, to kill them—it is imperative that we do not harm Gridlybone."

Its yellow eyes locked onto each of them in turn. "She was placed in the mountains not just to guard the stone, but to protect the lower villages from the trolls who once pillaged their towns and devoured their children."

The group stiffened at that revelation.

"A treaty was signed to confine the trolls to the Sabana Mountains, preventing them from wreaking havoc on the villages ever again. Gridlybone is not just a guardian of the stone—she is the barrier that keeps the trolls in check.

"However, the trolls are restless and are ready to end the treaty. Gridlybone's presence is all that is keeping peace on the eastern coast."

The group exchanged looks of concern. The Pilfert had often told them stories of Kazumeth's history during their dinners, and two lessons they all learned were to never fight a troll and to never steal from a dragon. Now it wanted them to do both.

"Emerson will be able to remove the stone without killing the dragon. I'm sure of it," the Pilfert said.

There was a silence as all eyes turned to Emerson, who tried his best to appear confident.

"So, what exactly does Akuramundo want with the stones?" Emerson asked, eager to shift the attention off himself. "If he's already as powerful as you say, does he really need them?"

The Pilfert's beak clicked. "Ah, but I've answered this before. The stones will allow him entry into your world, where he intends to expand his reach beyond our borders. But that is only one purpose."

It stopped pacing, fixing them with an intense gaze. "The stones don't just hold power—they are power. They have infused your very blood with magic. When combined, their abilities surpass anything we've ever imagined. Combined, their powers could make you the pious ruler of time—or, more commonly, the penultimate ruler."

They all stared blankly at the Pilfert. To Jack's surprise, Stefani was the only one who seemed to understand. She shot a wary glance around before fixing her gaze on the Pilfert. The creature began pacing in front of them.

"Collecting the sapphire is just a trivial task at this moment. We will set out, and with Emerson here, the stone will call to him for retrieval. But there are many moving parts in our turbulent climate." It paused. "The city of Mankato is on the verge of rebellion—whispers of a coup against Levestin grow stronger by the day. What was once a quiet resistance is becoming something much louder, and soon, the ruling regime will have no choice but to respond."

Stefani frowned. "What does their civil war have to do with making sure Akuramundo doesn't destroy the worlds?"

The Pilfert's head whipped around, its eyes sharp. "Everything. We are all connected! Every single organism—in our world, your world, and the other five as well. A civil war here will ripple through time itself."

It stopped pacing, uttering a string of beautiful yet foreign words, clicking its beak several times. As if in response, their olive-colored bags appeared in front of them.

"These bags carry everything you'll need for our journey," the Pilfert announced. As it spoke, several scrolls of parchment shot out, hovering in midair.

"Maps," it said, and the scrolls unfurled with a flick. "Books." Three large, weathered tomes with cracked spines appeared next. "And clothes." Long, draping dresses, tunics, and robes floated out, followed by tights and loose shirts without buttons. Tall skirts came next, along with corsets and other garments that, to Jack, looked better suited for a Renaissance fair or comic convention than actual everyday wear.

"You'll also find two other valuable items inside," the Pilfert added, "each chosen specifically for one of you." As it spoke, the books, maps, and clothes folded themselves neatly and slipped back into the bags.

Jack reached into his satchel and pulled out a long, jeweled sword. The hilt was etched with strange, otherworldly symbols, and just above three gleaming sapphires, the words *The Last Ruler* were engraved. He grinned and gave it a confident swing—only for the blade to hit the dirt with a thunk and stick there, unmoving.

His second item was a long, thin flute—or whistle—hanging from a flesh-colored string. The flute was no thicker than a quarter, its mouthpiece unusually wide. He pressed it to his lips and blew. Nothing.

He tried again. Still nothing.

Muttering a few choice words, he gave it one last attempt. This time, a smooth, sharp whistle filled the air.

The others stopped, turned, and laughed.

"Ah yes, Silfrado's Flute," the Pilfert said, eyes gleaming. "I invented this years ago for Barticus's brother. It served as a warning whistle to my clan whenever danger was near. We could communicate telepathically, but that takes time. This lets you speak to all those you've sworn allegiance to at once. Of course, only if you're within a reasonable distance, that is."

The Pilfert clapped its fuzzy hands eagerly. "Oh! And if you place it in your mouth while underwater, you can breathe for hours. Very useful when visiting the cecaelia," it added with a wink.

An axe, a shield, glass bottles containing colored liquids and herbs, and many other unique objects were passed around for each of them to inspect. Jack was particularly fascinated by a golden bracelet resembling several twisted snakes that Stefani received. It tightened its grip if the wearer was being deceived.

By the time they packed up to head home, the sky was aglow with stars, and the moon had shifted position. Adina and Jack walked side by side, discussing their new gifts as she whispered into what they had now dubbed his "panic pipe." As they trekked through the forest, Addison deliberately bumped into Jack's shoulder as he dashed past, turning to give Jack a questioning glance.

Jack shrugged, feeling slightly offended. He knew what Addison was insinuating, and he was wrong. Adina was just cool; she wasn't his type. Besides, he was still in love with Emma. No, he and Adina just got along exceptionally well, and their late-night conversations, which often stretched into the early hours of the morning, were always enjoyable—but it was purely platonic. Addison didn't know—

But Jack's thoughts were abruptly interrupted when he collided with the back of Addison's tall, solid frame.

"Why'd you stop?" Jack snapped.

"I need you to head north," the Pilfert said quietly, its voice tinged with fear. Jack moved to see what had caused this sudden shift in the Pilfert's tone. His heart sank as he saw that the tree they had been calling home was now nothing but a burning stump.

"Take the hopper stone to Ealu," the Pilfert instructed. "Once you're within the walls, you'll be safe. Wait for me there. I will meet you."

"Who did this?" Jack demanded, his insides igniting with anger at the sight of yet another home being ripped away from him.

"Get to Ealu now. Run, fly, fade, do whatever you must, but you need to flee." The Pilfert pointed to his right, its eyes wide with urgency. "Run," it yelled. But before they could move, they were surrounded.

"Ahh wud'n' roon . . . if Ahh wuz yuu," a high voice called as Jack looked up to see a green, lumpy giant looming over the Pilfert. The giant's coin-sized nostrils sniffed the air as his bulging, silver eyes swiveled, scanning each of their faces. "Danks fer takin' care o' our mast'r's guests . . . but we kin take 'em from 'ereh," he finished in a grunt, his spit flying from his gaping, toothless mouth.

Chapter Ten

Escape to Ealu

"So, the rumors are true," the Pilfert said casually. "Akuramundo has bought you by granting you the power of infinite speech."

Jack edged closer to the rest of the group, who were all huddled behind the Pilfert, desperately searching for any kind of opening in the circle of creatures that surrounded them.

"More'n any'un's ev'r done fer us," spat the shorter of the two green men. He, too, began sniffing the air, his hungry eyes locking onto Emerson, who, at that exact moment, seemed to have swallowed something particularly unpleasant.

"What are you whispering, boy?!" screeched a tall, lean woman with pointed ears. "You think you can escape us? You're surrounded, child!" she barked at Jack, who had just whispered something to the others. Her curly brown hair, adorned with golden trinkets, stiffened and flared, resembling snakes poised to strike.

The Pilfert made a slight motion with its staff, and suddenly, all predatory eyes shifted back to the small creature, their gazes fixated on its walking stick.

Seizing the distraction, Jack made a quick signal to the others. Without missing a beat, they charged between a half-bull, half-gnarled man and a wiry-haired wizard, whose frail form looked like it could snap in half like dry spaghetti. They collided, knocking the wizard to the ground as they tore through the gap.

Jack shot to the front, sprinting down the sloping hill, the sound of his pounding feet reverberating in his ears. Cracking whips and heavy footsteps echoed all around him, from both friend and foe.

He pushed himself harder, heart pounding so loudly it drowned out everything else. Flashes of light, flickering flames, and thick clouds of smoke erupted around him. Jack rolled beneath a flying gray sphere and dove behind a massive tree, taking a split second to survey the chaos behind him.

The forest was in full-blown pandemonium: trees burned, their skeletal remains cracking and toppling in fiery bursts; sparks and debris shot through the air like rogue missiles; explosions ripped through the underbrush, sending splinters of jagged wood raining down like daggers. A large chunk of wreckage impaled a snarling, troll-like figure mid-charge, dropping it with a sickening thud.

Jack's gaze snapped to the Pilfert in the distance, its scepter cutting through the air as it unleashed spells in every direction. Some ricocheted harmlessly off golden enemy shields; others dragged pursuers backward, as if yanked by invisible hands.

Nearby, Emerson grappled with a squat, vicious-looking troll. Addison raced toward them, axe raised—only for a massive, hairy hand to snatch the weapon mid-swing. In an instant, Addison was lifted and hurled into a tree with bone-crushing force. His body crumpled on impact, his head hanging limply against his chest.

Jack was about to charge into the action when the sharp crack of a whip split the air. Emerson stood where the troll had been moments ago, flushed and straining, his eyes blazing with the same unchecked fury he'd shown on their first day of training. The troll writhed, trapped in thick, twisting vines pulled tight by Emerson's rage.

The ground continued to tremble as roots from the surrounding trees tore free, snaking toward a charging minotaur—its massive axe raised high, aimed straight at Emerson's exposed back. Just as it closed in, the roots struck—slamming into the creature's legs and yanking it to the ground with a thunderous crash.

"Run, you idiot." Stefani's voice cut through the chaos. She leapt through the flames, dodging bursts of silver and gold sparks that exploded around her like wild fireworks.

Jack snapped to attention. He slung his bag over his shoulder and darted from behind the tree—just as it splintered in half, crashing down with a deafening roar.

He whirled, searching for Emerson, but the fallen trunk had completely blocked his view. He had to help. He had to get to Addison. But before he could move, flames roared from the log, climbing higher than the limbs above.

Jack swerved, changing course in an instant. He dove into a roll as another tree shook off flaming branches, sending them cascading down like burning spears. His bag was ripped from his shoulder, skidding across the warm forest floor. He lunged for it—but was too late.

Something heavier than wind slammed into him, knocking him forward. The ground shuddered. Stones skittered across the scorched dirt. Before he could react, thin, sinuous vines lashed around his body tightening with eerie precision.

The elven woman with the angry hair stood over him, a wicked smile playing on her lips as she brandished a long, silver wand with gleeful malice.

"*Fuck,*" Jack cursed, twisting desperately as the knots tightened around him. They squeezed harder, forcing the air from his lungs. "Help!" he gasped, but his voice came out thin—barely audible.

His bag—just out of reach—mocked him from the ground. Jack's eyes locked onto the flute peeking from beneath the flap.

Then, as if answering his unspoken plea, the slender piece of wood slid across the forest floor and straight toward his mouth.

The woman loomed above him, her outline fading in the smoke and fire. Through the haze, Jack could barely make out the smirk spreading across her face.

"I told you," she said in a calm voice, "you couldn't escape."

Then her voice cracked—an inhumanly high-pitched squawk tore through the air around him. Jack took advantage of the momentary distraction. He tilted his head and spoke into the whistle. He half expected the Pilfert and the others to come rushing to his aid—but instead, all he saw was the cruel-looking woman, standing just feet away as her terrible squawks echoed to the heavens.

"What are you doing?" Jack asked, as if they were simply having a cup of coffee.

"This would've been so much easier if you weren't so impetuous," she sneered. "This ancient forest wouldn't be burning now if you'd just listened." Her voice screeched again, then returned to its natural, unnerving tone. "Oh, but we have big plans for you."

He didn't ask what those were as his attention had shifted. Something had moved behind the flames—a pockmarked face flickered through the blaze. Jack was about to call out, but before he could, Emerson pressed a long, thin finger to his lips.

Silently, he stepped into the circle, and for a brief moment, the squawking woman paused, her eyes narrowing at his tall, lanky form and round eyes. Before she could register what was happening, a burning branch fell from a nearby tree, trapping her beneath it.

Then, the ground began to rumble and crack, as if it were collapsing beneath them. Jack felt the roots that had ensnared him slide back into the quaking earth.

"Thanks, man, you saved my life." Jack grinned at Emerson as he snatched up his bag and hopped over the parting flames. "Where are the others? Where's Addison?"

"He's okay, Jack. They're this way." Emerson pointed to his right. In an instant, their legs powered forward, tearing across the ground.

They passed the Pilfert, who was fending off several hooded men and a minotaur, a look of deep sadness on its face as it watched one of the abandoned homes being swallowed by a widening hole.

"Keep going. I'm going to help him," Jack called out.

Emerson raised his eyebrows but nodded in understanding as Jack darted toward the Pilfert's side, sword raised high.

"Get out of here. Get to the hopper stone now!"

Jack ignored the Pilfert's warning and stood his ground beside his mentor, swinging his sword at the relentless tangle of creatures attacking. The Pilfert spun its staff in rapid circles, binding the attackers together and unleashing spells with precise, vicious strikes.

As Jack turned to check on the Pilfert, he was suddenly confronted with an unpleasant surprise.

SWOOSH!

A long blade cut through the air, missing Jack by mere inches. Reacting quickly, Jack swung his own sword at his attacker's neck but was met with a resounding clang as steel collided with steel. The clash echoed through the crackling forest, the sound of metal ringing as the two opponents circled, leaped, and parried each other's blows.

"You may be a good fighter, kid, but you'll be no match for me," came the rasping voice of a man not much older than Jack. "It's unfortunate I'll have to kill you—you would've been an excellent addition to the cause."

Jack ignored the taunt, his blade banging into his opponent's with more force behind every blow. The man moved closer, his dirty face and shaggy facial hair just inches from his own.

Then, something hard slammed into Jack's knee, and a sharp *SNAP* echoed in his ears. Pain exploded through his leg as he collapsed, clutching his knee, his breath coming in ragged gasps.

A choked cry escaped him as cold steel ripped through his shirt, the point of the sword pressed jaggedly to his chest. He stared into the cold eyes of the long-haired attacker—but the man wasn't looking back. His head was turned to the sky, where something dark had begun to eclipse the moon.

A high-pitched caw pierced the air, and the leaves around them began to swirl violently. Light flickered back into the thinning trees as Jack rolled to his side, knocking the sword from his attacker's hand. The man didn't try to retrieve it; instead, he fled, rushing away from Jack, desperate to escape the circle.

"Did you see that? *Did you see that, Pilf?! I totally kicked their—*"

"Run," the Pilfert shouted, eyes wide with terror. "Run!" Its voice cracked with urgency.

Jack scrambled to his feet but collapsed instantly—the pain in his knee was overwhelming. The Pilfert raised its staff, and a golden light enveloped Jack's leg. He felt his knee slide back into place.

"This will help temporarily until I can fix it," the Pilfert said quickly. "Get out of here now. I have to check for the others."

Jack hobbled away as fast as he could, but the task proved difficult, even with the warming support of the brace the Pilfert had given him.

As he ran forward, favoring his injured leg, Jack swerved past the man who had kicked him. He glanced over his shoulder and saw the man slide a thick hand beneath his sea-gray tunic. When it resurfaced, a gleaming glass vial was clenched between his filthy fingers. The man hurled the bottle directly at Jack's feet. At once, the ground beneath him gave way, and he tumbled through the air as the earth hollowed.

Jack crashed to the forest floor, his body aching as he scrambled to crawl forward. The man continued to throw his glass bombs, and the forest exploded into a frenzy. Pieces of wood, clumps of dirt, and tumbling plants swirled around Jack, cutting into him and making it nearly impossible to see through the dust cloud. Blood dripped from his chin into the swirling chaos, but Jack kept crawling, staying as low to the ground as possible, hidden by the storm of debris.

"Jack, help," a familiar, high-pitched voice screamed from his left. Jack's head snapped toward the sound, but all he could see was a jumble of different legs—some hairy, some stout, others green, hooved, and stockinged. It wasn't until one of the stockinged legs shifted slightly that Jack realized they were surrounding a long, thin body, flailing helplessly on the ground.

"Help!" Emerson screamed again.

Jack tried to stand, but it felt as though the very air was collapsing in on him, pressing him back to the ground as the forest around him swirled in a violent storm. Darkness descended as the wind howled louder, the pressure building in his ears. Then, just as suddenly as it had begun, everything stilled.

Jack staggered to his feet and stumbled forward, running blindly into something large and solid. His eyes widened in astonishment as he took in the sight before him: long, sharp, gleaming blades in place of feathers protruded from the side of a massive bird. Its golden beak was already pecking at the ropes binding Emerson's struggling legs, while its blood-red eyes gleamed hungrily, shifting from the boy to his anxious captors.

"He's not dinner, you devil. We have to take him to our master," screamed the witchy elf, her red, irritated skin a welcome sight to Jack. The bird emitted a high-pitched screech and plunged its head toward Emerson, scooping the ropes into its beak and propelling itself back into the sky with such force that its talons left deep craters in the earth.

Jack charged into the clearing, ignoring the sharp pain in his knee, and lunged for the witch, who stood cackling as leaves swirled around her.

"Bring him back. Bring him back," Jack shouted, his voice tight with desperation. "Bring him back now or I'll kill you."

"Ha! What in Kazumeth could you do to me, child? Get off," she sneered, and with a flick of her knife, she cut into his arm—a burning pain erupting deep inside in a place the blade hadn't touched. "Be glad that I am not allowed to kill you, child." With a kick, she shot up into the air and out of sight.

A fist seemed to be squeezing Jack's lungs, and it felt as if it wouldn't stop until it caused them to pop like balloons. The pain in his face and leg paled in comparison to the suffocating pressure inside him. Time felt distorted; everything around him continued to move while he lay there, dying, unable to breathe. He was blacking out. Jack barely heard the footsteps behind him. He reached for his sword, but it wasn't there . . .

"Get up, Jack," Adina urged frantically. Jack watched as a flash of steel and jewels slipped into the tiny sack. She gathered his scattered belongings and slipped the bag off his neck, tucking everything into her own.

"Come on, they're coming," she barked, helping him to his feet. Jack's eyes darted around the forest, now ablaze as their enemies fled. Then, Jack turned, and what he saw made the fist squeezing his lungs open its fingers and claw deeper into his body.

The Pilfert was yards away, fighting the flames with water from its staff. Yet Jack was sure the water dripping from its fur came from its eyes, not its scepter. Jack knew he needed to help.

"Come on," Adina said, pulling Jack close. Before he could protest, before his weak legs could carry him to the Pilfert's side, he was lifted into the air. Held by Adina, they ascended high into the smoky sky.

The sensation was surreal—the cool wind against his scorched skin, his stomach flipping for reasons he couldn't place. Jack coughed, smoke burning his lungs, as Adina soared higher. He looked down to see blood dripping from his face into the dark clouds below as the smoke began to thin.

As they crossed over a field, Jack caught sight of Stefani, locked in combat with two trolls who were leering and circling her, making crude, suggestive gestures. A massive purple tree loomed nearby, with mossy boulders scattered in front.

"Adina, we have to help her. We have to save the others . . . let me down," Jack begged weakly, the pain in his leg starting to cloud his mind, dragging him toward unconsciousness.

"The Pilfert told me to get you out." Adina's voice reached him distantly. "She'll be fine. The hopper stone is right there." Her tone was calm, though Jack could hear the uncertainty beneath her words.

"No, Adina, stop. We have to help her. The stone is destroyed. Stefani will die . . . or be tortured into submission, just like Emerson," Jack said, his surroundings blurring as his windpipe constricted to the size of a coffee stirrer. The dream he'd so hoped was just a dream was becoming reality.

"She'll be fine. We need to get to Ealu. That's where it told us to go. They'll all be there soon, Jack. Don't worry."

They kept flying. Jack's thoughts became as contaminated as the smoke below. Emerson was gone. Stefani was fighting alone. Where was Addison? Jack closed his eyes, and as he did, he slipped into someone else's mind—someone else who was also soaring through the night sky miles away.

They were flying—but where, he didn't know. All Emerson could see was that the smoke had cleared, and the golden beak from which he dangled gleamed brightly in the night. He turned his head and, to his horror, saw three other people flying beside them, none supported by wings.

"Where are you going? We're supposed to be going to Dartmoor," barked the dark-haired woman, her voice causing Emerson to flinch in fright. The giant bird opened its beak to respond, and to Emerson's relief, he began to fall. The treetops quickly neared, their branches reaching up as if trying to catch him. With a flash of silver and a sharp pain across his back, he found himself gripped tightly in the bird's long talons. The creature retracted its legs, positioning them horizontally to its body, and Emerson noticed a patch of regular feathers just within his reach.

"This is a shortcut, Gara," the bird said, its voice dripping with frustration. The witch snarled at the bird and shot forward at an alarming speed. Emerson's body shuddered as the bird flapped its giant wings furiously in pursuit of her.

To his right, a figure with gray hair and a gnarled face gave him a wicked grin before veering off in the opposite direction. Emerson's heart pounded in his chest, so fast he feared it might burst. Then, as smoothly as he could, he reached up and plucked a few feathers from the bird's body. The creature turned its ugly head and snapped its beak in warning, but Emerson didn't care. He grinned as a feather slipped from his fingers and fluttered down through the air toward the forest below.

Emerson closed his eyes, and everything went dark. He was falling—falling from the sky. He was going to crash, and it would all be over. He'd be free of everything.

"Wake up, Jack!"

Jack's eyes fluttered open slightly before snapping shut again. He was lying on his back on what seemed to be a rock, something hard and wet pressing against his ribcage.

"Open your eyes, Jack, before I actually lose it and kill you myself, you drama queen. It's just your leg," Adina said, her voice low but laced with bite.

Jack's lips curled into a sweet, taunting smile. "You threaten all your patients, or am I just lucky?" he retorted, his eyes meeting a rather flustered Adina leaning over him. To his left, he noticed a large black stone with silver etchings. As he looked around, he realized it was a dull gray morning. The second sun was struggling to rise, its light smothered by dark clouds that had gathered to save the burning forest.

The sound of rain bouncing off the stone road broke the silence. Adina knelt over Jack, who felt water dripping from the great leaves of the tree under which they had taken cover.

"Where are we?" Jack asked, pushing himself off the solid ground.

"Ealu. Well, at least outside the gates. That damn goblin wouldn't let me take you in like this. Stefani arrived a bit ago and is waiting inside with Addison." She pushed his hair back and removed a thick splinter from his cheek. Jack cursed as a burning pain filled the spot she'd just pulled the wood from.

"Hey, cut that out. We're being watched," Adina warned. "Do you think you can stand on your leg?"

Jack looked down, and the moment he did, pain coursed through his body like lightning in water. Green pus seeped from the deep cut made by the stymphalian, and he could see just where his knee had been dislocated by the kick from the grungy man.

"The Pilfert still hasn't arrived, but I want to get inside sooner rather than later. I put a healing solution on the wound, but it doesn't seem to be helping. That stymphalian did quite a bit of nerve damage. It looks really deep." Adina shook her head in amazement, pulling Jack's arm around her shoulder. "I still can't believe they actually exist." She looked Jack in the face as she tried to lift him up. "Alright, Thiccums, you're gonna need to help me out here," she said, sounding a little winded as Jack gathered himself onto his feet.

They walked along a tall wall that stretched as high as a skyscraper. There were dark stones with elegant gold and purple markings, towers jutting from it with clocks that seemed to have stopped working, and vast windows too high for anyone to peer from. They searched for an entrance, wondering if they would be as safe inside as the Pilfert had suggested. After all, the harbored forest was supposed to be safe for them.

They splashed through deep puddles until they stumbled upon the vague outline of a door. Above it, a fat-faced man stood in a small hole, with white hair shaped like an ice cream cone.

"Can we get in now?" Adina asked the guardian of the gate.

"And what is your purpose?" he called back, eyeing them suspiciously. One eyebrow rose to the top of his head while his eyes shot down dramatically.

"We were just attacked and need a place to stay. Our friends are waiting for us inside."

"Attacked?!" the bearded man's high-pitched voice rang out as he nearly fell from his post. "My JiJi's! Are you being followed? We have no rooms for troublemakers within these walls. Ealu is the grandest and most peaceful city. Trickery within these borders will not be tolerated—nor will thievery, violence, or any other naughty, naughty behavior. You will not bring your terrors here, young girl! Goodbye," he barked, pulling a tiny curtain down.

"Please! The Pilfert sent us."

The guard raised the curtain and peeked out sheepishly. He placed both hands on the ledge and peered down at them. His yellow eyes glowed like beacons in a dark well.

"Very well," he said, and at once a light emanated from a very small door, which snapped open. Adina bent down and crawled through it, turning to beckon Jack to follow. Jack, unable to bend due to the throbbing pain in his knee, sat on his butt and scooted through like a dog with an itchy bum. Once his feet cleared the entrance, it swung shut, and Jack felt four hands help him to his feet. Addison and Stefani greeted him with tight embraces.

"God, Jack, you had me so worried," Stefani said, pulling away and kissing Jack on the cheek. Adina moved forward, pulling Jack's arm around her and shooting Stefani a reproachful look. Addison rushed to the other side, threw Jack's arm around his neck, and the four of them moved down the street.

The road was long, jagged, and curvy. Old stone homes and breweries lined the street, contrasting with the large, colorful, and oblong buildings looming in the distance. Streetlamps were spaced regularly, the flames inside flickering dimly in the early morning sheen. Tiny green goblins stumbled out of bars, laughing and speaking loudly in a language that sounded like a mix of lip smacking, clicking, and low grunts. A few of them stopped to stare as they passed. Jack gave them a welcoming smile, which made a few of them break into feverish giggles. One laughed so hard he fell over, pounding his tiny fists on the cobbled road as his feet flailed behind him.

"Beer for breakfast? Oh, honey, I'm home," Addison said, relieving some of the tension within the group.

"Which way do you guys want to go?" Jack asked as they reached an intersection. One way was illuminated by bright lights and colorful storefronts; the other was a dark alley with glowing red light that seemed impervious to the blossoming morning. Beat up, tattered, and wet, they stood smiling and made the obvious choice.

The street stretched for over a mile to a vast body of water, where enormous seahorses—like carousel creatures come to life—carried passengers from the distant sea into the river that flowed through the city. A small stone bridge arched over the water, where pedestrians waited as the seahorses playfully sprayed them with mist. The sound of loud bangs and children laughing filled the air.

As they walked down the street, Jack watched a young elven boy with pointy ears pick up a kaleidoscope, hold it to his eye, and disappear. As the scope fell, Jack's gaze shifted to the cart behind it, which had a large purple sign with words emblazoned in gold:

Ms. Celleanous's Mazes – One hour entry for four herots
If you finish before the hour is up, you get your money back.

"Woah, it's like a magical carnival!" Addison exclaimed, watching a witch perform flips, dips, and spins in the air, ten other brooms latched on behind her, each carrying creatures clearly unfamiliar with flight, all clinging on for dear life.

Vibrant toy stores and candy shops lined the road. Jack caught sight of colorful treats: bubblegum rat tails that gave you an actual tail, one that spun like a propeller from the seat of your pants and lifted you several feet off the ground; newt eyes that burst with fruity flavor; lollipops in every hue; and candy dust capable of shrinking you to the size of a grain of sand.

He knew it must be popular as he heard the faintest noise from the cracks in the cobblestone below his feet—then a loud bang, as two adults exploded into life before him, smoothing their clothes as they stumbled past him.

The neon lights began to dim as the sun took over the street. Tiny fairies, which had been lighting the signs, flew up to a tree that stood atop a grand building. Yawning, they settled peacefully on the leaves, awaiting their next shift.

"I don't think we should go much further. Maybe we should hang around an inn for the Pilfert? Any suggestions?"

"Ah, well, I hear the Good Thief is a rather cozy spot to grab a bite and escape your troubles," came a voice Jack was pleased to hear. Their furry mentor was hobbling across the bright city floor toward them. "I've always hated these roads," it said, wrenching its staff out of a tiny hole. "Move, let me take a look at the boy."

Adina and Addison lowered Jack to the ground, and he sat with his leg stretched out as the Pilfert examined it. "Did you get stabbed by another sword? I thought I had trained you better than that. No matter. You'll have time to practice before we head to Veilage Platts. Unfortunately, the spell I used for your brace is only temporary, and I see it has already dissolved. But your face . . . what happened to your face?"

"Got cut. Also, it wasn't a sword: I was cut by the giant bird with wing-blades . . ." His throat closed as he remembered. He had to tell the Pilfert now, before it was too late. "They took Emerson! They got him, they're taking him to . . . to . . ." He closed his eyes, trying to remember the fleeting words from Emerson's mind. "Dartmoor!"

The Pilfert continued digging in its bag as if it hadn't heard Jack at all.

"Didn't you hear me? Akuramundo has Emerson. They're going to torture him. I've seen it. He's either going to die or be—"

"Yes, I clearly heard you. I'm forgetful, not deaf," the Pilfert interrupted, giving a half-hearted smile as it continued examining Jack's face. "Also, you said they're *headed* to Dartmoor. Doesn't sound like Akuramundo has him *yet*. However, there's nothing I can do for him here. *You,* however, I can help."

It pulled out a small bottle and uncorked it with its beak. "Sit still. This might sting a bit."

The creature poured the liquid over Jack's leg, and pain worse than ever before throbbed through his body. He clenched his jaw as he held back his scream. The Pilfert traced its finger around the wound, murmuring words in a beautiful, complicated language.

Then, suddenly, the pain stopped. The Pilfert pulled out another tiny vial, sprinkled something cool on Jack's leg, and splashed the rest onto his face. The stinging subsided immediately. Jack looked down as his torn muscles and skin began to stitch itself back together, leaving only dried blood on his clothes.

"Thanks," Jack said absently, his mind still on Emerson. "Now, what's our plan for Emerson? How are we going to save him?"

The Pilfert gave Jack a mournful look.

"There is nothing we can do if he is indeed going to Dartmoor. Once there, he cannot be helped."

"We can fade; we can get him back. And what do you mean 'he cannot be helped'? We must save him. We can't let him die," Jack protested, feeling increasingly frustrated at the lack of support from his friends.

"There's no need to worry; his life will be spared. Based on what you told me during our early days of training, though, what we really should be concerned about is his mind," the Pilfert said. Its wide, fearful eyes only deepened Jack's anxiety.

"That said, we shouldn't stay lying here much longer—Ealu has strict rules about having fun. So I'll take no more questions until we reach the Good Thief. Once there, I urge you to rest. We'll talk when you wake. Now, please—follow me."

The Pilfert led them past another colorful shop shaped like a giant fluorescent hairdo—the headband above the entrance flashing the words Wiley Womper's Wig Shop. The creature made a sharp turn, pulling them down a side street. This part of town felt vastly different: stone buildings with neon signs and red window displays stood in stark contrast to the bleak, dreary avenue. Jack glanced into the windows as they passed, spotting a scandalously dressed goblin bathed in red light, her leg propped on a small wooden stool. Next door was another shop displaying clothes that might have been considered too daring even for a fetish ball. Jack exchanged a look with the others, who were all staring with wide, disbelieving eyes and drooping mouths.

"Ah, we're here," the Pilfert sighed as they turned a sharp left corner. They now stood in front of a tall, elegant building. Gemstone windows glowed warmly, casting shadows of famous witches and goblins across the stone road. Through intricately painted doors, Jack could see a colorful bar that was being transformed into a small dining room. The Pilfert approached the front desk and booked them several rooms with the grayish-green woman working there. Her red hair was pulled up high, cascading into a ponytail that swayed behind her large, pointed ears. Her green eyes gleamed brighter than a streetlight, and the golden jewelry around her neck hung loosely. She wore a barmaid's dress, stitched tightly up the front, accentuating her large chest. Jack thought, for a goblin, she was surprisingly beautiful—and she winked at him as she handed over the room keys as if reading his mind. Jack smiled widely.

"Keep it in your pants," Adina muttered as she grabbed her key and headed for the staircase opposite him.

Jack made his way to his room, changed out of his damp clothes, and slipped into the dry pajamas waiting on the big, feathery bed. He paid little attention to the gown he was wearing, his focus shifting instead to a small mug filled with a steaming purple liquid on his bedside table. He lifted it, inhaled the sweet pastry scent, and brought it to his lips. A warm, tingling sensation coursed through his body as he drank, emptying the mug with several quick gulps. He slammed it back onto the stand, then fell onto the bed. His thoughts drifted to Emerson, but soon, the warmth of the drink lulled him into a deep, dreamless sleep.

The early sun was already beginning to set when Jack stirred, his peaceful dreams now replaced with troubling visions of minotaurs and giant birds. He lay there, trying to remember where he was, when an image of Emerson lying alone on a dungeon floor crept into his mind. He leapt out of bed, ripped open the door, and dashed down the hallway, knocking on every door until he found Addison.

"Nice dress," Addison called, pulling his door open slowly. Jack smirked, noticing that Addison had already changed into freshly cleaned clothes.

"Where are the girls?"

"Sleeping, probably. Ready to go get Emerson?" Addison added slyly.

"Let's go get them first. I want to talk about what happened. We can eat downstairs at the bar and plan something—since the Pilfert clearly isn't going to help," Jack said, noticing Addison's eyes shift to the bowl of warm mush that had just been delivered.

They ran to the other side of the inn, knocking on random oak doors. They stopped when a large ogre yanked one open, club raised in one hand and a menacing green toddler swinging from the other. After dodging several blows, the ogre slammed the door shut. A second later, another door flew open across the hallway. Adina emerged with a disgruntled look on her face, which shifted to a scowl when she saw Addison standing nearby.

"What do you want?" Adina asked grumpily.

"I thought we could go downstairs and talk about Emerson," Jack said, stepping around Addison. The smallest hint of a smile tugged at Adina's lips, though it quickly faded.

"I'll go grab Princess Stefani . . . she's still out. We'll meet you down there in a minute."

Jack made a quick stop back at his room, swapping the wrinkled gown for his red vest and cloak. He ran a hand through his hair, gave himself a half-approving look in the mirror, then hurried to meet Addison, who'd already ordered food for the table, in the dining room. They chose a table in the corner, opposite the only other person in the bar—an old, lonely figure huddled at a table, her arms sprawled out and silver hair in disarray. They had just sat down when Adina and Stefani joined them.

"I want to know what happened," Jack demanded before their drinks had even arrived.

"I'm just getting up. Do you think you could give me a second?" Stefani groaned as she pushed her hair out of her face.

Jack gave her a warning glare, but it was unnecessary—Adina had already aimed a swift kick at Stefani under the table.

"Ow! Sorry, I'm always crabby when I get woken up," Stefani added, rubbing her leg. "Fine. Well, I was running like everyone else. I was doing just fine, but then several of those ugly bull-men showed up out of nowhere. I ended up facing off with them while you two leisurely flew by without offering any help. Whatever, I'm not even—" she waved a dismissive hand. "I eventually got out of it. Had a broken rib, but I fixed it using a potion Adina concocted and a spell from my book. When I got here, I ran into *Useless* over here." She nodded curtly at Addison. "He was unscathed and clueless about where you two were, so I left and went searching for you."

"Yeah, I made it here first," Addison said, "but I didn't know you guys were in a battle until Stefani showed up. Emerson did something to me after I hit that tree. I don't even remember how I got here."

A goblin waddled over, slammed their drinks on the table and stretched out a thin hand, revealing a palm with a swirling black tattoo. Jack realized he had no money to pay her.

"Just put it on the tab," Addison said, barely looking up.

She scurried off as another group of goblins sped past their table with a large bucket of water. They poured it over the gray-haired woman Jack had noticed earlier. Her sopping wet hair flung back as she gasped for air. She looked frantically around the room, her gray eyes locking onto Jack's.

His eyes widened and his mouth dropped open as he heard her murmur in a voice he had heard many times before:

"Blood of a brother is unlike any other."

CHAPTER ELEVEN

THE FAMILIAR STRANGER

"YOU'RE ONLY HERE BECAUSE you're a guest of the Pilfert, madam. We won't allow you to tarnish the name of the Good Thief. Get out, you spirituous woman," the goblin screeched, yanking on her long, gangly arms. His feet were planted firmly on the side of her chair. With one final tug, he found himself somersaulting across the room and landing spread-eagled. He wiped his hands on his apron and muttered curses under his breath as he stomped back into the kitchen.

But Jack didn't notice any of this. His gaze was locked on the woman he thought he'd never see again. His body moved toward her as if drawn by an invisible force. He couldn't believe he hadn't recognized her sooner—the wild hair, the weathered face. He had spent countless hours in her home during a time that now felt like a distant memory. Jack gently lifted her head, his hand clasped on both sides of her face as his thumb stroked it gently. There was no denying the striking resemblance she shared with her son.

Jack gasped in disbelief. "Ms. Garcia."

How on earth could she be here? The Pilfert had said that only those directly descended from the Sovereign Five could survive Ogof and enter Kazumeth. If she were a direct descendant, she should've died at Emerson's birth—just like all the others.

Then, a sudden thought flashed through Jack's mind: What if all their parents were here in this inn? What if that was why the Pilfert had told them to wait here? What if the Pilfert needed their help to rescue Emerson as well? Strength in numbers, after all. Hope ignited in Jack's chest, and his excitement grew. Would he see his mother too? His eyes scanned the bar, half-expecting to see her sitting in the opposite corner, observing this place with that familiar, judgmental glare.

"Jack Hackley," the enthusiastic woman cackled, her sodden face lighting up with a broad smile. "Come here, you little shit." She opened her arms and pulled Jack into a tight embrace.

The moment Jack stepped away, a crash and a bang rang out behind him. Turning back around, he saw her head sticking out of a wooden bowl, the soupy mixture dripping into her lap.

"Is this Emerson's mom?" Stefani asked, her voice full of curiosity as Jack wiped Ms. Garcia's face clean.

"Yeah, but why is she here?" Jack muttered, triggering a series of confused shrugs from his friends. "Ms. Garcia," Jack said, his tone formal. It didn't quite feel right. "How in the hell did you get here?" He shifted, eager for an answer.

"The magic we assert becomes Ogof's dessert," she sputtered in one of her usual annoying quips that Jack had never quite understood.

"Right . . ." Jack muttered before turning to the others. "What the hell does that mean?"

"Well," Stefani said quietly, "we know Ogof brought us to Kazumeth, so she must have met the snake. But we were also told that only those who possess magic in their blood could enter Kazumeth. Those who don't . . . well, they'd be killed."

Ms. Garcia's gray eyes widened, her mouth twitching. Jack shot Stefani a pointed look.

"Clearly, she didn't lose all her magic. There are no other options. The Pilfert said it itself."

Ms. Garcia nodded before, quite suddenly, warm chunks of scarlet and brown slid across the table. A goblin, who had finally squeezed his way between their legs, slammed a bucket down onto the empty seat beside her.

"She's your responsibility now, giant," he snapped at Jack, tossing a towel at his face. The small goblin hopped off the table, crawled back between their legs, and dashed to the opposite end of the bar to flirt with the hostess.

Jack ignored the bucket and pressed on. "So, again, how is it that you're here?"

Ms. Garcia grabbed the bucket and dunked her head inside, gagging and retching until the last remnants of her dinner splashed the bottom. She lifted her head, wiped the residue off her face with a napkin, and flashed Jack a grin.

"The magic we assert becomes Ogof's dessert."

Jack grimaced, his expression tight. Before he could say anything, Ms. Garcia twirled her hands above her head, summoning two frothy beverages in clear glass mugs from across the room. The disgruntled barmaid, who had just poured the drinks for other guests, started to chase after them but gave up halfway, raising the two long fingers at the center of her four-fingered hand before returning to her station. Ms. Garcia slid one of the ales toward Jack with a wink.

Jack took a long gulp, then stared at her cracked face as more questions bombarded him: Did this mean she had somehow kept the magic in her blood after giving birth to Emerson? Or had she gained it another way? If she was a direct descendant, how was she still alive when all the others' fathers were dead? Or were their fathers only dead in their world, but still alive here? Nothing made sense.

"So, you've managed to keep some of your power as a direct descendant, I take it? Did any of the others?" Jack asked, hope rising in his chest as he prayed to finally meet his father.

Ms. Garcia shook her head, her hands gripping the table for support.

"I'm special, you see. Magic grows in me." She slurped down some beer, and a moment later, let out the loudest belch Jack had ever heard. "No, honey, your father's dead. All of them are dead! Dead, dead, dead!" She booped each of their noses as she said it.

Jack's eyes widened as he glanced at his friends, their stunned silence louder than any cry. None of them had ever known their fathers, but hearing it said so plainly still carved something hollow in their chests.

Jack swallowed the ache, straightened up, and leaned forward as the others settled comfortably on stools they'd pulled from neighboring tables.

"They were too weak. The moment you were born . . . poof. Well, not really poof — the bodies stayed. Buried deep, deep, deep. But something left. Something returned." She whispered the last part dramatically before bursting into giggles. "Magic's funny like that."

Jack looked around at the others, all of whom stared back at him with faces that suggested there was nothing funny about this story.

Something returned? What did that mean?

No — you can't think about that right now. Focus.

"They're still trying to figure out how I didn't succumb to the same fate," she continued, her tone shifting as she paused to sip her drink. "Maybe it's because I'm the first female descendant on Earth to pass on the gift . . . or maybe, maybe it's because I'm a hoot. Who knows? Boop!" She tapped Jack on the nose, then erupted into frantic giggles again.

"As the years went on, my dreams of this world became more vivid," she said — all trace of laughter gone. "I became obsessed. The folks back home thought I'd lost my mind. Maybe I had. No . . . they're the insane ones—insanely narrow-minded!" She barked the last words before taking another swig from her drink. "I tried to teach Emerson about this place. I tried to educate him, but he never took me seriously. Such a little ass-hat. At least he still listened."

Her face fell, and a deep sadness crept into her expression. She looked Jack in the eyes. "They've got him, haven't they? The others. They stole my boy, didn't they?"

Jack nodded grimly, a familiar pain twisting in his stomach. He had to rescue Emerson — but the Pilfert had left them stranded. It claimed Emerson would survive. Jack wanted to believe that. But that wasn't all that haunted Jack. It was the betrayal.

The group sat in silence, sipping from their glasses as tension thickened around them, each of them shifting uncomfortably beneath the weight of what hadn't been said.

"Are you going to save him?" she asked, her voice thick with emotion.

"I don't know how," Jack admitted.

"You don't know how? Can you feel that magic in your veins?" she said, grabbing his wrist and tracing her long, broken fingernail up his arm. "It's a lifeline. Tell me, what are your skills? Come on, all of you." She snapped her fingers.

They each began to explain their special abilities, but it wasn't until Jack spoke of his talents for exploring others' minds and seeing the future that she became truly intrigued.

"A skill like that, and you tell me you don't know? Use your mind—or should I say, use your *gift*. Save my son."

Guilt hit Jack like a crashing wave. The weight of her words dragged him under—his lungs tightened, his stomach knotted, and fear clawed at the edges of his thoughts. But Ms. Garcia's gray eyes had already shifted focus.

"And you. You can fly?" she asked, her voice soft but sharp. Adina nodded in response.

"You could fly there in three days' time. You were given gifts, maps, and books? They're your survival kits—use them! It's like the Pilfert was setting you up to do just this."

A spark ignited within Jack, a surge of courage breaking through the fear. She was right, a coach only takes you so far; the rest is up to you. He needed Adina to get him to Dartmoor. From there, they could track down Akuramundo and rescue Emerson.

"Thank you," Jack said, the words rushing out of him.

Just as he spoke, Ms. Garcia gave one final, violent spin, and then her head slammed against the table with a sickening thud. Jack rose, ready to help her to her room, but before he could move, several goblins screeched and leapt across the bar.

"I've got her. I'm sorry! I'll take her up to her room now . . . but, er . . . do you happen to know which number it is?"

"406. Just get her out of here," the goblin snapped crossly, scowling as he walked away.

"Right, can you guys help me?" Jack asked. "Let's take her to her room, and then we can all meet back in mine."

They carefully carried her limp body upstairs and laid her gently on the cluttered mattress. Stefani quickly cleared the books and random objects from the bed, piling them onto the table before covering Ms. Garcia neatly with a blanket. She blew out the candle that lit the room, and then they all dashed down the hall to Jack's.

"Adina, I have a favor to ask," Jack blurted out immediately, before the door had even shut behind Stefani.

"Let me guess," Adina said, her lips curling into a knowing smile. "You want me to take old crazy's advice and fly you to Dartmoor? Well, I'm not sure if I can support your weight for that long of a journey, but sure, yeah, whatever. We've gotta get my fellow nerd back."

Jack grinned devilishly. "Right, and Addison and Stefani, do you think you could—"

"I'm not going anywhere," Stefani interrupted, her voice sharp. "We're supposed to be in bed waiting for the Pilfert! It said we'd discuss our options when it gets back. It knows this world better than you, Jack. Stop trying to be a hero and realize that this is a bad, bad idea. Things don't always work out like they do in the movies. You should know that."

Jack shot her a scathing look. "Luckily, that's exactly what I want you to do, Stefani. Addison, do you mind?" His tone softened. "Can you stay here until the Pilfert arrives and tell it where we've gone?"

"No, I want to go," Addison said stubbornly, shaking his head. "We all should go."

Jack gave him a shifty look. He knew Emerson and Addison had started moving past their high school distaste for each other, but there was no need for extra bodies—especially ones that couldn't fly. Besides, if something happened to Adina and him, at least two of the five would remain and hopefully be able to stop Akuramundo.

"It'll be easier with just two. Adina can't carry us all. Listen, I'm certain the Pilfert will come looking for us the moment you tell it where we've gone. Please just stay with Stefani."

Addison fired back, "But honestly, don't you think the Pilfert can see what you're up to now? After all, it can read minds, and it has better control of that power than you do."

Jack exhaled sharply, but Adina jumped in. "Alright, let me break it down for you, Ginge. I'm about . . . one forty-five? The two of you together would weigh double that and then some. It's just not physically possible for me to carry you both that far. Honestly, I don't even know if I can manage with just Jack. Flying exhausts me more than any other skill—and that's without carrying someone."

Addison looked away bitterly.

Jack didn't have time to deal with it. He was certain Addison was trying to make up for missing the action earlier, but this wasn't his mission. Addison didn't share the same bond Jack and Emerson had, nor the overwhelming guilt of leading Emerson into capture in the first place. Addison was being stubborn—but before Jack could say this, Addison reluctantly agreed to stay behind.

Adina and Stefani left for their room as Jack quickly undressed and changed into the lighter clothes folded neatly on his chair. He pulled on khaki bottoms that tucked into his boots and slipped into a tunic-like cloak in ocean-green and salmon, leaving the top of his chest exposed. He reached into his bag and pulled out a thick brown belt, fastening it around his waist before sliding his sword into place. He quickly covered it with a cloak and ran back downstairs to wait for Adina, feeling surprisingly comfortable—and slightly feminine—in his new attire.

He checked the clock on the wall, frustration rising: the numbers had been replaced with ancient runes and symbols he didn't recognize, and the timepiece had no hands. Instead, a tiny ball moved around inside, bouncing off three specific points, crossing the center each time and glowing yellow as it spun its way to the next stop.

After what felt like an hour, Adina burst through the front door. The chattering in the dining room fell silent as everyone turned to stare at the wild-haired girl in a wrinkled, dirt-smudged dress, bounding across the room like she'd just escaped some disaster.

"What took so long? And why are you so dirty?" Jack called out, eyeing the grime streaked across her sleeves. The goblin behind the counter shot him a warning look. "Well, I hope you're comfortable wearing that," Jack hissed.

Adina rolled her eyes. "Oh, whatever, that's not important. We're going to need money, Jack. We're going to need food and supplies! It's a three-day journey—*minimum*. That's what I've been working on."

Jack raised an eyebrow. "And what's your solution?"

She leaned in. "I've got a plan. I've collected a few things that might help us along the way, but we still need money. I happen to know the perfect spell to get into that till. You used to steal stuff from the—oh, don't act like you didn't. I've heard the stories."

Jack opened his mouth to protest, but she barreled on.

"That's not the point. I think we can take whatever's in that till if we keep the staff distracted. A bunch of drunken patrons—it'll be easy to start a fight. You'll have to get into the till—you're quicker and more athletic. I'll fly us out of here. I've got everything else ready. It's an easy heist."

Jack didn't look convinced.

"I get it. They're goblins. It wouldn't be hard to take them down," he said slowly. "But Adina, I just can't."

"And I get it. I feel terrible about it too. But this place is called *The Good Thief!* Honestly, Jack, they're just asking for it."

Jack frowned at her.

"Fine, what's the spell?"

She pulled him to a corner and whispered the details of her scheme into his ear, teaching him the spell and appropriate motion for enchanting the till.

"Alright. Start that fight," Jack said, already realizing just how risky this plan was.

"Oh, that's your job too. I'm handling the kitchen. Get inside that ogre's head." She nodded toward the table beside them, where a small, green ogre with a wide nose was boasting about his winnings from the card game he was playing.

"Tell the big guy beside him that he's been cheated—make him paranoid. He looks ready to explode already."

Jack slipped into his mind, placing the subtle suggestion that he had been cheated. The response was instant. The tall, muscular ogre with fiery eyes grabbed the smaller one by the collar and hoisted him into the air.

"Think yer clever, do ya?" he slurred, swaying as he stood.

The smaller one blinked. "Wha' now?"

"Don' play dumb wit' me," he growled.

Jack barely had time to react before the tall ogre dropped the smaller one and smashed a wooden chair across its back.

At the same time, chaos erupted in the kitchen—smoke poured from the service window, followed by a crash and panicked shouting from the back.

"Go," Adina hissed as the goblins behind the counter rushed off to help, running toward the boiling catastrophe in the kitchen.

Jack took his cue. He sprinted to the bar, vaulted over the counter, and landed in a crouch beside the till.

"Keys, keys . . ." he muttered, patting his pockets.

Adina stared at Jack in disbelief at his poor memory. She snapped to get his attention and made the hand motion again.

Jack mimicked her, murmuring the counterspell he'd learned. The lock clicked and the till slid open.

A rush of relief hit him as he snatched fistfuls of odd-shaped golden, bronze, and emerald coins, and shoved them into his bag. They'd done it!

As he dove to grab more, a shrill sound far harsher than any fire alarm pierced the air, echoing through the bar. Jack slammed his hands over his ears, momentarily forgetting they were robbing the place.

Adina's eyes widened. "It's jinxed. It recognized the spell!"

"No kidding!" Jack snapped.

The goblins turned—their faces twisted in rage.

"Thieves!" one of them bellowed.

They bolted into the street, but it was too late—echoing shrieks filled the air as hordes of goblins, clad in dark-purple uniforms and cavalry hats, spilled out of shops and windows. They charged toward Jack and Adina—some running down the street, others climbing rooftops, and still more skittering up walls like insects.

Realizing what was happening, Jack grabbed Adina and dragged her into an alley beside the inn. The path twisted and turned so frequently that he lost all sense of direction. Dimly lit rooms flashed past as tiny, green hands pulled back pink, chiffon curtains to see what all the ruckus was about.

The goblins' battle cries grew louder from every direction, blotting out any chance of escape. Jack's chest tightened. He scanned desperately for a way out—they had seconds before they would be surrounded.

Then he saw it—his eyes caught a sliver of space between two buildings, directly across from Wiley Womper's Wig Shop.

"This way." Jack yanked Adina's arm. They sprinted toward the alley, but just as they passed the wig shop, a blur of green shot up the wall beside them. A small goblin—no taller than Jack's calf—leapt from the bricks, knife drawn, aiming straight for Adina's shoulder.

Jack shoved her out of the way and dove behind a dumpster. His back slammed against the street, and a sharp pain ripped through his shoulder as he flung the goblin into a wall. The creature kicked off and landed on its feet, smiling gleefully as it wiped a scarlet smear from its knife.

Jack charged at him, but something sharp dug into the back of his leg. Another goblin had pierced a much larger knife into his calf. He yelled as he fell forward; his vision flared white-hot, pain exploding through his body.

The goblins closed in. Jack rolled, desperate, reaching for anything he could throw. His hands landed on a heavy garbage bin.

With a grunt, he shoved it forward. The full weight of the trash and rotten food barreled into the goblins, sending them toppling like bowling pins.

Adina took the distraction, scrambling to her feet and throwing spells behind her. Green bodies fell, but others trampled over them, snarling in pursuit.

"Adina," Jack called, his vision blurring. "Adina, save..." But the words faded as his mind went blank. He slumped against the wall.

Suddenly, he found himself standing in front of a black gate, dark clouds swirling ominously behind him. Whispers drifted from the shadows. He turned to his side and froze—face-to-face with a black, metallic wing. A pale, pockmarked face stared back at him with defeated eyes.

Jack blinked hard and found himself back in the alley, his body screaming in pain. Goblins swarmed the narrow passage, and Adina was nowhere in sight. Gritting his teeth, he pushed himself up onto his throbbing leg. Agony flared through every muscle as more goblins—these with gleaming gold badges—poured from every crevice, closing in around him.

"Hey, bug-eyes, I'm up here."

Every goblin's head snapped upward at once, their necks twisting with a sickening crack.

"Creepy," Adina breathed. She hesitated just a second, wide-eyed—then grinned. "Looking for this?" She dangled the sack of coins that had fallen from Jack's shoulder.

"Thievery is not tolerated in Ealu!" the tallest goblin, who barely reached Jack's hip, shrieked.

"Alright, I hear you! I'm sorry. Go fetch!" Adina shouted as she tossed the sack, which somersaulted through the air before one of its leather straps caught on the "y" of the Wiley Womper's Wig Shop's fluorescent sign. The goblins abandoned their pursuit, scattering in chaos to retrieve their stolen treasure.

"Let's get the hell out of here," Adina said, landing beside Jack.

"What are we going to do without the money?" Jack asked feebly.

"Don't worry. I combined our stuff. That one just had a few coins. We still have plenty. Let's go before they—"

A shriek echoed through the air, and bright lights flashed down every street.

"Thieves!" a goblin hanging from the tail of the "y" screeched, holding the small sack of coins in his hand. The rest of the crowd picked up the chant in a haunting chorus.

"Put your arm around my shoulders," Adina demanded.

Jack complied without hesitation.

The goblins whirled toward them, eyes ablaze with their twisted sense of justice. They surged forward again, now within club-swinging distance. Just as one raised a bludgeon, Adina kicked off the ground, lifting them into the cool night air.

"Once we're beyond the gates, they can't do anything. We'll be outside their borders," she said, shifting Jack's weight as they soared above the city.

Below, the streets were crawling with goblins—climbing buildings, leaping from rooftops, and skittering across the cobblestones. Jack's heart pounded.

"Fly higher!" he shouted, but it was too late.

A goblin launched from a nearby roof, grabbing hold of Jack's legs. He struggled, trying to shake it off, but the goblin squeezed tighter. As Jack kicked again, he felt Adina lose her grip. Suddenly, he was falling—plummeting toward the cobbled road.

Everything froze. Jack hung suspended in midair, just above a tiny cottage. He tried to kick the goblin off, but it sank its teeth into his already injured leg.

Jack screamed in agony.

Adina dove beneath him, lifting him once more.

"Stay still, Jack. I think I know how to get rid of him."

The goblin, now on Jack's shoulder, pressed a knife to his throat.

"Ready to breathe your last breath, thief?"

"Adina, I got this," Jack grunted, jutting his head upward.

The knife slipped from the goblin's hand, slicing across Adina's cheek. It loosened its grip and spiraled into the night, a sickening crunch following its descent.

Jack didn't have time to process what had happened before he saw the towering gate ahead.

"Jack, I can't go any further . . . It won't let me. The gate keeps growing," Adina gasped, her face pale, tears rolling down her cheeks.

The golden sun was rising behind the mountains beyond the border.

"Then we go through the door, but we have to be quick," Jack said. "When we land, we run for it. Once we're out of the gate, we need to get as far as we can."

As their feet touched the ground, a sea of goblins swarmed toward them like seagulls on a picnic. Jack and Adina sprinted for the tiny door in the darkened wood—the one they had crawled through earlier.

Adina made it through first, turning to help Jack.

"Adina!" he yelled, his upper body halfway through the hole. "One of them has my leg."

"What the hell is up with you and that damn leg?" she grunted, pulling on his hand.

Moments later, with a soft thump, she landed on her backside with Jack sprawled on top of her.

"Let's get the hell out of here," Jack muttered.

As he staggered to his feet, he could hear the gatekeeper's screams echoing behind them.

"Oh, shut it," Adina roared, swooping Jack up and flying them toward the mountains.

Early morning sunlight glinted off the snowy peaks ahead. Jack was certain this was the wrong direction—nowhere near Dartmoor—but he didn't care.

They were safe. They were alive.

Adina looked down at him, her face solemn.

"I'm sorry I couldn't stop the goblin. I'll heal you. I've been reading about tons of healing spells, and I promise—I'll take care of you, Jack. Don't worry."

"I know, Adina. Thank you."

He smiled weakly, hating how helpless he felt. But he pushed the thought aside and let the cool, peaceful air wash over him.

Chapter Twelve

A Pilfert's Decline

The warm rays of the first sun trickled into the cloudy room, casting a soft haze over the quiet pub. It was nearly empty, save for one couple huddled in the corner, their hands cutting through the air in quick, silent rounds. The darker hand of the woman froze in a wide-open palm before slamming the table, rattling the silverware and empty goblets.

"Stop . . . doing . . . paper!" Stefani whispered through gritted teeth, swatting Addison's outstretched hand away.

"You stop doing paper," Addison retorted.

They raised their fists again, but before they could begin, the front door of the inn burst open. Addison froze as their drenched and exhausted mentor stood hunched over its staff, its fierce, yellow eyes narrowing in on them from the doorway.

"What happened?!" the Pilfert demanded.

"Why don't you tell us?" Addison snapped back. "Where were you last night when the city was nothing but alarms and screeching goblins, huh? Where were you when that overfed eagle took Emerson from our group? And why are we still sitting here, doing nothing to save our friends? I thought you were supposed to be helping us."

"I had other important matters to attend to," the Pilfert retorted sharply. "I thought I could trust you to heed one simple request. I thought the four of you had enough sense to follow my orders. I thought what happened in O'Keen would prove to you just how dangerous things currently are—especially for you. But I guess I should have known better than to trust a blue dweller's judgment. Idiots!"

"And what exactly were you doing that was so important?" Addison demanded.

"What I was doing is none of your concern, Mr. Stempinski," the Pilfert snapped. "I expected Jack and Adina to go after Emerson—it needed to happen. However, I hoped Ms. Garcia would've kept them from doing anything reckless."

"Wait . . . what? How come—" Addison started, but the Pilfert held up its hand to silence him.

"There's much to be done, and we must act quickly before we meet with the elves. I can still keep a very close eye on them—if Jack doesn't shut me out," the Pilfert added, at the confused and worried looks crossing both Addison and Stefani's faces.

"First, we eat," the Pilfert said, walking to the desk where he was greeted unenthusiastically by a waiter.

Several minutes later, three large plates filled with poorly prepared food slid across the table. The goblin who delivered their meals didn't even acknowledge them before scurrying back to the kitchen. The Pilfert bit into a flaky pastry covered in yellow syrup that looked as if it were several days old. It offered a forced smile of satisfaction as the bright-red filling dripped down its wet, matted fur.

"You're not going to have the energy to make it through today if you don't eat. Now please, we'll finish the discussion after breakfast."

They ate the terrible food in silence, the only sound the occasional clink of fork against plate. Addison kept his glare fixed on the Pilfert, struggling to understand how it could be so indifferent. Jack and Adina had barely hesitated before throwing themselves into their terrible rescue plan, yet the Pilfert had just stated that it knew they'd go after Emerson—as if it were foretold. As if their choices were just predictable steps in a game it refused to explain.

Frustration tightened in Addison's chest. They'd come to help a world they hadn't even known existed, yet they were being treated like battered tools — relied on in the moment, forgotten the next.

Then a memory surfaced: his conversation with Emerson just days ago. Emerson had been skeptical from the start, questioning how much they could really trust a creature that kept holding back the truth. Addison had dismissed his doubts then. But now? He wasn't so sure. Had Emerson been right all along?

After breakfast, the Pilfert instructed them to grab their bags and change into clean clothes. Addison marched upstairs to his empty room and pulled on the green, leather vest, fastening it over his chest before tossing the brown cloak over his shoulders.

A few moments later, the Pilfert appeared at his door with Stefani in tow. Addison joined them, and together they made their way down the hall. Inside the Pilfert's room, a long, curvy candle flickered on the bedside table, casting dark shadows along the angled walls. Addison walked over and sat on the neatly made bed, which had been unused the previous night.

"Before we head to Veilage Platts, we must travel back to O'Keen," the Pilfert said, lifting its hand before Addison's question could break through his lips. "There are a few things we need to gather for the journey—and one thing in particular must be protected at all costs. I believe, aside from you, it was the reason for the attack on the ancient forest."

"But what if something happens? What if Jack and Adina get into trouble? What will you do then?" Stefani asked. Jack and Adina were alone in a world they barely understood. She wasn't exactly best friends with Adina, but she'd grown to like her—maybe even care about her. More than that, these strange circumstances had made them a family, and family looked out for each other.

"I can travel much faster than anyone here," the Pilfert said, fading into nothingness and reappearing behind them. "If something does happen, I'll be there in seconds. We'll leave shortly. But before we do, I need a word with Ms. Garcia."

"Take your time," Stefani said, knowing it would take a while to get any answers out of her.

"Look, we need to go after Jack and Adina. We have to find Emerson," Addison whispered desperately the moment the door closed behind their mentor.

Stefani shook her head, pulling away. "The Pilfert expected this, Addison. It told us as much. Jack and Adina had to go after Emerson for whatever reason. The Pilfert probably saw their rescue—or read about it in some prophecy or something."

"Or maybe it didn't." Addison snapped. "What if there is no prophecy? What if it's guessing—manipulating us—just hoping it's right? If they die out there, that leaves just us to stop this guy and his army. And let's be real—neither of us is skilled enough with magic to stand a chance against a bunch of magical creatures. If we're supposed to be these great Guardians, we need every single one of us. If this Ak guy is as powerful as the little man says, we don't stand a chance. We need to trick the Pilfert into—"

"Into what? Second-guessing itself? Thinking it doesn't already know what we're going to do?" Stefani's voice was firm, her arms crossing as she sat on the bed. "It knew they'd leave. It knew we'd stay. This is part of the plan, whether we like it or not. I'm going with the Pilfert, Addison. I won't change my mind."

Addison let out a frustrated breath. "Stefani, this isn't some book you can just flip through. This is your life. Just like you told Jack, we can't expect things to work out like they do in books and movies. We can't just sit around and wait for something to magically fix itself. You're acting like a child."

Stefani shot him a reproachful look before turning toward the mirror. She hummed softly as she fixed her hair, trying to drown him out. She knew he was right—but fear held her still.

This wasn't her life. It was never supposed to be her life. She was supposed to be in school, performing in shows, making her dreams a reality. Not standing at the edge of a war in a world she didn't belong in.

A sliver of light slipped through the cracked door, and a voice spoke from the shadows.

"Are you ready to leave?" the Pilfert asked, sidling back inside.

"Yeah, sure, whatever," Addison muttered in defeat, turning to face the Pilfert. They filed down the old, rickety stairway—different from the one that led to their rooms—and crossed into the pub. The Pilfert waved goodbye to the goblins working that morning, but they merely glared back with bulging, red eyes.

"That's not good," the Pilfert whispered.

As they walked down the street, more and more faces with pointed features and dangerous expressions pressed against windows. Every nod was met with a turned back, every wave with an obscene gesture.

"What's their problem?" Stefani asked, trying her hardest to melt them with her own glare.

"They must've realized we came with Adina and Jack. We're associates of the thieves. This won't be an easy exit, so if anything happens, you follow any order I give," the Pilfert answered.

Just then, Stefani jerked forward as a sharp pain shot through her left shin. She looked down to see a goblin with long, silver hair standing beneath her, holding a thick stick it had been using to cross the road. The goblin finished crossing, its eyes shooting daggers at Stefani as it clambered onto the sidewalk.

"Stop being so tense," Addison said quietly. "It just left The Grouchy Goblin. Had to be the service. I doubt it had anything to do with our friends—or the fact you almost crushed it," he added with a wry smile, which Stefani returned.

"So, do they drink all the time here?" Stefani asked as several men and women of all sizes poured into the streets, singing and waltzing.

"This city is Kazumeth's biggest entertainment hub and vacation spot, so yes, they do."

They approached the gate, where a small door shimmered into view.

"Did we come this way last time?" Stefani asked, gaping at the strange entrance. The Pilfert nodded, and she shrugged before ducking through.

As Addison moved forward, the door shrank with every step. By the time he reached it, the top barely reached his knees.

"What did you do that for?" he asked accusingly, glaring at the Pilfert.

"I haven't done anything, my boy. The door is simply a reflection of how you feel inside."

"What do you mean?"

"Most people enter Ealu through a very tiny door," the Pilfert explained. "They come to escape or reflect, seeking relief from the stress of their lives. After a night here, they leave feeling elated, ready for the next day's journey. That's when the door stretches into something large and exquisite. If it hasn't changed, the mayor offers a complimentary stay until they feel fully recharged. However, don't expect such a pleasant extension from O'Glorian today."

"Right. Stupidest . . ." Addison grunted as he began army crawling through the hole. "Thing . . . I've . . . ever . . . heard!"

"What are you doing on the ground?" Stefani laughed as his head peeked out the other side.

"I'd rather not talk about it," he said, clawing through the mud. When he stood up, he saw the Pilfert wiggling through a cupboard-sized hole behind him. After wiping the muck off, Addison began to walk away, staring up at the mountains where he was certain his friends must be.

An odd noise, like a metal fork spinning in a garbage disposal, drew his attention. Looking up, he was surprised to see the toad-faced guard from the night before. His pleasant demeanor had vanished, replaced by an air of solemnity.

"I assume you have something to tell me, Guardian of the Gate?" the Pilfert said grudgingly.

"O'Glorian Del-Butnik has asked me to relay a rather unfortunate message," the guard said. The Pilfert's face sagged as the man dramatically unfurled a tiny sheath of parchment.

"Dear Pilfert, you are hereby forbidden from entering the third of the last remaining capitals of Kazumeth. Should you attempt to breach the walls of Ealu, what I've been guarding for your protection may inadvertently fall into the hands of its seeker. Heed this warning, fur-ball. Good day."

The guard coughed, then, voice dropping several octaves, added, "Sorry to hear we won't be having any more of our little chats. I've always enjoyed your company. Goodbye, friend." He waved dramatically, tears welling in his bulging eyes.

The Pilfert nodded once, then turned toward the trees to the south.

"What does that mean?" Stefani asked anxiously.

"We're no longer welcome in Ealu. But worse—we've lost some important allies. Shall we walk?" The Pilfert gestured for them to follow as it waddled down the road.

"What about the thing she's guarding? What was that about?" Stefani pressed.

"Oh, nothing we can discuss in such an open place," the Pilfert replied, its voice shaky with frustration. "You never know who might be listening."

Stefani gave it a peculiar look. As far as she could tell, they were alone on the path. But she brushed it off and shifted her focus to the roadside as they walked.

Not even a few minutes later, something rustled behind a cluster of flowering bushes, catching her eye. She hesitated, wondering if she was just being paranoid.

But as her gaze lingered, the familiar blooms tugged her into a memory. A cold shiver of loneliness washed over her as her mother's garden filled her mind—and the spring evenings and summer mornings spent reading in the grass. Then a flood of memories broke through the wall she'd been building: dancing with friends, singing around the family piano, senior prom with Addison, and her first concert with Emma.

When her mind shifted to Emma, a deep sadness consumed her. It was a grief she had managed better when Jack was around. After all, if anyone had loved Emma—who felt like the sister she'd never had—more than she did, it was Jack. A taste of humility filled her empty soul, igniting a fire within her. They'd find Jack and end this nightmare, even if it meant never returning home. *God, please don't let that be the case.*

She cast a rebellious glance at Addison, which he returned with a nod. Without speaking a word, they silently sealed their pact: at the first opportunity, they'd ditch the Pilfert and find their friends.

The Pilfert, lost in its thoughts about the warning from a former friend, didn't notice their shared glance or silent exchange. It wasn't until they reached the old forest that it snapped back to the present. Blackened trees and toxic air filled the space around them, the stench clinging to their lungs as they trudged forward.

Stefani raised her hand to her mouth as she gazed at the remnants of her transitory home.

A light cough and subtle movement to her right pulled her attention to the Pilfert. She couldn't tell if it was sorrow or fury. It wasn't until one fat tear fell that she realized it was both. She stretched out her arm to comfort it, but before she could reach, the Pilfert jerked away and moved forward into the charcoaled clearing.

They pressed on, stepping over fallen branches and red coals that still burned with an insistent need to breathe. As the forest deepened, the trees grew thinner, darker — their bark marred by black streaks that peeled back to reveal an odd, orangish-gray beneath.

"Treachery, torment, and hate," the Pilfert muttered, its fury tinged with sadness. "It's all that Akuramundo has ever known. He's responsible for everything—why you were torn from your families, why I was torn from mine."

"What exactly happened to your family?" Stefani asked.

"Horrors I hope you'll never witness," the Pilfert said, its voice dropping to a haunting whisper. "Horrors he'll inflict upon your friends and family if we fail. Fire and destruction. They are . . ." It tensed suddenly, its body rigid. "We're being followed."

Almost on cue, a rustling noise came from behind a splintered tree. A scruffy-faced man with long hair stepped out, holding a book. He was only visible for a brief moment before he vanished into nothingness, but he shot the Pilfert a wink before he did so.

"What should we do? Are we about to be attacked?" Addison asked, readily pulling out his axe.

The Pilfert smiled, but it was twisted and cold. "There's no need to worry. He didn't hear anything of importance. If I'm not mistaken, Renago just revealed where his true loyalties lie. But come, time is running out. Let's gather our things and head to Veilage Platts."

It moved from the stump and stood beside a small hole in the ground. "After you." It motioned to Stefani.

Stefani stepped up to the hole, feeling her body slink into the ground. Addison followed, casting the Pilfert an interrogative glare before he, too, was swallowed up. The Pilfert stumbled in behind them, colliding with Addison's legs and sending him toppling forward onto an overturned table.

As Addison regained his footing, he looked around in shock. Ash covered everything, and the place looked like it had been ransacked. Chairs, tables, books, and maps were torn and scattered, and broken glass littered the floor, ready to rip into their flesh.

"I think someone was searching for something," Stefani muttered, voicing the obvious.

"And they found it. The grimoire. We already know this," the Pilfert said, tapping its staff on the ground. A glowing light appeared between its tangled ends as it plowed through the wreckage. It flipped over broken furniture, tossed papers aside, and stirred the ash so much that Addison had to hold his breath to avoid inhaling it.

The Pilfert reached into a tangle of roots that unfurled at its touch and dug around desperately. When it withdrew its hand, it looked as if something had bitten it from inside the hole.

"It's here. The pages are protected," it said. Its eyes flashed with something dark. "Dear Renago. I knew his heart was pure. The grimoire will be useless without what's hidden here. It shows that even the purest of souls can fall to darkness. He'll go to his grave a redeemed man."

Addison and Stefani waited for the Pilfert to elaborate.

"That book holds information more important than what one can find in the chambers of Blueca," the Pilfert continued. The gravity of the statement hit them like a brick. It was talking about spells, secrets of portals, and other knowledge that had been protected for years by its family. "It will be of great value to Akuramundo, but what he truly wanted from the grimoire is still well out of his reach. Still, this complicates things. The knowledge left inside that book could cost us everything."

Addison exchanged a glance with Stefani. He could see she was ready to leave this all behind, but he felt differently. He had always planned to join the army after graduation, just like his stepfather—to be a hero, to gain respect—even if it meant dying for it.

But now, as the memory of war and how it had ripped his family apart resurfaced, Addison realized something. He had lost so much to war before, but now, there was a chance to make things right.

"We'll win this fight," he said, the words firm in his chest. "We'll follow you to these meetings, but right after that, we go find Emerson, Jack, and Adina. Understood?"

The Pilfert nodded solemnly. "Right. Let me grab a few more things, and then we can leave here . . . forever."

The Pilfert's voice cracked, but Addison didn't comment. When it reappeared, it looked slightly different—no longer wearing the broken crown.

"Take my hand, but only my hand. I can transport you both where we need to go, but I can only do it one at a time. Ladies first, if you don't mind?" The Pilfert extended its hand to Stefani. She nodded, and the two of them vanished.

Addison stood alone in the ashy remains of the home he had lived in for the last two months. For the first time in his life, he felt utterly powerless. He sank to the floor, his mind racing. What had changed on Earth since he had been taken?

He thought of his stepsister, who cried at night for a father who would never come home. He wondered if his mother would ever step up and care for the girl, or if she would continue to bury herself in work, as she had since his stepfather's death. And then, he remembered the last conversation he had had with his mother.

"Where are you going?" she called from her office as Addison skidded down the hallway, his book bag swinging wildly on his shoulder.

"Over to Jack's—just working on a project."

"Well, make sure you're home to put Fanny to bed. She doesn't sleep when you're not around."

"Yeah, about that, Mom ... I might be out later than expected. Can you make sure she's okay? She needs to start adjusting to me being gone, anyway. If I'm not back tonight, will you tell her ..."

"I'm in the middle of reading a report, honey. Just go and be back by nine ... no later!"

"I love you, Mom."

"Uh-huh. Bye, kiddo."

Addison stared blankly into the void, his eyes burning, as the Pilfert materialized in front of him.

"Alright, are you ready to go?"

Addison's body acted of its own accord as he held out his hand. The moment his fingers touched the Pilfert's, it felt as though he were being torn apart by a violent force. He flew through space faster and faster, the heat of it warming his body—until he stood before a giant, glass tower.

A guard in silver and gold robes stood before him, arms outstretched, as if welcoming them with a hug.

"Welcome to Veilage Platts: the City of Light. Please, follow me."

Chapter Thirteen

Gara's Prediction

Emerson had lost track of how long he had been flying;
all he knew was that when the monstrous bird finally made its
descent, he couldn't have been happier to feel solid ground
beneath him. His body was icy from the wind, his stomach
churned with nausea and hunger, and every muscle ached
from the constant whiplash and shivering. Tiny scratches
and nicks from the bird's rough talons marked his skin.

Finally on land, he lay there, trying to unthaw and savor
the silence—until it shattered with a deafening clanking
sound, like that of an old wooden roller coaster. Two metallic
doors slid open, revealing a bleak, oppressive landscape
beyond.

"Stand him up and wipe the blood off his face. He needs to
look presentable," a shrill, commanding voice snapped from
somewhere to Emerson's right.

Suddenly, he was yanked to his feet by two rough,
calloused hands. The dark-haired elven witch who seemed to
be in charge walked up to him, spat in his face, and began
scrubbing it with a vile-smelling, threadbare rag. Emerson
narrowed his gaze, staring into the hollow darkness of her
eyes. Her face split into an evil grin before she turned away,
moving toward the metal-feathered predator.

"Get out of here, you ugly pigeon," the wild woman shouted, but the giant bird remained. Its complaint about payment was quickly silenced by the crack of a lion tamer's whip.

A harsh metallic scrape rang out as the Stymphalian's talons dragged across the stone road as it launched itself into the air. A rush of wind from its massive wings slammed into Emerson's chest, knocking him off his feet. He hit the ground hard, the impact stealing his breath.

"Get up, you," the witch snapped, bending over to yank Emerson up by his hair. "We haven't properly introduced ourselves. I'm Gara," she said with a sick smile, stepping back to give him a better view. Her face was pale brown with light freckles, her large, dark pupils ringed with gold. Her nose was small, and her smile stretched unnervingly wide. She held out her hand.

Emerson's arm hung stubbornly at his side, refusing to reach for it. Without warning, her hand cracked across his cheek, the sting blooming instantly.

"Try again," she hissed, and before Emerson could react, his arm jerked as though pulled by an invisible string, reaching for hers. She seized his hand and twisted it behind his back, then grabbed the other and bound them together. Emerson felt a sharp, metallic coldness as scratchy cuffs weighed down his arms. Pain flared through his veins when a slender pin sliced shallowly across his skin.

"The boy's cuffed. Let's move," Gara called, her voice dripping with sadistic pleasure.

As they marched toward the open gate, Emerson's heart began to race. Something sinister awaited beyond it. If he could go back in time and choose between being eaten by the bird or walking through the gate, he'd choose to be the worm.

He stopped just before crossing the threshold into the smoky, gray city. A thick hand prodded him from behind, snapping him out of his mounting dread. With a resigned sigh, Emerson stepped over the invisible line separating Dartmoor from the rest of the world. And the gate shut with a click, sealing off all sound from the other side.

The city stood breathless and eerie, its roads sprawling like a massive cobweb toward a distant tower; dim silver pathways shimmered beneath their feet, and dark stone buildings clung to the streets like flies trapped in its threads. Crumbling shops lined the main street, their windows displaying grotesque images, bulbous cauldrons, ancient books, and dangerous weapons. Dreary houses with cold, lifeless windows and gray curtains stood in the barren patches of land where grass had long since died. As they walked past these homes, Emerson noticed strange shadows shifting behind the candlelight in the windows.

His attention was averted as a couple in dark, flowing cloaks appeared before them. Their faces were pale and powdery, with charcoal eyes that gave them a ghostly, eerie appearance. Emerson couldn't tell their gender, but they both had on skirts with multiple leather belts, and they each wore a purple handkerchief around their ankles.

As they turned a corner, Emerson caught a glimpse of his reflection in a shattered window. His skin appeared ghostly pale, nearly translucent, with deep cuts on both of his cheeks. His eyes were burdened with dark baggage, and his hair was matted, wild, and wet.

The road beneath them was cracked, steam seeping through the stones. The gravel crackled like dry bones beneath their feet. The air was thick with the stench of burning flesh, churning Emerson's stomach. As he scanned his surroundings, his eyes fell on a young boy a few feet away dressed in Sunday attire, hunched over. The boy radiated innocence, and for a moment, Emerson felt a brief sense of peace.

But then their eyes met; in that instant Emerson realized what the boy was doing. Every meal from the previous day surged up in a wave of nausea as the child drove a silver knife into a cat-sized rat. Wearing a dark, tattered suit with missing buttons, the boy looked at Emerson with a cruel, daring smile, his gleaming red eyes piercing into Emerson's own.

I want to go home.

A stooped man carrying a long pole with a burning amber flame hobbled down the street, followed by a horse-drawn carriage that splashed through the puddles. The tall, thin wheels drenched the man, snuffing out his lantern in an instant.

Emerson stepped back, but the carriage stopped just in front of him. Its door creaked open, and three silver steps unfolded with a hiss.

He ignored the stairs, his attention caught by the strange creature hauling the carriage. It looked like a horse—same lean build, same heavy hooves—but something was off. Its mangy black coat clung to bone, and its gaze shimmered red and silver. Two eerie eyes flanked a small, worn-down stump on its forehead.

Then it hit him: this wasn't a horse, it was a corrupted unicorn.

"Akuramundo expected you an hour ago," the driver said, her lips tight and wrinkled.

"The Stymphalian isn't as fast as it once was. When its hatchlings are large enough, it will be my glorious duty to kill the beast," Gara muttered, shoving Emerson into the carriage before climbing in after him.

The door slammed shut just as the carriage jolted into motion.

Jaw clenched and brow tight, Emerson stared with fierce concentration at the thin back of the driver and the swaying tail of the hornless beast ahead.

"If you're trying to use magic, it's no good," Gara said, eyeing him with a knowing smirk. "You can't do anything within these walls, boy. Not with those." She nodded toward the heavy cuffs.

She knocked twice on the window. "Is there any way to make this go faster?" she snapped, then turned back toward him with a huff.

"My master will be pleased to see you," she said, her tone darkening. "Unfortunately, I'm not sure your survival is important. But," she paused, watching him closely, "I sense great power in you. If he makes you an offer, things may be better for us all."

When Emerson didn't respond, she said, "You can talk, you know."

"I . . . I don't know what you want me to say," Emerson stammered, staring at his feet.

"I said you could conceivably join the strongest magical force in the world. The world would fear you. Admire you. And yet you have no response. Hmm."

Without warning, her hand lashed out again, striking his face.

"Now you'll look at me when I speak to you, won't you?"

Emerson's eyes brimmed with tears as he lifted his head.

"You are powerful, and I can sense it." Gara paused. "I shouldn't be telling you this, but it's important. While I studied in Burkank, I transcribed a prophecy. It spoke of the Guardians' return. More specifically, yours."

She leaned in, her shadow casting over him like an eclipse.

"You will defy all magical law. And you alone will accomplish something we have only ever dreamed of."

Emerson's voice was small. "And what exactly do I do that defies all magical law?"

Gara shrugged, smiling flatly. "I have no idea. I only ever received the outcome. That's why it's crucial you join our side. Whatever it is that you possess—it will change the outcome of this war. Your blood is important. But I sense there is much more to you than meets the eye, son of Ulysses."

Emerson blinked, masking his reaction. *Son of Ulysses?* They must think he was Jack. What would they do when they realized the truth—that he was the heir of Hernando, not Ulysses?

There was a knock on the window, and Gara magicked it down with a flick of her wand.

Emerson's eyes darted to it. He'd never seen a wand before—and couldn't understand why anyone would need one.

"We can use a very different kind of magic than what you've been taught," Gara said, as if reading his thoughts. "With a wand, we can do extraordinary things. Unfortunately, wands have been banned—something Akuramundo hopes to overturn. For now, they're reserved for a select group."

Emerson registered the words, and while a part of him wondered what kind of magic she meant—or who the "select group" even was—he couldn't shake the gnawing jealousy twisting in his gut. Jack was meant to change the world forever—and he was just a supporting player.

What else is fucking new.

"We're here, Miss." The door swung open, and a long tuxedoed arm extended for Gara's delicate hand. She floated gracefully from the carriage, and Emerson stumbled after her. He stood there for a moment, staring at the two women. In that moment, he realized that beneath Gara's menacing façade, she was incredibly beautiful. The carriage driver kissed Gara before she returned to her seat and quickly disappeared down the crooked road.

"Where am I?" Emerson asked, gazing after the carriage, wishing he were back inside.

"The home of the greatest ruler Kazumeth has ever known: Akuramundo."

Emerson swallowed hard; he could feel the dry lump in his throat.

A tall, ghostly-lit tower stood atop a hill, the fortress appearing abandoned, with thick webs covering every rounded angle of its cemented structure. There were few windows, and the only ones showing any light came from the inverted lantern that formed the base of the tower. Cracks and overgrown plants traced their way across the deteriorating walls.

A crack of lightning, and this would feel like an old black-and-white monster film.

Gara moved ahead, past the unhinged gate at the end of the twisted footpath. She beckoned for Emerson to follow. They walked up the gravel road toward the dark tower, its silhouette looming ominously across the path.

"I have a question," Emerson asked as he tripped over a knot in the road, forcing him to grab the old, rickety railing that curved along the path. "What exactly do you need the blood of Ulysses's heir for?"

"Well, Akuramundo is after the stones—I'm sure you and that mangy little relic have pieced that much together," Gara said with a smirk. "But there are only two ways to possess them. He can either steal them himself, at great personal cost, and risk them not working properly, or one of the Sovereign can retrieve the stone and gift it to him. However, the stone of Ulysses is different. He hasn't confirmed how, but we all have our guesses."

She smiled faintly at him. Emerson noticed a tragic glint in her eyes. Unsure whether she was about to strike him or offer a comforting look, Emerson raised his eyebrows. When her arm didn't move, he offered her a small, uncertain smile in return.

The closer they got to the doors, the more ominous the tower appeared. Its walls stretched endlessly, as if waiting to swallow him whole. The hairs on Emerson's neck had long passed the point of merely standing up; now, they felt as though they were actively trying to dislodge themselves from his skin.

They approached the massive, dark opening that concealed a door in its depths. Gara grabbed the golden knocker hanging from a brass dragon's mouth and banged it three times. The doors broke apart with a loud creak, revealing an old, dusty, and cobwebbed entrance hall. It was completely empty, except for a rusted chandelier hanging from the ceiling and several suits of armor standing at intervals around them.

Gara grabbed his arm firmly and pulled him through the foyer. She jerked him sharply to the left, right through what appeared to be a solid wall.

They descended a steep, spiraling staircase, with torches hung sparsely along the windowless passage, granting the demons of the night free reign. Emerson swore he brushed against something slimy and hairy as he felt his way through the dark with his free hand.

"Stay here," Gara demanded in a cool whisper when they reached the landing at the bottom. "I'm going to inform Master that you've arrived. Do not touch anything," she warned before darting away into a corner chamber, her cloak billowing behind her like a curtain in the wind.

He waited until he was sure he was alone before he turned around and sprinted back up the staircase—he wanted as much distance between himself and *her master* as possible. However, Emerson had barely climbed twenty steps when the stairs dissolved beneath him, sending him tumbling back to the cellar floor.

He quickly glanced around the room to make sure no one had seen him. He was still alone, except for a tiny mouse frantically scurrying across the floor, looking for an escape. Emerson watched as the little creature slid into a crack in the wall.

"Lucky," he muttered to himself.

At that exact moment, fire burst to life along the walls, making Emerson spin around, his heart hammering in his throat.

One by one, torches ignited in steel brackets with a sharp whoosh, like the flare of a summer grill. Under the nearest bracket stood a tall, wide glass case, with a long, derelict bookshelf beside it. Emerson crept closer, checking behind him with every silent step.

There had to be a thousand books scattered across the decomposing shelves. Thick scrolls of parchment were rolled neatly, resting atop leather-bound spines. Unfinished books, broken quills, and shattered ink bottles littered the bottom shelves. Emerson's eyes roved over the vast collection of literature and history stored within the timeworn pages. He reached for a gilded-spined book that glimmered in the torchlight.

Just as his hand was about to touch it, he pulled back, remembering Gara's warning.

He walked past the glass case filled with pictures of jewelry, stones, and garments. Further down, he found another glass cabinet with six ominous-looking locks running from top to bottom. Inside was a piece of silver armor suspended in the air.

As he drew closer, he flinched in horror. The collar and sleeves of the armor were adorned with inverted blades along the hem, each one sparkling with crimson rust. He closed his eyes, only managing to hold back the bile rising in his throat because his heart seemed lodged in his neck, blocking it.

"I thought I told you not to touch anything," Gara's high-pitched voice whispered from the shadows.

"I didn't touch anything. I swear!" Emerson replied quickly, his voice earnest as he moved toward her, desperately trying to rid his mind of the image of himself wearing the death-trap armor.

"He'll be with you in a few moments," she said, smirking. "But he asked me to show you into the chamber."

She grimaced as her cold, long-fingered hand grasped his arm, pulling him to the back of the room, past the chamber from where she had just emerged, and far from the warmth of the torches.

"Sh-shouldn't we b-b-be going back upstairs?" Emerson stuttered.

"Until we know that you can be trusted, you'll be staying down here with the other guests," she said, her voice laced with irony as she emphasized the last word.

They stood before a stone wall, the bricks grinding as they sidled out of her way to reveal a new passage.

"Well, go in," she snapped, pushing him forward with her cold hand against his back.

Emerson stumbled and found himself submerged in darkness once more.

I am going to start sleeping with all the lights on if I ever get out of this.

"Come with me. I have specific instructions to follow. Don't worry—I can see."

Gara gripped Emerson's warm fingers with her cold ones, pulling him toward the center of the room. Each step felt like moving through ice, and his teeth began to chatter.

"When am I getting out of here? How was I supposed to know the Pilfert—"

"You be quiet, Renago! We'll deal with you later," Gara called to the raucous voice several yards away.

Emerson's heart raced faster than a film reel flipping through its frames. He tried to think of what the heroes in his favorite movies would do in this situation, but his mind was too weary to form any coherent thoughts.

Suddenly, he felt the tendrils of his hair pull away from his scalp as his head jerked back. Cold tin forced his lips apart, and warm liquid slid down his throat, sending a rush of euphoria through him that left him at ease, elated, and happier than he had ever been.

Gara raised her wand, maneuvering Emerson into position. "On the count of three. One . . . two . . ."

SNAP!

Chains shot up from the floor, clamping onto his arms and legs. Before he could react, they yanked him down onto his knees.

Gara's sickly cackle echoed off the stone walls as she spoke, her voice filled with cruel delight.

"I'm going to go talk with Master now. It'll only be a few minutes."

A torch flared to life as she turned away, her silhouette dissolving into thin air.

Emerson barely had time to register that she was gone before the ground began to tremble. Iron bars burst up from the floor, closing in around him.

Alone, Emerson's head fell to the floor, his heart sinking into a pit of despair.

Chapter Fourteen

Survival of the Dimmest

THE EARLY MORNING SUN stretched its warm rays across the cool, snowy mountainside, coaxing the sleeping flowers to awaken. Its light bounced off the snow, scattering over the wild grass and bathing the landscape in golden warmth. The rays eased along the mountain, their gentle touch stirring the sleeping hills and the narrow valley below. But then, they faltered, reaching an unusual sight: a small plateau where nothing had ever lived was now home to a long, hollow log and a tiny pile of smoldering embers. The sun hesitated before reaching out to illuminate it—and just as its light crept forward, a frizzy, disoriented head poked out from inside the log.

She looked like a groundhog peeking from its burrow, blinking against the light as she brushed dark hair from her pallid face. The girl quickly extended one leg with as much force as she could muster toward the opposite end of the log.

"*Ow!* What the hell, Adina?" Jack's voice echoed through the hollow wood as he rubbed his side where she'd just struck him.

"We need to get up, eat, and start moving," Adina replied, her voice scratchy from sleep.

"Next time, just tell me to get up," Jack muttered as he crawled out onto the snowy hill. "Holy shit, where are we, and where did all this snow come from?"

They were in a bowl-shaped valley between two sloping hills. To the right, Jack saw towering pine trees sweeping across the mountain's crest. To the left, a desolate, bleak landscape met his eyes. An odd scent lingered in the air, warm and sweet like freshly baked cookies, carried on the harsh wind. It made him think of a hidden village beyond the hill, something impossibly cozy, like it belonged at the North Pole.

"We're in the Sabana Mountains, according to this map. How's your leg feeling? The spells drained me a lot the first night. I had to give you another sleeping potion so your body could heal. I struggle with healing potions, so I think I made it too strong. You were out all day yesterday. Thankfully, I found a hopper stone that got me to Alors. It was a little damaged, but there was just enough of a gap to drag you through. I had to eat some roots to keep going. It was the only way I could've kept moving. I flew up a ravine, but there are a lot of creatures still hunting us. I had to hide us several times with protection spells, sometimes in caves, sometimes in trees . . . Once, I buried you under a pile of twigs and leaves."

She tugged a twig from Jack's curls and flicked it into the fire. She'd said it all so fast, Jack couldn't help but smile—she'd clearly been waiting for someone to listen.

"My . . . holy fuck. I totally forgot I got shanked. But, two days? Adina, you did too much. Please, let me . . ." Jack stood and glanced around the campsite, searching for something he could do.

But he really had nothing to offer—she'd already done it all: a small wooden bowl filled with plants and berries rested near the fire, beside an open, abandoned book, and a clothesline was strung between two trees, several blood-soaked towels fluttering in the breeze.

"What? Because I'm a girl, I don't know how to camp or start a fire?" Adina snapped defensively. "Yes, I did this all by myself. I managed to mend your leg, get you in that log, cast protection spells, and . . ." She took a deep breath. "I even started working out a plan to rescue Emerson."

"I feel useless," Jack murmured as he walked over to a rock near the clothesline. He grabbed their bag and rifled through it, coins slipping through his fingers as he dug to the bottom. Finally, he pulled out a map and unfolded it. "Where did you say we were again?"

"The Sabana Mountains. I checked last night and did some research." She picked up the book that had been wrapped in a towel beside the dying fire. "These hills are home to a clan of trolls that once terrorized a nearby town. According to this book, sleeping in logs is a good way to avoid being eaten—they don't like to scavenge for food. When men fled Drysmian during the coup, they were said to sleep in logs and bright valleys because trolls have sensitive skin." She tossed the book over to Jack, who glanced at the cover and chuckled.

The title read *Top Ten Places to Visit Before Your Chariot Arrives* and was accompanied by an illustration of creatures with blue and pink fur lying under an umbrella on a beach.

"Before your chariot arrives?" Jack asked, flipping through the tiny, thirty-page illustrated book. He couldn't fathom how Adina managed to read it—the font was minuscule and seemed to change shape constantly, making his head ache.

"Are trolls dangerous?" Jack asked, thinking back to the one they'd encountered in the forest.

"Yes, or . . . well, it depends. There are different tribes. But I did notice that trolls in the Sabana Mountains kill children, sometimes even their own, to eat them in honor of Naga Manchu, one of their gods. It's in here somewhere . . ." Adina said as Jack flipped through the pages. "Either way, it's sick stuff. These are the trolls from the Treaty of Alors the Pilfert told us about. They now capture those who wander into their midst and make them face off against the dragon to gain their freedom. None have survived."

Jack's stomach twisted. The Pilfert was leading them straight to the dragon. Emerson was supposed to get past it—not slay it. But the news that no one had ever survived sat heavy with him. The Pilfert claimed Emerson could and would succeed, but how much could they really trust a creature they'd only just met?

Adina gave Jack a nervous smile. He wiped the image from his mind and looked at her with a bemused expression.

"Have you even slept?" Jack asked, still in awe of what she had achieved. "I mean it, you really get this world, Adina," Jack said softly, smiling at her. "It's like you were always meant to be part of it."

Adina's cheeks flushed, and it wasn't from the warmth of the fire.

"We're all meant to be a part of it, Jack. You need to accept that." Adina heaved the log they had slept in into the fire, snuffing out the remaining embers. She glanced at Jack and, when he wasn't looking, swept her hand through the air, coaxing tall flames to rise from the wood. When she turned back, she caught a slight curve on Jack's lips as he peeked up from the map.

"Busted!"

"Oh, suck it," she grunted, digging through their bag.

"Hey," Jack exclaimed, looking down again. "Dartmoor isn't on this map."

"I noticed that too. These must be outdated. I remember the Pilfert said Dartmoor only came into existence after one of the capitals fell completely into Akuramundo's hands. It's the northernmost one . . . I forget the name." Adina shrugged casually. "But Jack, with how little sleep I've had, I'm in no shape to fly both of us today. The food we have isn't very filling, and I ate most of it yesterday. I didn't feel comfortable leaving you behind to fly into town—not when we're still being sought.

"The overexertion to fly us here at all took its toll," she added. "I could use the roots again, but I'd rather save them for when we get there. We're going to have to tackle some of this journey on foot. I figured we could cross the mountain today and set up camp in that valley where the trolls can't follow. Tomorrow, I'll fly us to Drysmian. We can disguise ourselves, stay in an inn, and figure out the rest of the plan. I think Dartmoor is a short flight from there."

Adina handed Jack some food from the bag, and they ate in silence, studying the maps and books. After they finished, Jack slung the bag over his shoulders, and Adina extinguished the fire, turning the log into ash. Jack kicked the remaining coals around in the snow.

Instead of climbing the nearest hill, Adina made a quick decision. "We'll cross the bowl and move away from the woods to avoid the trolls."

Jack opened his mouth to protest, ready to argue that it would leave them more exposed, but Adina was resolute. "Trolls can't stand direct sunlight," she said, glancing up at the pale sky.

For the next few hours, they trudged through the endless, wintry expanse, battling waist-deep snow and navigating narrow, ice-cold creeks. The wind bit at them, numbing their limbs and sapping their strength until it felt as though they were dragging their bodies through thick, frozen syrup.

By midday, the landscape changed. A wall of trees appeared on the horizon—tall, quiet, and welcoming. Adina froze for just a second, her eyes lingering on the forest she'd once sworn to avoid. Then her pace quickened, and her voice was steady, touched with resignation. "We need to escape some of this wind if we can, Jack. We're crossing into the forest."

Jack, relieved at Adina's shift in the plan, broke into a run, eager to take shelter from the biting wind. "So, would they still call these evergreens?" he called over his shoulder, breath forming clouds in the frigid air.

Adina didn't answer at first. She slowed and stared at the trees ahead. These weren't just any pines: they were an odd mosaic of colors—deep greens, fiery oranges, muted blues, and smoky grays, all interwoven with streaks of vibrant yellow.

Some branches were even dotted with exotic purple flowers, their petals dusted with snow. It was a strange, otherworldly sight—like nature had decided to paint with every color in its palette.

"They're . . . so beautiful," Adina breathed, her voice soft and tinged with awe.

Jack glanced back at her, pausing just a moment, but Adina had already moved forward, pushing through the thick pines. The snow hit her face, cold and sharp. Without thinking, she stuck out her tongue, catching a few flakes—only then realizing how thirsty she was. They hadn't stopped for food or water in hours. Her stomach clenched with hunger, and her mouth felt parched. She bent down, scooping snow into her hands and shoveling it into her mouth, cheeks puffing like a chipmunk trying to store food.

Jack watched her, one eyebrow raised. "Well, if you're done, I think we should move on. We need to find something to eat and some fresh water. There's gotta be a spring nearby," he said, his stomach growling loudly—a cruel reminder that it had been half a day since their last quick meal of tough, fibrous vegetables.

Adina nodded, wiping the snow from her lips. Jack pushed through the branches, his muscles protesting as they walked deeper into the forest. The silence was heavy, broken only by the crunch of snow underfoot, Adina's chattering teeth, and the distant growl of Jack's stomach.

"Jack . . ." Adina's voice trembled. "Can we stop and build a fire? I can't keep going like this. I'm freezing, I'm exhausted, and I'm starving."

Jack stopped and turned, his face softening with concern. "We've got a little food left—it may not be very filling, but it's something."

She looked down at her frozen hands. "I'm really cold, Jack. I just need a minute. If you like, you could always find something else for us to eat. There are wild birds and other creatures . . ."

Jack frowned, his mind racing. "I don't think separating is a good idea. What if the trolls manage to walk through your shield? What if—"

Adina cut him off, her voice strained but steady. "We're fine. I haven't seen or heard anything for hours—just us and the birds. Besides . . ." She hesitated. "I promise, the enchantment is strong."

Jack studied her, still unsure. He'd been so useless these last two days. Then a thought struck him. "What if I carry you? I'll wrap you in a blanket. With my body heat, it should help keep you warm."

Adina's eyes widened. "I'd rather be eaten by trolls."

"I'm serious," Jack insisted, ignoring her glare. "Just for a little while—"

"The hell you will," she exploded, ducking under his outstretched arms. "Go find food! I'll stay here and build the fire. I'll be fine. If I feel like I'm about to be snatched up, I'll scream," she added, rolling her eyes.

Jack hesitated, torn between trusting her and his own need to protect. But in the end, his instincts won. As she scratched her nose, he lunged forward, caught her by the waist, and in one swift motion, lifted her over his shoulder.

"Put me down! Put me down right now, Jack Hackley! Jack, let me go!" she shrieked, legs flailing wildly as he ducked under a low-hanging branch.

"For someone who's so exhausted, you sure put up a fight," Jack said with a smirk. "Now can you please stop thrashing? It's making it really hard to carry you against your will."

Adina huffed, crossing her arms but turned her head away hiding the small tug of her lips.

Jack carried her effortlessly through the winter landscape until he spotted a thick, enclosed circle of trees. The branches wove so tightly together that it was impossible to see beyond them. Perfect.

Lowering her gently to the ground, he pointed. "Alright, if you want shelter, crawl under that lowest branch over there. Stay hidden. Like you said, trolls don't like searching for food, and this is impossible to see through." He hesitated, then reached into his bag, pulling out Silfrado's flute. "Whisper into this if you need me."

Adina nodded, slipping beneath the tangled branches. Jack watched until she was out of sight before shifting his focus.

"I'm going to cast the disillusionment spell and light a fire. Let me know if you can see anything."

Minutes passed in silence before Adina's voice broke through: "Well?"

Jack grinned, relieved. "Perfect! I can't see a thing."

Adina yawned. "Do you think I could nap? I didn't get much sleep last night . . ."

"I need you to stay awake, just for now. Give me half an hour. If I'm not back, get out of here. We can always move to a new spot." His voice was edged with urgency. Every second they spent camping could be the very second Emerson was taking his final breath or making the deal to betray them.

Shaking off the grim thought, Jack moved quickly through the forest, his focus narrowing as he scanned for any sign of life. Minutes passed before he spotted it: a rabbit, digging frantically into the snow. His heart skipped. He looked around for something to use to stun it, but everything was buried. His sword felt ridiculous for such a small animal. Magic? But it's illegal to kill with magic. There was only one option left . . .

He'd have to kill it with his bare hands. The thought turned his stomach. But they needed food, and they couldn't afford to be picky, not until they had Emerson back.

With the practiced quiet of a hunter, Jack crept closer, his every movement deliberate. He was just a few steps away when the rabbit sprang into the air, its oddly powerful legs sending Jack sprawling backward onto the cold snow. He grunted as the impact rattled him, but by the time he regained his footing, the rabbit was already bounding away.

Frustration clawed at him. He was supposed to be good at this—strong, capable, the one who got things done and took care of others. But here he was, failing at something as basic as catching a damn rabbit. It wasn't just about food. It was about proving—to himself, to Adina—that he could still pull his weight—that he belonged here.

Teeth clenched, he pushed on, heart pounding. Then, a scent hit him—smoke, rich and savory, the unmistakable scent of grilled meat. Civilization. He moved cautiously, eyes darting ahead, scanning the thinning trees.

As he peered through the branches, his eyes widened. Before him stretched a large, barren field, shaded by the towering pines. In the center, six massive trolls were wrestling, their movements shaking the ground with each impact. Jack froze, watching them in stunned silence.

They were unlike anything he'd ever seen. Each troll had four long, muscular arms and a thick ponytail. Orange hair sprouted from their heads and bare shoulders, and their ears were long and floppy, extending comically from the sides of their skulls. Their noses were round and bluish, looking like they had been stolen straight from the faces of his childhood friends on *Sesame Street*. They wore tattered, yellowish loincloths that barely reached their knees, and which Jack was fairly certain hadn't been washed in ages.

His gaze shifted to the edge of the field, where several large rocks—angled intentionally—soaked up the rare sunlight filtering through the canopy. Atop each stone, slabs of meat sizzled, while near the largest rock, a wooden platter held thick, juicy slices already cooling in the shade.

His mouth watered as he dropped to a crouch, creeping forward, and staying low. He could barely contain the urge to run. The scent of herbs, spices, and warm, buttery meat was too much.

As he crept closer to the fighting in the clearing, the snow gave way beneath his foot. Snap. The sound rang out like shattering glass, echoing across the clearing.

All six trolls stopped. Their massive heads twisted, eyes narrowing as they scanned the area. Jack ducked behind a large stone, his heart hammering as their gazes swept over the spot he'd just vacated. His pulse thundered in his ears.

Time to go.

He dashed for the platter, grabbed two steaks—each as long as his arm—and sped off into the trees. His heart pounded as the thunderous footsteps of the trolls followed, their massive hands swiping dangerously close.

Jack's mind raced, adrenaline flooding his veins as he shoved the steaks into his bag and dove behind the nearest tree. Bark scraped his shoulder as he pressed against the trunk, barely breathing.

The trolls thundered past, too focused to notice him. Jack didn't wait. He spun on his heel and tore back toward the thicket where he'd left Adina.

"Hey, it's just me," he called out breathlessly as he crawled under the branches. "I grabbed a couple of steaks from the trolls. Thought we could melt some snow—"

His voice faltered.

The space where Adina should have been was empty. The fire had gone out, and broken tree limbs lay scattered across the clearing. *I thought they didn't search for food!*

Panic gripped him as he scrambled forward, scanning the shadows. He closed his eyes, reaching out with his mind—searching for her thoughts. But instead, a flicker of something else struck him: a pale boy, trembling with fear, and a shadowy figure looming over him like smoke. The vision vanished as quickly as it came, leaving Jack chilled to the bone.

When he opened his eyes, the world was inverted—the snowy forest floor loomed above him, while the sky and tangled branches stretched endlessly below. Turning his head, he spotted Adina beside him, bound to a long stake. Two grotesque trolls, their warty bodies covered in boils, carried her between them.

"Hey, Jack, how's it hanging?" Adina called out, her voice laced with irony. She seemed unfazed, hanging from the stake like a piece of meat.

Jack looked up to see the same troll from earlier, its cruel eyes gleaming as it dangled him upside down by the legs with its upper arms.

"Oh, just hanging . . ." Jack said with a wry grin, trying to keep his tone light. "But I guess we can talk later—looks like you're a little tied up."

Adina gave him a tight-lipped smile, her eyes filled with both determination and faint amusement. "Terrible. I expected more," she said dryly.

Jack felt the weight of his own guilt pressing against his ribs. Why did he leave her behind when he knew it was a terrible idea? Why did he feel the need to prove himself to her? She clearly didn't need protection or help. If it weren't for his need to feel needed, she wouldn't be in this mess.

Trying to mask the panic rising in his chest, Jack leaned his head back slightly and whispered, "Why didn't you use the flute?"

Adina raised an eyebrow, her lips curling into a faint smile.

"I tried," she said, her voice strained as she shifted in her restraints, "but this one"—she shot a glance at the troll with the long, muscled arms— "had me before I could even get it to my lips."

She began to squirm again, more violently this time. "Hey, ugly, where the hell are you taking us?"

The troll in the back turned its head slowly, flashing a wide, grotesque grin—no teeth, just a cavernous, drooling mouth that sent a chill down Jack's spine. He clenched his jaw, forcing himself to suppress the revulsion tugging at him.

A low growl rumbled from the trolls, followed by a string of guttural clicks. Jack glanced at Adina—her usual calm was gone, replaced by wide, nervous eyes that made her seem smaller, almost fragile. He opened his mouth to reassure her, but before he could speak, the troll dropped him.

He hit the ground hard. Pain shot through his back, and the air fled his lungs as the world snapped upright.

Now's my chance.

Jack scrambled to his feet, heart pounding. The cold, shadowed forest was gone.

In its place stretched a vivid, unfamiliar landscape. The snow had vanished, revealing a lush, fog-draped field that rolled into the distance. On the horizon rose a golden hill, its base split open to reveal a gaping cavern. Above it, a tree with white and purple blossoms swayed in the breeze, its roots tangled in vibrant grass. The air was thick with the scent of salt and earth, and the distant sound of water flowing softly over rocks whispered from a small river nearby. A large tent stood near the edge of the wood with a tunnel they must use to avoid direct light during the daytime.

"Hey, Jack, enjoying the view?" Adina's voice cut through the haze. Her pole had been placed in the center of the field, as though she had become part of the landscape.

Jack's stomach dropped. A dozen trolls surrounded her, their massive forms shifting like restless boulders. But what sent a cold spike through his chest was that *he* wasn't surrounded. He wasn't bound. He wasn't even acknowledged. *Why weren't they coming for him?*

His eyes flicked to Adina—still calm, still smirking. She was counting on him to get her out of this, and he wouldn't let her down. Finally, it was his turn to do the rescuing.

Knowing exactly what he needed to do, Jack flexed his mind.

The pull came fast—a sudden, sharp tug that nearly buckled his knees as the world lurched around him.

He was no longer seeing the trolls—he was seeing *through* them.

Their thoughts crashed into his like a tidal wave, a storm of guttural noise and primal instinct. Colors burst behind his eyelids: greens, blues, and the deep, throbbing red of hunger.

Leave her alone. She's not dangerous. Untie her.

The command cut through the chaos, but trollish language crashed around it, pulsing with each mind he touched. His temples throbbed. The pressure built with every word, every grunt, every burst of raw emotion.

He tried to push through—tried to make himself heard—but it was like shouting underwater.

His focus slipped, and his strength poured out after it, as if he'd just been uncorked. Before he could stop it, his mind slipped into someone else's— someone trapped, scared, and bound, pleading for release. *Not now.* The moment was fleeting but familiar, like a dream from another lifetime.

Snapping his eyes open, he forced himself back into the present. The trolls were watching him now—fifteen sets of glowing eyes, each one filled with malice. They roared in unison, raising their bludgeons high as they charged.

Instinct took over. Jack drew his sword with the golden, sapphire hilt. He swung it with practiced force, slicing through graying flesh. Blue blood sprayed the air, but it barely slowed the trolls. More arms came at him, but he danced between them, slashing, moving toward the center of the field. Adina was still struggling with the ropes, smiling faintly despite the chaos.

"Oh, you came to rescue your fair maiden?" she teased.

Jack scowled. "I—"

"Never mind, just cut me loose—I can't magic my way . . . Jack, behind you!"

Too late.

Jack watched the ground vanish beneath him as he was hurled through the air. He hit hard, skidding several yards before coming to a stop. Pain exploded through him, but his powers kept him from being shattered. He forced himself upright, breath ragged. Across the field, Adina was already tearing through the ropes herself, grumbling under her breath.

Jack staggered to his feet—just in time to see a small troll barreling toward him. As the creature reached him, he swung his sword with everything he had—but the troll snatched it from the air, gripping it between two of its monstrous hands. The silver blade flashed as it was wrenched away, spinning out of reach.

Before Jack could react, he was lifted off his feet and tossed through the air once more.

His body was twisting as the ground rushed up to meet him, but before the impact could shatter his bones, vines erupted from the earth, coiling around him and easing his fall, cradling him like a fragile child.

Groaning, Jack tried to push himself up, but his body refused to cooperate. Then, without warning, his mind slipped again. He found himself somewhere cold—staring at a deep-blue light reflected in a cracked mirror. His heart skipped a beat as the danger seemed to fade, and for a moment, he let himself believe he would survive this.

Jack shook his head and as he opened his eyes, he saw that a soft hand had reached down to him. The voice attached to it was sharp and commanding.

"Get. On. My. Horse!"

Jack blinked, dazed, still struggling to focus.

"Has something happened to his brain?" the unfamiliar voice asked someone else nearby.

"Unfortunately, no," Adina's voice rang out. "He's just like this."

Finally, he looked up. The woman before him was striking, her long, dark-blond hair cascading around a face that seemed illuminated by some otherworldly glow. Her honey-brown eyes locked onto his with a sharp intensity.

"Take a picture, it'll last longer," Adina teased from her own horse beside the woman, looking slightly disheveled but still defiant.

"Get up. I'll ride you," the woman instructed.

Jack whispered, almost breathless, *"Please do,"* as he reached for her hand. The moment their fingers brushed, it felt like a spell, an electric current that pulled him from the depths of confusion.

"Wrap your arms around me. We need to move," she urged, her voice all business. Jack hesitated before sliding his arms gently around her waist. Her scent, soft and floral with a sea-side edge beneath it, flooded his senses. But before he could savor it, she yanked his arms tighter around her, her strength surprising.

They galloped through the valley, Jack's thoughts still spinning. Behind them, the field was littered with fallen trolls—some lying motionless, knocked out, others groaning in pain. One even had a spear embedded in its skull. They rode onward, crossing golden sands that stretched toward a vast, dark body of water crashing against rocks.

As they approached a meadow that felt quietly enchanted, the horses slowed. A weeping willow, its long branches swaying in the breeze, stood atop a grassy knoll.

They dismounted near the ancient tree, its gnarled trunk offering shelter. The woman turned to Jack, her expression unreadable.

"Who are you?" he asked, still grappling with the surreal turn of events.

"My name is Jerica," she said, voice calm and regal. "Heir of Levestin."

Jack blinked, his mind still racing. "And the trolls? How did you find us? Did the Pilf . . ." His voice trailed off, unwilling to reveal too much as he remembered that the Pilfert was concerned about Levestin. He suddenly grew mistrustful.

Jerica's smile was gentle but firm. "Relax. Sit. Eat." She gestured toward a small fire where she was already beginning to prepare food. "You both look like you could use it." She pulled out a small vial and handed it to Adina. "This is a remedy I acquired from Veilage Platts. Their fountains hold the richest waters known to man, with magical properties even the elves haven't fully uncovered. With some incantations and the proper ingredients, all of which have been added, it'll hydrate you and heal injuries. The Pilfert managed to pass me some before I set out to help. Keep the rest; you'll need it for the journey ahead."

Adina uncorked the vial, taking a sip. Instantly, her posture relaxed, her wounds began to fade, and the fatigue drained from her face.

Jerica turned to Jack, offering him his own vial. He drank it eagerly, feeling it burn like liquid fire as it coursed through his veins.

"I'll answer your questions, Jack," Jerica said, stepping aside to tend to the horses. "But after we eat."

As she prepared their meal, Jack watched Adina, her wounds already fading. "Are you okay?" he asked softly.

"Yeah, totally fine," Adina replied, her grin playful, though she quickly tugged her sleeve down to cover the thin scars on her forearm. "I had just peeked out to see if you were coming and they grabbed me by the head and dragged me out of the trees," she added, her voice light, but there was a hard edge in her eyes.

"You were right about those needles—sharper than razor blades."

"Did it hurt?" Jack asked, his voice quiet.

"Not really," she replied, her gaze growing distant. Then, her expression hardened as Jerica returned with food. "But I like to think I'm the queen of pain."

"I wasn't talking about the trolls," Jack said softly.

Her face went still as Jerica set the pots beside them; Jack could tell she wasn't ready to talk about the scars that went deeper than skin.

"Dinner's ready," Jerica announced brightly. "No plates, though, so we'll eat straight from the pots. Hope that's alright."

Each container already had three spoons sticking out. She grabbed a thermos, unscrewed the cap, and revealed three silver cups tucked inside. Pouring a shimmering liquid into each one, she said, "This is my remedy. Something I learned in secret—magic is forbidden in Levestin, after all. It helps replenish blood, relax your muscles, and clear your mind."

She met their eyes, her gaze distant. "With the right ingredients or incantations, it can fight infections—even stop deadly illnesses. It's rare and hard to make, but you need it." She exhaled, staring into her cup. "I've always wanted to share this with your world, to protect your people from the sicknesses that plague you. But that's not possible anymore, for many reasons. Akuramundo, of course, wishes to change that. He wants to offer this to your people too—but at a price they can't afford."

She stared off pensively. Adina made a mental note to ask more about this later. Without hesitation, she grabbed her spoon, smiling at Jack, who was already digging in.

"Alright, let's start with when you first arrived in Kazumeth—the day the Guardians came . . ." Jerica said.

"Guardians?" Adina interrupted, confused.

"Yes, Guardians . . ." Jerica's voice was filled with disbelief. "Didn't you know? Because of your blood, you two are now considered the new Guardians of Kazumeth." She glanced between them, appearing perplexed. Jack and Adina exchanged a glance, both shaking their heads.

"Well, you are," Jerica continued matter-of-factly. "It was foretold that the Guardians would arrive when Kazumeth needed them most. Things have changed drastically in the last fifty years, ever since Akuramundo's rise. It's dangerous now, and we've been living in fear for far too long. Akuramundo controls three of the five ruling capitals, and he's captured many cities in the Winterlands. Every day, he grows closer to reaching his goal of expanding Kazumeth's borders . . ."

"And destroying anyone he deems unfit to survive in his new world, right?" Adina interjected, giving Jack a reproachful look as he stared at Jerica with drooping eyes.

"Exactly," Jerica confirmed, her voice as chilly as the breeze. "If you already know all this, then perhaps I should be on my way. I have other matters to attend to before I slip back home."

"No, please—we don't know everything," Jack said, his voice apologetic. "How did you find us? And what happened when I blacked out back there?" He cast a warning glance at Adina, who rolled her eyes and crossed her arms.

"We'd been expecting you," Jerica replied steadily. "We needed your arrival to remain undetected, because we knew Akuramundo would be after you the moment he sensed your presence. Your early arrival has disrupted his plans. The Pilfert held council with the remaining trusted leaders and asked for our help. It didn't need us to recover you—that part of the plan was already in motion. But it needed us for something else. It foresaw that a great rift would occur—that you would eventually leave its side to fulfill a part of a prophecy it deems critical. It asked us to keep an eye on you as you set out on your separate journeys."

Jerica paused, taking a breath. "I was in Veilage Platts when the Pilfert approached me. It handed me vials and told me to head straight for the Sabana Mountains. It said you'd need my help by the next passing of the suns. Luckily, Kira is the fastest steed we own. I arrived just in time. You had just fallen from a bed of flowers, and Adina was choking a troll with the ropes around her arms." Adina flushed as Jack raised an eyebrow in astonishment. She'd saved him again.

"I honestly don't know what to do with you anymore, Adina. You've saved my life way too many times." Though his words were grateful, he wriggled uncomfortably, his fingers tightening around the hem of his cloak. He was the protector—always had been. But more and more, it felt like he was failing.

Adina smiled and shrugged, then turned her attention back to Jerica.

"I threw a confucian track into the air," Jerica continued.

"A what?" Jack and Adina said in unison.

"It's a powder that spreads faster than pollen. It penetrates the minds of those you wish to confuse. By the time I reached Adina, the track had already taken effect, and the trolls were fighting amongst themselves. You were no longer important to them. I took that chance to get Adina onto my other horse before they killed Kakuzaman." Jerica's voice darkened. "Once I saw him fall, I knew we had seconds to escape before they turned their attention back to us."

"What do you mean?" Jack asked, brow furrowed.

"Kakuzaman was the Kakunon of the tribe . . . the troll king," she added quickly at their blank stares. "As long as he was alive, you wouldn't have been killed. He was trying to calm them and keep them from murdering you when I arrived. He was one of the few allies we had among the Sabana trolls—the only reason Akuramundo hasn't been able to sway them like other clans. Once he was dead, we had to move fast. I got you on the horse, and now we're here."

Jack absorbed this news, his mind racing with questions. "What about the Pilfert? Were Addison and Stefani with it?"

"The Pilfert has other matters to attend to. As for the other Guardians, it told me they're safe. They're currently learning from Eldomar, who is teaching them how to manipulate the waters." Jerica's words brought Jack some relief. "But it's getting late. I have a long ride ahead of me and won't make it home until after the golden sun begins to rise again. You two are safe here. Get some rest before you begin the next part of your journey."

Adina paused, a question on her lips. "The Pilfert didn't ask you to bring us back?"

"No," Jerica said with a quiet smile. "It has seen your reunion and knows you'll succeed in your quest for your friend."

"We rescue Emerson from Dartmoor?" Jack asked, astonished. "Did it say how?"

"No," Jerica replied, her grin widening. "But even if it did, I couldn't tell you. Until we meet again." With a wink, she swung onto her horse and spurred Kira into action, the horse galloping swiftly across the beach as the sinking sun cast long shadows over the crimson sand.

"This place is beautiful," Jack said softly, picking up Jerica's empty pot and slipping it into his bag. Adina moved closer, her gaze fixed on the horizon as the golden and red suns embraced.

"Put your arms around me. I'm getting chilly," she said, shifting closer.

Jack wrapped an arm around her and pulled her into his warmth, feeling her fit perfectly against him—just like Emma had. A queasy guilt curled low in his gut as he looked down at her dark hair.

Adina glanced up at him, noticing his sudden tension. "What's wrong?"

"Nothing," Jack replied quickly, his voice distant. "Just tired." He looked back at the ocean, trying to focus on something other than the mix of feelings inside him.

As the suns dipped below the horizon, they sat in silence, letting the beauty of the moment settle around them. After a while, Adina stood, breaking the quiet.

"We should set up camp, don't you think?"

Jack nodded absently. Adina walked toward Jerica's other horse, where a folded note caught her eye. She picked it up and read aloud:

> *Because you two clearly can't make it out there on your own, I'm leaving these behind. I bought them for some of the women in Mankato, but they'll be more useful for protecting our Guardians. Stay warm tonight, and please: Do not stare out at the*

water. Beauty-obsessed mermaids lurk beneath the surface. They feed on youth and spirit to maintain their beauty. They don't need to feed often, but they are many. Beware.

P.S. I left Ivory with you. You can send her back if you don't need her, but I thought you might need a break from flying after all the exertion today.

Adina looked up at Jack just in time to see him staring out at the water.

"Stop!" she yelled.

Jack was mesmerized; his eyes locked on the sparkling lights dancing above the water.

"Look at them. They're like land stars. So beautiful," he murmured, tone distant and entranced.

Adina grabbed his arm, pulling him back toward the tree. "Hold up there, cowboy."

Jack blinked, shaking himself out of his trance. "What's wrong?"

"Read this," Adina said, thrusting the note into his hand.

Jack took it, his confusion deepening as he read. "Well, that's concerning. I've never felt more peaceful in my life—and that's saying something."

"Look, let's just get some rest and head out first thing tomorrow. The Pilfert has seen our reunion. We'll be fine," Adina urged.

Jack slumped, his earlier excitement drained. "Alright," he muttered, unrolling a blanket and lying down. He stole one last glance at the lights above the water as he wrapped another blanket around himself.

"G'night, Jack," Adina said softly, curling up on her side. For a moment, they shared a look. She hesitated, her lips parting for a second, but nothing came out. She simply rolled back onto her back and stared blankly at the stars.

"Good night, Adina," Jack whispered. He watched her a second longer, then closed his eyes as a strange warmth settled through him, stronger than anything the lights had stirred.

Chapter Fifteen

The Bargain

THE NORTHERN SUN ROSE first, its gentle rays cutting through the clouds, stretching long, delicate fingers across the shimmering water—extending a quiet invitation to its companion hidden behind an opposing mountain. The ethereal white lights that had hovered over the lake throughout the night unraveled into nothingness, vanishing with a sound like parting lips.

Nearby, on the warming beach, a disheveled mass of dark hair rustled through a haversack abandoned beside the remnants of an extinguished fire.

Adina's pale hands withdrew a thick slab of meat and placed it carefully on the golden grill Jerica had left for them the night before. She ignited fresh flames beneath the bars, then walked to the lake, filling a silver container with water, her gaze wandering over the vast expanse that still stirred something tight within her.

"Good morning," she said, her voice gentle as Jack wrestled beneath his blanket. "Sleep okay?"

She placed a teacup of water beside his head. Jack blinked at it with bleary eyes.

"Don't worry. The container purifies the water."

Jack reached for the cup and drained it in one swift gulp, clinging to the fading remnants of a dream—his last night with Emma.

"There's more in the canteen if you're still thirsty."

"How long have you been up?" Jack asked, his voice thick with sleep.

"Not long," Adina replied. "I was just starting to have bad dreams."

Her dark eyes lingered on his, and for a moment, Jack couldn't tell whether she was telling him not to ask more—or silently begging him to pry further.

"Care to tell me about them?" he asked cautiously, a careful response he'd learned during his years with Emma.

"Maybe later," she answered, her tone distant. "Not the best subject for morning conversation."

She returned to the grill, tossing seasoning over the steak as she flipped another with her other hand.

"Hey," Jack called, sitting up and squinting at the water. "Where'd the lights go?"

"No idea."

"Huh. This place is strange. Do you think it's safe to wash up here? Or should I stay out of the water?"

"I wouldn't go in," she replied. "But you can rinse off a bit from the shore. Your pits, my friend, need to be reunited with some deodorant."

"Oh, eat me," Jack grumbled. "You'd think there'd be a spell for that, but I've found nada."

He sniffed his pit and nearly recoiled as he headed toward the shore. Yanking off his shirt, muscles flexing, he tossed it aside and knelt to rinse himself clean at the water's edge.

Adina exhaled softly, a flash of longing passing over her face before she deliberately focused on the grill. She was just finishing the steaks when she heard him approach.

"So, how's the food coming along?" Jack asked, walking toward the fire with his shirt slung over his shoulder.

Adina, frowning slightly, was hacking through a stubborn piece of meat.

"Want me to take a stab at it? Don't want you losing an eye."

Jack took the knife from her, slicing through the steak effortlessly. Adina scowled but accepted the piece he offered.

Jack smiled as he picked up his own steak, holding it in two hands and ripping off a mouthful.

"The whole point of cutting the steak was so we don't look like barbarians trying to eat it," she said, her eyes fixed on his face, fighting the urge to glance lower.

Jack grinned, taking another large bite.

"I have no idea how you landed Emma," Adina said dryly.

Jack flexed his bicep, the muscle rippling beneath his skin, the size of a grapefruit. Adina rolled her eyes.

"I'm not sure how far I'll be able to carry you today," she said as she wiped her hands on a cloth, "but we should at least make it to the outskirts of Drysmian, like we planned."

She scanned the camp, noticing the horse grazing peacefully nearby, its coat glowing in the morning light. She walked over and untied the ropes from its neck.

"Hey, buddy," she whispered. "Do you know your way home?"

To Jack's surprise, the horse neighed in response, tossing its thick mane as though to confirm.

"OK, go home and be safe. Thanks for trusting me yesterday," she murmured, kissing the horse on the nose before it galloped away, its hooves kicking up sand as it disappeared into the distance, swallowed by the mountains.

"Ready to go?" Adina asked, stepping up to Jack, who had just slung the bag over his shoulder.

He bounced on his feet, grinning.

"This is amazing," Jack said. The bag felt lighter than it had the day before, even after he'd crammed two golden grills inside.

"Grab my waist," Adina said, her voice steady. "It's easier when you're on my back."

Jack wrapped his arms around her waist, and with a firm push, they ascended into the sky. The cool wind whipped past Jack's face as they soared above the glittering waters.

Jack marveled at the landscape below as the sun bathed the mountains in soft, golden light. As the morning passed by, they flew over ships crossing the sea, tiny villages nestled between cliffs, and wide expanses of open water.

Just as he was beginning to relax, something caught his eye: a woman floating far from the shore, so distant that his first instinct was to look for a sinking ship. Her long navy hair swirled around her neck like ink in water, and her dark eyes gleamed like rich, chocolate pools against her mahogany skin. She was breathtakingly beautiful, but there was something terrifying about her—as if she were an angel fallen from grace.

"Do you see that?" Jack whispered, pointing toward the woman.

Adina gasped as she caught sight of her. The woman lingered a moment—then flipped backward, a decaying gray fin breaking the surface before disappearing beneath the water.

"Mermaids . . ." Adina breathed in awe as Jack's mouth formed a wide, understanding "O." "We must be getting close to Drysmian."

Jack's gaze followed the ripples in the water, and his stomach twisted when he saw what swam beneath the surface—gray, withered faces were staring up at him, their features twisted and jagged. Their noses formed crooked ridges, while their mouths were mere thin, puckered lines, nearly swallowed by the shadows that consumed them. Their eyes glinted from the depths, never once leaving him.

He quickly averted his gaze, and to his relief, a massive rocky cliff rose ahead.

They descended toward a crumbling tower, its wide, arched windows shattered and its jade-colored roof punctured with holes. Vines clung to the building's sides, dragging the ancient stones back into the earth as if to reclaim it.

"Do you think there are guards?" Jack asked, eyeing the dilapidated structure.

"Does it look like it's been used in the last thousand years?" Adina replied dryly, her breath slightly ragged as she landed. "If anything is in there . . . it's definitely not human," she added as a rounded shadow slunk past a broken window.

"So, where exactly are we?"

"The outskirts of Drysmian," Adina said quietly, her voice heavy with the weight of the place.

"Nice," Jack replied, though he had no idea where that was.

"Clearly, you haven't looked at any maps or books since we've been here, have you?" Adina shot back, raising an eyebrow.

"I skimmed through that one yesterday," Jack admitted sheepishly.

"Drysmian is a city," Adina continued. "It's governed by one of the many races of Kazumeth. Could be elves, witches, men, Eraquis, Atnos . . . Hell, it could be something else entirely. This place has a bloody history, so it's hard to tell who's actually in charge right now."

"Yet 'Kazumeth is the most peaceful place,'" Jack mimicked the Pilfert, his tone dripping with sarcasm. A small seed of doubt about the Pilfert's trustworthiness was starting to dig its roots in his mind.

"Is it going to be safe for us to pass through?" Jack asked, shifting his attention as he walked around the rocky cliffside.

He glanced down and noticed more of those ugly, gnarled faces staring up from the water, their sagging white eyes fixed hungrily on them. He kicked a stone off the cliff, and after a moment, the sound of it crashing into the depths below echoed back. The creatures scattered like cockroaches, their movements quick and unsettling.

"I think it's our safest bet," Adina replied. "It'll be way easier to blend in with humans than another herd of trolls, don't you think? Plus, there are places to eat here. We can grab a bite in a pub, plan our next move, and save some of our food for dinner."

Adina seemed to have regained some of her energy. Just as she placed her hands on the ground to push herself up, Jack reached over, grabbed her hands, and pulled her to her feet.

As they passed by the withered stone tower, Jack noticed shards of broken glass still clinging to its circular windows, jagged like a shattered smile.

"OK, this place looks creepy as hell," Jack said, eyeing the tower. "We should climb through one of those windows and check if anything's—"

"You're not entering that building, Jack," Adina interrupted, pulling him away from the structure. "You have no idea what's inside there. Besides, it's only a matter of time before that roof caves in."

They climbed up the rocky cliff, past rows of green trees, until they reached a narrow dirt road. Fields of pumpkins, in every size and shade of orange and white sprawled along the winding road. Old cottages lined the perimeter of a weathered city visible in the distance.

Jack remembered from a late-night conversation with Adina that pumpkins were Drysmian's main export to Strega. Witches used them not only for food but for deeper magic, too.

"It's beautiful," Adina said softly as they approached the chilly city.

The buildings crowded together in a haphazard jumble, which, to Jack, made it look like a giant accordion. Great stone structures in faded colors twisted into old wooden cottages, banners flapping from the windows. The angles of the streets and the streetlamps had a peculiar elegance, leading up to a towering gothic cathedral that loomed over the city. The flying buttresses, horse-sized gargoyles, and darkened arched windows made the cathedral feel haunted—like it belonged to another age.

As they walked, Adina started pointing out shops and gasping at the clothing displayed in windows.

Jack wasn't listening.

His gaze remained fixed on the cathedral. He couldn't shake the pull he felt toward it—a sensation he hadn't experienced since the cave, which now seemed like a lifetime ago. There was something alive in those walls. Something he needed to see.

Thunk!

Jack walked straight into a dangling shop sign, a knot instantly forming on his forehead.

Adina doubled over in laughter, but it was short-lived. A heavy gust of wind swept up the alley, lifting her dress over her head and exposing a flash of pink fabric. She immediately pushed it back down, her face turning crimson.

Jack's eyes widened in delight.

"Don't even . . ." she warned, glaring at him.

"Oh, come on. Pink?" Jack teased.

"If you say one more word about them, Jack, I'll give your head another knot so big trolls could live on it."

"They're cute," Jack insisted, barely holding back his grin.

"Suck it," Adina huffed, storming off a few paces.

Trying to shift the conversation, Jack said, "So, this city kind of reminds me of the dingy alley in Ealu, don't you think?"

"Maybe at one point . . ." Adina responded in a whisper.

Some of the shops did resemble Ealu, but the vibe of the city couldn't have been more different. As they ventured deeper into town, the beauty of the streets began to fade. The air grew cold, and it wasn't just the wind rattling the signs. There was a heaviness to it—a palpable sense of unease.

Adina's eyes flicked from side to side, her unease growing. Every window they passed displayed the same red flag with a golden "A" in the center, surrounded by the crossed symbols of a wand, a staff, a sword, and an arrow. Her stomach turned.

The suns were no longer shining. The gray buildings cast a dull, oppressive shadow that seemed to suck the life from the sky. The only light came from the flickering lamps in front of the cathedral, adding to the cold, lifeless atmosphere.

"Look," Jack said, his voice low, pointing into the grimy window of a nearby shop.

Adina's stomach lurched.

Inside, a woman in black robes, wearing a wild, spiral hat in shades of green, purple, and black, was furiously chopping the head off a long, strange-looking salamander. Its many legs wriggled helplessly in the air as she pinned it down with one hand.

"Yeah, maybe we should just move on from here, Jack," Adina said tightly, spinning around to face him. "Jack?!"

He was standing a few yards away, holding open a shop door.

"We might as well get some lunch while we're here," he said casually, completely oblivious to the uneasy feeling creeping up Adina's spine.

"Okay . . ." Adina muttered as she pushed past the creaky door to the dimly lit tavern.

Jack-o'-lanterns flickered on every table, their faces grotesque in the shadows. A haze of smoke curled through the air, and the room smelled of stale tobacco, damp wood, and a lingering trace of cinnamon. Adina navigated her way to a corner table, but as they passed, Jack couldn't help but notice the eyes of a group of four burly dwarves sitting at the booth behind them.

They were covered in thick, silver-and-red beards, their glares lingering on the two strangers with a mix of suspicion and disdain. All except for the youngest—his face was gaunt and serious, with an odd solemnity that didn't belong to someone his age.

"Your beard will grow in, Gilliad. Patience, lad, you're only six," said the dwarf beside him, whose voice rumbled like stones.

"But Ma, BilJim already has three inches! I'm the class joke," the boy muttered, crestfallen as he stroked the faint beginnings of his own.

Jack's eyebrows shot up into his hairline. He blinked.

"Six years old and already growing a beard? Impressive," Adina said aloud.

"Not nearly as impressive as his mother's," Jack muttered under his breath as he twirled a finger around his non-existent beard. "What do you think? Could I pull one off?"

Adina's lips twitched at the image of Jack with long, untamed facial hair jutting from his dark, chiseled face. But neither of them laughed. The air inside the tavern was colder than the streets outside, heavy with unease. Jack turned to the window, watching as the dark clouds that had loomed all day finally broke, unleashing a torrential downpour.

Before either of them could speak, a repulsive figure waddled up to their table. He was portly, with a wild, matted beard that looked like it hosted more creatures than hairs. A clipboard hovered beside him, suspended by some unseen force.

"Ve haff no specials tonight—no beer, no ales. You vill drink vater," he grumbled, his voice thick with a heavy accent. "Food? Bah. No appetizers, no desserts. Just dis—" He slapped a dingy scrap of parchment onto the table, its surface smeared with what looked like grease and hastily scribbled words. "Main courses. Take or leave."

"Oh, fantastic," Adina said, her voice dripping with sarcasm. "A stunning selection." She pointed to a dwarven word on the menu she didn't recognize, and Jack followed suit, picking the dish below it. As the man turned to leave, he muttered something in a language neither of them understood.

At that moment, the soft tinkle of the bell above the door rang out, signaling a newcomer. A man in a brown traveling cloak entered, his face hidden beneath a hood. He stalked to a table in the corner by the fireplace and unfurled several pieces of parchment from his bag, scribbling furiously with a long, silver quill. Jack's eyes locked on the man, but just as the stranger's gaze flicked up to meet his, Jack turned away, a knot forming in his stomach. There was no mistaking it—this man was watching them.

Jack leaned closer to Adina, his voice barely a whisper. "I think that man is watching us. Should we go?"

"Aliases, Jack. We're already here—it'll look more suspicious if we get up and leave. Just don't use your full name."

Jack nodded apprehensively. "How many languages do you think they have here in Kazumeth? And how does everyone seem to know English?"

Adina gave him an exasperated glance. "Not everyone does. But we understand the languages because of the Vocation Stones. When we're engaged with someone, the stones help us understand and speak back."

Her eyes scanned the room once more. The man's gaze had returned to his parchment, but Jack couldn't shake the unsettling feeling of being watched.

Adina pulled a map and another book from their bag. "Anyway, forget that. We need to focus on Emerson. Let's talk over a plan to save him."

Jack straightened in his seat as she slid the book across the table. He groaned inwardly. "You want me to read this?"

"Honestly, I'm amazed you got past the first grade. Open the damn book," she snapped, not giving him an ounce of sympathy.

The hour passed as they flipped through the brittle pages and ate their way through a large, savory pie. It was filled with strange spices, vegetables, and meat—heavily seasoned griffin meat, according to the waiter. Jack winced, but the food was so good he looked past that gross detail.

"The food in this world is something else. I just wish all these amazing creatures didn't have to die for it," Adina added.

"It's just like home. Maybe griffins are as common as chickens here," Jack said, hoisting his fork for one final bite.

"Yeah, because how chickens are treated at home is so just."

"Point taken."

Adina grew serious again, flipping through the book. "We'll camp in the forest north of the city tonight. If we leave early, we should reach Dartmoor on foot by midday. Once there, we blend in—then make our move toward Akuramundo's tower.

I've researched Dartmoor. If we wear dark robes, we should be fine until we reach the city center. After that, we'll probably have to fight. Can you manage those spells?"

Jack looked down at the book in front of him, the words already starting to blur. "Definitely. Are you ready to go?" He glanced toward the corner. Jack noticed the man's posture shift as something stirred beneath his cloak. Jack stiffened, suspicion prickling at the back of his neck.

Adina followed his gaze, then quickly slid some coins across the table. "We need to move. Now."

Jack hesitated, his hand lingering on the coins as he looked to the waiter, whose eyes were still fixated on them. The waiter didn't speak, but his lips curled into a strange, knowing smile as he shoved the coins into his pocket, tossed his apron on the counter, and sprinted out the front door.

"We may have over-tipped," Jack muttered as they stepped out onto the slick, rain-soaked alley.

They hurried on before veering off onto a gravel path, their footing shifting beneath them as the heavy air pressed in on them. Adina's gaze flicked to the looming cathedral, its dark silhouette stark against the bleak sky.

"What do you think that building is?" Jack asked, mesmerized.

"I don't know, but I don't like it," she said, her voice a low murmur. "It feels dangerous."

"Always the optimist" Jack replied with a grin, trying to lighten the mood.

But Adina didn't smile. Her eyes stayed fixed on the shadows ahead before she suddenly broke her stare and grabbed his arm. "Come on, we're going this way," she said, pulling him down a side street.

They followed a winding path, weaving through the city's darker corners, until the faint glow of a carriage appeared in the distance. The horse's erratic trot echoed through the alley, its lantern swinging wildly with each jolt. At the sight of it, Adina yanked Jack into a recessed doorway, both of them pressing their backs to the damp stone to avoid being seen.

They stood still, holding their breath as the carriage clattered past. Once it was gone, they slipped back into the alley, keeping low, eyes darting to every shadow as they moved deeper into the darkness. All they could think about was escaping the eyes that seemed to be on them at every turn.

"Who do you think was in that carriage?" Jack asked, noting the tension still etched across Adina's face.

"I don't know," she muttered, eyes flicking to the dark windows and narrow alleys behind them. "But that carriage had Akuramundo's mark—and we're wanted, Jack. We need to start acting like it. People were watching. From windows, from shops. That guy in the tavern. It feels like entire town has eyes on us now."

"Where's all this coming from?" he asked, raising an eyebrow.

"This place gives me the creeps. And the sky—what happened to the daylight? It's like someone hit a switch. Why is it already so dark?" Her tone dropped as she glanced over her shoulder. "I know we planned to stay at an inn, but I don't think we should stop. Not here."

Jack chuckled at her earnestness but stopped short when she shot him a look so sharp the darkness couldn't obscure it.

"I've been meaning to ask," Adina said after a beat, her boots echoing softly as they moved beyond the last crooked buildings. The road had opened up, leading into a long, empty stretch flanked by weedy ditches and the silhouettes of distant trees. "Have you tried entering Emerson's mind lately?"

"Yeah, well, sort of," Jack admitted. "During the troll attack, I think I was inside his head for a bit . . ." He shared the brief visions he'd seen, pausing to gauge her reaction. "Since then, things have been a bit hectic. I haven't really thought about trying again."

Adina nodded, her brow furrowing as they walked in silence. Behind them, the city had vanished into a curtain of shadow, its dim glow swallowed by thick clouds and steady drizzle. Ahead, the road slipped into a pale mist, and for the first time in hours, light began to return—not just from above, but from the land itself. A soft, golden shimmer hovered near the tree line, as if the forest had lit a lantern and was quietly waiting for them to arrive. As they stepped beneath the first low-hanging boughs, Jack felt the tightness of anxiety loosen its grip.

The trees here were colossal and ancient, their trunks ranging from wagon-wide giants to slender, spiraling columns wrapped in moss. Branches arched high overhead in graceful sweeps, forming a canopy that fractured the dim light into shifting patterns of gold and green.

The air grew sweeter, thick with the scent of damp bark, ripe fruit, and something floral—wild, familiar, and untamed. Somewhere deeper in the woods, a warm, pulsing glow flickered like a heartbeat, calm and welcoming. Jack felt it settle into him, soft and sure, and for the first time in what felt like days, his shoulders dropped.

He inhaled deeply as the weight he was carrying seemed to lift with the warm air around him, and for a fleeting moment, the idea of rescuing Emerson—breaking into a dangerous city and pulling his friend out—felt not only possible, but easy, like the forest itself was convincing him it would all be fine.

They walked for hours, the forest stretching endlessly around them, shifting in color and sound with every bend. Jack marveled at the strange creatures that crossed their path: large, furry dogs that came up to his chest, earless bunnies that hopped on a single leg, and other oddities that blurred the line between flora and fauna—each one stranger than the last.

Eventually, Adina veered off the path as she heard the faint trickle of water. She found a small river where they paused for a quick meal and to refill their canteen.

"Oh my god," Jack exclaimed, smacking Adina's arm.

"What?" she snapped, whipping around.

"Adina, it's a unicorn!" Jack said breathlessly, as though he were meeting a childhood hero.

"Don't point! It's rude," Adina hissed, though her gaze softened as she nodded at the majestic creature, which nodded back before gracefully disappearing into the trees. Its mane shimmered like winking stars, and a spiral of gold and silver curled from its brow like a natural crown.

"We should be far enough from Drysmian by now, and close enough to Dartmoor that we'll make it by midday on foot."

They moved back onto the road, but instead of continuing down the path, Adina cut across to the other side, crushing several fallen branches underfoot as she disappeared into the forest. Jack followed unquestioningly. Ahead, he saw a small clearing he hadn't noticed before.

"This looks like a good spot to camp, don't you think?" Adina asked.

Jack surveyed the area. The trees here were thinner, allowing the moon and stars to shine through. He noticed the surrounding bushes glimmering with small lights, like glowing crystals—moonlight, rose, and topaz hues that seemed to pulse with their own energy.

"Fairies," Adina explained, as though reading his mind. "They're harmless."

"Ah. How did you know this spot was here?" Jack asked, raising an eyebrow.

"Intuition," she replied with a playful wiggle of her fingers, as if casting a spell.

"Right," Jack said with a half-smile, dropping his bag to the ground with a soft thud before sinking down beside it. Within moments, Adina had conjured a fire with a wave of her hand. The flickering light danced across her pale face, casting shadows that sharpened the quiet tragedy in her features. She handed Jack one of Jerica's blankets, and as she walked back to her spot, she began muttering a soft incantation. Jack assumed it was a protection spell, but he couldn't help being enchanted by the flow of the unfamiliar words.

When she finally lay down, head resting on her bag, Jack followed suit. He curled onto his side, blanket pulled up to his shoulders, and watched her across the fire. The flames painted her in shifting hues—amber, gold, deep blue—and for the first time, he noticed how peaceful she looked in stillness. He was surprised by the quiet warmth blooming in her presence.

"Thank you, Adina," he muttered softly. "For coming with me. You've been a bigger help than Addison or Stefani would've been." His voice darkened as he thought of them, feasting with the Pilfert while he and Adina were almost troll food. "We should've stayed with the Pilfert. We have no real plan. How are we going to infiltrate the most guarded city in Kazumeth and defeat the strongest force in this world?"

The optimism he'd felt earlier—as light as the forest's glow—had now dimmed, swallowed by the hush of night.

Adina's eyes flickered with amusement. "Don't be such a bore. We're the freakin' Guardians of Kazumeth. We can do whatever the hell we want. Now, close your eyes. You need to catch up on your beauty sleep. Your skin looks like it's about to give birth to a pimple."

He ran a hand over his face, smiling to himself when he realized she was just joking.

There was something about the way she moved through the world — steady, unbothered, always a step ahead. He admired that about her. The way she wouldn't shrink. The way she spoke the truth and didn't apologize for it. And there was a quiet beauty, too — something he hadn't noticed at first and now couldn't seem to ignore.

As if in protest, thoughts of Emma stirred: angry and disapproving of him looking at someone else. Then, Adina let out a soft sneeze, blowing all thoughts of Emma from his mind. He exhaled, let his body sink into the earth, and allowed sleep to pull him under.

Jack had no idea what time it was when the forest sounds roused him, but when his eyes snapped open, he could just make out the reddish clouds in the early morning sky. Adina was still lying where she had been the night before, the fire crackling softly between them. Jack groggily got to his feet, brushed dirt from his boots, and rolled his blanket before slipping it under her head. He took her bag and dug into it, retrieving a handful of coins that he quickly shoved into his pockets.

He adjusted the blanket over her shoulders, slung her sack over his own shoulder, and stepped to the edge of their small camp. Closing his eyes, he waved his hands through the air, chanting softly—a quiet incantation meant to mark their hiding place and guard Adina until he returned.

With one last glance at her, Jack stepped away, the twisted trees rising around him, tall and unmoving. Vines hung like snakes from the branches, and moss-covered boulders the size of houses dotted the landscape. Jack felt an unsettling sense that something lurked beneath them.

Once Jack stepped out of the woods, the gloomy cityscape emerged in the distance, cloaked in mist and shadow. He took a steadying breath and closed his eyes, focusing on his destination.

When he opened them again, the forest was gone. He now stood just outside the city limits, the massive cathedral-like structure rising before him, its spires stabbing into the sky.

The sky above darkened as storm clouds gathered, casting the city in an oppressive gloom. The stone buildings stood drenched and miserable, and Jack couldn't help but wonder: Did the sun ever shine here?

He deliberately kept his back to the alluring building, but it still tugged at his attention—a persistent pull he couldn't shake. He quickened his pace, trudging down the sodden street, determined to reach his destination.

With a reluctant sigh, Jack stepped into the dimly lit shop, the bell above the door chiming softly as it closed behind him. The air was heavy with the scent of damp fabric and incense. Dark robes hung stiffly on iron racks, flanked by shelves lined with hoods and gloves.

He moved quickly, grabbing two full sets of dark robes, fingerless gloves, and leathered pants, desperate to get out as quickly as possible.

The shopkeeper stood behind the counter, rigid and wordless, his eyes fixed on Jack with an unblinking stare.

Jack handed over the coins, a chill crawling down his spine. As he turned to leave, he could still feel the weight of that stare pressing into his back.

Unnerved and eager to return to Adina, he made his final stop: Mallory's Meat Market.

He pushed open the door and stepped inside—the smell of something sour and metallic, poorly masked by herbs, hit him in a wave.

Behind the counter, a brittle, wart-covered woman with a long, thin nose and frayed gray hair greeted him with a hunched posture.

"I've never seen you around here before," she croaked, her voice a rasping, damaged whisper. Her spider-infested, tattered, burgundy hat swayed atop her head, and a dark veil slipped free, partially obscuring her eyes—pale, sagging orbs that seemed to struggle to stay in their sockets.

Jack felt his skin crawl as she shuffled closer, her withered hands reaching for the small wooden door behind the counter and pushing it open with a creak.

He instinctively took a step back as she wobbled toward him, brushing against one of the glass cases and sending several large flies buzzing around the aged meat inside.

"Careful, my dear. You wouldn't want to break my things, would you?" she cackled, her voice thick with ancient malice.

"Me? No, never," Jack said, recovering quickly as he moved toward the front of the shop, positioning himself near a wooden desk. Suddenly, a loud, screeching noise tore through the room, coming from the very space the woman had just vacated.

"What is that?" Jack asked, trying to sound unfazed.

"We caught a Siren today," she replied, a sickening ecstasy lacing her words. She extinguished a candle on one of the old, cracked stands as her lips curled into a smile. "Sly little creatures they may be, but no one escapes my JubJub when he has his eyes on a prize. No, not my JubJub."

"Ar . . . aren't Sirens part human?" Jack asked, his curiosity betraying him.

"Just the head," she answered with a rasp, her voice thickening into a grotesque chuckle. "We don't use anything from the head. That would be cannibalism." She laughed again, a dry, wheezing sound. "No, no—it's the mutated anomalies that are truly delicious. And very rare." Her long, slick tongue snaked out, tracing her cracked lips as her mind seemed to drift, lost in some twisted reverie.

Jack, stomach turning, inched closer to the door, searching for an excuse to leave. But before he could move, she lunged, her bony fingers snapping shut around his wrist.

"You surely aren't leaving without making a purchase, are you, my dear?" she crooned, the sweetness in her voice laced with an underlying threat.

Jack quickly grabbed the two cleanest slabs of meat he could find, along with several eggs, and placed them on the counter.

"That will be seven herots and two selacs," she rasped, eyes glinting. Jack passed over a handful of coins, but she left them on the counter as he started to make his way toward the door.

"Just one more thing before you go," she added with relish as she vanished behind the counter.

Jack turned, his hand already on the door handle, hoping to slip out before she returned. But the knob wouldn't turn. He jiggled it—still nothing. He pressed his shoulder into the door, but at that same moment, a cold wind swept through the shop, snuffing out the candles and the fire in the pit across the room. His breath caught as heavy footsteps began to move out from the room the witch had just disappeared into.

"Tell me, Jack, Guardian of Kazumeth," the witch's voice rasped, thick with venom. "Did you really think you could wander into my shop and not be handed over to my master?"

The shop darkened further as she stepped into the doorway, her frame now stretched, blocking the candlelight from the other room. Jack didn't even have time to think before he was hurled across the room, crashing through several glass displays. He hit the ground hard, pinned by long, gnarled claws curling tightly around his throat. Her face loomed over his, breath hot and foul, thick with the stench of garlic.

"Those idiots captured the wrong boy," she muttered darkly, eyes narrowing. "I told them this. You even smell like the Pilferts. Oh, how I miss the taste . . ."

Revulsion twisted through Jack as her long tongue dragged up his cheek, leaving a cold, slimy trail.

"No matter," she purred. "Once he's done with you, I'm sure he can spare just a little for me . . ."

Suddenly, a metallic screech tore through the room as the window exploded inward in a shower of glass, shards spraying across the witch. She loosened her grip, and in that brief moment, Jack shoved her off and rolled beneath a table.

He looked to his right, heart leaping as a dark, hooded silhouette climbed through the shattered window, sword in hand.

"Get out," the man growled.

Jack didn't need telling twice. He scrambled toward the window—food, clothes, and bag completely forgotten—as he vaulted over the broken frame and took off down the road.

He could hear glass crunching beneath the man's boots as he glanced back—just long enough to see the figure raise his sword and charge the witch, who was lengthening like a shadow. Jack caught a flash of ancient runes etched along the blade but didn't stop to study them—he kept sprinting down the street, desperate to escape the chaos.

He stumbled as he rushed down the gloomy road, breath ragged in his chest. He passed the dark building that seemed to call to him, but he forced himself to keep going, cutting through side alleys and narrow lanes until the stone gave way to gravel. At last, he reached the dirt road on the outskirts of Drysmian.

He closed his eyes and took a deep breath—then came the familiar sensation of bursting through space, like scattered ash on the wind. When he opened his eyes again, he was standing beside the stream where he and Adina had eaten the evening before. A rush of frustration rose in his chest, tangled with fear—his power was still unpredictable, slipping through his fingers no matter how hard he tried to hold onto it. And worse, after everything Adina had done for him, he still hadn't found a way to repay her. He was leaning on her more than ever, still not standing on his own, still falling short. And now he'd only made things worse—their bag, their food, even the disguises he'd risked everything to get were gone, left behind in the chaos of his escape.

They had nothing.

As he walked forward, something caught his eye. A feather as long as his forearm drifted gently across the ground, carried by the chill morning air. It was unmistakable—this was a Stymphalian's plume. Without thinking, he snatched it from the air, and the moment he touched it, his body collapsed, crumpling beneath him.

Emerson lay cold and stiff on the floor, his body sore from days of deprivation. It had been at least five days since his kidnapping, and the only sustenance he'd received were bottles of supplements. He hadn't seen anyone since Akuramundo had made his offer. The only sign of life in the grim chamber was a possible corpse hunched in the corner. The stench of decay hung heavy in the air, choking him.

A sudden loud clank echoed through the hollow chamber, the sound piercing the silence—louder than a thousand cymbals crashing.

"Who's there?" Emerson called into the dark.

A woman with curly brown hair stepped into the faint blue light. Emerson's breath caught in his throat.

"Gara," he murmured, the nervousness evident in his voice.

"Master has invited you upstairs to dinner," she said coolly. "He has another request he wishes to bestow upon you. You are to be bathed and dressed within the hour. Wear these." She held out a black-and-silver tunic, its fabric glinting in the low light.

"These were meant to be his," Gara added, nodding toward the place where the man Emerson had heard violently breathing for days now lay silent.

Gara bent down, unshackled him from his chains, and placed a cold hand in his. She led him from the darkness up the stairs and into the cool light of the foyer, where fate awaited.

Jack sat up, sweat dampening his forehead as the vision faded. The nightmare—a fragment from a time when life felt simpler, when his only worry had been Emma's ever-shifting moods—lingered in his mind. Akuramundo's interrogations of Emerson came flooding back vividly, and Jack remembered the cryptic mention of the Pilfert and his heritage.

He'd done it. Emerson had made the deal. Jack stared ahead in stunned disbelief.

He pulled himself to his feet, heart racing, and tore through the trees, waving his hand to clear the protective barrier Adina had cast. He shook her awake and explained everything, his words tumbling out in a breathless rush that made Adina's tired eyes snap wide open in alarm.

"Jack, that was honestly the stupidest thing you could have done! Why would you go back into town without me?"

"We needed food. We needed clothes to slip into Dartmoor," Jack panted, "and I need to keep practicing my fading."

Adina's eyes narrowed. "Wait . . . you did it? You faded?" Her voice held a mixture of disbelief and awe that made Jack feel even more useless.

"Not very well the second time. But did you not hear me? I was getting gnawed on—without my consent, by the way. The food is probably lying on the floor back there, with, well, everything else . . ."

"Great," Adina muttered, her tone exaggerated and dry. "So what now? We just wing it with no books, no food, no weapons, and no disguises? I mean, our plan was shit before—but now what?"

Jack gave her an apologetic smile. His desire to prove himself was just causing problems. Admitting defeat, he knew he had to let Adina take charge from here on out.

"We have to get the bag back, Jack. I'm useless without those books." Her voice broke off as she suddenly turned, her eyes darting to the space behind him.

"What—?" Jack started to ask, but Adina placed a hand over his mouth, her posture stiffening as she peered into the dense foliage ahead.

"I'm not here to hurt you," a low voice called from within the trees.

Jack froze, twisting his head toward the voice, but the clearing was empty—no one was there. Adina moved cautiously, extending her hand as she searched the shadows, her gaze flickering from left to right.

"I have your bags," the voice continued, a hint of amusement in its tone. "And food. Unfortunately, the eggs didn't survive the dance with old Mallory."

"That's the guy who saved me," Jack whispered to Adina, his voice low with a mix of confusion and curiosity. "How did he get here so fast?"

"And how did he find us? Show yourself," Adina called, her voice steady but commanding.

A figure stepped out from behind a tree, his cloak shifting to blend with the surroundings before it reverted to its natural brown hue. Beneath it, he wore gray trousers and a leather vest, the lacing of it tight against his lean form. He pulled back the hood to reveal a sharp, angular face—thin and clean-shaven, with a pronounced jawline, dark eyebrows, and intense eyes that seemed to gleam with secret knowledge. A mole sat above his thin, unsmiling lips.

"Who are you?" Jack asked, eyeing the stranger warily.

"My name is Osric," the man replied smoothly. "I'm a member of the Shadow Clan, and a friend to the Pilfert."

"Well, that's fine with me," Jack said, his tension easing somewhat. "Come have a seat." He gestured toward their small, struggling fire, its flames dancing weakly in the breeze.

Adina, however, studied him with suspicion, her gaze sharp. "You're from Levestin, aren't you? I've read your name somewhere."

"I am," Osric said, his tone light. "And I'm sure you have. It's good to see one of you does their research." His smile faded almost immediately, as if the effort of smiling had exhausted him. "I saved your friend, but if you don't trust me, I understand. The stories they tell about me aren't exactly flattering. But I've come with a warning."

"Adina, if he was going to kill us, he would've done so already," Jack said, his voice gentle but firm. "Please, Osric, sit down."

Adina gestured for Osric to join them, though her expression remained distrustful.

"Thank you," Osric said, dropping his rucksack to the ground and pulling out the shredded meat. Jack retrieved the golden grills, and Adina reignited the fire with the calm skill of a Girl Scout who had never missed a badge.

"As I said, my name is Osric," the man continued, stirring the food in a pan as the smell of grilled meat and spices began to fill the air. "I lived in Levestin, but I left many years ago."

"Why'd you leave?" Adina asked, eyeing him carefully. He didn't look any older than thirty, yet his words carried the weight of someone much older.

"There are many reasons," Osric said, his tone darkening. "Things are not right in the kingdom. I've been recruiting others to help overthrow my father. Kazumeth isn't the perfect place the Pilfert likes to paint. The Pilferts, once some of the wisest creatures in the world, have a tendency to romanticize things."

"Do you mind elaborating?" Adina asked, her curiosity piqued despite her wariness.

"Impetuous, aren't you?" Osric chuckled, but there was no humor in his eyes.

Adina glared at him.

"The city of Levestin has fallen under a dictatorship—one set in motion by my grandfather, though my people don't seem to realize it. The residents aren't free to leave. The island of Mankato, to the east, has become a slave colony for those who oppose the leadership. But worse things are happening there—things no one knows about. Trade to and from Levestin has been halted for years, and valuable resources have all but disappeared." He stopped, his eyes hardening.

"The Pilfert will tell you more, as it plans to send you there once you're reunited and the sapphire is collected from Alors." He glanced at Adina's bag. "Do you happen to have any ale?"

Adina passed him the jug wordlessly, and he took a long swig before pouring some into the stew. Adina's face contorted, not pleased about the backwash that may now be floating in their breakfast.

"Thank you. Now, you must heed my warning," Osric said, his voice dropping to a grave tone. "I'm sure you're aware of how valuable you are. The King of the North seeks you, as do many other rulers and powerbrokers across our world. The 'Kids of Destiny,' the future Guardians of our land, are highly sought after. Flaunting your way through a city that hosted the Great Burnings, that's also this close"—he held his fingers barely apart—"to falling under Akuramundo's control? It's not wise. You saw the clouds above the city—they're a constant reminder of the evil that transpired there long ago. Clouds from the gods, sent to wash away the horrors that led to the near extinction of the Pilferts."

He paused, his gaze intense. "You must not go to Dartmoor."

Jack and Adina exchanged uneasy glances.

"Well, my dude, one of our friends was captured and taken there," Jack said. "So . . . that's kind of the plan. You know. After we eat. And this whole chit-chat, of course."

"And what plan is that?" Osric's voice was low and knowing as he grabbed one of Jerica's blankets and lifted the grill from the flame.

Adina and Jack looked shiftily at one another.

"I have heard your intentions, but it takes much more strategy than marching into Dartmoor and demanding he be handed over. I have friends—acclaimed Futurians—who have written of your captures and deaths. You have to promise me you won't go."

"Interesting . . ." Adina muttered, glancing at Jack before looking back. "We've heard differently. We've been told that we succeed in our quest."

"Futurians can see multiple outcomes, depending on your actions," Osric countered. "Their prophecies aren't set in stone.

Those who study at Burkank can trace the different paths laid out in the oracles' writings—but right now, your story is heading straight for a dead end. You mustn't go to Dartmoor."

Jack wiped his mouth and swallowed a bite of the hearty dish Osric had prepared. "We know it's not going to be easy, but—" he paused mid-sentence, his mouth full, then gestured with a wink, "—this is amazing. Adina, take note—we're adding this to the menu."

Adina rolled her eyes. "I might cook better if I wasn't constantly taking care of you," she muttered, a jab that affirmed she was thinking the same thing he was.

"How can you be so sure the Futurians are right? They just sound like educated guesses to me."

"It's strange magic," Osric replied, his tone distant. "Something born from the Yellow."

"Born from the Yellow?" Adina echoed incredulously. "What does that even mean?"

Osric's smile was enigmatic. "You have so much to learn."

"That may be true, but you already said the Pilfert has seen our reunion."

"That is correct. But it doesn't happen in Dartmoor, love," he added to Adina, almost condescendingly.

Jack saw the rage rising in her and quickly tried to interject before she could let it boil over.

Still, the conversation spiraled into heated arguments about their plans and Osric's warnings. Adina's patience wore thin, her cold silence growing more pronounced with each passing moment. Jack, knowing Osric wouldn't leave without a promise, gave it—fingers crossed behind his back.

When the meal was over, Osric helped them clean up camp, methodically camouflaging their tracks. As he turned to leave, he extended a dirty hand for them to shake.

"Until we meet again," he said, his voice grim. "You will see your friend again. Find the Pilfert. Dartmoor will be your end."

Before they could say another word, Osric vanished into the trees with startling speed.

Jack and Adina walked in silence down the trail as the world around them grew unnervingly quiet, as if it shared in their uncertainty. The air hung heavy, almost suffocating. Leaves spun in the stillness, branches cracked without a sound.

Just as Jack began to feel slightly unnerved, a sudden gust swept down the path, carrying a long feather that drifted into his outstretched palm.

The moment his fingers closed around it, his body went rigid. His knees gave out, and his eyes rolled back as he collapsed to the ground.

"No one has come for you, Emerson. They don't care about you like I do," the tall, lean woman said in a voice that dripped with maternal affection. Her words were soft, but there was an unsettling edge beneath the sweetness. "Trust in us, and we'll take care of you."

Her cool, smooth hand lingered on his cheek, brushing away the tension that seemed to cling to him.

"I have something for you," she whispered, her voice barely a breath, as she slid a long, slender package across the oak dining table.

Behind Emerson, the fire cast flickering shadows across the dim hall. The flames danced lazily, their warmth never touching the chill in the air. Emerson's pale fingers hovered for a moment, then trembled slightly as he reached out and took the package.

As he did, she turned and began to walk toward the fireplace, her heels clicking softly against the stone floor. Candlelight shimmered across the table's polished surface, throwing restless patterns on the walls.

"What is it?" Emerson asked, his voice low with awe. Despite the woman's unsettling presence, her sudden shift in demeanor didn't surprise him. Somehow, it felt inevitable.

She didn't turn around. "Open it and see, my love."

The soft crackle of parchment filled the space as Emerson peeled the paper back slowly, revealing the thin piece of wood nestled inside. His breath caught, a spark of childlike excitement igniting within him. Without thinking, he dashed to the fireplace and flung his arms around her gooselike neck in an exuberant, almost frantic embrace, his long fingers pressing into her skin.

"Your carriage awaits," she said with a sweet smile, her fingers adjusting the collar of his tunic. "Let's get you outside."

The words felt like a command more than a suggestion, and Emerson found himself following her without question, his mind clouded with a strange sense of yearning.

As they reached the door, she spoke again, her tone soft but unmistakably commanding.

"The moment we step beyond these walls, let go of the person you're speaking to now. We all don masks when the world looks on; we must hide our truths behind our carefully crafted façades. You understand this, don't you, my dear?"

Emerson nodded, though a strange unease twisted in his gut.

She smiled at him, the expression both knowing and secretive, before she pushed open the door.

A flood of bright, golden light poured in, blinding him for a moment, and as he stumbled forward into its warmth, he felt an intruder—a shadow in his mind—one he forced out just as the light swallowed him.

Chapter Sixteen

Follow the Feather-Clad Trail

"Did you have another vision?" Adina asked, not taking her eyes off him.

"Yes," Jack whispered, his eyes distant. "And it wasn't good."

They had been too late. The images from his vision played over and over in his mind. Emerson had betrayed them. He'd joined forces with the very ones threatening their worlds.

Jack couldn't fathom it. There had to be some mistake—some trick, some lie. He refused to believe it. It had to be a deception. A way to survive. A way to protect them.

"What happened?"

"I'm not sure. It was just flashes. I couldn't make sense of it all," Jack lied, the words tasting bitter on his tongue. He couldn't afford for anyone to doubt Emerson before he had the chance to confront him. He needed the truth. He had to believe Emerson was trapped, forced to make an impossible choice to survive. That was the only explanation Jack could accept. Emerson wouldn't betray them. He couldn't. *Could he?*

Adina watched him carefully, her gaze sharp. "Oh," she said softly, but her voice didn't carry the suspicion Jack feared. Jack knew she could tell he wasn't being honest, but she didn't press him.

"Well, we can't just stand here," she said, changing the subject. "Let's go to Dartmoor!" Adina howled, like they were heading off on some grand vacation.

Jack smiled.

"We'll also want to go over some basic spells I've learned. You'll need them. We have to blend in—but also be ready to move quickly and fight when we arrive."

"Okay," Jack muttered. He still couldn't shake the image of his friend—thinner, hollow-eyed, his once-bright gaze now tinged with a troubling red, like their first training day in Kaluna. Jack's stomach twisted, and his thoughts darkened with the memory of Emerson's uncontrollable rage.

Adina caught the subtle shift in his mood and offered him a soft, understanding smile. Without a word, she turned and started walking, her boots crunching softly over damp leaves as mist clung to the forest floor.

"So, if I take a guess, will you tell me what you saw in your vision?" Adina asked.

"I already told you—" Jack began, but she cut him off.

"You don't think I'm stupid enough to buy that hogwash, do you? Did they finally get to him?"

"Hogwash? Who says that?" Jack chuckled as the tension eased for a moment.

"Oh, suck it. I'm trying new things. Emerson would totally appreciate it," Adina said with a playful glint in her eye. Jack smiled despite himself—she was right, Emerson would.

"Seriously, though. Am I right?" she pressed.

"I think so, but it's hard to say for sure. The visions don't seem to follow any order, and there are huge gaps in between," Jack said.

"I figured as much." Her expression was sympathetic but firm. "Something is different about your power. You're strong, but something seems off."

"I'm not weak," Jack shot back.

"I literally said you're strong and that it doesn't have anything to do with your skill. Something is going on with it. The Pilfert even said that Ulysses did something unique with his stone. Maybe it affects the way you channel from it. Anyway," she said, watching Jack tense, realizing what it was he must be feeling. "Until we get that figured out, you should just trust in me a bit. I think I get the Mallory situation now." She paused as she looked directly into his eyes. "You're not used to leaning on others, but sometimes you just have to."

Jack remained quiet, her words lingering, unwelcome, but true.

"I just wanna say one last thing about Emerson. He's loyal, Jack. He was just put in a situation where he had to make a choice. He made a deal to save himself, but once he realizes we're still on his side and the Pilfert will protect him, he'll break that deal. I don't know exactly what you saw, but I do know he's wise and a survivor. Believe in him, Jack, just like you've been believing in me."

Jack frowned. "What do you mean?"

"You've trusted me to fly you over a vast body of water with who-knows-what lurking below. You've trusted me to lead you through this unfamiliar world, even though I don't know any more about it than you do. And you trusted me to heal you when you were at your weakest," Adina said.

"Well, first off, I was unconscious and didn't exactly have a say in that. And secondly: are you seriously telling me you don't know where we're going right now?" Jack asked, equal parts incredulous and relieved that she might be just as lost as he was.

"I know where we're going," she shot back, rolling her eyes. "But let's be real, Jack—I didn't exactly come here on vacation. I'm winging it just like you."

Jack paused, realizing just how much she had learned in such a short time. It was impressive, given she had only arrived a few days before him.

Adina sighed, her eyes distant for a moment. Jack noticed and, feeling playful, poked her gently in the side.

"Want to do some spell work?" he asked with a mischievous grin.

"No . . . well, yes," she replied, but her attention drifted as a long plume drifted across the soft earth ahead.

"What do you want to tell me?" Jack asked, sensing the change in her mood.

Adina's face darkened. "Never mind that for now. I'll tell you in a bit. Try holding this. Every time you've touched one of these, you've seen Emerson. Maybe it'll help."

Jack took the quill from her hand, his fingers closing around the smooth, pointed shaft. The moment he touched it, a familiar shift coursed through his senses. His brown eyes darkened to black, and his eyelids fluttered.

Adina hovered nearby, just in case. She watched as his body jolted, muscles tightening beneath his clothes. A second later, Jack snapped back with a sharp inhale, muttering a curse under his breath. His eyes had returned to their usual shade.

"What happened? Is everything okay?" Adina asked, her fingers flexing like she didn't know what to do with them.

"Everything's fine," Jack muttered, though the strain in his voice told a different story. "It was Emerson. The carriage from last night—it was him."

Adina's breath caught, eyes wide. "What? How do you know? Jack, why aren't your visions . . . visions?"

"I don't know," Jack snapped, frustration bubbling over. His hands clenched into fists. "This is bad, Adina. He could be anywhere now. We have to start over. All of this has been for nothing."

With a heavy grunt, he dropped to the ground, the crisp sounds of autumn surrounding them. The weight of failure settled hard on his shoulders.

"At least we don't have to go into Dartmoor anymore," Adina offered, her tone brightening despite it all. "That's a relief. Our plan was a disaster—I was just pretending it wasn't."

Jack gave a tired, crooked smile. "So, we turn back?"

"Exactly," she said with a spark of enthusiasm. "Can you try reaching out to his mind without the feathers? Maybe that will work . . ."

Jack shook his head. "This whole thing was a waste. We could've stayed with the Pilfert—been safe, like Addison and Stefani. I shouldn't have dragged us out here. I'm sorry—"

"We took a chance," Adina said, cutting him off gently but firmly. "Don't apologize. What if Emerson hadn't been released, and no one came to find him? We did the right thing."

She offered her hand to help him up. Jack took it, pulling himself to his feet and brushing off his clothes. But instead of letting go, he held on.

"What are you doing, Jack?" she asked, raising an eyebrow as he placed her hand into his.

"I want to hold your hand," Jack said, like it was the simplest thing in the world.

Adina blinked, taken aback. "Jack Hackley, are you hitting on me?"

Jack stumbled, suddenly flustered. "Oh . . . uh, if you don't want to . . ."

Adina's voice softened, "Let's just walk, Jack. I've never held hands with a guy before. I want it to actually mean something when I do."

Jack grinned, his earlier frustration slipping away. "Seriously? Never?" he called, hurrying to catch up.

"Guys don't really look at me like that, Jack." Her words carried a quiet honesty, but Jack found them hard to believe. Still, he didn't press her.

"Now come on, let's go get Emerson back," Adina said, shifting the conversation with ease.

They walked side by side, lightheartedly teasing one another about the absurdities of their journey. Jack tried to steer the topic toward Adina's love life—or rather, the lack thereof—but each time, she deftly swerved the conversation in another direction, a playful deflection in her voice. They walked happily for half an hour, the road stretching out before them like an open invitation, until a sudden, creeping shadow surrounded them.

Adina looked up, narrowing her eyes as three women swept across the cloudy sky. Two had hair as red as fresh blood; the third streaked past with golden locks.

"Jack, we need to get off the road." Her voice was urgent, but Jack didn't respond—his body had already collapsed to the ground, wracked with violent tremors.

"Dammit, not now . . ." Adina muttered under her breath, panic rising as she scrambled to grab his convulsing form. Her strength was fueled by fear as she dragged him into the underbrush, the leaves and dirt scraping against them.

She hid them just in time as the three women landed lightly on the road, their movements eerie in the quiet of the forest. They immediately began searching the area, splitting off in different directions. Their noses flared, sniffing the air, and their lips murmured dark incantations.

"It smells like the boy the master has already captured. It may be him or another one of the Kids of Destiny, but the master no longer needs them," the tallest said, her voice sickly sweet. Adina couldn't bring herself to look at her.

"Come. We have other orders." With that, the women took off into the sky without another word.

Adina waited a beat before lowering her hand, dispelling the protective shield she'd summoned around them.

"What did you see?" she asked, her voice hoarse.

"Just snow. Snow everywhere. I couldn't see a thing." Jack's voice was strained, his chest still heaving from the seizure.

"Do you think he could be in the Sabana Mountains?" Adina asked, trying to make sense of the fragmented vision. "After all, that's where his stone is. Maybe Akuramundo released him to retrieve it?"

"I don't know. Maybe," Jack replied, ignoring Adina's suggestion.

They decided it was safer to avoid the road and continue through the trees, cloaked by Adina's charm. Their movements were swift and careful, the occasional rustle of leaves the only sign of their passing. Unseen creatures stirred in the shadows, sniffing the air or pausing mid-step, confused by the sound of motion where no figures could be seen. Curiosity crackled in the underbrush—but none of the animals dared to venture closer.

"What's that?" Jack asked, pointing toward the east as Adina let down her shield for a moment of respite. She was clearly starting to feel the drain of magic pulling at her limbs—they'd already spent most of the day traipsing through the woods, uncertain of where to go next. They'd only paused briefly to share some leftovers and a handful of berries they'd found near a stream.

Their conversations kept circling back to the same question: what to do next. Jack had tried again and again to reach Emerson's mind, but each attempt felt like slamming into a wall. Even the whistle had failed—but deep down, they had known it would. The Pilfert had warned them the day O'Keen was attacked that its call could only carry so far.

Ahead of them stood a wall of weathered stone, half-hidden among the trees, surrounding a crumbling tower that reached several stories high. The structure looked out of place—ancient and forlorn in the midst of this desolate part of the forest. Broken statues, worn with age, had become one with the foliage, like forgotten remnants of a once-vibrant place.

"It looks like an old watchtower," Adina mused as they approached the wall. Jack effortlessly hoisted himself over the stone, then turned to help Adina.

The moment they crossed into the enclosure, they were met with an unexpected sight. The space inside, overrun with nature, thrummed with life. Wildflowers in brilliant hues tangled together with dense shrubs, and vines had completely overtaken the ancient stone, swaying gently in the wind. Tiny creatures, their eyes large and curious, clung to the vines, scrambling like children at play.

Jack stepped closer to investigate one of the creatures—a strange little being with two long, spindly arms and a stout body that lacked legs. Its tiny face was adorned with four marble-sized eyes, two nostrils nestled between them, and a wide, toothy grin that was oddly adorable.

Jack wasn't scared—in fact, he found himself smiling back as the creature flopped around, climbing the vines with a kind of joyful abandon.

Adina pulled out her canteen and handed it to Jack. "We're near the edge of the woods, Jack. You can see the road that leads into Drysmian just a few yards ahead," she said, pointing toward the south. "Let's rest for a minute. I'm starting to feel the burn."

"Okay," Jack said reluctantly, still unwilling to fully abandon their search until Emerson was found. But even he could sense that they needed a break.

"So . . . this morning, when you sounded shocked about me believing in you and your skills," Jack said, his voice low, careful. "I wanted to ask you something."

Adina didn't flinch. "Ask away," she said, her breezy voice at odds with her wary eyes.

"It just . . . it sounded like no one's ever said that to you before." He hesitated. "Don't take this the wrong way, but . . . have you ever had a real friend?"

"I did . . . once," she said flatly. "But it ended like these things always do—my mom decided who I was supposed to be and wouldn't let me see him anymore."

She glanced down, her voice tightening.

"She said that whenever I was around him, I acted like a feral little boy. No one loves feral little boys. So I had to be softer. Prettier. Quieter."

Jack said nothing.

"That went for her love too." Then, mood shifting completely, she looked up with a hollow smile. "So I learned to shut up, smile wide, and disappear when I wasn't spoken to."

She rolled her eyes and laughed. "God, she was awful. I quickly learned to dress like a funeral and bite back. Upside: no one asks you to twirl in a dress if they think you'll bite."

Jack looked confused as she said this but didn't interrupt.

"And now here you are, chipping away at a perfectly good wall I spent years mortaring with eyeliner and spite. I don't know if I can forgive you for this."

"I didn't mean to—"

"You're fine. I'm joking," Adina interrupted, her voice steady again. "But I won't lie, it's not something I'm used to, and I don't know how to truly feel about it yet."

The silence between them thickened, and for a moment, the noise of the forest seemed distant. Jack wanted to reach for her hand again, but didn't.

"I'm gonna tell you something I've been holding in since Willow Wisp," Adina said, her voice barely above a whisper. "But don't get all soft on me, okay? I don't want your pity."

Jack didn't say anything—just held out his pinky.

She hesitated, then linked hers with his. Her grip was tentative at first, then firmer—like she needed it more than she wanted to admit.

"You don't have to tell me," Jack said gently. "Only if you're ready."

"I am." She drew in a breath, her gaze flicking to his. "I just need you to listen. No fixing. No flinching. Just . . . listen."

"I can do that," he said, steady and warm. "I've got you."

She nodded, her chest rising and falling with a steadying breath.

"Okay," she whispered. She locked eyes with him, her voice quieter now, almost tentative. "I've never had anyone in my life like you, Jack. I've never told anyone this story." Another deep breath. She seemed to brace herself. "Do you remember how I was gone from school for several weeks in March?"

Jack frowned, thinking for a moment. "Not really," he admitted, shaking his head. "Sorry."

"Of course not," she replied, her voice soft and knowing. "Well, I was . . . in the hospital."

Jack gasped dramatically, hand flying to his mouth like he'd just witnessed a royal scandal.

Adina's eyes narrowed. She jabbed him in the chest. "Don't joke about it. Not yet." But even as she said it, a tiny chuckle slipped out.

"I'm sorry, I'm sorry!" Jack grinned, then softened. "But alright . . . hospital. Why were you there?"

Her smile vanished. "I tried to kill myself."

The words landed like stones. Jack's face dropped, all the air seeming to leave his chest. Whatever he'd expected, it wasn't that. In the fading light, his expression turned solemn—guilt written plainly across it.

"Don't look at me like that," Adina said quickly, voice sharp. "I told you—no sympathy. Forget it. I shouldn't have said anything."

"No—wait." He extended his pinky again. "I'm not judging. I'm not pitying. I just . . . didn't know. That's all."

Adina hesitated, then wrapped her pinky around his again. This time, her grip tightened, and she held on longer than before.

"There's no breaking the sacred bond of a pinky promise," she muttered with a crooked smile. "But if you get weird about this, I reserve the right to punch you."

Jack smiled faintly. "Deal."

She took a long breath. Her shoulders rose, then fell, as if shedding armor.

"Ever since I can remember, my mom's tried to turn me into some porcelain little princess. When I was a kid, she'd make me watch Cinderella over and over, even though all I wanted to do was watch Power Rangers. She'd curl my hair every morning, make me wear those ugly dresses to school, and parade me around like I was her delicate angel—the daughter she thought she deserved. She treated me as if I was a doll she could pose, not a person.

"When I turned eight, the pageants started. Dance recitals. Talent shows. Hours in front of mirrors, being trained how to smile on command." Her voice turned bitter. "The other girls loved it—drowning in glitter and competition. But not me. I wanted to climb trees and chase thunderstorms. Not stand under stage lights next to six-year-olds with fake lashes and spray tans while moms stuffed their dresses like it was some twisted costume party."

She looked up at Jack, a flicker of emotion crossing her face. "It felt like I was being erased. Like there was a 'right' version of me that got rewarded—and whoever I actually was . . . didn't make the cut.

"Still, I did okay—or I thought I did. I never won the crown, but I was usually a runner-up. My mom played it humble in front of others, but behind closed doors, she'd blame me for being 'too chubby' or 'too loud,' and then it was back to strict diets in preparation for next year's pageant. When I turned nine, we were right back at it. Thankfully, that year was a little better.

"A boy named David, who was a year younger than me, joined my dance class. We became best friends right away. After class, Mom would drop us off at his house, and for the first time,

I got to experience what it was like to actually be a kid. We'd play kickball, four-square, tag—anything we could think of. On rainy days, we'd play video games. I would always take a bath there, just to get myself clean before my mom showed up. I knew the rules—dirty meant grounding. And I hated it.

"I even made David's family lie. Told them to say we'd spent the whole day rehearsing routines. They didn't get it, but they did it anyway."

Jack watched as she paused, steadying herself. The words were spilling out so quickly, but he didn't care. He wanted to drown in them—wanted to take away whatever pain she had been carrying alone for so long.

"Then, during one of my pageants, I looked out and saw David sitting in the front row with his dad and brothers. I had just finished my first two rounds, and it was finally time for a break. The other girls were gossiping with their mothers, but all I could think about was the park across the street."

Her voice lightened briefly, almost nostalgic.

"When my mom went off to schmooze with the other pageant moms, I ran. I played until I forgot the time. Forgot the hairspray, the fake smile, the schedule. When I got back, I was caked in mud, ribbons falling out of my hair. My mom was pacing backstage, fuming that I was filthy. We had no time to clean me up as I barely made my number."

Adina looked at Jack now, something darker flickering in her eyes.

"But I didn't care. I ran straight past her and onto that stage. Muddy dress and all. I did my dance. And the crowd went wild. Like it was some big dramatic entrance. An art piece of some sort." She let out a short laugh. "And honestly, it was the first time I felt like me on that stage.

"But backstage? My mom lost it. Said I humiliated her. Told me I wasn't allowed to see David or his family again. Said I acted like a wild animal. Unladylike. Embarrassing. She pulled me from pageants right then and there. After that, we barely spoke. She fed me, but that was about it. I basically raised myself.

"I was twelve when I stopped wearing bright colors. You don't see much black in beauty pageants.

"We moved to Brookville when I was seventeen. She'd met this guy, Ed. He had a daughter—Ana. And Ana was . . . perfect. Porcelain skin, perfect hair, fake-sweet voice. Cheer team royalty. She was the daughter my mom had always wanted.

"I became the wallpaper. I could do whatever I wanted, come and go—no one cared. The only rule in the house was: don't bother Ana. That was the only time they even remembered I existed."

Her jaw clenched as she gave a tired shrug.

"Home was unbearable. School wasn't better. No friends. Failing grades. Constant bullying. I stopped caring. About everything."

Then, calmly, as if narrating someone else's story: "That's when I started cutting."

She rolled up her sleeve. Jack kept his face still, though it took every effort to do so. He had to honor the promise.

"The emotional pain was too much, so I turned it into something I could see—something I could control. It was the only time I felt. The only time I could shut out the noise. The loneliness. The nothing. I didn't know how bad it was until I tried to die."

She pulled her sleeve back down—casual, practiced.

"I've worked through it. Mostly. But it was hell. I remember thinking . . . if I disappeared, who'd even notice? Who would care?"

She looked at Jack.

"No one did. So, I guess I was right."

Jack had been silent through it all, completely absorbed. And then, as if pulled by something beyond him, he reached out and gently took her by the shoulders.

"You weren't invisible," he said, voice steady but thick with emotion. "I noticed—"

But Adina pressed a finger to his lips, silencing him.

"You already said you didn't even realize I was gone when I was in the hospital."

Her tone wasn't accusing—just tired.

"It's okay. You didn't know me yet."

Jack tried to offer a smile, but it faltered before it could reach his lips. The words he wanted to give her were stuck—lodged somewhere between guilt and awe. He had noticed . . . but way too late.

Adina looked away for a moment, gathering herself, and then she spoke again, her voice barely above a whisper.

"One day, after my mom came home with bags overflowing with new clothes for Ana, but not a single thing for me . . . I just couldn't take it anymore. I went outside, sat on the back stairs, and cried. I heard her go into her room, completely oblivious to the girl she was supposed to love, sitting there, broken."

She paused, her lips trembling as the weight of her words hung in the air.

"And that's when I decided—I was done with it all."

Her eyes darkened as she relived the moment.

"I grabbed the saw from the garage, and I went straight for Ana's tire swing. I hacked at it until it fell, cutting through the rope right above the knot that held it in place."

She inhaled sharply, then looked up at Jack, her gaze distant.

"I had been researching this for months by that point, and when the tire fell to the ground, I made my noose. I climbed the tree, wrapped the rope around the branch several times, then slid the rope around my . . ."

Jack shifted uncomfortably, his voice low.

"Yeah, I think I know what happens next—you don't have to finish that part. Who found you?"

Adina hesitated, her eyes far away. "I'm not sure. I heard a scream just before my fingers slipped from the branch, and the next thing I remember is waking up in the back of an ambulance." She paused, her voice soft but steady. "I recovered in the hospital, then was transferred to a psych ward. I spent hours staring at walls, listening to the schizophrenic guy screaming down the hall, hating the world for thinking I was anything like those people. They had real mental illnesses. I just had a lousy rope around my neck."

Her gaze sharpened, a quiet fierceness there. "But I never let myself sink that low again, no matter how lonely I felt. I kept working with my therapists, my counselors. I found a new purpose, a new fire inside me. I burned and rose like a phoenix. . . from ashes to eyeliner and a big ol' middle finger to the past."

Jack reached for her hand—slow, gentle, as if asking permission. She glanced down, then sideways at him, meeting his eyes. For a moment, the storm inside her seemed to settle.

She gave him a half-smile. "Guess I'm more flame than funeral now."

Jack didn't speak. He just held her gaze, silently stunned by what she had just given him. She had opened a door no one else had ever seen behind. And somehow, she had done it with both fire and grace.

He wanted to tell her that. To say something worthy of what she'd shared.

But all he could think was, *What story do I have that could possibly compare?*

Adina stood and brushed the dirt from the dark pants of her Dartmoor disguise. Jack followed, and without thinking, reached for her hand. This time, she didn't pull away. She let him lace his fingers through hers.

They walked together, side by side, down the quiet path through the darkening trees. When they emerged onto the road, the sky above was stretched wide and streaked with deep blue, the fading suns casting fire behind the drifting clouds.

After a while, Adina broke the silence. "What are we doing?"

Jack instantly dropped her hand, feeling suddenly foolish. "I don't . . . uh, sorry."

"You didn't have to let go," she said, her voice soft.

Jack turned his face away, discomfort creeping up his neck.

"You like me," she said. Not a question. Her tone was bold, unfiltered, and unapologetic.

"I—what? No. I mean, I still—wait, what?"

Emma's face flickered in Jack's thoughts. But it was quickly eclipsed by other images: Adina flying barefoot through moonlight during their training, hair streaming like smoke behind her, eyes lit up with something fierce and free; her sharp smile; the way she looked at him when she wasn't pretending not to care.

"Adina, you can't just say something like—"

Before he could finish his sentence, her body collided into his—her hair a wild curtain of shadow as she smashed her lips to his. Her tongue punched through his mouth like Ogof in its cave, all sudden and aggressive, and just as terrifying. Her arms wrapped around his waist like she was trying to hold herself together, and for a second, Jack lost his breath.

"What are you doing?" he asked, pulling back, dazed.

Adina's face flushed red. "I . . . I thought—" Her voice trailed into a whisper. "I'm sorry. I've never kissed anyone before."

Jack blinked. "Yeah . . . that was obvious."

She looked like she wanted to dissolve into the ground, but Jack stepped closer.

"Hey," he said, tilting her chin up. "It's okay." He cupped her cheek, steady now. "This is how you kiss someone."

Then he kissed her, slow and gentle, like he was learning her instead of taking anything—as if he understood everything she hadn't said. Adina's leg lifted slightly, her body leaning into his as if gravity had finally picked a side. The wind tugged at her hair, curling it around them like a dark halo. The forest blurred as time forgot itself.

The kiss deepened with the weight they both now carried. When they finally pulled apart, they were breathless.

They simply stood there, forehead to forehead, eyes locked in a world that felt completely their own.

Then Adina laughed—a real, bright, colorful laugh that cracked the last layer of tension between them. It filled the road, echoed against the trees, and wrapped around Jack like sunlight.

"Oh look, we made it out alive," Adina said, voice playful.

The moment was over before Jack could even begin to process the storm unraveling inside him. He still loved Emma—that hadn't changed, wouldn't change—but whatever had just happened with Adina felt like the beginning of something different, beautiful, yet terrifying.

Then, a breeze swept across the road, carrying with it a single feather, which twirled gently before landing intentionally on Jack's boot.

"Well," she said, hopeful this would give Jack a full, accurate vision of where Emerson currently was. "Pick it up."

He reached down and picked up the feather, thankful for the distraction, the forward motion, anything to outrun the thoughts he didn't have the tools to fix and the guilt he didn't have time to feel.

"No one even came to find me!" Emerson's voice cracked as he stormed through the snow, each step pounding into the frozen earth. Powder burst beneath his boots like shards of glass, scattering into the wind.

"I could be dead—rotting—and I bet not a single soul would care. Not even him!" He spat the last word like venom, his pace quickening, fury burning with every step.

"Gara was right. No one cares about me. They only care about what I can do. That little fur-ball—it doesn't want me. It wants my power. That's all."

He threw himself backward into the snow, his hands flaming as they tore into the ice. Fistfuls of snow flew into the air, vaporizing into steam the instant they left his grasp. A roar tore from his chest as he screamed into the storm. In response, the ground trembled beneath him, as if his anger had awakened something deep within the earth. The sound of distant drums echoed—the rhythm unsettling and heavy, reverberating all around him.

The pale boy turned his head, his wild hair swooping over his eyes and blurring his vision. He swiped at it, but before he could clear the way, several strong hands gripped him. Without warning, they lifted him off the ground, and the world around him faded to black.

Jack's body jerked as if pulled from a nightmare, his breath coming in sharp gasps.

"They've got him!" he shouted, eyes wide, springing to his feet. "They have him . . . the trolls . . . Akuramundo. He's really angry, Adina. He doesn't think we've been looking for him . . . and the trolls—the trolls have him. They took him, just like they took you!"

Adina's face drained of color as she grabbed Jack's hand, already pulling him with her.

"We have to get to Sabana now! We need to tell the Pilfert. Do you think you can break into Addison's mind? Control it, like you did during training?"

Jack hesitated for a heartbeat, his breath unsteady.

"I . . . I don't know. He's so far away. I think I can only do that when I'm close to—"

"Jack, now is not the time for excuses," Adina snapped. She halted abruptly, spinning to face him with fierce intensity. "You can do this. Make Addison tell the Pilfert that Emerson has been captured. That he's in the Sabana Mountains. We need their help. You have to concentrate."

Jack closed his eyes, his face scrunching in concentration. He tried to focus, reaching out with his mind, pushing past the distance, but the connection felt strained.

Suddenly—CRACK! A deafening burst of thunder split the sky. A blinding flash of lightning lit up the darkness, and Jack's body convulsed, as if the storm had struck him directly.

He was on his back, soaked to the bone, the rain coming down in sheets. His chest heaved with exertion.

"Shit!" He heard Adina curse from somewhere in the distance, her voice barely audible over the howling wind.

His body trembled violently, every muscle screaming as if the very air were too heavy to breathe.

As Jack's body stilled, he found himself lying in the middle of a dirt road, its once-dry surface now slick and coated in sticky mud. Adina's face was drawn with worry, and the protective shield she had conjured had dissipated, weakened by her concern.

A carriage loomed in the distance, its wheels sinking into the thickened sludge, sending clumps of mud flying with every turn. A lamp on its side swung violently in the wind, the flame flickering dangerously, threatening to die out.

"We have to get out of here, Jack—quick! Before that carriage sees us," Adina urged, her voice tight. She leaned over him, her damp hair sticking to her pale cheeks like a matted mop.

Jack scrambled to his feet, and together, they dropped low, running through the grass, hoping the rain and the smudged windows of the carriage would keep them hidden.

"I'm going to fly us out of here," Adina said, her voice determined. "I know we're not safe in the air, but we're not safe here, either. Did you manage to get into his mind?" she asked quickly, not slowing her pace as she pulled a silver root from her bag, replacing the whistle she had used moments ago in a desperate attempt to reach their minds. Even though it failed earlier she felt it was worth a try.

"No," Jack muttered, his face flushed with embarrassment.

Adina bit off a piece of the root, looking at Jack with concern.

"I didn't even have time. When did all this happen?" he asked, pushing his damp curls back from his forehead, gesturing to the dark clouds looming overhead.

"You were out for at least five minutes," Adina shot back, eyes wide.

"Five minutes? I didn't—"

"Now, put your arms around me and try again while we're flying. You've got this," she encouraged, smiling at him through the storm.

She raised her arms, and with a sudden, graceful motion, kicked off the ground. The two ascended together, the freezing rain whipping against their skin.

Jack closed his eyes, summoning every ounce of focus he could muster. His mind stretched, and the world around him melted into a sweeping panorama: snowy hills, a chilling lake, shadowed tombs veiled by towering mountains, distant villages—each scene flashing by in an instant.

At last, he broke through a towering glass gate and found himself floating above a bustling street. The cobbled road was lined with stone gargoyles, water fountains, and elegant shops. In the heart of the street stood a magnificent glass building shaped like a tree. A boy with fox-red hair stood by a window on one of its upper floors, the structure jutting out like a branch. He wore a long coat with vivid, lilac pants, his back to Jack.

Jack concentrated, pushing everything from his mind except the messy hair in front of him.

With a sudden pop, Jack slipped inside.

He saw the Pilfert seated by a roaring fire, the warm glow casting long shadows across the pristine, white room. A golden-framed picture of an elegant family rested atop a table beside a delicate wooden chair.

Addison's voice broke the silence.

"Listen up, guys. Emerson's been captured . . . again . . ."
His eyes rolled slightly as the last word slipped from his lips.
"The trolls of Sabana have—"

"Emerson was captured by Gara. We all know that. Jack
and Adina are looking for him," Stefani said, her voice
cutting in from the shadows—clipped and calm in that way
only a fed-up sibling could manage.

She moved to stand beside the Pilfert, and Addison's
jaw nearly dropped. She was more beautiful than Jack had
ever seen her: a simple purple dress, a thigh-high slit, straps
winding around her neck, and golden fabric tied around her
waist. Bangles of various colors climbed her arm.

"Didn't you hear me say he's been captured again?"
Addison's voice was tight. "This is Jack speaking right now,
so just listen. He was released from Dartmoor . . . well, I'm
not sure when, because my visions have been all over the
place. We need to talk about that," he added, turning to
the Pilfert. "Point is, Emerson's captured again, and it's not
looking good. We need your help."

The Pilfert stood, reaching for the staff hanging above the
mantle on golden hooks that emerged from the wall.

"Jack, why have you closed your mind to me?" the Pilfert
asked, its voice trembling. "I haven't been able to see inside
your head since your dinner at Drysmian. We believed you
were dead until I spoke with Osric."

"I . . . what? I haven't done anything! Just meet me and
Adina in the Sabana Mountains. We can explain everything
once we have Emerson back."

The Pilfert nodded grimly—and then, in an instant,
the image around Jack began to swirl. The colors blurred
together, and with a lurch, his eyes snapped open.

They were still flying through the torrential rain,
skimming over stormy waters.

"They're on their way!" Jack shouted above the roar of thunder and howling wind.

"Excellent," Adina murmured, her voice strained with exhaustion. Jack wrapped his arms around her more tightly.

"We're almost there," she added, her voice trailing off as the rain turned to sleet. The orange sun was peeking beneath the dark clouds, but the heavy storm was pulling it back into the earth's shadow.

Jack's thoughts flickered to Emerson—how abandoned he must feel, just like Adina had once felt with her mother. He leaned forward and pressed a soft kiss to the back of her neck. Her cool skin sent a shiver through him, but the warmth of her body slowly seeped in, chasing away the bite of the cold.

"You're amazing, you know that?" Jack whispered, as they landed on the icy edge of the mountain.

She giggled—a soft, almost unnatural sound—and Jack felt a familiar knot of unease twist in his gut.

"Yeah, I do," she recovered quickly. "Do you know when the Pilfert will be arriving?"

"I may be short in stature, but I assure you, I'm not invisible. I'm right behind you," said a familiar voice.

Adina turned, rushing toward the Pilfert and bending to squeeze it affectionately, but it held out a hand. She hesitated, remembering the Pilfert didn't like its fur to be touched.

Its bushy eyebrows furrowed in alarm as it looked at Jack. Addison stood next to it, grinning.

"I must go. Stefani is waiting," the Pilfert said, and vanished in a blink.

"You two look like hell." Addison grinned, embracing Jack before giving Adina an awkward pat on the back.

"I may not have had the luxury of five-star hotels like you, but I'm pretty sure I still look better than you," Jack shot back, his bitterness barely masked behind playful words.

"I tried to get Stefani to come with me right after you left, but she refused," Addison explained. "When the Pilfert said it wasn't coming after you, I really . . ." His voice faltered.

"It doesn't matter. I shouldn't have—"

"OK, Jack, just because Emma isn't around doesn't mean you should stop looking after yourself," Stefani's cool voice interrupted.

Jack smiled. She winked, and he nodded, silently appreciating the connection.

"We'll have time to catch up later. For now, we need to get to Emerson," the Pilfert said, cutting through the conversation.

They trudged through the snow until they reached the cold circle of evergreens atop the hill. The Pilfert conjured a small fire, and they huddled around it, shivering.

The Pilfert paced before them, deep in thought, as silence stretched around them, broken only by the harsh winds.

"Jack, you say you saw Emerson captured by the trolls?" it asked, eyes narrowing. Jack nodded grimly.

"I don't believe this is a coincidence. Akuramundo has his men in these hills, waiting to steal the stone from Emerson the moment he possesses it."

"So, this is some kind of trap?" Jack asked.

"Oh yes. Akuramundo knows much more than I realized," the Pilfert replied, voice darkening. "We must ensure Emerson keeps the stone—and that he doesn't hand it over to Akuramundo's forces. We also need to be prepared for an attack. Emerson is angry; he's been lied to. My insider tells me that, though he faced cruelty in Dartmoor, he left glowing—as if he had been reprieved. The parting was . . . amicable."

Jack glanced nervously at Adina, who shook her head in disbelief.

"As you know," the Pilfert continued, "the Treaty of Alors has complicated relations between man and troll, especially after Gridlybone was forced upon them by the kingdom of

Lebendor. She was placed at the border to guard a treasure that resides within their territory."

"Wait—if we already know Emerson will slay the dragon, why does he need our help?" Adina asked, frowning.

"Because Emerson must not slay the dragon," the Pilfert replied, as if explaining something simple to a child. "The prophecy I've shared with you all speaks of a weapon—one that will change the course of history. It will be won by the son of a Guardian. That weapon is the dragon. Emerson is being misled. We must remind him of the plan: Don't slay the dragon; retrieve the stone."

A heavy silence fell, the weight of its words sinking in. The Pilfert paced restlessly, muttering to itself.

"I believe Emerson and Gridlybone will share a connection, but it will be weak," it continued. "Though the blood of Hernando runs strong in Emerson, he'll be tired from his journey. We must heighten his senses, strengthen him . . ."

"The roots," Adina blurted. She fumbled inside the sack around her neck, pulling out long, sinuous silver plants.

"Ms. Maynard?" the Pilfert's voice was filled with quiet awe.

"I flew back to Kaluna the night we were attacked in the woods and asked the tree for these," Adina explained. "It let me dig them up, and you were right—it was harder than I thought, but I managed."

The Pilfert's eyes lit up.

"Brilliant. This is exactly what we need." It clapped its hands. "Now, we will need someone to walk among the trolls as an equal . . . disguised, of course. Ah . . ."

Suddenly, the sound of a gong rang through the forest, followed by the shattering of glass. Jack's stomach twisted in fear as the Pilfert turned toward him, its yellow eyes alight with a strange spark.

"Come here, Jack," it said softly. "You're our best chance."

Chapter Seventeen

The Trolls' Sacrifice

"Why do I have to do this?" Jack whined, tugging the leathered shirt he had been wearing from around his shoulders and tossing it onto the frozen ground.

"Because, with that stupid look you always have on your face, you'll fit right in," Addison teased, earning a crude hand gesture in response from Jack.

"The magic I'll be using to transfigure you is rare, and it will be draining," the Pilfert explained, its voice serious despite the levity in the air. "Shapeshifting is not only difficult, but it's also illegal and incredibly dangerous. Taking someone's identity entirely is a heinous crime—almost impossible to master. But changing into a creature, like an avatar, is less so. Once this transformation is complete, you will temporarily be a troll.

"After the transformation, you'll be able to speak and understand their language. No magic can distinguish their primitive dialect. However, we also need someone who can telepathically communicate with Emerson. Since I've been unable to enter his mind, but your bond is still strong, it has to be you.

"Don't worry—the enchantment will only last a few hours. Stand up, Jack. You might want to take off your pants too. This robe should fit over you afterward."

With a wave of its staff, the Pilfert conjured what looked like a large, furry tent from the branches above.

"Now put this over you and undress."

Jack placed the large canopy of fabric around his shoulders, leaving just the top of his head exposed. He kicked around inside his new ensemble, searching for the bag in which he could stow the rest of his clothes.

Adina moved to assist, but Jack stumbled back, eyes wide.

"This is insane. You can't honestly expect this to work," Jack exclaimed as he pulled off his pants and shoved them deep into his bag. He stood shivering in the cold, the chilly wind breathing against his neck. "I don't know anything about these creatures . . . What if I make a mistake and they realize that I'm . . ."

"Oh, shut up and take your pants off," Adina demanded.

"I already did. You want to check?" Jack shot back with a wink.

Adina rolled her eyes, visibly exasperated. "I can't believe my first kiss was with a child."

"You two kissed?" Addison exclaimed.

"Jack, how could you? What about Emma?" Stefani asked sharply, peering at the small bit of Jack's face that was exposed from under the canopy.

Jack sighed, his tone flat. "How can I cheat on someone I'll never see again, Stefani?"

"Enough," the Pilfert snapped, cutting off any further discussion. "We can't waste any more time. Emerson needs us. Now, on the count of three . . ."

It lifted its staff high, and before Jack could even process what was happening, the world seemed to collapse inward.

Pain seared through his body. It felt as if someone had ripped off his head and was slamming hot coals down his neck. They were burning him from the inside out. His arms began to stretch as they pulled him down to the ground, and his blood transformed into cement. His skin began to rip, and no sooner had his raw muscles been exposed than greenish-gray scabs began to cover them.

He fell to his knees in the furry brown toga, screaming in agony and clawing at the ground as his body morphed. Then, just as quickly as it had begun, the pain dissipated.

Jack staggered to his feet, gasping for air. He was taller now by at least five feet. He looked down at his broad, callused palms, each nearly the size of his mom's breakfast griddle; his thick, olive-colored fingers twitched awkwardly, resembling overcooked sausages as he flexed them. He ran a hand over the mangy fur throw clinging to one shoulder, draped across his chest like a toga that hung just above a pair of knobby, bulging knees.

Addison gave him an appraising look, as if admiring a painting in a museum.

"Yeah, see? That dumb look really ties the whole thing together," he said, as he framed Jack's dumbfounded expression with his fingers.

Jack bent down, his massive head now level with Addison. He tried to speak but only grunted in frustration.

"Ugh, dude. Did you brush your tooth with Colgate dog shit?"

Adina stifled a laugh, but the Pilfert wasn't amused.

"Adina," it said, gently, with an edge of command. "Jack's right, too much could go wrong with just him. I think you should take on the same guise. Go together, and it will be easier to blend in. If things go south, at least you'll have each other to get out safely."

"Wait, why can't I do it?" Addison piped up, his voice suddenly eager. "Jack and I could—"

"No," the Pilfert interjected, raising a hand to silence him. "You'll stay with me. You're more useful on the sidelines. We need our stronger magical forces inside the trolls' domain. We can monitor and intervene if needed."

It hesitated, eyes flicking to Jack. "Sorry, Adina, but I also need you take your clothes off."

Jack's oversized face split into a wide grin as he looked down at Adina from his new height. She looked mortified, quickly turning away and tugging at her shirt.

Before she could pull it off, the Pilfert conjured a tall velvet tent around her, its sides flapping in the frigid wind.

Jack gestured dramatically at the enclosure and then pointed at himself several times, grunting vehemently. The Pilfert gave him a wild-eyed look.

Addison chuckled. "I think he wants to know why you didn't do that for him."

"Because we all know you don't mind showing off your body—or sharing it, apparently," Stefani remarked coolly, folding her arms across her chest.

Jack shot her a glare, which she returned, a challenge in her eyes.

The Pilfert remained impervious to their commentary, already deep in concentration as it cast the enchantment over Adina.

Adina's screams filled the air, but only for a few seconds before her new troll body began to stretch and grow, breaking free of the small, purple tent. Like Jack, she now wore a brown, fitted toga that clung to her new form.

"How do I look?" she asked Jack, her voice wavering with nervousness.

"Hideous," Jack replied bluntly.

The two new trolls stared down at the Pilfert, who was practically bouncing with excitement beneath them. Stefani and Addison stood behind them, mouths agape, stunned at the sight of their transformed friends. The clearing now rumbled with low, guttural grunts, which vibrated through them all.

"You two look excellent," the Pilfert said, grinning ear to ear. "Now, the task ahead of you is simple: slip the roots to Emerson when no one's looking, but make sure he knows it's you. Do whatever it takes to ensure he eats them. You cannot risk him thinking it's anyone else," it added, its tone taking on a more serious edge. "The enchantment will only last a few hours, so time is of the essence. Now go. We'll be waiting for you on the cliff above the hollow."

Without another word, the Pilfert vanished with Stefani in tow.

Jack exchanged a quick, purposeful glance with Addison before grabbing Adina's chubby, stubby hand.

"Let's do this," Jack grumbled, a strange mix of determination and discomfort in his voice as he pulled Adina through the dense foliage.

The walk didn't take long thanks to their newly elongated legs, which gave them both an awkward, lumbering gait. Jack's heart sank as they reached the clearing—right where their journey had begun, the same field where Jerica had saved them. Now it was their turn to do the saving.

The two trolls trudged across the soggy grass, passing the large tent Jack had noticed a few days before. Ahead of them, a new, larger tent had been erected near the center of the field. This one looked more ceremonial, and Jack's heart raced as he realized what it might mean.

Then, a memory long buried surfaced: a rainy Father's Day, sitting by the window, staring out at the yard and dreaming of playing ball with his dad. His mother had come in with two circus tickets as a surprise, and the joy he'd felt then surged back through him — only now it was shadowed by the weight of the moment.

He paused, caught in the memory, until a tug on his arm pulled him from his thoughts. Adina was already creeping toward the back of the tent.

"Where are you going?" Jack called after her.

"We have to get the roots to Emerson. We don't know how much time he has left. Stay quiet or you'll get us noticed," Adina whispered, pulling back the tent flap just enough to peer inside.

Her breath caught as she saw the interior.

Inside the tent stood an army of large, suited trolls, all wearing matching brown togas that crossed their chests and hung low around their midriffs.

"Jack . . . if we go in, there's a strong chance they'll figure us out. Please, just follow my lead," Adina hissed under her breath as she dropped the flap.

Jack, his body heavy in his troll skin, reached for her. He pulled Adina into an embrace—his large, awkward arms curling around her smaller, misshapen frame.

They stood together in the shadow of the tent, sweat streaking down their warped brows, their breath shallow in the thick heat. Jack's thoughts dragged like stones through mud, dulled by the transformation creeping deeper into his mind. The weight of it all: the mission, the failures, the fear that Emerson had become Akuramundo's puppet, pressed harder with every breath. *Would any of this work? What if they were already too late? Jack gripped her tighter.*

And Adina didn't move. She didn't pull away or crack a joke to break the silence. She just held on. And Jack didn't try to lead. He let her hold him up, and for a moment, it felt like breathing for the first time.

A rustle in the trees shattered the moment as two massive trolls burst from the shadows, charging straight at them. Jack spun around just as one loomed inches from his face. It had a grotesque head, bulging red eyes, and nostrils flaring like a bull's. Its jagged grin revealed four splintered teeth, and its rancid breath made Jack gag.

Without a word, the creature seized Jack by the arms and dragged him toward the tent. His mind raced, the world spinning around him. He twisted to look for Adina—only to see her limp in the other one's grip, unconscious.

As they entered the tent, Jack did his best to appear composed, though his insides churned with anxiety. The trolls lining the path bowed low, kissing the ground—paying homage, perhaps, to some higher power. Then he saw Emerson, and his heart leapt.

The thin, long-haired boy stood near the center of the tent, clad in heavy armor, looking every bit the warrior he was meant to be. A helmet rested on a nearby table beside a sword, an axe, and a bow. Jack's pulse quickened. Time was running out—and the roots hung useless inside Adina's robe, a failed lifeline he couldn't reach.

Just as panic began to claw at Jack's insides, the troll holding him barked something in a guttural, unnatural language. Jack furrowed his brow, but the words were incomprehensible.

Then a voice boomed from deeper within the tent—a low, rumbling voice that cut through the murmur of the crowd.

"My, my. We have quite a lot of unexpected visitors today," a short, squat troll whispered as it moved through the crowd. "Who are you? And why have you come to Sabana?"

The creature's tone was rude, but to Jack's relief, the language it spoke was one he could understand.

"I'm Ortok, from the southern region," Adina's voice rang out from behind them, rough and gravelly. "And this is Glamboot. We've come to watch the boy defeat your torturer, as it was foretold many years ago by a member of my tribe. You may remember—it was your own cousin who made this prophecy, Kabula."

Jack froze, stunned. *Kabula?* Where had Adina learned all this? Had she truly been knocked out, or was it just an . . . *Ah. She'd been faking.* The Pilfert must be speaking through her like a ventriloquist. Just as Jack was meant to do now—with Emerson.

"Ah, you're a boulder dweller . . . Hmm. Quite tall for boulder dwellers . . ." muttered the obscured troll, repeating himself as he shoved through the crowd to the front. His eyes narrowed, scrutinizing them both. Jack needed to break through to Emerson—but doing it here, in front of the king, felt like a surefire way to get caught.

Instead, he locked his gaze onto the king now standing before him. Though he was knee-high compared to the other trolls, his aura was unmistakably terrifying. There was a heavy presence around him—a quiet power that commanded immediate respect, if not outright fear.

His body was broad, rippling with muscle, and a long violet cape draped around his stumpy neck, moving with an unsettling fluidity. The red fur lining the neck of his robe twitched, as though it had a pulse of its own. Beneath the cape, he wore a silky, blue tunic buttoned just below his chest, with long, white hair spilling from the neckline. His short, uneven dress pants ended above his pungent, calloused feet.

"Yes, they sent us to bear the news that you've finally captured the heir of Hernando," Adina said. Though her voice was still rough, it brimmed with confidence. "You'll be free from Gridlybone's reign at last. The treasure of Sabana will be yours, and revenge on the ones who enslaved you will be rightfully earned."

The king regarded them for a long, unsettling stretch of time, studying their every move, word, and expression.

Then, after one particularly bizarre moment—when Jack was forced to his knees and the king shoved a finger up his nose before licking it clean—the king finally looked satisfied.

Jack, on the other hand, was feeling anything but.

Before turning to leave, the king raised one thick hand, signaling for silence.

"One more thing. What say you, other visitor?" he asked, a sly smile tugging at his cracked lips. He turned toward the shadowed corner of the tent where a lone troll stood, partially obscured by a pillar of smoke. "You say you are from the southern tribes as well?"

The troll gave a slow nod, and murmurs rippled through the crowd.

Jack stiffened. He hadn't noticed the other figure before—tall, composed, and far too relaxed to be a prisoner.

A chill slid up his spine. This troll wasn't from here; he was a visitor, like them. But unlike them, he actually belonged to the tribe they were pretending to be from. And if he spoke up, the king would know in an instant, that they were impostors.

"Well, are they boulder dwellers?"

The tall troll nodded, giving Jack and Adina a stare that sent a shiver down their spines. He knew—whoever this troll was, he knew who they were. Adina grabbed Jack's hand, ready to react.

However, before anything else could happen, Kabula turned back to them and said, "You die if he dies." The king's voice was sadistically casual as he turned away. "I hope you enjoy the festivities. We've worked hard to ensure this day is celebrated."

The room filled with guttural chatter, and Adina took the sudden outbreak of noise as her cue.

"Jack, you need to get into Emerson's mind—*now!*" she hissed.

Jack squeezed his eyes shut, diving into Emerson's racing thoughts with ease.

Emerson, we've come to help you. Adina and I are disguised as trolls—the ones who just . . . Hey, fucker, I'm in your head, so I heard that, Jack snapped, reacting to Emerson's thought: *Well, at least now your body matches that stupid expression you always wear.*

We're giving you the roots of Kaluna. They'll help in the fight. The Pilfert, Addison, and Stefani are waiting on the cliffs above to assist if things go south. Oh, and the Pilfert asked me to remind you: don't kill Gridlybone. Use the connection you two share. You've got this, buddy.

Jack hesitated a moment before adding, almost against his will, *I missed you.*

He felt his cheeks burn as he pulled back from Emerson's mind.

"You just said you missed him, didn't you?" Adina observed, her eyes narrowing with a sly smile.

"How did you—"

"Your face. Even as a troll, your emotions are written all over it."

Before he could respond, the squat troll re-entered the tent, flanked by two guards, and strode to the table beside Emerson. His cape was now a deeper shade of purple, and orange swirls had been painted across his exposed skin.

He stretched out his cape, trying for a dramatic reveal as he attempted to cover the table—but with his short arms, most of it was already on full display. Undeterred, he moved to Emerson's side, fixing him with a bloodthirsty stare.

"The weapon selection," he bellowed, his voice booming in the common tongue.

Emerson eyed the table cautiously, studying the weapons before looking up at the troll with a steady gaze.

"I choose the sword," he said, voice unwavering.

The king grinned, his golden tooth flashing in the dim light.

"Very well. We will alert you when your time comes."

He turned away, his mouth curling into an unsettling grin.

"Looks like he's dismissing us to the field," Adina whispered, as the trolls began moving toward the exit, which was flapping catty-corner from the hole where they had entered.

"This is our chance," Jack whispered, glancing toward Emerson. "Give them to me. I'll go now."

But as Jack turned to look at Adina, he saw her transfixed by the guards standing at the doorway. The two trolls were clearly stationed to ensure Emerson didn't escape.

"I don't think it's going to be that easy," Adina muttered, eyeing the guards, who were now glaring at them, their expressions sharp with suspicion.

Adina handed Jack the roots, which she had tucked into her belt. Then, with an exaggerated sway in her hips, she began walking toward the guards.

Jack's face twitched as he realized what she was about to try. Before he could stop himself, a laugh burst out—high-pitched and awkward. He smothered it quickly with his large, fat hand.

Adina, her movements deliberately exaggerated, tossed back her thinning dark hair and ran her fingers through it seductively. The troll she faced looked confused, but the other guard, whom she had just accidentally splattered with sweat, shifted his gaze from Jack to Adina, mesmerized. She giggled an unnaturally high, trollish laugh, and the guards seemed to forget about Jack entirely, fixating only on her.

"Disgusting," Jack muttered, as he silently moved toward Emerson.

There, alone in the corner, his friend sat with his face buried in his hands. Jack approached and placed his massive, troll-sized hand gently on Emerson's back.

"Is it time?" Emerson's voice quivered as he lifted his head to look up at Jack.

Jack shook his head and offered Emerson the roots, placing them carefully in his lap.

"Jack? Is that you?" Emerson asked, his voice caught between nervous tension and unexpected relief.

Jack nodded and held out his other hand. Emerson bolted forward and grasped Jack's leg, his grip strong.

"Thank you."

Jack pointed at the roots, but Emerson's gaze had drifted somewhere else—distant, like he was listening to someone only he could hear. A tense silence passed before Emerson muttered, "I don't want them. Not yet. I want to try this on my own." He tossed the roots aside like a spoiled child rejecting a cheap gift.

Jack felt a surge of frustration but picked the roots up and shoved them back into Emerson's chest.

Take the damn roots, Jack thought forcefully into Emerson's mind.

Why? Why help now? Emerson responded, each word laced with the fury he fought to contain. *You didn't even bother to come looking for me when you . . . Will you stop? I'm not eating them now.*

He stuffed the roots into his pocket with a defiant air.

Jack felt his face flush, the weight of Emerson's stubbornness bearing down on him. But before he could respond, Emerson's gaze grew distant, as if he were being pulled away from the spot.

"They're onto us. We have to move," Adina muttered, already at his side.

Jack turned just in time to see two massive trolls storming toward them. He and Adina bolted for the tent flaps, pressing their backs against the canvas on either side. A moment later, the guards burst through, charging past them into the forest, their bodies igniting with searing burns from the setting sun.

Jack and Adina slipped back into the tent and out the other side, moving unnoticed through the crowd. As they took their spots, the flaps opened again, and the red-tinged guards reappeared, their faces twisted with malice.

"What happened?" Jack asked in a hushed whisper, catching his breath.

"I guess twerking doesn't work as well with trolls as it does with the trolls in our world," Adina said, causing Jack to snort loudly. Several trolls shot them confused glances.

"Real smooth, Jack. Draw more attention to us."

They stood in line with the others, trying to remain inconspicuous as the atmosphere buzzed with anticipation. Jack wasn't sure what was in store for Emerson, but he hoped his friend would swallow his pride and eat the roots.

As the crowd settled, Kabula climbed onto a grand, colorful stage. Crimson banners hung above him, adorned with spiraling, silver script; the podium was emblazoned with a bold, green "G." Kabula raised his arms to the crowd, his voice triumphant as he bellowed his exuberant speech.

The air was thick with excitement, but Jack and Adina couldn't shake the weight of the looming tension.

Then, as Kabula stepped off the stage, the crowd fell into an uneasy silence. The structure was quickly dismantled and carried back into the tent. One of the guards approached the king, but as he bent to speak, Kabula hushed him, gesturing toward the broken podium. The guard picked it up and tossed it into the crowd, where trolls scrambled to claim it, fighting like children over a brand-new toy.

Suddenly, the earth shook.

Jack turned as flames burst through the stone, and an enormous head the size of a shed emerged. Gridlybone unfurled, long slanted horns forming a crown on her forehead, her violet skin glowing in the early moonlight as the twin suns sank behind the cliffs. Her white eyes blazed with hunger, and her jagged mouth split open, sending flames into the sky as a high-pitched, tormented scream filled the air.

Jack's blood ran cold.

"She's huge. There's no way. We're getting him out of there," Jack hissed, eyes wide.

Before he could finish, the sound of a gong split the air. The tent flaps tore open, and Emerson, head bowed, stepped onto the field. He scanned the crowd, searching for Jack in the sea of monstrous shapes. But all he saw were hungry eyes staring back at him with predatory intent.

His smile faltered. As he lifted his gaze, his heart stopped.

Towering above the horde, the dragon bent its long neck low, a wicked, toothy grin fixed squarely on him.

Chapter Eighteen
The Rescue

EMERSON STUMBLED, HIS FOOT catching on the uneven ground before he rolled backward, spread-eagle, onto the dirt. He gazed up, his eyes locked with the monstrous face of the dragon, whose piercing gaze seemed to study him with unnerving interest.

There was no way out. The only hope he had of leaving this field alive was either convincing the dragon to join forces—or slaying her.

His thoughts flashed to the day he'd battled a wooden dragon in the colorful, wind-swept fields months ago, with the Pilfert watching from the sidelines. His mentor's voice echoed in his mind: *Dragon riders never take the kill shot. Speak into its mind. Persuade—don't kill.*

But why?

He remembered the words, but not the reason. A conversation in a shop in Ealu—something important, something crucial—but it slipped through his fingers like soap.

"Move," the Kakunon, Kabula, bellowed to the horde of spectators.

In unison, the sea of green trolls shuffled backward—except for two awkward shapes that kept bumping into the others.

Both had turned a shade paler, their discomfort palpable—even from where Emerson stood watching. He shared a nervous, fleeting smile with Jack, but it did little to ease the tight knot in his stomach.

Kabula stepped forward, barking something in that harsh trollish tongue. Emerson didn't understand the words, but he understood the meaning well enough —the trolls were splitting into two groups, forming an aisle for him to approach the winged monster.

A tense silence followed as Adina nudged Jack back into line, her eyes already locked on Emerson with a look that said more than a thousand words. Jack, however, glared and jabbed a finger toward Emerson's pocket.

Emerson blinked, watching as Jack slipped a hand beneath his toga, pantomiming the act of eating with exaggerated flair. The broken-toothed grin didn't make him smile. He just shook his head, catching the flicker of annoyance in Jack's eyes as the hand fell.

Then—*thrum*. A sudden drumbeat split the air.

Emerson stepped forward, pushing through the odorous walls of thick, green arms and lolloping heads that had formed around him. As he reached the front, near the mouth of the cavern, the crowd behind him grew still.

Emerson stood there, sword trembling in his grasp, unable to raise it. His arms were too weak to wield it. His gaze locked onto the dragon's cold, calculating eyes.

The Pilfert had spoken of a bond—but in those narrowed, pitiless eyes, Emerson saw only severance.

A screeching sound—like the roar of squealing tires before a car crash—pierced the air. Emerson barely managed to duck-roll out of the way as an inferno rained down, heat licking at his heels.

There was no time to think. Heart pounding, he scrambled to his feet and sprinted toward the only hope he had: the unguarded cave entrance.

But then—a flash of pale violet. A glint of fangs.

In a blur, Emerson dove beneath her massive jowls, rolling hard into the dirt. He barely had time to catch a breath before instinct took over. His hand shot up, grabbing one of the curved horns of her wicked crown. With a grunt, he swung his legs upward, hooking his body onto the crown and hauling himself onto it.

Gridlybone reared with a guttural roar, her neck snapping like a whip as she thrashed to dislodge him like a flea. Emerson held tight, elven magic sparking beneath his grip as he called forth the wind to anchor him.

"I am the heir of Hernando!" he yelled, hoping to spark recognition.

Nothing.

He shut his eyes and forced his thoughts to still. As her head steadied for a heartbeat, he drew his sword.

There—just behind the crown—two pulsing earholes, wide as plates. Perfect targets.

This can't be this easy.

Then, without hesitation, he released the horn and slid down her neck, blade poised, aiming for the gap.

But just as he began his descent, Gridlybone surged upward with the force of a hurricane—launching into the sky and dragging him with her.

Emerson clung to her hide, wind screaming in his ears, the earth spinning wildly below. But the force was too great—he couldn't hold on. His fingers tore free.

The wind howled as the earth spun and blurred beneath him. Panic surged. He twisted midair, grasping for anything—claws, horn, magic—but there was nothing. Only air. For one breathless moment, he stopped fighting—ready to embrace the final impact as the ground surged up to meet him.

But instead, an odd, almost joyful sensation caught him. The earth bowed beneath him with a soft, trampoline-like give, breaking his fall with a gentle bounce.

As he steadied himself, his gaze swept the crowd of trolls near the cavern, then lifted to the hill above Gridlybone's lair—where Addison, Stefani, and the Pilfert stood, the creature's staff held high.

His stomach churned with rage —but there was no time to make sense of it now.

A shrill shriek pierced the air—higher and louder than before. Gridlybone was diving, her mouth unhinged, her neck stretched long and deadly.

Emerson bolted for the cave, slipping through the opening just as flames slammed into the hillside. The ground shook beneath him as he ran, the tunnel tightening, pressing in from all sides.

The darkness was suffocating.

"I need light!" he shouted.

Instantly, tiny orbs ignited around him, casting warm light across the treasure-strewn cavern. Piles of gold and gemstones gleamed in the glow—sharp and glistening like teeth.

Behind him, Gridlybone roared—her serpentine neck dragging across stone with a deafening, unstoppable grind. Ahead a flicker of blue light beckoned him forward: the stone. His stone. The very reason he was here.

Emerson's heart leapt as he reached for it. But just as his fingers grazed the air around it, a wall of flame erupted.

He stumbled back, shielding his face, lungs burning with each breath. As the smoke thinned, his eyes widened. He had entered a vast chamber—the ceiling arched high above, the walls stretching wider than any before: this was the heart of the lair.

A shadow shifted above. Gridlybone rose to her full height, wings brushing the curved ceiling, her neck coiling upward like a serpent poised to strike.

Then she stilled.

She loomed over him, her massive head tilting slightly, eyes glinting with strange, measured curiosity.

Emerson scrambled back, the weight of her presence pressing down on him. He held her gaze, breath shallow, as a low rumble rose—trollish grunts echoing through the cavern, their chants swelling until the stone beneath his feet began to shake.

Gridlybone's head tilted back, the sound fueling her fury. Fire rumbled in her chest, heat warping the air as she prepared to strike.

Seizing the moment, Emerson drove his fist through the rising flames and yanked the stone from the wall—but his grip slipped, and it clattered across the floor.

Too late to turn back, he snatched up a fallen shield and sprinted toward the exit with everything he had.

He was nearly there when a thunderous roar split the air behind him—Gridlybone's fury, unleashed at last.

A shockwave of heat hit him mid-step. Emerson stumbled, slamming into the stone wall, and threw up his shield just in time. The blast crashed against it, searing heat pulsing through the metal as flames curled around its edges.

The shield burned against his skin. His forearm, still locked around the handle, felt like it had been plunged into boiling oil. A scream tore from his throat. Then, as the fire ebbed, he crouched low and ran for the opening, pushing through the agony, and hurled himself out, tumbling into twilight.

A ragged cry of victory mixed with the sharp sting of pain escaped him as he staggered to his feet. Looking down at his arm, he watched in horror as the skin began to peel away like melted wax, exposing raw, tender flesh beneath.

His eyes scanned the area until he found a creek and plunged his arm into the cool, soothing water, biting down on his shirt to stifle the howl of agony threatening to escape.

As he lowered his arm deeper, he glanced back toward the cave. The dragon was trapped inside, her massive form too large to squeeze through the narrow opening. Only one nostril was visible, exhaling a plume of frustrated steam as her body thrashed against the rocks, making the ground tremble and sending chunks of the hillside crashing down.

Her tortured screech echoed through the air, rattling the very bones of the earth.

"No wonder the trolls wanted me to kill you . . . You're so damn annoying," Emerson muttered bitterly.

To his surprise, Gridlybone's roar faltered.

The dragon fell silent. For a moment, her piercing eye peeked out from behind the rocks, locking onto him with an unsettling, almost curious gaze.

Emerson turned away and was drawn instead to the unexpected beauty before him. The cliffs above were blanketed in thick pines, their dark silhouettes standing guard against the fading twilight. Below, a silver river wound through a vast, green valley, stretching toward a distant mountain crowned by a waterfall that tumbled into the stream.

That must be where Gara is waiting, he thought, recalling the words Akuramundo had whispered to him in the tent:

Emerson. Do not eat the roots. Not yet. The moment you do, the Pilfert will see everything—every secret you carry, every truth we've uncovered. A single bite, when I say so, is all you'll need. Gara is waiting near Gorman Falls. Go to her. Let the fool believe it has won. And then . . . let our plan unfold.

He cleared his mind, rinsing away the voice as his gaze returned to the dragon. Her single, massive eye still watched him through the crack in the stone—but she no longer seemed intent on roasting him alive, and Emerson found he didn't mind the attention. The lush grass beneath him swayed gently in the cool breeze, the vibrant reds and golds of the fields contrasting with the rocky terrain. A calmness washed over him as he took a deep breath of the crisp, frosty air.

The moment was short-lived.

"Emerson, what are you doing?" called a familiar voice, light and full of energy.

A flame lit up inside Emerson as he turned to see Addison running down the cliffside.

"The Pilfert told me that you need to go through with the plan. It said you'd know what I meant. It also asked for you to open your mind to it."

Emerson scoffed.

"Why? Why isn't it here talking to me if it's so important?" His voice was tight, his lungs constricting around the words.

He tried to mask the weakness, but a warmth bloomed in his chest as he looked at Addison's face—healthy, untroubled, perfect; a stark contrast to his own battered state.

"Jack and Adina are still back there," Addison said. "And the trolls are getting restless. If you don't go back and give them something to celebrate, they'll tear them apart. Trolls may be dumb, but they've figured out they're imposters. The Pilfert's watching over them, but the moment it steps in, a full-blown fight will break out."

"I don't give a damn," Emerson muttered, bitterness thick in his voice. "You think I care if the trolls tear them apart?"

Addison drew in a sharp breath, his jaw tightening—but whatever he was about to say faltered when he saw Emerson's arm.

"Did she burn you?"

"Obviously," Emerson bit out.

"Let me help." Addison extended his hand, and after a brief hesitation, Emerson gave it to him.

With gentle hands, Addison guided Emerson's arm back into the creek. He whispered something under his breath—a soft, melodic language that felt strangely like home. A faint ripple spread across the water where his voice touched it.

Emerson blinked. When Addison drew Emerson's arm from the water, the burn had faded. Only a blotchy, red patch remained above his wrist, the skin no longer peeling or blistered.

"I learned that from the elves," Addison said, offering a wink and a grin.

Emerson looked at the tiny burn, then back at Addison, his thoughts still a whirlwind.

"You need to face the dragon," Addison said, his voice steady yet urgent, placing a hand on Emerson's knee. "You need to follow the plan you and the Pilfert made."

"Why should I do a damn thing for that creature?"

The flame that had just begun to flicker out exploded back to life—his blood like gasoline, fueling the fire erupting in his veins. He flung Addison's hand from his leg as he stood, adrenaline making it impossible to stay seated. Then it burst out—his voice sharp and shrill.

"No one cared if I lived or died when that Stymphalian made off with me. No one came looking for me when I was tortured, starved, and left to rot in a dungeon cellar. No one cared that I almost died!

"So why should I care if Jack and Adina get ripped to shreds? Why should I help that *vile* creature? Why should I do *anything* when *nobody* helped me?"

The words, long pent up since his capture, melted the brightness in Addison's expression into something more somber.

"You don't know what you're talking about, Emerson," Addison said gently, stepping closer. "The Pilfert knows more than you think. And you're wrong. We planned to come after you the moment you were taken. Jack and Adina left that very night to find you. Don't play the victim. You don't have the whole story."

The anger still pressed inside Emerson, but it began to soften as Addison's words sank in. Jack had come looking for him. Jack had cared.

He looked back at Addison—and for the first time today, he saw something familiar in his eyes.

"Fine," Emerson said at last, his voice cool but edged with reluctant acceptance. "I'll go. But not because you told me to."

They set off without another word, beginning the steady climb toward the other side of the hill.

"One more thing," Addison said, tapping his temple. "Jack just told me you didn't eat the roots. You need to eat them now."

Emerson frowned, pulling the silver vegetable from his robes and dangling it between them.

"Nah, I don't need—"

"Eat them now." Addison cut him off, his voice suddenly sharp. "They might just be what saves your ass. We're almost to the other side."

Emerson's frustration simmered, but he didn't argue. He exhaled hard and let the roots slip from his hand.

"No."

Addison stiffened. His jaw clenched, and with a growl, he scooped up the roots and shoved them into Emerson's chest.

"What the hell do you mean, 'No'? Start chewing."

Emerson glared at him, hands clenched. "I don't need it. Didn't the Pilfert say elves were dragon riders? I'm not eating that."

Addison's eyes narrowed.

"Eat. The. Damn. Roots," he muttered through gritted teeth.

Emerson froze. His expression clouded, as if listening to something only he could hear.

A choice hovered in the silence: the Pilfert or Akuramundo.

He remembered what Akuramundo had promised—a way home, his mother waiting. But then came Kaluna, and those strange, fleeting moments of belonging with the friends he'd grown to love. And the Pilfert's promise—that defeating Akuramundo would save them all.

With a heavy heart, Emerson bent down, picked up the roots, and bit into them. The taste was bitter and unfamiliar, but he forced himself to chew, locking the small, stubborn morsel between his teeth.

Immediately, a rush of warmth spread through his body. A light, euphoric sensation wrapped around his mind as his muscles relaxed and the tension drained away. His thoughts snapped into focus, and the world around him seemed to shimmer—brighter, more vivid, almost unreal. For a moment, he felt invincible.

"How do you feel?" Addison asked cautiously, his voice edged with concern.

"Like Mario after catching a star." Emerson grinned, his voice bubbling with the new surge of energy. His brain was firing on all cylinders—every thought sharp, clear, and crisp.

He tossed the remaining roots at Addison with a flick of his wrist.

"Take these. You might need them more than I do if the trolls turn on us."

"There's my nerd." Addison smiled with a mixture of affection and amusement. "Come on, let's go."

Without another word, the two boys broke into a run, the adrenaline from Emerson's newfound strength pushing them faster.

As they raced ahead, Addison glanced sideways.

"Em, when you go down there—just know we've got your back if this gets out of hand. It's good to have you back. And just so you know . . . I wanted to go after you the moment I found out you were taken."

Emerson flushed. His throat thickened, the words he wanted to say tangled somewhere behind his heart. So instead, he just nodded—then surged forward, charging down the cliff.

As he landed back on solid ground, the trolls' angry eyes locked onto him. But two pairs of eyes—Jack's and Adina's—watched in fear.

Emerson smirked and threw them a quick wink. *I've got this,* he thought, riding the surge of energy still pulsing through him—so much so that his arm began to tremble, the one clutching the sword to his chest.

A strange vibration rose from his heart, flowing down through his shoulder and into the blade. The strings wrapped around the hilt began to stir, winding slowly up his wrist with the quiet, practiced care of a healer tending a wound.

The blade shimmered. Its edges rippled as the long, straight form bent inward, reshaping into a crescent curve. Gold, silver, brown, and blue swirled like wind around his fist—then red, glowing with dangerous grace. This was no longer just a sword. It was a weapon meant to fly, to return, to answer.

Gasps and guttural grunts rose from the crowd as Emerson raised the blade high. With a fierce cry, he hurled it into the sky. It spun in a flawless arc, curving like a boomerang—then zipped back into his open hand with a satisfying thrum.

The trolls erupted, howling in a frenzy, their voices echoing his in bursts of primal approval.

Emerson glanced toward the hillside just in time to see two figures leap into the air—Stefani and his mentor. Stefani's smile poured down like sunlight. Beside her, Addison tilted back his head and howled at the rising moon, his joy spilling into the night.

"Hey, dragon!" he shouted, his voice booming across the rocky expanse. "Come on out. I made a little upgrade to my sword—I'd love to show it off!"

The response came in a deafening roar, shaking the ground beneath his feet. Heat poured from the cave as the dragon's fury surged outward—the air alone might've knocked him flat, and if he'd been any closer, the flames could've turned him to ash. But he held steady, the newfound strength anchoring him like stone.

With a swift, fluid motion, he dodged the next wave of flames. Emerson's legs moved faster than ever before, propelling him up the hillside with speed and balance that felt almost inhuman. His strides were clean, his footing sure, each leap carrying him higher until he vaulted onto a jutting ledge.

Then, without hesitation, he leapt—soaring through the air and landing squarely on the dragon's long, scaly neck.

A roar of excitement tore through the air as the trolls watched in stunned silence. All eyes turned toward Emerson, who clung to the dragon's scales with ease.

The creature bucked and thrashed, trying to shake him loose, but Emerson held tight, swinging his sword in a wild flurry of silver and fire. Each strike slammed against her solid scales, but the blade only vibrated with each hit, ringing like a tuning fork rather than cutting.

"Behind the ears, remember! Behind the ears!" Addison's voice rang out from the hillside, clear and urgent.

Trolls grunted and pointed wildly toward the blossoming tree, shouting in alarm as they spotted the unwanted visitors.

"Foolish child," the Pilfert muttered, raising its staff as it crackled with dark energy, readying for the inevitable troll assault. "You did tell him not to kill the dragon?"

Addison's gaze stayed locked on the sky. His voice was low, steady. "As long as he lives, I don't care what he does."

The dragon's massive knees bent.

This is it, Emerson thought, adrenaline flooding his chest as the ground disappeared beneath him. *Now or never.*

He scrambled up the dragon's writhing neck, muscles screaming, grip slipping with every surge of motion. A deafening gust of wind hit him like a wave—he lost hold.

He slid, bouncing and tumbling, jamming his sword into the gaps between her scales in a desperate attempt to catch himself.

But it was no use. He slammed against the thick curve of her leg, the impact rattling through his bones.

With a grunt, he rolled onto his stomach and pushed back against the pull of gravity. Inch by inch, he climbed again, fingers raw, limbs shaking, the world spinning beneath him.

Below, the crowd began to stir—but he could no longer see them. The clouds obscured the tumultuous waves of green.

He simply focused on the scale just inches away from the dragon's ear—his one and only chance.

"We've drawn too much attention to ourselves. Look . . ." The Pilfert pointed a long finger toward the field.

Addison and Stefani turned from the sky. Below, the mass of trolls shifted like a writhing sea of green, surging toward the cliffside cavern. Amid the chaos, one troll broke away, slinking toward the edge of the forest and vanishing into the shadows. The Pilfert's eyes narrowed.

A ripple of recognition swept across the horde. Trolls glanced at one another. The performance was over. And now, they seemed eager to start their own.

The field exploded into a fury of swinging limbs and colliding bodies. What had been a crowd became a mob.

Addison blinked, his brain struggling to process the shift. It felt like something out of a Saturday morning cartoon . . . except the blood was real.

Stefani screamed as a long, scabby arm raised a club and smashed it down on another troll's skull. The head snapped off, bouncing across the dirt like a shattered melon; a thick blue substance gushed from the severed neck as the body crumpled with a heavy thud.

"What's happening?" Addison shouted, eyes scanning the field as the crowd surged toward Jack and Adina.

"I told you what would happen," the Pilfert snapped. "Trolls don't think—they react. Especially when war is in the air. One spark, and they burn everything around them."

It didn't wait for a response. With a frustrated huff, the Pilfert pulled a long, root-like strand from its pouch—something worm-like and glistening—and slurped it down.

"We need to get Jack and Adina out of there. *Now.*"

Addison and Stefani exchanged a glance, then followed, choking down their own bitter strands and charging after the Pilfert.

"I can't remember what they look like. Do you?" Stefani asked, voice taut with focus as she loosed an arrow into a charging troll's red eye. It burst like a grape, splattering dark blood across the mossy ground.

"Can't focus on that right now," Addison growled, his axe cleaving through the skull of another troll lunging toward her.

"Thanks," Stefani shouted, ducking and sprinting deeper into the chaos.

Just beyond the curve of the hill, Jack and Adina stood pressed against the cliff face, boxed in by a tightening wall of snarling trolls. Adina tried to flip her oily hair at them, but it was clear their bloodlust far outweighed their other lustful desires.

"Jack, what do we do?"

Jack didn't answer. His eyes were fixed, his brow furrowed. He reached out—not with his hands, but with his mind, probing the trolls like he had before.

But this time, his attempt was met with resistance.

We can feel you . . . It won't work this time . . . The voice came from the troll closest to him. *Our future king has granted us anacylin.*

Jack didn't know what it meant, but he understood enough: they were immune to his mental grasp.

"Hope you enjoyed the show," a nearby troll sneered, raising its club. But before it could strike, something moved beneath them.

Jack looked down to see Kabula, the Kakunon, weaving through the trolls' legs.

"Now, now," the troll king purred, his voice slick with glee. "These two belong to me."

Jack turned just in time to see Kabula drive his sword beneath Adina's ribs. Her breath caught. Then she collapsed, shrinking rapidly back to her normal size. Blood pooled beneath her—slow, dark, and spreading.

"What have you done?" Jack roared.

He swung a massive fist at his enemy, but the Kakunon danced aside, laughing. Jack's blow slammed into the ground, shaking the earth.

For a moment, the trolls froze as the small figure darted toward the treasure. Then chaos roared back to life. Vicious grunts and snarls filled the air as they turned on one another—greed ignited by the sight of their leader racing for the gold.

With a snarl, Jack scooped Adina into his arms and charged up the slope, away from the cavern entrance. The trolls, now blinded by greed, forgot their original target and surged after Kabula, their rage funneled entirely toward the promise of treasure.

She's okay. She just needs a healing potion. It's just a flesh wound, he told himself. But the blood soaking her side told a different story. Her skin now fairer and tinged with green.

I need my body back, Jack thought, and in the next breath, a sudden lightness surged through him. His troll form released him like a deflating balloon.

Back in his own skin, Jack scrambled for his bag, yanked out the whistle, and called into it, praying someone would come. He cradled Adina beneath the swaying limbs of a nearby willow, feeling like he'd let her down for the final time.

The Pilfert barely had time to react before a club smashed into the dirt beside it. With lightning reflexes, it spun its staff through the air, tangled wood unraveling like serpents and wrapping around the troll's arm. With a sharp crack, the staff snapped back into place, pinning the creature to the ground.

"Jack!" Stefani's voice rang out nearby, followed by a mental cry for help that hit Addison like a slap. He looked up just in time to see Jack crouched over a girl with dark hair, barely visible through the chaos.

"I'm on it!" Addison called.

Stefani loosed another arrow, sinking it into a troll's throat just before it brought a club down on Addison.

"Thanks!" he called over his shoulder. Then, like a fish darting through murky waters, Addison weaved between flailing limbs and crashing feet, slicing at troll ankles and dropping them one by one. The chaos—and the thuds of enemies falling—gave him hope. Maybe they *would* make it out of this alive.

But as he ran, his thoughts drifted to Emerson. *Where was he? And was he okay?*

High above, Emerson clung to Gridlybone's scaled back, swiping at her armored hide in search of a weakness. Every time he reached for a gap, she twisted, snapping at him with jaws lined with eighty serrated teeth. He had nearly lost a hand the last time.

Frustrated, he hurled his sword like a boomerang—it missed again.

You wish to kill me, elf lord? A gentle voice whispered through his mind.

She had just spoken to him—the connection suddenly open. But the shock of hearing her voice caught him off guard. His grip slipped, and he tumbled down her rough, scaled body.

Wind screamed past his ears as the sky spun around him—then a blur of violet streaked past him: Gridlybone, wings tucked, was diving. She surged upward from below, and he dropped straight into the nook between two of her large scales. Her wings boomed as she climbed higher, steadying herself in the air.

The fall through the sky had reminded him of his kidnapping by the Stymphalian just a week ago—when he'd been carried in giant talons, gripped by fear and helplessness.

But he wasn't helpless this time. He was tucked safely on her back.

And she had spoken to him—just like the Pilfert said she would.

Her voice was softer than he expected. Feminine. A voice he'd never heard before, yet it felt like family.

A little too much like family. And thinking about killing her now . . . he wasn't sure he could do it.

You won't kill me, elf lord, came the voice, calm and firm, weaving into his thoughts like an ancient lullaby. *That would be a foolish thing to do. We have always been connected . . . I just couldn't hear you before. Please forgive me.*

Then, with surprising gentleness, Gridlybone adjusted her flight. One wing dipped slightly as she tilted her body, cradling him more securely between her scales. A soft rumble vibrated beneath him—almost like a purr.

Emerson shifted, fingers brushing over the warm ridges of her back. Carefully, he pulled himself higher, swinging a leg over her thick neck and settling just above the curve of her wings.

A rush of wind filled Emerson's lungs as she rose higher. Her breathing matched his—slow, steady, and deliberate.

A quiet settled over him, deeper than anything he'd ever known. His mind was clear and calm. He was in control. And for the first time, he wasn't just clinging on to survive; he was riding the storm.

No need for apologies. My mentor told me we'd be connected, but I didn't feel it until now. So, no, please forgive me. But there's one thing I must ask of you.

Ask away, heir of Hernando.

Stefani, invisible in the chaos of the battlefield, wove through the troll-infested field like a phantom. Each arrow found its mark with deadly precision—trolls clutched their eyes and throats, stumbling in confusion. The air was filled with roars of rage as the trolls beat their clubs frantically, trying to locate the invisible assailant.

Beneath the cliff, the Pilfert was working its magic, casting spells that ensnared enemies in a transparent, shimmering sphere. As a new wave of trolls charged forward, movements full of fury, a sudden roar from above cut through the chaos.

All heads snapped up, eyes widening in shock as a great storm of violet and silver blazed across the sky.

Emerson and Gridlybone spiraled through the air, locked in what appeared to be a brutal midair clash. His sword flashed outward—a wide, theatrical swing that skimmed past her horn—before slipping from his fingers, spinning downward in a streak of silver light.

Below, trolls collapsed as the blade struck true. Emerson, without breaking character, reached for the curved weapon as it returned to his outstretched hand and immediately resumed slashing at Gridlybone's scales.

She roared, twisting hard as fire burst from her throat in sweeping, spiraling streams across the field. Emerson let the sword fly once more. He heard it hum through the air as it curved back toward him. He caught it without looking—already preparing the next throw. Steel sang through the sky as he continued the charade: another throw, another arc, more trolls toppling—hopefully enough to protect his friends below.

Then, through the flames, Emerson made out a figure on the ground—Addison, his auburn hair unmistakable. The boy was hunched over a collapsed lump. Emerson's chest tightened. Was that Jack or Adina? He steeled himself, ready to end this battle.

But he didn't know how. He didn't know what else to do.

Then, as if in response to his mounting anxiety, Akuramundo's cool voice slipped into his mind—smooth as smoke. *You can end this quickly. Just join Gara at the statue. I'll handle the rest.*

To the fallen statue. Hurry, Emerson whispered into Gridlybone's mind.

Without a word, she shifted, wings lurching hard as they soared upward, wind screaming past Emerson's ears as the battlefield shrank beneath them. The mountains rose ahead, jagged and cold, clawing at the sky.

They descended through the clouds, soaring over a silver river that twisted through the green valley below. The low roar of a waterfall echoed off the cliffs. Emerson's breath caught. It reminded him of home—of bathwater running, of his mother humming, before her mind betrayed her.

He closed his eyes and let the cold wind sting. *Focus.*

After several minutes of soaring, Gridlybone began their descent, landing gracefully on a patch of lush, green grass. Tiny yellow creatures scattered as she touched down and stepped lightly over them on her way to the river. She lowered her great head and drank deeply. With each pull of water, ripples spread outward, and as the level receded, several rocks emerged—displaced by her thirst.

"Thank you for bringing me here," Emerson said, his voice thick with gratitude.

"It was my pleasure, Emerson," she murmured, her voice gentler now, no longer speaking directly into his mind. "Hernando was the greatest of Kazumeth's five rulers. He protected my kind when no one else would."

She paused. "He believed all creatures of Kazumeth should live united. The prayer that hunters recite when they take a life was born from his words—spoken the day he was forced to kill my ailing mother to save his village."

Emerson blinked in confusion. "He killed your mother, and yet you still wish to help me?"

Gridlybone's gaze softened. A long pause followed before she answered. "She was dying. So were they. It was mercy—for both. I didn't understand it then. But time teaches us things rage cannot."

Emerson raised an eyebrow.

"Forgiveness," she said, "is the only gift worth giving."

A sudden crack shattered the quiet. Gridlybone's neck stiffened, her head jerking toward the sound, steam puffing sharply from her nostrils.

"I'll take it from here," Gara's voice rang out, cold and commanding, as she stepped from the shadows near the waterfall.

Gridlybone's lips peeled back, revealing teeth as long as Emerson's forearm. "Do we trust her?" she asked, low and dangerous.

Emerson studied the woman before him. Memories of his final days in Dartmoor surged to the surface—her cruel mood swings, the strange gifts she'd provided, and the deals that were made in the dark. And then: the Pilfert. The cryptic truths, the abandonment, and the strange protection only clear in hindsight.

Which of them has been playing the long game? He didn't know. But the game wasn't over yet.

The Kakunon's body lay sprawled atop a pile of fallen trolls, one hand still clutching his blade. His glassy eyes stared blankly at the sky, a crooked smile frozen on his face. For a breath, the battlefield held its silence. A strange, eerie stillness.

The remaining trolls, bloodied but wild with purpose, suddenly surged toward the mouth of the cave—where freedom and treasure would be plentiful. Their charge sent rocks tumbling from the cliffs above, loose stones scattering down the hillside like shrapnel. Stefani stumbled back, nearly crushed beneath the stampede.

"Don't let them reach the cave," the Pilfert barked.

With a sharp twist of its staff, the Pilfert flung her upward. Wind surged beneath her feet, lifting her effortlessly through the air. She landed beside the willow tree, near Adina's body, now covered by the toga, which barely stirred with her shallow breaths.

"Shoot from above," the Pilfert ordered.

Arrows rained down upon the battlefield as Jack and Addison re-entered the fray, having done what they could for their friend, hoping it was enough. They'd just leapt off the hillside when Jack felt a powerful blow—a green fist colliding with his side with the force of a wrecking ball. His ribs shattered, and he collapsed inward like a crushed bottle. The force launched him several feet into a stone wall. Broken and gasping for air, he watched the chaos unfold, reaching for a sword just out of reach.

Jack had no sense of how much time passed as he lay there, his body a heap of pain and confusion. All he knew was that, just before the world closed in on him, he saw—through blurred, cloudy vision—a tall, thin figure emerging from the mouth of the cave. In one hand, it held a pulsing sphere of blue fire. In the other, trailing behind like a broken banner, was a massive, lifeless serpent.

It was too much. Nothing made sense. And as the curtain of darkness fell, the last thing he felt was the brush of long, dark hair across his face.

"I'll stand guard. You go take care of Adina."

The low whisper brushed Jack's ear. At the sound of Adina's name his chest tightened, and panic flooded his mind.

"Jack, lay back down," came Addison's voice as he pressed down against Jack's shoulder, trying to ease him back.

But Jack didn't move. He clutched his side, pain cutting deep with every breath. His eyes scanned the hill—until he found her. There, standing beside Adina's lifeless body, was the Pilfert. The creature was waving its staff in slow, intricate circles, as ancient words in melodic tongue flowed from its beak.

Jack sat beneath the willow tree, its limbs stretching protectively around him. The ground beneath him rumbled softly, as if the earth itself were snoring. Through the branches, Jack glimpsed trolls moving in and out of the cave below—carrying fistfuls of treasure, shoving each other aside, and sending others crashing to the ground in chaotic fashion, their spoils spilling in all directions, reminding Jack of an old video game. But there was one troll who didn't move to join the frenzy. The largest of them all stood apart, his gaze fixed on the intruders hiding on the cliff.

"What happened?" Jack asked, his voice hoarse.

Stefani turned from Adina, her eyes rimmed red. "When you were hit, Adina flew down from the hill . . . but she didn't make it far. She crawled to reach you. We were outnumbered and had to abandon our positions to get to you. The trolls are free now but keeping you and Adina alive was far more important."

She paused, dabbing at her cheeks. "When we got to you, she was lying across your body—protecting you." Her voice broke. "We thought you were both gone. Jack, I thought you were dead."

And then the tears came heavier, spilling from her high cheekbones.

"Her wound had torn open again," she continued. "She lost a lot of blood. But the new Kakunon down there gave us space to breathe—you know, with Emerson giving them their freedom." She blinked, brushing away the last of her tears.

Adina's body lay still, her eyes closed, limp in death's embrace. But as Jack watched, he felt a warmth begin to pulse from her. The darkness around her face faded slowly, and the dried blood began to shimmer and evaporate into the air like dying embers of fireworks.

Her eyes flashed open and found Jack at once.

"Oh good," she croaked, her voice flat as ever. "You're not dead."

Jack stared at her, taking in every small detail of her features: the way the light played in her hair, the faint sheen of sweat on her brow, the way her lips parted as she caught her breath. The tightness in his chest eased as his stomach flipped.

"We need to get out of here. They're about to—" Addison interrupted before Jack had the chance to respond.

"I know," the Pilfert cut in, voice hoarse. "I'll speak to him. Stay here."

It moved slower than usual, hunched more than Jack remembered. The fight had clearly drained it. Jack and Adina watched as the Pilfert approached the enormous troll still glaring up at them, his fists clenched at his sides.

The Pilfert raised its staff, muttering in low, guttural tones.

"Do you think they'll try to kill us again?" Jack asked.

"Let them try," Addison grinned, nodding toward the massive dragon tail still sprawled on the battlefield like a flag. "Emerson just handed a dragon its ass and walked away. I doubt trolls are gonna top that. Plus, there are very few left. Most are already fleeing the hills."

Below, voices rose, both low and sharp. The tension between the Pilfert and the towering troll had reached it breaking point. Jack glanced down just as the troll stepped forward, chest puffed, rage simmering in his eyes.

Then, with a sudden leap, the Pilfert flipped into the air and brought its staff down on the troll's thick, lumpy head with a thunderous crack.

The massive creature stumbled back, clearly stunned. Jack couldn't help but laugh, though he regretted it immediately as pain shot through his side.

"I guess even Pilferts run out of patience," he muttered, grinning, as the Pilfert hobbled back up the hill. "Good work down there."

The Pilfert smacked Jack's outstretched hand away with a huff. "Violence is never the answer," it said, then paused. "But when you're dealing with a pack of poo-slinging barbarians, sometimes it shouts a little louder than reason."

The Pilfert approached Adina. "How are you feeling?"

"Better than ever," she said through a grimace, forcing a smile despite the lingering throb in her side where the blade had cut deep; the wound had already begun to scar but her insides still burned.

"Perfect. Come help me with Emerson. And Stefani," the Pilfert called over its shoulder. Stefani snapped out of her daze, jumping to attention. "We need some of the Alorian salt. We'll need to wake him."

Stefani grabbed the small bag and rushed over to the Pilfert, who was now standing over Emerson's prone form. It uncorked the bottle and held it under Emerson's nose.

His eyes fluttered open, like someone waking from a long, enchanted sleep. He lay still at first. But the moment his gaze landed on the Pilfert, his face tensed, eyes narrowed, and his jaw tightened. Jack couldn't tell what flashed behind that look—anger, fear, confusion—but it set him on edge. Emerson pushed himself upright too fast, his body trembling as his breath grew shallow. His eyes swept the ground, scanning for something.

"I don't know what's going on," Emerson said panicked, his eyes locking onto the faces around him. Jack watched him closely, his posture tight, fists clenching and unclenching, his gaze flickering like he was trying to piece it all together. His voice was raw, like it had been dragged through coals. It sent a chill down Jack's spine.

The Pilfert knelt beside him, its voice gentle but its gaze wary. "You've endured more than most. We'll need to hear everything—but not here. The remaining trolls are still unsettled. We don't want to be here when they grow bored with their treasure and notice their newest Kakunon has been knocked out."

With a flick of its staff, vines and grasses wove themselves into a stretcher, lifting Emerson with surprising care. The group moved in, each taking a corner of the makeshift frame. Their hands brushed over the fragrant vines, the silence between them heavy with things unsaid.

As they passed the fallen Kakunon, a wave of stench hit them—sweat, blood, and decay.

Emerson wrinkled his nose. "They smell awful," he said with a grimace. "I hope we never have to see these guys again."

That earned a half-laugh from group, and though no one said it out loud, they all hoped the same thing.

Chapter Nineteen

Ogof Returns

THE STARS IN THE periwinkle sky winked down at the Guardians, congratulating them on a job well done. Jack, Stefani, Addison, Adina, and Emerson sat around a fire, talking animatedly as the trees swayed in delight beneath the silvery moon.

Behind them, a ball of fur toddled up from the river, two large buckets in hand. Bulging eyes from scaly, unrecognizable creatures flopped inside, twitching and shifting.

"I caught us some bogsnaps," the Pilfert said, carefully setting the pails beside the stack of logs.

"Bog—what?" Stefani asked, leaning over a pail before recoiling, her cheeks puffed in disgust. Inside, fat, angular fish with yellow and purple scales writhed against flaking skin. Their long fins curled into triangular heads, each with four bulging eyes. Suckers along their bellies clung tightly to the sides of the tin pail.

"They taste better than they look," the Pilfert said, moving to prepare them. It knocked each one unconscious, whispering a quiet prayer of forgiveness.

An hour later, their plates were piled high with mushy orange risotto and colorful, spiced bogsnap filets. The only sounds were the rhythmic clinking of forks and the crackling of the fire.

The Pilfert, the last to finish, set its plate aside and stood before them.

"Well," it said, flattening its fur, "we've put this off long enough. Emerson, I know it will be difficult—but I need you to tell me everything you remember from the day we fled O'Keen."

Emerson's eyes narrowed, a shadow of dread flickering behind them. Jack offered an encouraging smile.

"Well," Emerson began, "when you told us to flee to Ealu, I stayed behind for just a moment to make sure everyone was gone. I caught up to Jack, who was closest. I managed to tie up a few of the creatures on his tail with help from the trees, but then more showed up, and I couldn't handle them all. I called for Adina, but she was trapped by two of the minotaurs. Everyone else was already deep in the forest."

His gaze shifted to the Pilfert, hardening as they locked eyes.

"I ran through the trees, dodging spells exploding all around me—bark, rocks, everything flying through the air. I made it through, barely. I was trying to outrun whatever was chasing me when I slipped on a wet patch of leaves. Flames erupted around me as I fell. I heard a cruel laugh—and then everything went dark. Something blocked the sun. It turned out to be the stymphalian that took me away."

He paused, the firelight flickering in his eyes as he scanned their faces. Emerson offered a faint smile, his voice steady as the words tumbled out—faster than he could shape them.

"We landed outside the gates of Dartmoor. They brought me in. They chained me up. Said it was for their protection. Then they gave me a drink . . . something strong and sweet.""

The Pilfert's eyes sharpened, shadows dancing across its furry face.

"He fed you anacylin," the Pilfert whispered. "You felt euphoric the moment it touched your lips, didn't you?"

"Yes," Emerson whispered back.

"I see." The Pilfert studied him, as if peering past the surface. But it said nothing more on the matter.

"What happened when you woke?"

Emerson's expression twitched.

"At first, I felt amazing. Clear-headed. Like I could breathe again. But after a few hours, it wore off. I'd spoken with Gara again by then. And then . . . Akuramundo came. We talked."

"About?" the Pilfert pressed.

"Things. You. The truth about the Great Burnings." Emerson's eyes shifted to his friend. "He told me the Pilferts weren't saviors. He said you—" Emerson turned, a bitter edge in his voice. "That you were the ones planning to wipe out anyone who stands in your way."

The Pilfert didn't move.

"Akuramundo said the Great Burnings started because the Pilferts wished to break the borders—make them wide open. He said that you were going to bring magic into our world—but not to help. To control. Cure our diseases, offer freedom, sure—but only to make us dependent. Then take everything."

Emerson's gaze met the Pilfert's, steady and intense.

"You're not telling us everything. You never have."

The Pilfert's voice dropped low.

"Emerson, you're not entirely wrong. Long ago, there were a band of Pilferts who dreamed of conquest. But they never left the island when darkness overtook it. I have no wish to extend our borders—you know that. Do you remember what I said in Ealu? When we trained?"

Emerson shook his head, jaw tight.

"What about what I said the night you arrived? Akuramundo will stop at nothing to claim you. All of you. Your Vocation Stones have given you power that rivals his—and in some ways, surpasses it. That is deep magic. Ancient. And dangerous in the wrong hands.

"You've been manipulated," the Pilfert said, stepping closer. "Please. Your mind is not your own."

Emerson's expression cracked. "I'm so lost," he whispered. "I don't know what's real anymore. It's only been two months since we arrived—two months—and I don't even know if we're helping the right side."

"I think visits to Blueca will be useful for all of you once you reach Levestin tomorrow night. In those chambers, you'll find the largest collection of unbiased knowledge in our world. But for now, please—continue your story," the Pilfert urged.

"I . . . I don't know where I left off," Emerson said. "But I remember him saying something about my blood. That he could smell something in it."

The fire popped.

"He asked about Jack," Emerson continued, his eyes darting. "About his . . ."

"His heritage?" the Pilfert offered gently.

Emerson nodded. "Yes."

"So, he already knows. Though I suspect he's known for much longer—ever since he retrieved the book from my home," the Pilfert said.

"Jack, there's something you must know," the Pilfert said, voice unusually gentle. "There are many strange tales about Ulysses's magical abilities. His stone is so well-hidden that no one has ever uncovered its location. Futurians have been tortured by seekers for years, trying to learn where it lies.

"But Akuramundo wants more than the stone. In Burkank, they say the heir of Ulysses will be the breaker of borders, the end of the world . . . and the bearer of a new beginning."

Jack stared into the fire. "Yeah . . . I don't want to be any of that."

The Pilfert tilted its head. "That may be. But this time, you have no choice. This isn't just a Futurian's prediction—it's a prophecy."

It stirred the fire with a stick, sending sparks into the night. "The Oracle sees the whole tree, Jack—every root, every branch, all the way to the final leaf. But it never reveals which branch is yours. That's left to the Futurians, who pore over its words like sacred script, each convinced they've found the true path—only to discover another interpretation hiding in the leaves."

It looked at him, eyes reflecting the flames. "Some trace your path to darkness—the tree burned to a stump. Others believe it blossoms into something new and wild and wondrous. The prophecy allows for both truths. The Oracle gave the vision . . . not the verdict. But the one thing no one questions is that it's you."

Jack's thoughts turned to the image in the cave: a hand marked with a K, crushing the earth as crimson rivers flooded the sea.

Why hadn't the Pilfert told him this sooner?

The weight of the world quite literally fell upon his shoulders. Two months ago, he was skateboarding through Pennsylvania. Now he was supposed to reshape the cosmos. He opened his mouth to speak—but nothing came. He felt hollow. Sinking. Like his insides had been turned to stone.

"I'm sorry, Jack," the Pilfert said softly. "But the night is growing late. We'll speak more on this before you depart for Levestin. For now . . . Emerson, please—finish your story."

Emerson nodded and went on. "After they interrogated me, they just let me go. We stayed in Drysmian that night, but the next morning—when no one showed—they ordered me a carriage and left me in Sabana. I was supposed to head through the mountains. They said you'd find me there." He glanced at the Pilfert.

"They used you as bait," the Pilfert said. "Their men had the city surrounded. You were their pawn. If my informants hadn't warned me, we'd have walked straight into their trap. Sending you through the mountains was their backup plan—hoping you'd fulfill the prophecy for them. That you'd deliver the stone."

"Great way to ask for help," Adina muttered, her hand still resting on the scar on her side.

Emerson chuckled lightly, and Jack smiled from the side. He would be all right. Emerson had chosen his side—Jack was certain.

"You know this next bit, so, we'll jump to Gridlybone. At first, I didn't feel any connection. I thought maybe you were wrong. That she couldn't hear me. That I was just hanging on for the ride."

"That was the anacylin," the Pilfert said. "It clouds the mind, severs magic. There's no cure—but the root you took helped temporarily."

"Right." Emerson swallowed. "Once I took that bite, everything got clearer. She . . . she spoke to me." His voice cracked, just enough to sound wounded. "Told me she was sorry she didn't feel our connection before."

He paused, gaze fixed on the fire. "And I remembered what you said—she needed to survive." He took a shaky breath. "But we were ambushed. It all happened so fast." His fingers curled around his knee. "Akuramundo's men . . . They killed her. She forced me to flee as they attacked, but I only hid, determined to find some kind of way to save her. Her cries were . . ." He paused again, his voice breaking. "They took her body. Only her tail was left behind, which I went back to retrieve . . . to bury."

A long silence followed.

The Pilfert didn't blink. Its eyes, wide and unreadable, stayed locked on Emerson a beat too long. Then it simply said, "I see. I will go back and bury her tail for you when I return to Sabana tomorrow."

Emerson nodded a silent thank you.

"So then, that is what they wanted. They hoped you'd release the troll clan—the ones who once terrorized Alors. They'll try to pin it on us, turn the people of Alors against our cause. But I will stop those trolls. As for the stone, we won't let that out of our sight."

Emerson's gaze shifted to the box where the Pilfert was keeping his stone, shielded by a transparent cage.

"But that's all settled now. We're here, well-fed, and alive," the Pilfert said, trying to downplay the unease. "I'm sorry for the troubles you had to endure, Emerson. But just like Hernando, you fought victoriously. With cunning and strength, you stand with us today."

The hill erupted in soft applause. Emerson's ears turned red.

"The day has been long. You'll need your rest," the Pilfert said.

The trees around them groaned and creaked, weaving into a dome—an interlocking canopy of leaf and branch.

"Don't you think this is a bit . . . obvious?" Stefani asked, gesturing around at the nest of foliage.

"No," the Pilfert replied flatly.

Adina raised an eyebrow, and the Pilfert sighed.

"Creatures of the night and wanderers may pass by and see only trees standing tall—never knowing they're actually cradling us, shielding us from the wind. But if anyone comes too close and uncovers our secret spot, I'll be ready."

Jack looked impressed as Adina lay her head across his thigh. "Is that the same spell from the night I went witch-hunting?"

Adina nodded, already half-asleep.

Emerson, blinking, looked to Jack. Jack just shrugged and gave him a tired grin before easing back into the grass, gazing up at the stars just barely visible through the canopy above.

The weight of the world seemed to lift slightly as the stars winked down at him. Though it was still there, he knew he wouldn't have to carry it alone.

And for the first time since entering Kazumeth, Emma didn't cross his mind.

Jack had just nodded off when he felt a sharp pain in his side that wasn't the lingering unease from the troll's blow. He opened his eyes to see the Pilfert beside him, staff held into his side, and one furry finger over its beak. It gestured for Jack to follow.

"I have some things to discuss with you, Mr. Hackley," the Pilfert said, stopping in a small clearing several yards from camp. It wiggled its staff into a nearby bush, sending several fairies shooting into the air, blowing raspberries as they rubbed tired eyes.

"And this couldn't wait until morning?" Jack mumbled through a yawn, watching the fairy lights flicker across the leaves.

"It cannot wait another minute," the Pilfert replied solemnly. "I don't want to have this conversation at all. But it's about Emerson—and about you, as well. As you know, I won't be joining you in Levestin. I have other matters to attend to with Barticus—and a massive troll problem that needs handling immediately."

"How will we know what we're doing without you there to help?" Jack asked.

"You didn't seem to have much trouble this time," the Pilfert chided. "I have faith in you. Besides, we'll discuss that in the morning.

"But since I won't be there, you need to understand how dangerous anacylin is. The first taste puts the sleeper into an enchanted slumber. The potion maker gains full access to their mind and can plant their own images. The drink also blocks any mind-sharing—no one but the potion maker can get through. It's a popular brew for that reason; many brew it for their own use to protect their thoughts.

"However, it's tricky to make. It takes a full year to prepare."

"If it blocks people out, how was I able to enter Emerson's mind in the tent?" Jack asked.

"An excellent question," the Pilfert replied. "I have a theory, but until I'm absolutely sure, I won't speak it here.

"But back to what I *will* say: Until a cure is found, you must keep a very close eye on Emerson. Akuramundo will have access to his mind at all times. And as their relationship deepens—as I suspect Akuramundo plans—Emerson may eventually leave our side and join him."

The Pilfert paused, seeing the shock in Jack's face.

Jack's mouth parted, but no words came. The thought of Emerson—*his* Emerson—joining Akuramundo felt impossible. Wrong. He'd never . . . not after what they did to Gridlybone. He shook his head slightly, as if trying to rid himself of the preposterous idea.

"He wouldn't," Jack said, barely louder than a whisper. "Not Emerson."

"I know this isn't easy to hear, Jack," the Pilfert said gently. "But it's the truth, whether we like it or not."

"So, Emerson is permanently tainted?" Jack asked.

"Until a cure is found—or Akuramundo is killed—yes."

Silence, as Jack let the words sink in.

"Emerson's strong—strong enough to fight. But strength cracks under the right pressure. And when it does, he won't even realize he's gone too far. During those times, I'll need you to be my eyes. Calm him. Bring him back. If he loses awareness, he'll sink into the darkest parts of his soul. You must be there to pull him out."

"I will."

"Secondly," the Pilfert continued, "I don't believe Emerson was completely truthful about what happened with Gridlybone. I didn't mention this before, but I plan to return tomorrow and inspect the area myself when I go to deal with the trolls. If a dragon has been slain, there will be signs—blood, scales, bone fragments. Slaying a dragon is no easy feat. If nothing is found, your task—keeping him grounded, keeping your eyes on him—becomes even more invaluable."

Jack's stomach churned. "Emerson wouldn't lie about that," he said quickly, remembering the grief etched into Emerson's face as he told the story.

The Pilfert ignored this and continued on. "Maybe. It wouldn't be unlike Akuramundo to manipulate the situation—to make it appear a certain way so I'd add extra protections and unknowingly push Emerson right into his arms. You must find out the truth—and you must do so inconspicuously."

The Pilfert's voice softened as it moved on. "Thirdly, the prophecies I mentioned earlier are of great importance. Legends surrounding Ulysses's Vocation Stone and the powers of his heir have long confounded the Futurians. Barticus, a friend of mine who worked closely with Ulysses, believes your powers are greater than we've seen—thanks to Ulysses's studies into other magical forces during his time at Strega Academy."

"He studied with the witches?" Jack asked.

"Yes. That's another reason spells should come easily to you. It's in your blood."

"So Akuramundo is after me because he thinks I can destroy him? But my powers are inconsistent. They're not strong."

"He's after you because he believes the prophecy shows you by his side. But more than that . . . he needs your stone to open the portals between worlds as we've discussed. Which brings me to my next request."

The Pilfert reached into the pouch around its neck and pulled out a jagged blue stone.

"Is that a piece of Emerson's stone?" Jack asked.

"Yes. I was wondering if you could reshape it for me—into a gem that would fit, let's say, inside a crown."

Jack furrowed his brow. "I don't understand. Can't you do this?"

"It has to be you."

"Why? Why break off a piece of Emerson's stone?" Jack asked, suspicion creeping into his voice as Emerson's earlier revelations echoed in his mind. Doubt, sharp and unwelcome, stirred beneath the surface—distrust of his mentor beginning to take root.

"An excellent question—one I believe may help answer the one you asked earlier. I understand if you don't want to help me. But I promise, it's for your benefit."

The Pilfert held out the stone, and Jack reluctantly cupped his hands around it.

"Close your eyes. Imagine the shape you want it to take. No spell. No chant. Just will it—reshape it like the world might reshape you."

Jack did as instructed, his thoughts drifting to the diadem the Pilfert had worn the day he first entered Kazumeth.

At once, an orb of blue light pulled the stone from his hands and spun it through the air. It hovered for a moment, then dropped back into his palm, lighter, warmer. The jagged shard had become a smooth, radiant gem.

The Pilfert's eyes gleamed with approval.

"It's as I suspected. Now, I must ask one more thing of you, Jack. Please don't tell Emerson about his mother. I fear what will happen when he learns she's here. Until this war is over, she must remain a secret. She's safe in Ealu, well cared for. But if Emerson finds out, the bond between them is so strong that he'll lose all sense of reason. He'd storm into Ealu—and thanks to you and Adina . . ."

Jack looked down, ashamed.

"A weapon held by O'Glorian will fall into Akuramundo's hands."

Jack nodded silently.

"Pilfert, something strange happened when Adina and I were heading to Dartmoor. Several witches found us—but they said Akuramundo isn't after all of us anymore. Is it because he's only after me now?"

"Jack, I don't think you're as clueless as the others believe." The Pilfert gave a beaky smile. "After everything I've told you, yes—he's after you. But not to capture or isolate you. To *use* you, when the time comes. Now that he has a spy—even if

Emerson's still truly with us—Akuramundo can see everything Emerson sees. That's all he needs.

"What he wants now is for each of you to retrieve your stones so he can take them for himself. I believe his men will be waiting at every turn to do exactly that. One of those men he believes is Emerson"

Jack opened his mouth to speak, but the Pilfert raised a hand.

"Jack, you must've realized the other visiting troll was Akuramundo himself. He didn't help us by keeping your identities hidden—he helped himself. He knew the trolls would turn against each other and that gets him one step closer to the stones. You're useful to him, Jack. That's the only reason you're still breathing."

"Akuramundo was there?" Jack said incredulously.

"Yes. He can shapeshift—and though I'm not certain how, I have my theories. Theories Adina and Stefani can help me uncover through their research in—"

A twig cracked nearby, cutting their conversation short.

The Pilfert moved swiftly, the light from the fairies casting a gentle glow as he checked a bush a few feet away. Finding nothing, he turned back—but Jack was certain he saw Emerson's slender frame slinking away.

"This is a good place to pause for the night. Rest now. We'll talk more in the morning."

They reentered the camp quietly, like shadows in the night. Jack gently slid the pack out from beneath Adina's head, letting her rest against his chest. But sleep eluded him, his thoughts tangled in a web of doubt.

Could Emerson really betray them? Had the Pilfert told him the whole truth—or just enough to keep him loyal? And when Emerson learned what Jack was hiding . . . what then?

He held Adina closer, grounding himself in the rhythm of her breath. She was the one thing that still felt certain.

He was beginning to understand: the most dangerous truths were the ones left unspoken—the ones hiding in the spaces between their words.

The next morning, camp stirred with playful disorder. Jack and Addison were wrestling in the dewy grass, tossing each other about and laughing, using magic to cushion their falls. Stefani was complaining about the food, threatening a hunger strike unless they found a healthier alternative to the constant bread and meats.

Adina, unbothered, swiped the spicy-sweet pumpkin bread from Stefani's plate, slathered it with cream, and savored each zing with delight.

The Pilfert ignored the chaos, its eyes fixed on Emerson as he sat alone, quietly folding his blankets and slipping them into his bag.

"How did you sleep?" the Pilfert asked.

"Better than on that stone floor," Emerson replied flatly.

"I'm sorry we couldn't rescue you sooner. It was out of our hands. As we explai—"

"Forget it," Emerson said, cutting off the Pilfert, his eyes fixed on the grass.

"Emerson . . ."

"Why am I not allowed to carry my own stone?"

"You are—I was only trying to—"

"Steal it? Control me?" Emerson snapped. His tone was sharp, but his hands remained steady.

The Pilfert offered the box. Emerson snatched it greedily, clutching it tight. But after a beat, his shoulders softened, and his face fell.

"I'm sorry," he said quietly, not quite looking at the Pilfert. "I just . . . after that drink . . . I'm just . . . I'll just feel safer with it close, that's all."

He opened his bag and dropped the small box inside, where it thudded against the row of books lining the bottom.

The two stood in silence, the Pilfert observing Emerson with quiet intrigue. Then, without another word, it turned and raised its arms, calling the others to gather.

"King Ricco is expecting your arrival today," the Pilfert began. "Jerica will meet us outside the borders to lead you in. I've trained you as best I could under the circumstances. From here on, you must sharpen your reflexes, strengthen your focus, and practice control the moment you enter the city. Do as Jerica advises. Tutors have been arranged to help develop your abilities.

"Push your minds beyond where they've dared to go. Train your bodies as though nothing can break them. Be strong. Be smart. If you succeed, you won't just retrieve the next stone—you'll help restore Levestin to its former glory."

The creature straightened, its yellow eyes darkening beneath its tangled brow.

"But I won't lie to you—this will be difficult. And it must remain secret. Levestin's laws on magic are strict. Years ago, during the regime change, magical beings and witches were driven out, hunted, or imprisoned. You will practice only in private, under the guidance of our tutors. Trust no one outside your circle."

The Pilfert's tone deepened.

"Now, to graver matters—Akuramundo is rising. We believe he's already infiltrated Ricco's kingdom, though we don't yet know how. Once he infects the minds of the people, gaining allies will become nearly impossible for us. While you live among them, protect them. Guard their hearts. Shield their thoughts from the false promise of Akuramundo.

"And remember—Mankato, the island where dissidents are imprisoned and enslaved, is on the verge of revolution. I won't ask you to—"

It stopped mid-sentence. Its eyes narrowed, voice catching in its throat. The group followed its gaze. Jack's hand went instinctively to his sword.

A horned, serpentine figure slithered from the shadows.

"Is that—" Addison started.

"That's the thing that ate us," Jack said, pointing.

"Silence," the Pilfert snapped. It stepped forward and rubbed the serpent's spiked head. "What happened? Why did you take so long to return, Ogof?"

The snake hissed in reply, its piercing gaze sweeping over the crowd. The Pilfert's eyes betrayed a flash of anxiety before it turned back to the creature.

"Where did she end up?" it asked urgently. The serpent hissed again—lower this time.

The Pilfert's expression tightened. "I see . . ." it muttered, mostly to itself. Then, in a clipped tone, "Come with me."

And without another word, both the Pilfert and the seminarion were sucked into a burst of light.

"What was that about?" Addison asked, flopping down onto the grass.

"I think someone else has passed through," Stefani said, thoughtful. "Did you hear it? It asked, 'Where did she end up?'"

Jack nodded, but Emerson just stared at the ground, his mind racing. Visions of his mother—lost and confused in the forest—flashed before him. His heart surged at the thought of seeing her again.

Addison thought of his sister, desperate to make sure she was safe. Stefani's thoughts turned to Emma. Jack and Adina exchanged a glance of indifference.

"What's going on?" Emerson asked sharply as the Pilfert reappeared on the hill.

"No time. Stefani—your bag."

Without hesitation, she handed it over. The Pilfert took it and disappeared again.

"Why'd it need your bag?" Jack asked, eyes narrowing.

"We made healing potions in the fountains," Stefani said. "Someone's hurt."

"You think she's dying?" Emerson's voice cracked. His thoughts snapped back to his mother—covered in snake bites, fading fast.

"No," Jack replied, though his stomach churned. Emerson didn't know his mother was safe in Ealu. But the truth must stay buried. He'd promised the Pilfert—and more than that, he'd decided his mentor was worth trusting.

The sun burned overhead, but it was the silence that scorched. Time slowed around them.

Then the air shimmered, heat rippling like water. A glowing bubble drifted toward them, a girl with long blonde hair suspended inside, caged in light. The seminarion, now smaller than it had been in the cave, was coiled around her protectively.

The Pilfert walked beneath the floating sphere, its face unreadable. As they neared, Jack's heart stalled.

"Jack!" a familiar voice cried out, high-pitched and raw.

Jack blinked, stunned. Emma's scent reached him before his thoughts could—warm, familiar, achingly real. He ran—but slammed into an invisible barrier. He rammed his shoulder against it again and again, desperate to break through.

"Emma!" he shouted, pounding his fists against the shield. "Pilfert, remove it! Right now! Emma!"

The barrier dropped and Emma floated to the ground.

Ogof bowed once to the Pilfert, then vanished in a ripple of smoke and wind.

Jack ran to her, wrapping his arms around her waist, pulling her close as if afraid she might vanish again. The sun bathed the hill in golden light as they stood there, holding each other. The war in Jack's mind finally ceased. A peace settled over him like feet finding solid ground. And in that moment, he kissed Emma without hesitation, lost in a quiet moment of unremitting bliss.